Ask for the Moon

a tale of love, growth and acceptance
as Idlewild comes of age

JuliAnne Sisung

ISBN-13: 978-1093576481

Published April 2019 by JuliAnne Sisung

Books by JuliAnne Sisung

Sophie's Lies

The Hersey Series

Elephant in the Room
Angels in the Corner
Light in the Forest
Place in the Circle

The Idlewild Series

Leaving Nirvana
The Whipping Post
Ask for the Moon

The North Michigan Series

Curse of the Damselfly
Beyond the Crooked Tree

Acknowledgements

The Idlewild books caused a parade of fears to find a place in my gut and fester until I faced and slew them. The fears were language based, and they caused sweat to seep from my pores when I faced words I'd never used: colored, black, Negro, the KKK, lynching, cross burning, Black Legion, Jim Crow, and so many others. Thank you all for my late education.

Micala Evans filled my head and heart with a great variety of information during a tour of Idlewild. Her knowledge is vast, and it settled into her bones early as she grew to adulthood in Idlewild. Ask her about a relative who ran the whistle stop.

Theresa Rose works tirelessly to grow Idlewild and has her phone connected to many Idlewild greats like Carlene Giles. Carlene is an infinitely beautiful woman who tells tales only she and a few others could know of Idlewild. She'll explain what it was like to entertain across the nation as a black performer prior to the middle sixties.

Thank you, Theresa, Micala, Carlene, and so many others who spent time with me and helped me understand Idlewild, the nation and myself.

Closer to home, I want to thank my family for loving my wild imagination and putting up with my flights of fancy, my friends who roll their eyes when I say I can't go here or there because I have to write or revise or edit, and my fans who keep asking when the next book is coming out. Keep on asking, please.

And finally, thanks to Larry Hale for continuing to look for continuity, search out repetitions, prune the flowers in my word garden, and still tell me I'm great. We have fewer fights, so *you* must be getting wiser, right?

Thank you all. I'm grateful.

Chapter One

1928

The usher, a dark-skinned colored man, met them at the entry. You'd think he would step aside, but he didn't. He stood in their way as they tried to move down the aisle of the movie house, forcing them to step around him and through the double doors to the general seating area.

"Telling you, sir. Negroes sit upstairs. Whites down here." Gold braid picked up light from the wall sconces, and his uniform showed care in the knife-creased pants and stiff white cuffs sticking out of his red jacket sleeves.

"Ridiculous." Abby spouted her irritation and straightened her spine. "We came together. We're going to sit together."

"Not in this theater, ma'am." He pointed the flashlight beam toward the door. "You can leave or sit separately."

Abby's back stiffened. "I'm not going. Michigan doesn't have stupid Jim Crow laws, and you know it." She grew taller and yanked her elbow from Samuel's hand when he tried to guide her back down the aisle and outside.

"We don't have the laws, just the practices," Samuel said, his tone irritatingly calm and academic. "We knew this would happen, Abby. I did, anyway. Let's give this man a break and let him do his job."

"But it's senseless."

"Much in this world is."

She let him take her arm and gave watchers in the lobby a conquering lift of her chin on the way to the door.

White couples shuffled in embarrassment or glared in anger – or possibly fear. Black couples headed for the door leading to the balcony where they would sit with their kind and looked away so their eyes wouldn't show hidden thoughts, reveal their biases and resentments.

Their histories.

Outside, Abby rubbed her upper arms against the afternoon chill, and Samuel wrapped an arm around her.

"Cold? You can have my coat."

She shook her head, anger staining her cheeks. "Mad. Not cold."

"Mad makes you shiver?"

He removed his suit jacket, anyway, and draped it over her lilac dress. She'd worn it for him for their only real date, one they had talked about for months.

Well, *she'd* talked about it, wanting to spend a few hours with him somewhere besides the hotel where her da and their friends were in constant attendance. She wanted to be anywhere they could forget Idlewild and be alone amongst strangers.

"Where do you think we could go, Abby?" he had asked when she'd prodded him.

"I don't know. Out to dinner? A movie in White Cloud or Baldwin?"

What happened inside the theater didn't surprise Samuel. In fact, he knew it would and, in a strange way, was glad for it. She'd seen the Ku Klux Klan in action and racist ignorance in arson and ugly hand-drawn pictures, but she hadn't come up against blatant, inflexible Jim Crow before.

Now, he watched her fight the battle, her only weapon a desire for change. But being powerless to right a significant wrong defeated her. It churned in the pit of her stomach, and she itched to throw something, hit somebody.

He turned her around to face him, and she couldn't tell if he was hurt or angry. His black eyes appeared serene, and his lips curved at the corners, possibly in amusement after she stomped her foot in frustration.

"Why are you letting this happen, Samuel? We should just go in there, give the man the tickets you paid for and sit down. Why can't we?"

"Time and place, girl. I don't want you hurt."

"Who's going to hurt me?"

Samuel smoothed a hand over his black mustache.

"You think you know about bias? About racial injustice? You don't Abby. You've just scratched the surface because you've lived in a small-town bubble and haven't been in the south. You haven't seen the 'Whites Only' signs on fountains, the 'No Coloreds' signs in diners and on restroom doors. You haven't had to take a leak and danced around because there was nowhere you could go. You haven't seen black children hauled out by their shirt collars when they made themselves go into a white restroom because it was better than the humiliation of wetting their pants."

His voice grew soft with sorrow, and Abby placed a hand on his shoulder.

"I'm sorry," she whispered.

A white couple strolled by, their eyes glued to Abby and Samuel.

"Ought a be a law," the gray-haired man said to the woman beside him who turned her face away as if seeing a colored man with a white woman was a disease that would infect and spread like chicken pox or measles.

"There is. In a lot of places," she said.

Abby whipped around to glare at the man and wished the woman would turn back so she could shoot eye darts at her, too.

"Not in Michigan, there isn't. And there shouldn't be anywhere. You're just Neanderthals." She stomped her foot again.

Samuel tugged her toward his Model T parked in front of the general store.

"You're courting trouble, Abby. Real trouble." He opened her door but thought again. "Feel like some dinner?"

"In a restaurant?"

"No. On the river bank."

He pointed to the store, and her shoulders slumped.

"I guess."

"You sound like I'm dragging you to a dog fight," he said and thumped her chin with a knuckle. When she nodded, he grasped an elbow and steered her inside.

A woman in a red cloche hat sniffed and moved around the aisle away from them. Another took her daughter's hand and pulled her close. People stared and scowled, but no one told them they had to leave or shop separately.

Abby's mood lifted as he pointed to the jar of ring bologna swimming in pickle juice and asked the man behind the counter for a thick slab of yellow cheese and a box of crackers to go with it.

"Something sweet, too," Samuel said.

"Me. I'm sweet," she said.

A black eyebrow lifted. "Not the word I would call you. Never, ever."

"I am, too."

"A-hah. This will sweeten you up. A pound of the chocolate covered cherries," he told the man behind the counter who piled everything in a box and took his money.

Memories of the usher and the hurtful words and looks fled Abby's mind as she skipped beside him to his vehicle. She put it all behind her and looked forward to a picnic by the river.

Abby liked being encased in Samuel's auto and the rumble of the tires on the road, the speed, the intimacy of the small space. She could reach out to touch him, and her hand moved through the air in his direction before she caught herself. It went to her hair, instead, and patted it as an alternative before returning to her lap.

As if he knew what she'd intended, Samuel's hand landed on hers. He squeezed it, ran a lazy thumb over the back of it, and let his fingers curl under hers.

The familiarity didn't surprise her. The quickening of her pulse did, and she straightened her fingers. He would either remove his hand or interlace his with hers.

He wove them together.

Without conversation, the stillness magnified breath and exaggerated swallows. She watched his Adam's apple move up and down and wondered how he could drive with one hand? How could he look perfect in the late sunlight after a lengthy day, and why were his fingers so long and slender? Did he ever love someone? Most likely.

"Are you done watching me?" he asked.

"I don't think so."

Her voice came out small, like a child's admission of wrong doing, but she was excited, joyful.

His lips quirked as he turned onto a two-track leading to the rain-swollen Pere Marquette River. Swift current ran close to the bank's rim and splashed over fallen trees, filling the air with watery music.

He spread a blanket on a dry spot near the river's edge and plopped the box in the middle. Abby's stomach grumbled as the scent of pickle juice wafted her way.

"Hungry?" he asked with a pointed chuckle.

She patted her flat stomach, embarrassed he'd heard the uncouth noise it had emitted. "Guess I am."

"I like a girl who can eat."

"We all eat."

"Not all women."

"They must, else they wouldn't survive."

She reached for a chunk of bologna he'd lopped off with a jackknife and followed it with a large bite of cheese.

"They don't eat in front of the man they're trying to impress with their feminine charms," he said.

"I guess that's true, but it's just silly."

She was glad to be talking about inane things, glad to have left behind the awkwardness she'd felt in the automobile - and at the theatre.

Abby had kissed him once - at the door of the hotel when he was leaving. He hadn't stopped her, but he'd not taken it as an invitation to do it again. He'd said she didn't know what real trouble was and warned her about the unimaginable hardship of what she was considering.

She knew he was right about the battle but believed he was wrong not to fight it.

Dusk chased the afternoon away, and Samuel wrapped Abby in a second blanket. Evening sounds crept close to them in the rustle of brush and skitterings and yips, and their voices grew softer in keeping with their surroundings. Samuel lay on his side, his head propped on a hand. The other moved over Abby's.

"Close your eyes and open your mouth."

She plucked a chocolate covered cherry from the box, plopped it between his lips, and closed his mouth with a finger under his chin.

He chewed with his eyes closed and savored the sweetness until he felt her lips on his.

"Sweetheart," he murmured with apprehension.

"Yummy. You taste like cherry."

"Yes, and now *you* do."

He pulled her to him and wrapped his arms around her for a real kiss, one he'd wanted for months, maybe years, and Abby's small moan was his undoing. He pulled on the ribbon corralling her auburn hair and ran fingers through the curls, cooling in the night air and cocooning them. He fingered the strands as they fell from her face, looked in her green eyes and saw passion reflecting his own.

"This is foolish, Abby, and you know it."

"More foolish than staying legally tied to a man who couldn't love me?"

"Probably a great deal more. You have no idea."

"I'm not listening, Samuel."

He kissed her again and lifted her away from him at the end. Her heart pounded, and her head swam. She hadn't known a kiss could do that, but she'd hoped, and now she knew.

"You should kiss me again," she said.

"No, Abby. I shouldn't, and it's time to leave."

"Can we do this again?"

Samuel packed the leftovers in the box and took it to the auto. He lifted a silent Abby from the blanket and shook the leaves from it. She watched as he folded and put it with the box.

"Are you going to answer me?" She slid into the passenger seat, a probing look in her eyes.

He didn't respond until he got in, turned the vehicle around, and started back down the two-lane path.

"I didn't answer because I don't know."

"Why not?"

"Because I'm more than concerned, Abby. I'm terrified."

She watched nightfall flicker in the lights of Samuel's automobile and show an unfamiliar explosion of insects drawn by the glare. They whizzed through the air and darted at the yellow glow in confusion, and Abby understood and commiserated with their misperceptions.

"Because of what happened at the theater today?"

"No. Because of what happened three hundred years ago." His words sounded harsh, staccato and angry.

Feeling chastised, Abby turned to stare out at the darkness, wanting to refute his words. But she couldn't. What he said was true. Accurate and hateful. Tears wanted to form, and she blinked to refuse them entry.

His arm snaked around her shoulders, and fingers crawled up the back of her neck and moved through the tendrils at the base of her skull. She stiffened, still in the throes of disappointment, but her head soon fell forward and gave his hand access to her bruised heart.

"I'm sorry, Abigail."

She patted his knee. "I know."

"I'll be in, in a minute," Samuel said as they pulled up to the hotel, and he reached across to open her door.

The bar was half full, and Charity frowned seeing her walk in. With Abby here, Jackson would lose his place behind the bar and return to waiting tables, which meant she'd have to go back to being a customer on a stool instead of helping out. She loved working the hotel bar – *dining room* since prohibition – and didn't want to give it up.

"Can't you go away?" she shouted to Abby who told her to continue what she was doing.

"I'm going to sit for a . . ."

Hands grabbed her from behind, and a gasp of surprise choked in her chest as she was lifted and tossed over his shoulder. It came out as an oomph.

He sprinted out of the bar and headed for the stairs, deep laughter spilling from him. She thought it familiar but could only see a man's behind as her head bobbed up and down while he ran.

"Who are you?" she bellowed.

He stopped at the bottom step. "Seriously? You don't know?"

"No!"

"So, you go upstairs with just any ole man who tries to carry you off?"

"No! As you can see, I had no choice in this matter!" She pounded his back with her fists.

He smacked her bottom as Samuel came through the door and stopped dead still, his hand clenching on the brass knob. Abby grinned at the irritation on his face. At the moment, she didn't care who carried her.

Samuel was jealous.

He slid her off his shoulder, and her feet hit the floor. She backed up a step, and her face lit.

"Yancy!" she yelled and threw her arms around him. "Where on earth have you been? What have you been doing? Are you here for a while?"

"I been north. I been south. I been west. I been everywhere. You wouldn't believe where I been."

They wandered back into the bar as he filled her in, and Yancy saw Bear rub a large hand over his face like he used to when Yancy got to talking too much.

"Don't you be gawking at me like that, Bear. I missed this woman. She shoulda been Mrs. Yancy, and you know it as well as me."

Yancy slapped a stool and told her to climb on it. Abby turned to look for Samuel, not wanting to end their night like this, and saw him take a seat next to Jesse Falmouth, Idlewild's other attorney. His look said he wasn't going to rescue her, and she drew her brows together in a quick reprimand.

"Where you been, girl? Don't you work anymore? Got the help doing it for you?"

"Sometimes I go out, Yancy. Every once in a while, a girl needs to get away."

He tilted his head toward Samuel and drew his brows together. "With him?"

"Yes."

"Hmmm. That so?"

"Yes. It is so."

She was saved further explanation by her da who came from the kitchen drying his hands and whistling.

"So, I see the lad found ye," he said. "Surprised?"

"I was, Da. I thought I was being abducted."

"I would if I could get away with it. Told you that before I left." Yancy gazed at her meaningfully, and she unconsciously inched away from the shoulder he'd pressed against hers.

"Tell me where you've been, my friend," she asked, changing the topic.

"Mostly big towns. Played some poker when the trees ran out. Doing odd jobs when the cards ran against me. It's a good life."

"Well, it's good to see you. I have to get behind the bar, though, and do my job."

She thought a frown swiped his face but told herself she was seeing things, imagining looks that weren't there, and slid from the stool to leave.

"Don't run off," he said.

She ran to her room to change into work clothes and run a wet cloth over her face, pondering the Yancy she'd known long ago. He seemed different, now, but . . . so was she. Time and life did that to people.

Samuel was leaving when she returned, and she put a hand on his arm to stop him.

"I didn't get a chance to thank you. Do you really need to go? Porch time won't be far off."

His mustache twitched in a half smile that wasn't reflected in his eyes, and Abby thought of the kiss they'd shared, wanting to repeat it right here, right now.

"That wouldn't be a good idea, Abigail."

"What wouldn't?"

"What you're thinking."

She twisted her head like her neck hurt, and it made a loud cracking noise.

He laughed at the sound. "I'm telling you, it wouldn't."

"You think you know everything, Samuel. You don't know what was in my mind."

He reached a hand toward her and let a fingertip touch her bottom lip for a brief second. She blushed fire red.

"So . . . What don't I know, Abby?" He patted her hand and turned to leave. "Have a nice night, sweetheart."

Samuel didn't always share the nightly porch sitting with the family but frequently enough that Abby missed his presence, even though Yancy filled his chair. Patrick introduced him to Charles Chesnutt when he came up the steps and explained Charles' place in the world of Negro literature. Yancy's brown eyes narrowed as he digested the news.

"Why would a white man write colored stories?" he asked, his confusion real and infused with dismay.

"But I am Negro, Mr. Yancy," was Charles' quiet response. He tilted his rocking chair and continued the slow dance shared by Patrick, Bear, Shorty, and soon Abby.

Yancy's head spun from Charles to Patrick, checked the faces of Bear and Shorty, and went back again to Charles, unsure if he'd been made sport of or not. He decided he hadn't. Mr. Chesnutt was a colored man who looked whiter than he did with his black hair and dark skin, the product of Latin ancestors back a couple of generations. And he didn't think of himself as anything but white.

Things were strange here in Idlewild, definitely not the same as Nirvana, with coloreds looking white and Irish Abby stepping out with a Negro. He hadn't wanted to ask if that was the way of things, but he would.

He most definitely would.

Yancy bent forward with a start, his chin jutting and eyes wide as he stared at a strange gray-haired woman strolling the lake's edge. Her flowing dress dragged the ground behind her, and a stream of cats followed single file. She poked in the lake water with a knobby stick and, every once in a while, brought something up on its sharp end and stuck it in her bag.

"What the . . . What is that?"

Whether she'd heard him or not, no one knew, but she turned and stared. They couldn't see her eyes in the dark, but everyone felt the pull of her gaze and was happy not to be the object of her attention.

"Who, not what," Bear said. "She is Cassandra. Our local healer. Our friend."

"You all seem to have a whole lot of different friends here in Idlewild."

Yancy's words in any other mouth might have sounded like admiration, but from his lips, they didn't. Patrick squinted as he tried to figure out his old friend's statement but shrugged and continued rocking, the click of wood on wood a continuous song without interruption, his mellow night-mind a peaceful place.

Chapter Two

She wasn't surprised to see Shorty in front of a bucket of potatoes with a knife in his hand. The big man had her apron hanging in front of him, but it protected only a narrow strip of his clothes. He whispered a good morning, so Abby assumed talk was permitted.

"You on the payroll, now?" she asked.

"Just helping Al."

"I'll take over, Shorty." Abby removed the knife from his hand and slid the apron from his head to hers. "Must have had your coffee already?"

"Not yet," Al said.

"Wow." She stared at him and wanted to tease but thought more words might be taking acceptable morning noise a step too far. She had too much to do this morning than to spend precious time perched on the high cupboard where he'd place anyone who disturbed the quiet before his coffee.

Love had changed her friend.

Al had made the difference, but Abby wasn't taking any chances, and as soon as she sniffed the chicory in Patrick's special blend of coffee, she poured a cup and set it in front of him. He sipped and nodded thanks.

Bear pushed through the kitchen's swinging doors as if the scent of coffee magically carried him. He wore Phantom, Abby's white cat, over his shoulder and carried Cleo, her sleek, black feline. They slept with Abby at night, but as soon as she opened her door each morning, they streaked down the hall to Bear's. He never closed his door entirely so they could have access to his room and him.

He was the *cat man.*

She poured coffee for Bear, said, "Step back, Al," and tossed the sliced potatoes into a sizzling cast iron frypan.

"Too hot," Al said and pushed it toward the back of the stove where the heat was kept lower.

"You're right. Damn, I'm really sorry. I don't know what's the matter with me. Hope it didn't splatter you."

She saw Shorty's eyes do a quick onceover, checking for burns, and Al reassured him with a look. Not a word had passed between them. They communicated without speaking because Al talked in two or three-word sentences and Shorty in hard to hear whispers and hardly ever in the morning before he saw the bottom of his coffee cup.

His cat, Nurse, climbed on his lap and stared into his eyes, doing the job he'd been trained to do – keep Shorty well. He'd been a gift from Cassandra while recovering from a beating that left him in a coma, and the orange tabby never left his side unless forced.

"This place is a feline menagerie," Abby said, as she refilled Shorty's cup. "By the way, how's the Oakmere coming?"

"Done in a couple of months. You ready?"

"Don't think I'll ever be ready. Wish Da hadn't taken on another hotel. One is enough."

"You tell him that?" Bear asked.

"No and you don't need to either. I'll manage. I've got some ideas how, but I want to run them by him before I say anything."

Al had six eggs on the griddle. She loaded two plates with sausage and bacon and slid three perfect sunny-side-up eggs next to them. When she set them in front of the men, Abby's heart pinched – just a nip, but a pinch all the same.

Sharing Bear and Shorty tweaked her in ways she'd never admit, and it shamed her. For years, all the way back to the Aishcum Hotel in Nirvana, they'd been all hers, the brothers she never had. She was the one who fed them every morning and night, and they had cared for her, protected her from things that could have been dangerous – like air and chipmunks.

Charity bounded in, her blond bob bouncing with each step. "Gotta cuppa?" she chirped.

"Morning. Help yourself." Abby stirred the potatoes and scooted Charity out of the way with her hip.

"Who's the man sitting at the bar?"

Abby gave her a blank look.

"Dark haired, kind of a deep, brooding type. Maybe he's brooding because it's too early in the morning. Don't know if I could tolerate brooding in a man. You know what I mean? But he's a handsome devil."

Al's eyes went to the corner of the room, and she yanked on the pink ribbon holding back her long pale hair and fled to the pantry.

"Now you've done it, girl," Shorty said to Charity.

Her eyes widened. "What? What'd I do?"

"You're a bit too chipper, a bit too early," Abby said. "From your description, the brooder could only be Yancy."

"Who's Yancy, and why is he sulking at the bar?"

"Later, Charity. Are the guests up and about?"

"Some of them. I saw . . ."

"Get started, then, and I'll be there as soon as Da gets up and down here."

"Go, Abby," Al said, slipping back through the pantry door, her hair retied in the pink ribbon.

Shorty stood, put his plate in the dry sink and lifted the large buffet bowls from the high shelf.

"Fill em, Al, and I'll carry when you're done."

Abby looked back and forth between the two and knew she wasn't needed. Al had been making the breakfast buffet for years, and Shorty had been watching it cook and eating it for more than that. They could handle the food table without her.

Abby filled a bucket with water for the washstand pitchers, handed Charity the empty one, and pushed through the doors. They passed Yancy on the way through the bar, and his head lifted and eyes lit.

"Morning, Abby. It's good to see your smiling face."

"Food will be out soon, Yancy. You must be hungry, up so early."

Charity poked her with an elbow.

"Ouch. That was hard and uncalled for."

She introduced them, and Yancy gave Charity the grin he saved for pretty, young women. Her lashes fluttered and her bob bounced as she put her hand in his.

"It's a pleasure," he said with a Latin inflection kept hidden until it was useful or he wanted to attract and impress.

Charity bought the charm, and Abby scrunched her face and tried not to groan.

"Come on, girl. We have rooms to clean. Grab the broom. See you later, Yancy. Breakfast will be right out."

They stopped at the cupboard for linens and towels and began cleaning the long row of guest rooms.

"Betty coming back to work after the baby?" Charity asked.

"Not sure, but I think so, why?" Abby changed the sheets since Charity always ended up a sheet-wrapped mummy on the floor. "Sweep and dust mop, please."

She never had to tell Betty what to do, but to be fair, they'd been doing rooms together for a long time, so . . .

"Just want to know if I'll be stuck upstairs forever." Charity opened her eyes wide like she'd stepped on a snake. "I mean. Not that I hate it. It's . . . I like working the bar better. That's all. There are more people to talk with."

"I know. I'm not offended. Some work is more pleasant than others and suited to certain personalities."

"Ma calls me a social butterfly, but she means I have a brain the size of one."

"You know that's not true, Charity. You're a smart young woman. You have a college degree, and you didn't pick it off a tree like it was a leaf just growing there."

"Pretty much did. It was easy."

Abby tucked in the end of the top sheet and turned to look at her, checking for fibs or facts. She wasn't fibbing.

"It was easy for you because you're smart. And don't let anyone convince you otherwise, not even your mother. Women have brains. And rights. It's about time we start fighting for them, too."

Charity swept dirt into the dustpan and tossed it into the trash, picked up the dust mop and dislodged Phantom who chased it across the room.

"Where did that come from?"

"Phantom?"

"No, the rights thing. You were talking about brains and all of a sudden you're soapboxing about women's rights."

"Sorry. I don't know where it came from. I get angry, every now and then, when folks' rights are stomped on. Makes me really mad."

She sailed out the door at the sound of Betty's voice calling her name and peered over the banister to see her standing next to Benjamin and a bulging suitcase. Betty rubbed her protruding belly, and her grin showed two rows of huge white teeth.

"What does it take to get some help around here? You got a room? I don't see the 'no vacancy' sign out." She moved to the lobby desk, pounded a fist on it and a flat hand on the silver bell at the same time. "Service, please!"

"What are you doing here? Do you really want a room, Betty?"

"I said so, didn't I?"

"Hello, Benjamin," Abby said. "Good to see you, too."

"Thought we'd be better off in Idlewild now her date is near. Closer to Cassandra and Dr. Dan."

"You're not just talented and pretty, Benjamin; you're wise, too. I'm happy you're here."

Abby ran down the stairs and looked at the check-in book to find an available room. "Right next to me. Perfect. I'll take you there." She grabbed the suitcase.

"I think I know where it is, Abby."

The grin never left her lips as she waddled to the stairs. Benjamin helped with an arm around her back, his face not conveying the same glee as his wife's. His smile, said, 'Help me. I'm terrified.'

"Women give birth all the time, my friend," Abby said to him. "Betty will be fine."

But she worried, too. Not all women made it through childbirth. Her own mother hadn't.

"They surely do. You hear, husband? But I don't mind a little spoiling. It's nice."

"How are things in Nirvana? Folks still trying to book rooms?" Abby asked.

They lived at the Aishcum, her da's old hotel a few miles from Idlewild. Patrick and Abby had left it, and the dying town of Nirvana, at the end of the lumber boom.

Benjamin, looking for solitude and a place to heal from WWI shrapnel wounds, had offered to care for it in exchange for a place to live. He'd found peace and health in the old place, and Abby visited now and then – always when she needed a bit of serenity.

"Folks still come. I think they want to watch Betty grow," he said. "She sits in front of the fireplace with a woolen blanket and her knitting, and people stop by for a drink and to spend time with her. She's a magnet."

"Not so. It's your piano music they want." Betty tapped his arm and groaned up the stairs.

"Speaking of that. Will you play while you're here?"

He cocked his head toward Abby and lifted Betty up the last step.

"You need some rooms on the ground floor. And, yes, I look forward to playing for you again."

"Do you need help settling in? Something cold to drink? Or hot? Food? You hungry? What can I do?"

Betty squinted her eyes at her.

"Um . . . You can *not* hover over me, boss. Go see what Charity's up to. You never know what havoc that woman will create if you leave her alone too long. She's most likely sprawled on somebody's bed taking a nap by now. Her pretty, red-painted mouth is making snoring sounds, you can bet on it."

"Sorry, I'm . . . darn," Abby stammered. She knew she was fussing over Betty, but she'd missed her – and she *was* worried. "Okay. I'll be just down the hall if you need anything. Anything at all. You hear?"

"I hear, boss. Al around?"

"She is. Want me to tell her where you are?"

Betty nodded.

"I'm glad you're here." Abby squeezed Betty's shoulder and went downstairs to the kitchen.

"I'll finish here, lass," Patrick told Al when Abby explained who their newest guests were. "You go on up to see our wee Betty."

Al's eyebrows rose when he said *wee*. Being taller than most females and extremely pregnant, she resembled a walking stick having recently made lunch out of a baby elephant.

She missed Betty, missed living at the Tatum farm with her – before she became Mrs. Chambers.

But her own last name was Tatum. And for good reasons, Betty had hated that name until she got to know the young woman called Strange Al. It was an unlikely friendship – tiny blonde Al, tall dark Betty and between them a horrific history.

It remained a rock-solid relationship, made of tested iron and admiration

Yancy sat behind a plate of breakfast and waved a fork at Bear and Shorty as they left the kitchen. They stopped to ask if he'd be looking for work in the area.

"Could use another hand," Shorty said. "Work will last until the new hotel is done."

Yancy lifted his shoulders like work didn't interest him much and went back to forking food into his mouth.

"Maybe when my poker money runs out." He grinned between bites and slapped Bear on the back. "You know how it is. Next week is for worrying about next week."

Bear shrugged off the slap and didn't respond. They left him at the bar and wondered if he would still be there when they got back from work.

"Does he seem a bit more Yancy-like than before?" Shorty asked, throwing a thick wool blanket over his gelding.

Bear knew what he meant. "Seems so. We'll see how he pans out."

"Yancy-like was never a real good thing, but tolerable. You know?"

"Maybe he'll get over it."

The sun had set when Samuel walked in. He took a stool by Patrick and gave Abby a nod. She brought a short glass of amber ale and even wiped the bottom of it before setting it in front of him.

"Looks busy," he said. "Thank you."

"For the quick drink? You're welcome."

"For wiping the bottom."

She tried not to grin. "Couldn't make you use those freshly starched cuffs tonight."

Benjamin's piano music filtered through the conversations, and Samuel left his drink when he saw Betty sitting in one of the porch rockers in front of a small fire.

"Just visiting?" he asked as he drew near.

"I'm here for the duration, Samuel. Benjamin wanted both Dr. Dan and Miss Cassandra to attend his son's entrance into the world."

"Son? You sure about that?"

"He is, and nothing's too good for his son."

"And his son's mother, I'm thinking. He takes good care of you, Betty."

"He surely does. Until he makes me about daft. Abby, too. Between the two of them, I can't walk across the room by myself."

Samuel chuckled. He could see that happening. Abby had seen her friend badly hurt, more than once, and she'd protect her with her last breath.

"Take advantage, Betty. We don't get spoiled often enough."

When Sue and Sally came in, they sat on either side of Patrick who flung his arms around their backs. Their red satin dresses were identical, but you'd have to look carefully to see it. Long, lithe Sally's draped over narrow shoulders in elegant folds and snugged her hips perfectly, while Sue's pulled sideways, stretching over the curves of her lavish proportions, periodically revealing more than encasing.

"On me, ladies. On the house. It's been too long. Where ye been all this time?"

"Working too hard, Patrick. And thank you for the drink," Sally said.

"If you'd come to our establishment, we'd offer one on the house to you, too," Sue said, tipping her head and fluttering black eyelashes.

"Sue," Sally said.

"What?"

Patrick bridged the moment. "I'd love to take you up on your generous offer, but I might never leave, ladies. And what would become of me poor daughter and the hotel?"

Sue giggled like a girl, and Sally sat straighter, if that was possible. Model perfect. She knew his words were accurate, even if he didn't.

At the end of the bar, Yancy lifted his drink toward Patrick and gave a slow and meaningful wink. Some of the whiskey splashed from the glass as he tried to set it down, and Patrick frowned. His old friend had been at the bar most of the day, and, as much as the leprechaun enjoyed a drink or two, too many was not acceptable.

He went to speak with Bear and Shorty about their friend, and Yancy slid into his vacated stool. But Sally's face darkened after fleeting introductions, and he left when she whispered in his ear.

"What'd you do to offend the ladies?" Patrick asked, coming up behind him.

"Nothing. Honest." His eyes went wide in contrived innocence.

"Should I be asking them?"

Yancy gave a disgusted snarl, and Phantom strolled down to bump his chin in affection. He shoved the cat in irritation, causing him to stumble and scramble to keep his feet. Cats don't do either, and Phantom, unused to such hostile treatment, glared at the offender.

Bear responded in an instant with a hand on his shoulder.

"We're going for a walk, Yancy. Get up."

When he tried to shrug it off, Bear took his arm and pulled him along, struggling to keep from punching the smaller man. Nobody abused Phantom, or any cat, not with him around. They were to be treated as treasures by all. He didn't speak until they were outside and away.

"Know why we're out here?"

Yancy's head wobbled from side to side, but, before he could stop himself, his mouth opened and stuff spilled out. He couldn't help it. "Cuz you're crazy?"

Bear let go of the arm and lowered his head.

Yancy shivered. He knew about the scars in Bear's beard, how he'd gotten his name after winning a fight with a mama bear, and tried desperately to figure out what he'd done wrong.

"The cat! That's it. The damned cat!" Yancy yelled, thrilled he'd remembered.

"So, you're not completely stupid."

"Aw, come on. It's a cat, and I didn't hurt it."

"His name is Phantom. Respect him."

They stood by the water's edge, and silence grew around them. Bear didn't add to his warning, and Yancy thought he might have said enough. He'd forgotten about the man's love of felines, but he'd remember from now on. For certain.

He was wondering how to end the discussion and get back to the bar and into his friends' good graces when his scalp prickled. His old childhood fear of the dark stole over him, and his head spun, eyes searching the shadows for a reason.

The strange woman he'd seen the other night stood behind him, and a long line of felines stretched behind her. He hadn't heard the woman approach, and her proximity unsettled him, especially after Bear's words of warning.

He swore her hot breath whispered over the back of his neck.

"This is Yancy, Cassandra, an old friend."

She looked him over, from his scuffed boots to the roots of his black hair. "I know."

"We haven't met," Yancy said, and quickly amended it. "I don't think, anyway."

"True. You don't."

Bear chuckled.

Yancy scratched his head, wondering what she meant but didn't want to ask. He shifted his feet and searched for something to say that wouldn't get him into more trouble. "You have lots of cats."

"A clowder," she said, still looking him over.

"Good to see you, Miss Cassandra," Bear said, and turned toward the hotel, leaving his old buddy scrambling to catch up.

Yancy didn't want to be alone in the night with that cat woman. Something about her scared him. She looked through his body as if probing for his soul, and she smelled of a scent he recognized but couldn't define. Not identifying it would drive him crazy later as he lay awake.

In the dark.

Chapter Three

Abby gave a sigh of pleasure and added four to the total as soon as she saw the buggy turn the corner by Foster's store. She calculated success by having to use more than the fingers of both hands. For too long, she couldn't get beyond use of one. Now she used toes, too. Full integration of the church services hovered out of reach, but not far.

James Gerard stepped from the Adams rig and reached a hand to help his wife, Mildred, and Emily Adams. Emily had been picking up Betty's parents since soon after her son's funeral. The Adams and Gerards had worked through a difficult relationship, given George died while brutally whipping the Gerards' daughter, but it was a friendship Emily needed.

She had failed her son, neglected to teach him about real strength and honor. Because of her negligence, she felt accountable for what he'd done to Betty and, ultimately, for his death. She would not let her responsibility lie fallow knowing she had much to atone for.

Her daughter-in-law, Cecily Adams, and grandsons, Chunk and Baily, leaped down the other side of the buggy. The boys ran off to play with other children, no longer concerned over the color of skin. Their father ranted when he heard about it, but they'd learned to keep their mouths shut, and he never came to church with them to put a stop to it.

Cecily looked for Abby, spotted her on the hotel porch and strolled in that direction.

"Still counting integration on fingers and toes, Abby?"

She nodded and grinned. "I can't help it. Wish I could. Glad Terry let you come."

"He doesn't have much choice. Ma Adams said we're going to listen to the colored preacher, and nobody argues with her anymore."

"I'm glad. I mean – to see you here. Not the other."

Yancy pushed the screen door open and let it slam behind him. Abby spun at the noise.

"Sorry, Abigail. Didn't mean to do that."

"No matter, Yancy. Do you know my sister-in-law?"

He shook his head. "You mean ex, don't you?"

"We're still sisters." She took Cecily's arm. "I'm going in to see if Betty needs help. Want to come?"

Cecily backed away and shook her head. "Better not. The boys."

Yancy followed her inside. "What's with you and these . . . people?"

Abby stiffened and stopped walking. "What people do you mean?"

He twisted his head and rubbed the back of it. "You know. I heard through the screen door. Why are you so anxious about the colored folks? It's a constant thing with you. Are you pretending to be color blind, or do you just not like white people?"

She felt her skin prickle, and the little hairs at the back of her neck stood up. This couldn't be the same man she'd known in Nirvana. It occurred to her to walk away and not give him an answer, but she changed her mind. Anger simmered.

"I like *most all* people. And few truly suffer that particular eye ailment. I see color just fine. I respect it and the people who own whatever skin holds their bones together, and I care about principles and rights. Civility, too. If you'll excuse me."

She watched Yancy stalk off, saw Betty at the top of the stairs and hoped she hadn't heard Yancy's words. She took the steps two at a time and got there as Benjamin came out of their room.

"I didn't think your man would let you walk down those stairs alone."

"Good Lord, no. And heaven forbid I even try to walk by myself on flat ground. I swear he's gonna spoon feed me next. And you surely gave that Yancy a piece of your mind, Abigail. Thought I didn't hear him, didn't you? Or maybe you were just wishing it."

Abby scrunched her face. "Yeah. I was hoping. Sorry. I don't know what's gotten into him. He's different than before, or maybe he's just more himself than he was then or . . . I don't know what I'm saying."

"Don't worry about it. Let's waddle on down. By the way, I hear their finishing the white church pretty soon. Reverend Evans is gonna be one happy preacher."

"I heard, too. The Klan didn't waste any time coming up with the money. He'll be one damned happy, fat and sassy pastor. Say that three times fast without tripping on your tongue." Abby ducked her head and turned red. "God, did I really say that? On Sunday, no less. Sorry."

Betty hooted, slapped her hip and hawed again. "You aren't either sorry. You meant every word, and I'm gonna tell on you. You can pray for forgiveness, but I don't think you'd mean it much, so it's not gonna work."

Abby peeked through her hands, saw Benjamin grinning, and scanned the lobby to see if anyone else had overheard her creative tongue twister. Samuel leaned against the registration desk looking up at her, his arms crossed, an ambiguous grin on his handsome face.

"Darn. Quit sneaking up on me." Abby twisted around to bend over the bannister and scowl at him, but playfully.

"I didn't sneak. I walked in quietly so I could hear your wicked words."

"What are you doing here, Samuel?"

"I thought I'd check on Betty and escort you to church."

She stuck a finger on her chin and looked at the ceiling. "Gee, keep the little women safe all the way across the road to the pavilion?"

"Guess not." Samuel turned to leave.

"Wait. I'm joshing. You're tough to tease, and I'm glad you came."

"You're looking good, Betty," Samuel said, eyeing her belly.

"Always wanted to put on some weight. I know how, now." Betty chuckled and caressed her stomach like the babe inside could feel her touch or she could feel the babe. Her eyes softened with mother-love, and Abby shoved aside a twinge of envy and berated herself.

"And she's going to share this baby with all of us. Right, Betty?" At the bottom of the stairs, Abby took Samuel's arm and turned back for Betty's response. "I said, right, Betty?"

"Okay, boss. You'll likely be sorry you asked."

Shorty and Al came from the kitchen, followed by Patrick who shooed them away with a long, wooden spoon.

"I can finish. Been doing it for years, so get on outta here." He waved the spoon in the air for emphasis, and his reddish grey curls wobbled. "Give the Irish a prayer if ye would."

"If we don't get moving, we'll miss all the praying, and we could use it." Betty headed for the door, grabbed her stomach and bent double.

Benjamin wrapped his arms around her and yelled. She yelled back, stood upright, grinned and resumed walking. A trail of liquid followed, and Abby stuttered.

"Betty! Benjamin, I don't . . . You're leaking . . . Something's wrong, Samuel! Do something."

"Dang." Betty said and headed for their room. "Don't think we're gonna say a prayer for the Irish."

She folded again halfway up the stairs, and Abby grabbed Betty's arm, Benjamin the other, and together they hauled her up the steps.

"Samuel, will you go for Cassandra and then Doctor Dan?" Abby shouted behind her.

The tires of Samuel's Model T kicked up plumes of dust, choking people under the pavilion waiting for Reverend Jenkins to begin the invocation. Heads and bodies tilted sideways as they watched the automobile fishtail down the road.

"What lit Samuel's fire?" the reverend asked. "Thought he'd grace us with his presence this beautiful morning."

"Where's Betty?" Mildred stood, her head spinning as she scanned the congregation. "Where's my daughter? And Benjamin?"

Understanding lit her eyes, and she shoved her way across the row of chairs, stepping on toes, stumbling and mumbling apologies. She strode across the lawn, down the road and up to the hotel porch like Satan was chasing, her husband James close behind.

"Hold on, Mildred. Betty's fine. You know she is."

Mildred stopped in front of the door and pounded on her heart. It thumped so hard her chest hurt, and she could see the buttons on her dress bounce in its rhythm. When James reached her, she'd gained some control of her fear, but it hadn't reached her eyes. They were wide brown orbs floating in distress.

He wrapped an arm around his wife and whispered into her hair. Whatever he said calmed her, even brought a quiver of a smile to her lips.

"I remember, James. I surely do. Can I go in and help with our grandchild's birth?"

"You ready to be a grandma?"

"Been ready a long time, Grandpa."

She waited halfway down her lane where a screech owl had caught her attention. Samuel had slowed down, not wanting to run over any of Cassandra's critters, and when he came to a stop, he opened the passenger door for her.

"I'm not getting in, Samuel." She pointed at the owl perched in a hollow tree, and it whinnied like a small horse.

"What on earth. You keeping ponies in the woods?"

"Screech owls. Park the automobile and walk down the trail with me. We'll have tea."

"Abby sent me to get you, Miss Cassandra. Betty's having a baby."

The woman's serene eyes sparkled with humor.

"I know. It started around nine months ago. Do we need to have *the talk*?"

Samuel rubbed his forehead. "What's with you and your sister? Bunny slaps the back of my head like I'm a misbehaving two-year old, and you both treat me like a boy in short pants."

"Sometimes you are." Her grin widened. "And it's so much fun to cause a crack in your perfect attitude of indifference."

"From the two of you, I accept mistreatment but only because I love you." His lips curved in a semi-grin. "I'm serious about Abby, though. She needs you."

"Not yet. Let's have tea."

"Cassandra . . ."

She threaded her arm through his and headed down the lane, forcing him to follow and leaving the vehicle where it sat mid-lane. A whitetail munched on shrubs, ignoring their presence, and Samuel pointed out two speckled fawns nestled in the grass behind her. Cassandra nodded and placed a finger on her lips for quiet.

"Artemis and Apollo appeared yesterday." Her voice was a soft, melodic whisper on the spring air.

"Did they tell you their names?"

She tugged on his arm rather than startle the deer with a slap to the back of his head. When they had walked a few steps further, she pointed to a stand of trees with thick scrub brush beneath the canopy of newly leafed branches.

"What?" he whispered.

"Wolf crawling."

He stopped to stare into the gloom of the shrubbery, trying to spot what she'd pointed out. If it hadn't moved to sit upright, Samuel would have missed the majestic creature. His massive head appeared above the low brush, ears forward, white muzzle gleaming and eyes locking on

Cassandra. "Behave." She slowly closed her eyes and reopened them, and he disappeared from view.

Samuel wondered if the animal had really been there or if the woman by his side had conjured him from her imagination. He knew better but turned to look at her, nevertheless.

"He is real, Samuel. He keeps the coyotes from harassing my clowder."

"I'd think your cats could do that all by themselves."

"They could. Makes the wolf feel useful, though."

The tea kettle began to whistle as they opened the screen door, and Samuel breathed in the scent of hyacinth overflowing from vases on every surface.

"Tell me about your warfare." Cassandra placed a steaming cup in front of him and sat. She crossed her hands on the table and waited, spine erect, countenance serene as if she had all day to wait for his response.

Samuel blinked in surprise but settled back and eyed her, determined not to be bested by the legend of her gifts. He lifted the cup to his nose and inhaled the unfamiliar, pungent aroma. Truthfully, he couldn't respond because he didn't know what she meant. What war?

Samuel had learned mastery of silence, of waiting and watching, letting other people grow uncomfortable and babble whether they had anything sensible to say or not. So, he waited. He sipped tea. He looked at the hyacinths and back at Cassandra.

But she must have taught the master. She didn't look around the room but gazed straight at Samuel's eyes and waited in stillness.

"Alright, darn it. What war?"

"Between you and Abigail Riley, of course."

"We have no war."

"You do. One that will be waged for another hundred years. Maybe more."

Samuel leaned in and put his elbows on the table, his chin on his tangled fingers. "I have no conflict with Abby. I care for her."

"And she for you, but you lie. There is conflict."

He untangled his fingers and rested his back against the wooden chair. He looked at his dark brown hands, at the deep mahogany hands of the woman across the table from him, and thought of pale Abby; Irish, auburn-haired Abigail Riley. He refused to use her married name as she wasn't anymore. Yes, of course, there was a battle, and it angered and concerned him. He picked up the teacup, drained it, and dropped it back on the saucer.

When he rose to leave, Cassandra put a hand on his shoulder. "Have you joined the Blue Vein Society? Or are you adding Abby's name to that illustrious group?"

Samuel's eyes narrowed. He knew he'd heard the terms before but didn't remember where and didn't like the way they sounded. An eyebrow rose.

"Mr. Chesnutt wrote about it in *A Matter of Principle*." She walked with him and watched his face as he processed the information and knew when memory penned the words in his mind.

"You're speaking gobbledygook, Cassandra. He wrote about an entirely different issue."

She pursed her lips and continued down the path in silence until they reached the Model T.

"Possibly. Tell Abby I'll be there within the hour." She smiled with knowledge. "A long, long while before I'll be needed."

Shreds of white cloud stretched across the sky, illuminated by a monster Flower Moon. They feathered over Lake Idlewild water, a duplicate sky rippled by feeding fish. Nocturnal critters were silent.

Chair runners made the only night noise as they banged back and forth on the wooden planks of the hotel porch, and they stilled with each of Betty's wails. It had been hours – but seemed like days – and Benjamin's step staggered when each scream began, and his pacing came to a halt every time they ended. His head tilted toward the upstairs windows, waiting for the next sound, praying to hear the sharp squall of an infant.

Shorty went inside and came back with a tray of small glasses. He set it on a table, grabbed Benjamin's arm, and turned him toward the drinks.

"Take one. I'm thinking you need it. We all do."

"How long does it take to have a baby? What's wrong? I know something's wrong, and you need to find out what it is."

His words spewed in a boiling mass of fear and anger. Never again, he vowed. Never. World War I hadn't engendered this much fear in him, and his wife had been through too much already. He wouldn't again be the man to add more.

"I hear first ones take a while." Shorty placed an arm over Benjamin's shoulder.

While he wanted to comfort the man, he was having some similar thoughts about Al. It'd break her for sure if she got pregnant with a child of his. He was too damned big, and she was the tiniest woman he'd ever seen. Maybe they shouldn't marry. Maybe he should just run off. He couldn't stand to think of Al in such pain, but he probably wouldn't even hear any because she wouldn't make a sound.

"What? What's wrong?" Benjamin said. "You know something I don't?"

"No, nothing at all. I've been here with you all night."

"Why'd your face look like somebody died, then?"

Shorty ran a hand over his shiny head and rubbed it. "I was thinking it could be Al up there. It wouldn't feel good at all."

Abby pushed through the screen door and everyone leaped from their chairs, hope holding breath suspended.

"No change upstairs," she said, "we just want some music. Will you play, Benjamin? Betty asked for a lullaby or two to help the little one into the world."

He nodded, happy for something helpful to do. Moments later the lulling sound of his music seeped through windows and doors.

"Should I get Doc Williams back here?" Samuel asked.

"Cassandra says Betty's fine. Just slow."

"Lass always likes to make a show of things. She likes drama." Patrick chuckled and tipped his chair back, content to enjoy the night. "Could use another wee nip of Irish if you've a mind, Daughter. Keeps away the night chill."

"Wouldn't want you to get sick from the cold, Da. I'll bring the bottle, and you can help yourself."

Another wail filled the air, and the lullaby stopped mid-note, paused for a heartbeat and began again. Rockers halted and resumed. Sentences were finished, and they all wondered how long one could endure the agony of childbirth. Themselves included.

Samuel followed Abby inside.

"You telling us everything?"

She grabbed the bottle and filled three small glasses.

"We could use some courage. And yes. I've been truthful." She moved close and lay her head in the crook of his neck, and he ran long fingers through her hair. He could feel her breathing even out like she was winding down for a rest.

"Tired, aren't you?"

"Yes, but you should see Betty."

"I could take over while you rest a while."

"You? A man up there?" She tried to grin but failed. "Thanks for the offer, though, and for the brief respite."

"I'll take the bottle out to the porch. You go on up." He walked her to the stairs and touched her arm as she put a foot on the first step. "Do you know *A Matter of Principle*?"

Abby's face went blank. "I don't understand. What principle? About men in birthing rooms?"

His mustache twitched, and he shook his head. "No. Never mind. I shouldn't have mentioned it."

"Samuel. Explain."

"No. Another time. You go on up."

Abby took her tired feet upstairs, muttering about principles and men. Betty rested quietly in between wrenching contractions, and Al pried an aching hand from her grip to dampen the cloth in cool water and wipe her sweat drenched brow.

"This babe's never gonna come. I don't think he likes me." Betty's words were faint from exhaustion, and Al ignored them.

"Want a sip of water?"

"I want some of the whiskey I saw Abby bring in."

"Nope."

She couldn't argue the matter as a moan took over and turned into a cry for help.

"Get her to sip the Bach flower and Skullcap tea," Cassandra said. "When the contraction is done."

Al took over, and Abby and Cassandra were shoved aside. Until the baby crowned, little could be done, and Al wanted them available but out of the way.

"Benjamin!" Betty screamed. "I need Benjamin!"

Al's eyes questioned Abby who shook her head. "It's a matter of principle."

Cassandra snuffled. "What is?"

"Men in birthing rooms, apparently."

"Girl, why would you say that? Men are there at the beginning, and many help at the end. Who gave you that bit of erroneous information?"

"Samuel. Or he could have meant men *should* be in the birthing room as a matter of principle. I don't really know."

Cassandra's eyes focused inward as she recalled the conversation with him about Charles Chesnutt's short story and nodded. It was a knowing movement that made Abby want to make a face at her, or tug on the bright scarf covering her head so it tilted over one eye.

She loved Cassandra, but she was tired, scared for Betty, and confused by Samuel.

Abby's chin rested on her chest as she nodded between groans, but she jolted at the sound of a baby's cry and leaped to her feet. The infant's lusty yell prompted the sound of boots on the floor and a fist pounding on the door.

"Give us a minute or two Benjamin," Cassandra said and handed the baby to Abby. The healer cut the cord, cleared the baby's mouth of debris and washed his eyes with an herbal solution.

"Wipe him dry and wrap him," she added.

Abby held the infant as if he was made of spun sugar and feared she might do him harm. When he was clean, she stared at the tiny fingers and toes, marveling at their perfection, and moisture clogged the back of her throat and crept into her eyes.

Knock it off, Abby. It's a baby. Don't you be one.

Benjamin's voice brought her back, and she finished the chore she'd been given by wrapping the child in the blue blanket. She handed the bundle to Betty, kissed her forehead, and said good night. Al and Cassandra followed her as Benjamin came in to introduce himself to his son.

He kissed his wife and stared into her dark brown, tired eyes, ignoring the baby she couldn't turn away from.

"I'm so sorry. So sorry."

"How can you be sorry when we have our son?"

He hadn't wept when he'd been wounded in the war or when he'd seen his friends die on the battlefield. He hadn't wept when they told him he may not walk again because of the shrapnel nesting near his spine. But tears choked him at the love in her eyes as she looked at their son.

"How are you?" he whispered.

"I'm perfect, and so is our son. He surely is."

Benjamin opened the blanket and stared. "Yes. He surely is, and so are you, my beautiful Betty."

Chapter Four

They called him Benji, and no child born to woman and man was more treasured. Betty insisted on the first name – after the love of her life – and gave him two middle names after both their fathers. The tiny, squalling infant was called Benjamin James Micah Chambers, and he made enough noise to be worthy of the long moniker.

She peered at her child for the hundredth time, pulled up the gown and ran a finger over his long, satin limbs. She hummed in amazement and admiration.

"I know what ebony means now. Never saw it before this child. He's beautiful, isn't he, Benjamin."

He patted her back and murmured agreement. "He's a Mali king, Betty."

"I'm not biased, right?"

He chuckled, but she couldn't hear it over Benji's squalls. He lifted his son and tucked the flannel around him. "Course not. I'll take him downstairs so you can get some rest. Folks aren't going to leave you be until they see him."

She grinned and wiped a hand across her eyes. Every muscle in her body ached, but she'd never felt better or stronger.

"I'm not letting you soak up all the credit for this." She wiggled a tiny toe sticking out of the blue flannel bundle in his arms. "How about we all go downstairs? I'll sit in a rocker while Benji sleeps, and everybody can croon over him."

"That's crazy, Betty. It's only been two days. You need to rest."

"I don't want to rest. I want to get out of this room and show him off."

"He's something to brag about, that's for certain." Benjamin's dark eyes melted as he raised a pinky finger wrapped in his son's hand.

"He's perfect. So damned perfect it scares me."

"He surely is, Benjamin. Get me into my robe."

He lay Benji on the bed and helped his wife rise and struggle to make herself presentable in front of the mirror.

"Let me do that," he said, taking the brush from her. He stroked her dark hair away from her face and kissed her nose. "You're beautiful. Hold my arm tight. I'll carry Benji."

By the time they reached the last step, a crowd had gathered, and everyone wanted to help. They pushed at each other to get closer to the royal threesome and grumbled when they got shoved themselves.

"Please, give me a path to the fireplace," Betty shouted. When they did, she raised her chin and led the way. "You'd think we were Mary and Joseph for crying out loud. I just want to sit in a chair by the hearth with my baby."

Her dictatorial words conflicted with the light in her eyes and grin on her lips. She enjoyed the attention and was eager to show off her son – their son.

Patrick pulled a rocker closer to the small fire and threw on another log to create more warmth. Shorty draped the chair in an afghan that had been left folded over the arm and steadied the chair while she sat. Abby smoothed the coverlet over her legs as if she was an invalid.

Betty's smile said she'd like to do this every day. Being a queen had something to offer. She raised her arms to receive her son, the prince.

Word spread, and it wasn't long before folks Abby knew only to nod at had gathered around Betty, Benjamin and Benji. The nearby table filled with gifts: a smoked ham, jars of preserves and pickles, a hand stitched towel with *Chambers* embroidered along the edge, a basket filled with dried herbs and one with pastel soap wedges smelling of lavender and spice.

Abby tried to serve the new arrivals, but they weren't in the bar for drinks or Patrick's food. They were there to see Betty and Benji and were eager to be part of the celebration. She made gallons of coffee and set it out where people could help themselves.

When someone magically produced a plate of cookies to sit next to it, Abby threw her hands in the air, gave up trying to run the show, and went behind the bar to watch. Betty or some unknown force was in charge, and she was fine with abdicating responsibility.

The door opened to a breathless Charity pushing the biggest, shiniest baby carriage Abby had ever seen.

"It came today! I've been waiting and waiting. Beautiful, isn't it?" She pushed it into the bar and up alongside the rocker holding Betty and Benji. "Here. Put him in it."

"He's asleep, Charity."

"Well, he can sleep in there. It's for him. And for you so you don't have to carry him around all the time."

"Thank you, friend. It's generous of you."

"You could come back to work, too, and push him from room to room. Be like old times only with – um, him in there instead of your belly. You know?" She pointed at the carriage to make her point.

"She doesn't need to work, Charity," Benjamin said.

Betty turned a sweet smile his way to soften the words she'd been holding back. "But I want to, Husband. Abby needs me, and I like my job."

He strolled to the piano, and Betty heard the beginnings of the song he'd created for her, *A Pretty Woman.* She smiled, and her mild distress floated off on his sweet notes.

Benji succeeded in maintaining the focus of attention at his baptism by multiple-octave howls of displeasure after Reverend Jenkins dipped his body in the lake. Much of the town of Idlewild encircled them, some in the water with them, and ignored his wails in a sincere attempt to hear the reverend's prayer for his soul.

"I was baptized. Right here." Sue slapped a flat hand on the water and beamed in remembered ecstasy, her cheeks bunching into a grin and spreading across her face. She dipped herself further into the water, entirely soaking the green satin dress, and poked Shorty who stood next to her. "I learned not to fear the Lord and the water all on the same day. You should try it."

Sally put a finger across her lips. "Hush, Sue. This isn't about you today."

"Nobody can hear me over Benji's wailing." Sue pouted but couldn't be dejected for more than a moment. Her essence demanded good humor. "He's a good-looking boy, though. Lusty lungs, too."

As godmother, Al stood next to Betty in water up to her waist because she was such a tiny thing. When Reverend Jenkins handed Benji to her, he grabbed a fistful of long blonde hair, quit yelling and tried to eat it, his eyes focused on the fascinating nearly white mane falling over her shoulders.

"I know how to shut him up, now," Betty said. "Can I cut a bunch of your hair and make a toy out of it?"

Al rolled an eye and adjusted her grip on the baby who worked to fill his other fist with the rest of her hair.

Shorty tried to help by pulling it away from her face, but she told him to give it up. Benji could have it. When the Reverend tried to take him back for the final dunking, he set up such a wail that Al told him to dip them both.

"I've been wet before," she said.

He did. He put an arm around her back and one on Benji's head and lowered them both into the water. White hair spread around their heads like halos shimmering in the ripples.

"They're gonna drown," Shorty said, nudging the reverend.

Startled, he yanked them from the water, his face reddening in embarrassment. "I'm sorry. They were so beautiful, so holy looking, I was mesmerized. I apologize."

"I understand. She is – I mean, they are."

Benji didn't even yell. He still had two hands full of Al's wet locks and was happy. They waded from Lake Idlewild, Betty and Benjamin trailing but keeping a careful eye on their child.

His Grandma Gerard waited next to Abby's former mother-in-law, both of them wearing out the grass in their impatience. Emily Adams' eyes followed Benji as if he were prey and she predator. When they neared, she took a long step to stop their progress and reached out large knuckled hands for the soggy bundle.

"I have a dry blanket," she said and turned to grab it from Mildred. "He won't want to be cold."

"Don't think he cares right now, Mrs. Adams. He's got Al's hair."

Betty's chuckle sounded half mirth – half concern as she watched the older woman's eyes on her son. They weren't angry but could have been. They weren't miserable but could have been that, too. She didn't know what Emily Adams' eyes expressed, but she knew captivation and fixation on her child when she saw it.

When it became clear Benji was determined to stay put in Al's arms, Emily gave in and wrapped the dry blanket around his back. She tilted her head to look at his face, searching for a streak of blue in the dark brown of his eyes, for a tilt of the nose, a birthmark shadow under his left ear.

While she searched, others watched her and wondered. She focused on him out of realistic proportion. Folks liked to see babies, but . . . Mildred patted her arm and linked it with hers, drawing her away.

"What are you doing, woman? What you looking for?"

Emily blinked like she'd forgotten how and her eyes had grown dry. "Nothing. I wasn't looking for anything. Just looking. Everybody looks at babies."

"Emily Adams, I don't hate you anymore, like I said, but you can't lie and expect to be my friend. What were you looking at?"

"Nothing. It's not there."

Mildred Gerard scoffed in the back of her throat, pulled her away from the others and turned to face her. She pushed out her chin like she was about to stomp her foot or slug the other woman.

"You tell me what, right now, Emily Adams. What isn't there?"

She watched the woman's shoulders drop and her head follow. This is what defeat looks like, Mildred thought. This is what despair looks like, and a little forgiveness crept into her heart, a little mercy she never thought she'd feel for the mother of George Adams. She had no compassion for a rapist, but his mother . . . maybe. It had been blossoming.

"I'm such a fool," Emily whispered. "I hoped."

"My God." Mildred slapped her forehead in understanding. "You were looking to see blue eyes, weren't you? I don't believe you!"

She watched Emily shrink and didn't know if she could stop herself from punching her. She still didn't know when her hand raised and came down on the other's shoulder, gently. She pulled her into an embrace and prayed for a little of the mercy she'd felt a moment ago.

"I'm sorry, Emily. For you, not for Benji. He's Benjamin's son, and you know it."

"I know. I knew."

She wanted to weep but couldn't. Tears had long since dried up and left her vacant and hopeless. She'd latched on to the ridiculous idea this child might have some of George in him, and part of her son lived on. The timing wasn't perfect, and she knew it. Plus he hadn't raped Betty that last time. But . . .

"I really am a fool, Mildred."

"You love like a mother, Emily. A foolish one."

No smile softened her words, and she spun and headed for the hotel, eyes on the ground, bent forward at the waist like she always did. When she realized Emily hadn't followed, she turned back. "Come on, you old fool. Let's go get some of Abby's tea."

The room reverberated in good will, friends and family, jokes and memories of other baptisms and other celebrations of love and life. Patrick sliced his Irish tea cake into smaller pieces than planned, not expecting the number of well-wishers filling the bar. He groaned when the door opened again, and Gus filled the frame. His booming voice turned heads.

"You could have invited me! Why'd you leave me out?"

Patrick shuffled his way with a piece of cake held out in apology. "Not really a party, Gus. Today is Benji's baptism."

Gus was bigger and darker than anyone Patrick knew, and he could frighten even the toughest of men with a simple lift of an eyebrow, no glare needed. He ducked into the room and softened his voice.

"I can do baptisms." The entire piece of cake went into his mouth, and he swallowed and grinned when he saw Al. "There's my little pocket girl."

"Don't ye be messing with Shorty, now. He gets riled easy over Strange Al."

"I know. That's what makes it fun."

He lumbered over, picked her up and swung her around, her feet nearly slamming into anyone close enough to get clobbered. Al didn't yell or fight him. She simply hung there until he stopped whirling and put her down.

"Where's that baby?" Gus asked.

She pointed to a circle of people bent over making silly sounds, and he wandered to them.

"Kinda looks like me," he said, glancing at Benjamin whose fingers stalled on the piano and then picked out a funeral dirge that brought smiles to everyone who figured it out.

"Sounds like you don't care for the idea, old man. He's an outstanding boy." Gus bent over the carriage where Benji lay and planted a sloppy kiss on his forehead, an odd move for such a hulking man. "Thank the good Lord he looks like his momma."

"Sweet, Gus. But I think he looks just like his papa. What you doing here on a Sunday?"

"Picking up an order tonight and was looking for my pals to ride with me."

Yancy eyed him from his perch on a bar stool, wondering who the man was and why he could walk in, swing the little blonde around, and no one did anything to stop him. He wondered, too, if his size had anything to do with it but figured Shorty was probably close to as strong as the big colored man.

Nobody bartended, since this wasn't a normal day, so the empty glass in front of Yancy went unfilled until he slipped behind the bar and helped himself.

Fingering his drink, he sipped and watched Abby swing through the kitchen doors and refill the punch bowl. Samuel followed close behind with a platter of cookies. It seemed anywhere Abby went, that man trailed close behind. If not, it wasn't long before he showed up. Yancy's eyebrows drew together, his forehead wrinkled, and his foot bobbed up and down with energy demanding release.

He watched the big black man amble over to Abby and pick her up. And she let him, even smiled and patted his face. Something sprung inside, and he leaped across the room and stood in front of Gus with clenched hands.

"Why in hell do you think . . . Get your hands off her!" His voice cracked on the last word and made him feel like the boy he must appear by comparison. The picture in his mind made him madder.

Gus lowered Abby, pushed her behind him, and turned to the scrawny stranger who raised his fists into the air in front of him and spread his legs – a fighting stance.

"Don't believe we've had the pleasure," Gus said, his voice a calm salve to soothe the irritated man. He'd seen bantam roosters before, and they never knew how much damage mere heft could do, or they wanted to prove they weren't impressed with size.

"I don't care to know . . ."

Abby slid from behind Gus and pulled at Yancy's arm. "Stop it. What are you doing?"

He stumbled with Abby's yank on his arm and tried to hold his posture, embarrassing himself further and getting angrier.

"Not gonna put up with men mauling you. It's time somebody stopped it."

"Yancy. You can't do this. These people are my friends."

"Another one, huh?"

The words resonated, and for a moment she saw her ex-husband standing in front of her. He would have said the same thing, *had* said them, and she hadn't known about his biases until it was too late. Yancy's had been hidden from her, too, because nothing had brought them out; there had been no cause in Nirvana.

Gus stiffened as he processed Yancy's words, and Samuel wondered how long he should let this go on. Somebody could get hurt.

"What does that mean?" Gus asked.

"I think you know, mister." His eyes narrowed. He knew exactly what he'd meant, and it didn't occur to him the man wouldn't.

The collar of his shirt went skyward, and the belt around his waist tightened, squeezing his stomach as his trousers pulled up between his legs and he was walked involuntarily toward the door.

Bear spun him around and pierced him with a glare as soon as the porch door shut behind them.

"You're acting the fool." He rubbed at his scarred beard and waited for Yancy to find some sense.

"I'm just watching out for Abby."

"She doesn't need you looking after her."

"Seems she does with all these men bothering her. One after another. They don't leave her alone."

Bear moved to the porch rail and looked out over the lake, then took Yancy in tow and led him away from the hotel. A few fishing boats dotted the water, and several determined children splashed in the shallows of the sandy shore. In a short while, the sun would head too far west and force swimmers ashore, purple with cold and goose fleshed.

Bear didn't want to turn from the tranquil view and face a feisty old friend. He faltered, knowing reason wouldn't work, but figured force might. He corralled his thoughts and gave it a try.

"Leave Abby to live her own life. You hear me?"

Yancy staggered and thrust his shoulders back as far as they would go. "Don't think you can be telling me what to do, Bear."

"But I am." He moved into Yancy's space and forced the smaller man to look up. "I'm telling you right now. Are you listening to me?"

"This time she's gonna marry me like she shoulda done before. I told her then Frank wasn't right for her. You'll see. All those . . . The colored men flocking around her can just . . . Stop it, Bear! Damn it! What are you doing?"

The smaller man seemed to take forever to hit the water, and the splash he made was suitable given his thrashing arms and legs. In a good five feet of water, it took his boots a moment to find bottom, but Bear stood by, waiting. He didn't even get his own wet because he'd thrown him high and hard over his head.

Folks might have thought Bear's face sported a grin at the sight of a flailing Yancy – if there had been anyone close enough to see it and comment.

And there was, and she did. Cassandra and the clowder hovered in the growing dusk, her knobby walking stick pointing to the rippling circle growing around Yancy.

"Nicely done, Cat Man."

Chapter Five

The nightly regulars filed out of the hotel, led by Patrick who ran a knotted hand over his scruffy face and made a rasping sound like he was sanding a piece of wood.

Charles' eyebrow rose. "Taking up wood- working?"

He was smooth shaven no matter what time of day it was, and his friend didn't stand close to the razor unless he was directed there by his daughter.

Patrick cocked his head and grinned. "Thinking I'll be ready for winter and won't get cold like all you tidy folks. Ye don't see naked animals in the forest. When it gets cold, they grow thicker fur; they don't rub it off."

"Guess you're right about that. Doesn't it itch, though? Or smell like moss growing on the side of a tree?" He sniffed, smiled, and rubbed his own chin in thought. "And it's only July, Patrick."

"Ye used to be such a bonny lad."

"I haven't been a lad since you've known me. Glad about that, too. I'm happy those days are done."

Following them out the door, Bear and Shorty slid into their chairs and listened to the beard banter. Bear fondled his own and remembered the animal who had scarred it with white lines amidst the black bristles.

"Sitting off by yourself tonight?" he asked.

Yancy had pulled two of the rockers close together and was perched in one. He'd grown damned tired of the others monopolizing her attention and had gotten there early so he could be sure to get the seat by Abby, away from the rest.

When she came out, he grabbed her hand and said, "Sit." He didn't rise, simply pulled her into the chair next to him.

"What are you doing, Yancy? Let go of me."

She tumbled into the chair and stared at him. "What's going on?"

"Nothing. Just wanted to talk. We never get to cuz someone else is always around and in the way. Always talking at you. Like him." Yancy pointed at Samuel.

"Why is he always here?" He tempered his voice, but it didn't come out a whisper, either.

Abby stiffened and felt a twinge as Samuel made his way to another chair. He always took the one next to hers, she expected it – he expected it. But she didn't know how to remedy this situation without making a big deal of it.

She sat back, trying to relax, and watched the night deepen. Fish made circles in the water and dinner of insects on it. A coyote yipped a response to a faraway query, and Abby wondered if someone else occupied his chair, too. Or maybe a mate objected to being apart from him? If so, she hoped *she* had the courage to get up and go sit in whatever spot she wanted.

Night in July was pungent with the scent of wet earth floating in the air and coating your skin and hair. You could taste it on the back of your tongue as if you'd sipped from nature's cup. Like no other smell, it was the aroma of summer in northern Michigan. Abby let the scents take her around the lake to the critters whose talk she interpreted. His sudden words startled her.

"Come ride with me tomorrow, Abby. Or go for a nice meal out of town with me?"

"It's a work day, Yancy."

"Get that Charity girl to work for you. She loves being in the bar, making eyes at all the men."

"Be nice. And she's working upstairs. We're short-handed with Betty off."

Yancy shifted, and his hands tightened their grip on the arms of the chair which had ceased its rocking. When Abby turned his way, she saw anger flash in his eyes before vanishing.

"Well, then, how about you figure out a day or night when you can get away, and we'll ditch this town and go have ourselves a good time? Name the day, Abby. We'll maybe go dancing, too. I recall you like shaking a leg."

"I'll try to find an hour or so. I promise, but let's just take a nice ride, okay?"

She glanced at Samuel, who ignored her as if he hadn't been shunted aside or cared if he had, and tried to pick up the conversation they were all having – without her. She heard the murmuring but not the words.

Why are they being so quiet, tonight?

". . . a nice restaurant. You know he can't even get into one."

Abby swung back to Yancy with enough force to make a loud crack. She grabbed her neck and rotated her head as an ache shot down her back and into her heart.

He was right, she knew, but he didn't need to say it or sound so darned happy and superior about it.

"If you want to remain my friend, Yancy, I never want to hear you speaking drivel about my friends again. Jim Crow is immoral, and Michigan should be above those southern practices."

She had whispered, but her words penetrated with significance, and, when she sat back and raised her eyes, Samuel's were on her.

"You live in a fairyland, Abby," Yancy said, his voice harsh and inflexible.

Without regard for the man next to her, she scooched her chair closer to the others, scraping the runners on the wood and drawing eyes her way. She sat back with a miffed groan. Maybe Yancy would think about what he'd said. Probably not, but she could hope.

Cleo left Bear's lap in a single leap and landed on hers. She turned her sleek, black body in a circle, glared her golden eyes at Yancy, and lay down. She pretended to sleep but left one eye slightly open to keep tabs on the man who had angered her mistress. Her purr comforted and rumbled, adding to the night sounds.

"It damn well isn't just another club like the Elks," she heard her da say. "I don't care what some folks want you to believe." Patrick was mad, and the reddish-gray curls on his head jiggled with each word. "The Herald said over fifteen thousand flocked to Grand Rapids like buzzards picking at fresh bones. They want a Klan governor like Indiana? That's . . . It's . . . I can't even find words."

"Wow, Da. No words? You must be riled. Not much gets your goat." Abby thumped his arm, teasing the tensions away as the rest recognized her presence with nods.

So this had been their subdued conversation.

"They said some three thousand of those hooded idiots marched through the city's west end. Guess they're trying to keep the immigrants and Catholics in place," Edna threw in for effect and looked around her. "Looks like some folks are right down there on the bottom rungs of society with us coloreds."

She was mad, too, but her voice matched the night. Its velvet caressed in an effort to soothe boiling tempers. Her husband, Jesse, had wanted to take off for Grand Rapids right after reading about the march. She knew the angry eyes smoldering in his dark face would not have been well received even though his education and culture matched any man's.

"It's not just about us," she added, reminding him the Klan hates people who aren't colored, too, but probably not as much.

Perhaps his rhythm was off, or possibly it was deliberate, but tonight, Yancy ignored the harmony of synchronization and the rhythmic rocking practiced on the porch and emphasized his differences with his chair as he leaned it back and held it there, his legs extended and rigid. "Sounds like they were having a little July fourth entertainment," he said.

"You find Klan marches entertaining? How about cross burnings and lynching? You find that fun, too?"

Jesse stood in front of Yancy, his hands itching to do something besides clench. Edna moved to her husband's side and pulled him toward the steps. He didn't resist her tug, but he didn't quit staring at the new hotel guest, either, and stopped before descending the stairs.

"Never thought I couldn't be a friend to a friend of Abby's, but you're close to bellying up to that bar – friend."

"I was making a joke. That's all. You people are so touchy."

A bead of sweat rolled from Jesse's brow and gathered above his lip, tasting of salt and disgust on his tongue.

"And what people might *you people* be?"

Edna yanked, and Jesse obeyed. In the yard, they waved themselves away without words or backward glances.

Abby stood, stomped on the toe of Yancy's rocker and he shot forward, his head bouncing off her hip.

"Go to bed, Yancy. Now."

"But I . . . I . . ."

"I know. It's all about you. You're a two-year-old. Go on, now. Go to bed."

He rose from his chair, trying for tall and dignified, and when Abby's finger pointed at the door, he puffed his chest and left the porch. He didn't even let the screen door slam as he left. A quiet *snick* as it closed announced his departure and separated them from the thoughtless, ignorant man.

Charles lifted his eyebrows and resumed the rhythm Patrick had never broken. Samuel's thumb and forefinger smoothed the narrow mustache over his lip, his black, granite eyes lighting with a suggestion of a smile.

"What's so funny?" she demanded. Her toes tapped the gray painted wood in an irritated rat-a-tat.

"What do I find amusing?" he asked.

"Yes. That was my question? Yancy was not humorous. He needs a spanking. He was being obnoxious, and I think you're smiling about it."

A long arm shot out, and her finger pointed to the door as if Yancy still hovered nearby. "How was he . . . How was that stupidity humorous?"

Samuel pulled a gold watch from his vest and flipped it open. It caught a sliver of moonlight and flickered a couple of times off the white columns lining the long porch before he snapped it closed and pocketed it.

"You're still smiling," she said.

"Not at him."

Her arm bent to point the fingers at her own chest.

"At me?"

The smile moved from his eyes to his lips. "Yes. At you."

Abby dragged her chair over and plopped into it, a sheen of sweat glazing her forehead and cheeks.

"I swear, Samuel. You're . . ."

She quit talking and regarded the rush of insect tweets and twitters she hadn't heard earlier. The night worked correctly, now, as it should, as *she* should. Here in this chair by Samuel, she could enjoy the evening.

"I understand." He rested a hand on her arm and listened to snickers from the other four men on the porch. "But Abby, you sent a grown man to bed. And he went. It was kind of funny."

"I guess. I didn't think you'd find anything about the Klan rally entertaining."

"I don't."

Shorty's chair stopped its motion and, ignoring Abby and Samuel, he leaned toward Charles. "Were you in Idlewild the day they marched here?"

The gentle man had little patience with violence, especially the stupid, pointless kind practiced by the Klan and other bullies. They could hear the anger hiding in his soft voice.

"I was," Charles said. "Right here on this porch, listening to Betty tell them off from the upstairs window and watching Abigail come close to de-hooding her husband and the rest of the Adams men right here in the street."

"I wanted to. I really did, and I would have if Samuel hadn't stopped me."

"Should have let her, Samuel," Charles said. "Why'd you stop her from exposing their faces? Men should have to stand by their choices. Women, too."

"Wasn't the right time."

His eyes drifted in the direction of the stable where Edwin lived. He could have identified the man under the hood as the one who'd sold him a dead man's horse, and Samuel couldn't let that happen.

They rocked in silence, listening to the crickets rub their legs together, bat wings flutter across the sky, and the clatter of their own thoughts as they meandered or leaped from cliff to cliff and point to point.

"I read a story you wrote," Shorty said.

He was in a reflective mood tonight, and it centered on Charles. He rubbed his bald head as if shining it, patted the orange cat on his lap, opened his mouth, closed it, and started again.

"It's about the 'Blue Veins Society' and light-skinned colored people. I'm trying to understand. Want to just tell me what it means so I can stop hurting myself trying to think it out?"

"The Wife of My Youth?" Charles glanced at Samuel after acknowledging Shorty's nod. "What do you think it means, Samuel? Does it tell the truth?"

"Depends."

"On what?"

"On what you think it tells us." Samuel smiled, knowing he wasn't going to let Charles drag him into this particular discussion. It was too close to home.

His home.

"You wrote it, Charles," Shorty said. "Why don't *you* tell *us* what you were getting at?"

"I wasn't getting at anything. I was simply starting conversations, exploring relationships within my race. A lot changed after the Civil War. If people didn't want to be married anymore and their wedding occurred before the war, marriages could just be ignored. Folks climbed to new heights as upward mobility became available – for light-skinned men with light-skinned wives. Or so it seemed. I wanted us to reflect on the issue, to talk about it. I don't desire to tell anyone what to think or do."

"About marrying light skin?" Samuel asked.

Charles grew older, worn-out in the glimmer of a moment as he thought about his next words. "No," he said. "About what we thought of dark."

"Not a commentary on miscegenation?" Samuel said.

He patted his vest pocket but refrained from pulling the watch from it. A glance at Abby told him she'd seen and knew it was his equivalent to biting a lip or chewing a fingernail. But did she know why?

"No. Miscegenation is not a theme in any of my work. That involves a sexual relationship or marriage between two races. I write only about my own – in all of its vibrant and varied hues." His glance grazed Samuel's troubled eyes. "Why would you ask? Do you think it's wrong?" Charles asked.

The watch tumbled as it came from its satin nest and landed on his lap where it lay reflecting the moon.

"No," Samuel said, "but my beliefs oppose convention, and the weight of them pales in comparison to the rest of society's. My ability to shield mixed race couples and their progeny from harm is sadly lacking. Even less than deficient. I am powerless."

He refused to look anywhere but at Charles as he spoke and, when finished, he picked the errant watch from his leg, flipped it open, peered at the tiny photographs lining the back, closed and returned it to the pocket. He hated his father's watch as much as he loved it. A finger caressed the edge before leaving it to its slumber.

Around the two men, four faces regarded them, understanding more than the poignant words spoken. They peered at the lake when their conversation came to an end and waited for someone else to fill the void.

Shorty cleared his throat. Bear caused Phantom to purr with a scratch behind his ears, and Abby prayed for her loon to wail or a fish to leap.

Patrick ceased his ceaseless rhythmic rocking.

"We've had no nightcap, lass, and I'd like to make a toast to our friend, Charles. Would ye do us the honor of bringing a tray?"

"Don't be making something of me I'm not, Patrick. I'm just doing a job like everybody else. That's all my writing is and no more."

Patrick tilted sideways, thinking as he gazed at the slender, handsome man.

"Some of us do jobs, Charles. Some of us have careers, and some of ye have a calling that makes ye do the work whether ye want to or not. I think that's your gift and your curse."

Abby kicked at the screen door, holding a tray of small glasses filled with Patrick's favorite Irish whiskey. Samuel leaped to open it.

"Want me to take it?" he asked.

"Nope. Not heavy. Grab one, and we'll wait for whatever Da has planted in his wee brain. I never know." She headed for her father.

Patrick held his glass high, and when the others had one in their hands, he began.

"To Charles and to the heavy work of thinking ye make us do. Keep writing stories. Ye have a revolution to perform, not in the whole world, but right here in Michigan. In Idlewild."

He downed his drink in order to make the toast more powerful and the exhortation come true.

The others struggled not to choke on theirs when they heard the word revolution. What was Patrick thinking? Was he calling for an actual revolt? A war? Against whom?

"Whoa, there, my friend. I'm no revolutionary. I prefer to think of myself as a scholar, a quiet one at that. And I'm about done writing. I'm in my sixties and tired out."

"You are not," Abby blurted and tried to cover her shock with a cough.

"That's neither here nor there. And age is no matter," Patrick said. "I'm not saying a revolution with weapons. I'm talking about ways of thinking, changing the way ye see the world and folks in it. And that's a calling. Ireland has been doing it for centuries, sometimes with guns. Not asking ye to do that."

Crickets and bats continued to fill the night with sound, but their twitters sounded lonely for the space of long moments without voices for accompaniment. Patrick shifted his chair into motion. Bear followed, and before long all six chairs were again in peaceful sync.

They were glad for an opportunity to think about something other than revolts when the clowder and their mistress appeared. Phantom and Cleo leaped to watchful positions on the rail posts with only a few back hairs raised in alarm as they followed Cassandra along the lake shore with their gaze.

Her long, robe-like dress moved about as if a tempest stirred it, flipping the sleeves back and forth and tossing the skirt. She raised her walking stick in the air, pointed it at the group on the porch, and braced her other hand on her hip. She spread her legs like she was preparing to do battle with walking stick-sword in hand.

"Is she challenging us?" Abby asked, her voice soft so Cassandra's extraordinary senses couldn't pick up her words.

Cassandra scoffed. "I am demonstrating approval." She didn't raise her voice, but the sound carried to them in mud-scented air wafting on a curious cloud.

"How'd she hear me?" Abby said, and wondered if what she tasted when she licked her lips came from Cassandra's sack.

"Don't know. She's without explanation," Samuel said. "But she apparently agrees with us."

"But agrees with what? Revolt? Irish Whiskey? Miscegenation? We've been everywhere tonight. What does she agree with?"

Samuel's eyes twinkled in the moonlight. He enjoyed Abby's frustrated confusion. "Ask her tomorrow. I think I already know."

"Tell me, then."

"No."

"Brat."

He nodded, said goodnight and blended into the darkness in a few long steps. Abby shivered.

"Silly woman," she whispered, and heard Cassandra's chuckle even though she could no longer see her or her clowder.

"Um . . . I was talking about me," she added and looked around for the woman even though she knew better.

Bear poked her and growled. She jumped, and he laughed.

"You're a brat, too."

"Not nearly often enough."

Chapter Six

Frank stood well over six feet and refused to let age bend his back. White hair grew thick and curled over the collar of his work shirt, and large-knuckled hands gripped with the strength of youth. His nose and chin jutted out in expressions of command and demand.

Emily watched her husband, as she did frequently, and wondered how he could remain youthful when she'd grown old. Losing two of her sons had wrinkled her skin and grayed her hair, but knowledge of her role in their departure had broken her soul.

"Where you going, Frank?"

He had an old quilt draped over his shoulder and carried a sack bulging with angular shapes. He heard but didn't respond and shuffled to the pantry and disappeared. When he returned, he had a second sack hanging over his other shoulder.

"I asked where you're heading? Where you carting all that stuff off to?"

Frank's eyes were hollow when he turned her way. "Just moving some stuff. Taking it out to my place."

"This is your place. Please put down the sacks, and have a cup of coffee with me. I'll do these later." Her voice cajoled, hoped.

He walked out the kitchen door without responding, and Emily shook her head, shrugged and continued washing the breakfast dishes. She didn't know him anymore. He wasn't the man she married – or maybe this man had been in him all along, and she didn't recognize him.

Outside, she grabbed the bucket of chicken feed. She didn't need to call to her hens; most of them were flocking around her feet, clucking impatiently and hungry. She fed them later than before because things were different on the farm, now.

Terry took care of the fields and the repair of buildings and fences, sometimes with the help of his two little boys. Cecily milked the large herd of heifers, and Emily cared for the young calves and chickens and the house.

They worked hard, all of them, and not much time remained for play, but they didn't play much anyway. They never had, and Emily regretted letting that happen. It didn't seem important at the time because work took precedence, and she blamed herself. A game of cards in the evening wouldn't have hurt anybody, might even have brought them all together, made them laugh, helped them love.

She tossed a last handful of chicken feed and tilted her head in thought. She didn't remember them doing that. Laughing.

Emily paused at the door to the milk parlor and sniffed the sweet, damp scent of molasses and warm cow. It could be comforting if you took a moment to let it.

When her eyes adjusted to the lack of light, she saw her daughter-in-law squatting on a milk stool, her head resting on the swollen side of a heifer. Milk twanged against the side of a metal bucket.

"Do you know where Frank goes, Cecily?"

"No, I don't, Mother Adams. He never says."

"Does Terry know?"

"I don't know that either. *He* never says."

"Nobody says anything around here, do they?"

Cecily didn't bother to respond. Her bones ached. Her heart hurt, and she didn't know what to do about it. What to do about anything.

"Sorry, girl," Emily said, and placed a hand on her shoulder. "I didn't mean anything. You're a good wife. A good daughter-in-law."

She saw him tramping out of the woods, edging sideways down the bank so he wouldn't tumble in, and kneel at the edge of the river. He tossed in a bucket, let it fill it with clear, cold water and drew it back with a rope tied to the bail. When it rested on a flat rock, Frank pulled an object from his pocket, removed his clothes and waded in.

Abby didn't want to see her ex-father-in-law stripped down to his birthday suit, but she couldn't look away. She tried not to see, but the idea of Frank bathing in the river compelled her eyes to stay focused on the long, white body as he scrubbed it pink, dipped into the water and rinsed the lather away.

Frank's brown head and neck didn't belong to the pale body they attached to, and his dark hands extended from white arms that looked a lot like a long-sleeved shirt. A pinkish-white one.

She chuckled and clapped a hand over her mouth, not wanting to reveal herself. It was too late for that.

Yancy finished hobbling his mare and came up behind her, whistling. Abby stood, stepped behind a tree to hide from Frank, and held a finger to her lips to shush him.

"We have to go," she whispered and tried to turn Yancy back toward the buggy.

"We just got here. What're you doing, Abby?"

"Sshhhh."

She hurried him back toward the mare, not wanting to say why and not wanting him to see the naked man. For an inexplicable reason, she wanted to protect her ex-father-in-law from humiliation. It was hypocritical because *she* had looked, but Frank Adams was a proud man. He'd be mortified.

Back at the buggy, Yancy whirled around.

"What the hell?" he said.

"I know, and I'm sorry."

"What changed your mind?"

"I . . . Well, it's . . . uh." She giggled and tried to get the words out, but they stuck.

Yancy balled his fists, and frustration flushed his neck red. Black eyes flashed anger, making her step back until she bumped into the buggy.

"You promised a ride and a sit by the river. I've waited a long time for this, and now you're cutting out on me? You're a tease, Abigail Riley. That's what you are."

"Let's go somewhere else, please. Someone is on the other side of the river, and we don't need him to see us."

She hadn't wanted to take the ride with Yancy in the first place and didn't like much about him at the moment. She'd agreed because they used to be friends and, for some reason, felt an obligation to an old friendship. She wished she hadn't and hesitated at the step of the buggy.

Yancy glowered, stewed about the turn of events, and thrashed around in his mind over who it could be. Probably that Samuel man. She wouldn't want to disappoint *him*. Not her *good friend,* Samuel.

"I don't care who sees us, Abby. I'm not ashamed to be seen with you. Is that it? You ashamed of me?"

"Of course not. Don't be silly."

"Silly, am I? Well, I'm getting what I came here for."

He grabbed Abby's shoulder, turned her around and planted his lips on hers, hard. She pushed against his chest, but anger strengthened him, and she couldn't shove with enough force. He dragged her to the ground, lips still attached to hers, and forced his tongue into her mouth. She bit down, and he yelled. She pulled up a knee, and he yelled harder.

Abby didn't think twice about taking his mare.

"It's my buggy," she yelled back as he rolled on the ground in agony. "I don't think he cares," she told the bird racing alongside. The bright ruby-throated hummingbird stayed with her until she pulled up to the stable.

"Looks like you traded in Yancy for a good luck bird."

"I did, Edwin. It was nicer."

"Should I take the rig and go get him?"

"Absolutely not. A walk will do him good. Cool him off."

Edwin's grin and the sparkle in his eyes said he approved. He snapped a suspender twice with one hand and unbuckled the mare's halter with another.

"Then I'll just take care of this old girl. Glad you're back safe."

"Sure, I'm safe. Why wouldn't I be?"

"Never know about some people. I got taken in before, so I know it happens."

"What are you getting at, Edwin? If you're trying to tell me something, spit it out."

"Nope, Miss Abby. I'm gabbin' like a fool is all. It's what old fools do."

Abby tossed her tussled head and headed for the hotel with a satisfied stride. In the kitchen, she sniffed chicory coffee and saw Patrick and Betty at the table with their heads together.

"What are you two up to? Cooking up trouble?" She tugged at her da's curls and bent to peer at Betty who ignored her. "What's going on?"

Betty leaped to her feet, unable to carry on the sham any longer.

"I'm coming back to work! I was supposed to say I was quitting to tease you, but couldn't do it, and I can't sit around feeding this little piggy anymore."

She dipped a hand toward the pram next to them, the extravagant, but well used gift from Charity. Abby peered at the wide-eyed, pudgy baby gurgling at her.

"Guess you've been doing more than a bit of feeding from the looks of him." Abby raised eyebrows at her. "You mean it about coming back?"

"Course. I always mean what I say. Assuming I can bring Benji, that is. He won't be any problem. He's a good boy."

"What about Benjamin?"

"No. Not bringing him."

Abby laughed out loud, showing big, white teeth, and it felt good.

"Smarty. I meant, will he be okay with all this?"

"Sure. Probably be relieved to get some time to himself. You know how men are."

"No. Actually, I don't think I do."

Her thoughts flew back to Yancy. To the kiss., to the bite, to the knee in his groin. No, she really didn't know men. Not at all.

Betty eyed her boss.

Abby swore the woman had a sixth sense, or eyes in the back of her head, or she could summon information like Cassandra. "Don't do that."

"I don't know what you mean." Betty rolled her black eyes toward the ceiling corner, and Abby giggled like a little girl.

"God, I've missed you. When are you coming back?"

"Does tomorrow work?"

"Perfect."

Patrick hummed as he stirred the huge pot of savory smelling soup. The sparkle in his daughter's eyes always made him want to sing.

"Where you been?" Betty asked.

The color left Abby's cheeks. "For a ride."

Patrick's spoon stopped. "I plum forgot. Where'd you leave wee Yancy?"

Abby's lips twisted sideways as she bit her cheek and wondered what to say, how much to say. Maybe she shouldn't have left him. And he sure wasn't so darned wee.

"Um . . . at the river. I had to get back, and he wanted to stay for a while."

It wasn't a lie. Was it? I needed to leave, and he was occupied with rolling on the ground and moaning.

"Quick trip," Patrick said, prodding.

Color flooded back into her face. "I need to clean up and get to work. Things to do."

"You're keeping secrets, boss."

Abby fled the room, calling platitudes over her shoulder. "Good to see you. Glad you're coming back to work. You're just in time to help with the big wedding."

Betty swung back into the job like she'd never left. Once again, crisp white sheets floated down in perfect rectangles on the guest room beds. Again, they worked in harmony, without words unless they had a desire for them.

Benji cooed from the corner, contented in his carriage until hunger prompted a wail. Betty hauled him off to the rocker in Abby's room, fed him, and returned to work. The baby didn't notice when they wheeled him from one room to the next and slept through the rest of the morning.

Abby emitted a hushed shriek the first time she saw Phantom stretched out in the carriage next to him, but by the time Cleo joined them, she'd gotten used to it. Betty even encouraged it because it kept the cats from chasing the dust mop or making beds out of the guests' clothes in closed armoires and drawers which they could open and often did.

Abby grabbed the buckets in one hand and dragged the mop with the other. Betty had already left for the last room.

"Forgot your baby," Abby said as she walked in and watched the sheet hover in the warm, lake scented air coming in through the open window.

Betty's head popped up, eyes round and frightened.

"My God, I did. What kind of mother am I? Be right back."

Abby giggled and Betty sailed out the door.

She pushed the shiny, blue carriage into the corner and peered into it. Benji slept with the cats curled next to him. One fat hand locked around Phantom's leg like it was a rattle he might shake when he woke.

Betty made hospital corners on the top sheet but kept a watch on the carriage. "You gonna be good without Al and me this Saturday?"

"Why? What's Saturday?"

"What's Sat . . . Surely you know what Saturday is."

"The day after Friday?" Abby's eyes lit with fun.

"Abigail Riley. Two of your best friends are getting married, and I – another best friend – am standing up as a witness. Like a matron of honor. Imagine that? Who would have thought it a few years ago? Strange Al and me, best friends."

Abby couldn't respond around the odd lump lodged in her throat. She blinked back moisture and swallowed, moved to the window and watched geese pull at the grass. More came every year, and, as much as she loved them, they made a mess. She took her time musing about messy geese and swallowing.

"You alright, boss?"

"Sure," she croaked. "Like all old ladies, I want things to stay the same. And they don't, not ever."

"You? Old?" Betty snorted. "That's just plain crazy."

"Sometimes I feel terribly old. You're married with a baby. Shorty and Al are getting married. Shorty will move out . . ." She banged her forehead on the window frame.

"I'm so selfish. I want everybody here. With me." Betty's hand on her shoulder brought more swallowing, and she smiled around it. "I'm Edwin," she said with a hoarse chuckle.

"Now I know you're crazy, Abby."

"I know," she said through a wet giggle. "Sorry. He said he was an old fool, and that's what I feel like. I'm Edwin."

"You're not losing anybody, Edwin. We're here every day, like always."

Abby sucked in some air and thrust her shoulders back. "Let's get this room done so you can get home to your handsome husband. Is he picking you up?"

"Yup. Maybe we'll stay for some of the colcannon Patrick was stirring up, and Benjamin can play for a bit."

"I'd love it, but you don't have to, Betty. Really."

"What? Eat? I surely do. How else can I feed my Benji?"

"You know what I . . . Never mind. You're a good friend."

From behind the bar, Abby kept an eye on the door, still looking for Yancy. He hadn't been back to the hotel since the river incident and didn't sleep in his bed anymore. They dusted his room and changed the water in the pitcher, as usual, but Abby was thinking about letting it out to another guest soon. Just pack his things up and store them.

"Why you worried, Abby?" Shorty ran a finger down the still full glass and watched her eyes.

"I'm not worried."

Bear raised one eyebrow.

"Okay, I am. He left all his stuff here. I hope nothing happened to him."

"He's been seen at Foster's store, hanging out with Joe and whoever comes in and stays to talk. Don't know where he's sleeping, though," Samuel said.

He'd stayed out of the conversation until now, and his senses twitched, letting him know something was going on he didn't know anything about and might not want to.

"Could be he's staying at the whistle stop. Miss Evans takes in roomers, usually for just a night until they can get to the resort, but you never know," Shorty said.

"Could you find out?" Abby's eyes pleaded. She was mad at Yancy, but . . . He'd been part of their lives in a quieter time and place.

"He's a big boy, Abby. Some reason he should stay away from here?" Samuel asked.

"Course not. I don't think so."

Abby moved down to the serving station where Jackson waited with an order, glad for a reason to leave. When she glanced back, Samuel's eyes followed, and she turned away.

Chapter Seven

The sun blessed them with good weather and the right amount of breeze. Edna's daughter Daisy, hired to chase the geese away from the pavilion, ran around waving her arms and yelling. Her mother and a taskforce of women decorated the wedding site with ribbons and a variety of blooms from their gardens. A riot of color speckled every corner and flowed over the makeshift altar.

"Think they'll have babies?" Mildred asked Emily who had driven the buggy to retrieve her friend, as well as the giant dahlias taking over her garden. Together, the two of them had become a natural scene in Idlewild, and folks no longer stared or commented about the unlikely friendship.

"Why shouldn't they? They're a young couple like most newlyweds." Emily straightened with a hand on her back and a groan. "Certainly wish I could say that about me. Young, that is."

"But they're not like most. Not at all. She's no bigger than a minute and he's . . . well . . . big. Nice and soft spoken, but really big."

Mildred's words were hushed like she was speaking out of turn, and her eyes darted about looking for interlopers who might overhear and think her a gossip. Bunny, coming unseen from behind, tapped her on the shoulder, and she spun like a child's top.

"You look like I caught you blaspheming."

Bunny's beautiful head wore a bright red turban, and her face bordered on solemn. But when her smile turned on, the skin over her high cheek bones tightened, her eyes flashed, and the light she shined made you feel blessed by something extraordinary.

"I wasn't swearing. You know me better, Bunny. Where's your sister. She's bringing the herbs and we need to twine them in the flowers," Mildred said.

"Cassandra will be here with baskets of lavender for devotion, Ivy for fidelity, dill for good spirits, and calendula for health. Told me this couple didn't need herbs at all, but she'd bring those for the multitude of less spiritually blessed folks in the audience. I agreed with her."

In Abby's room, Al stood at the window and watched the activity at the pavilion. She sipped a cup of steaming tea and wondered why they didn't hop on Shorty's horse and elope. Come back when the deed was done.

"Are you nervous, Al?" Betty asked. "Cuz that'd be understandable. Did anyone have *the talk* with you?"

"What talk?"

"You know - *the* talk. The one mothers have with their . . ." Betty smacked a hand over her mouth, remembering Al's had died in childbirth.

"I'm sorry. That was dumb. Maybe Abby can do it? No, not Abby. Maybe Ma? Or Edna? She might be the best one to . . ."

"Stop. I lived on a farm."

"So? What does that have to do with anything?"

"I know about babies."

"Oh. Well, sure, but . . ." Betty couldn't finish, couldn't say what she really wanted Al to comprehend. She moved beside her at the window and stared out of it, but didn't see the children at play, the women at work, the shrieking geese as they fled the crazy little girl who screamed at them.

She remembered Abby's dead eyes when she talked about her husband taking her but not loving her, about not ever being touched with affection. Betty didn't think Shorty would be like him, but who really knew?

"I can hear you thinking," Al said. "Say it."

Betty drew in a long breath and let it out through fluttering lips.

"Women have the right to say what happens to their bodies, and when it happens, and they have the right to be loved. Tenderly and passionately. You can have that, but you might need to say so. If you do need to, that is, if Shorty doesn't treat you right, you have to say so. Promise me?"

Al didn't turn toward Betty, but her eyes rolled her way, and she grinned.

"I didn't hear you, Al. Promise? Let me hear you say you promise."

"Shorty's the best man ever." She didn't need to say anything else.

Betty snorted in relief and grinned, happy the talk was over. "Second best."

In Shorty's room, Bear snarled at the nervous groom and picked up his orange cat for something to do. He'd been trying to keep the man from leaping out the window, saddling his horse, and running off.

"You know I'm right, Bear. I don't know what I was thinking. I'm too old, too big, too, hell, too everything, and she's a sweet young woman – one who deserves a hell of a lot better than me."

"It's you she wants, you big dumb brute. You know that's true."

"But sometimes you don't always know what's best for yourself."

"Al? She knows. Always has. I'm going down to pour us a medicinal whiskey. You'd best be right here when I get back."

Abby was giving Charity instructions for the day when he arrived, and Jackson was zipping around the room smiling for tips. Normalcy flourished in the bar, unlike in Shorty's room. Bear ordered the drinks from Patrick.

"Medicinal," he said.

"Shorty feeling a wee bit a chill on his feet?" Patrick grinned, looking like the happy leprechaun he claimed to be.

"The usual. Want to join us for a drink?" Bear nodded to Abby. "He'd welcome you, too."

Charity, happy to be in charge, scooted around the bar and poured four, put the glasses on a tray, and tilted her head in the direction of the doorway.

"You're off for the day, Abby. Go on up with your friends."

"You thought you needed reinforcements to keep me from running off?" Shorty whispered when they barged through the door.

"Brought some cheer."

Bear put a drink in Shorty's shaking hand, and Patrick took one from the tray and lifted it in the air.

"May your right hand always be stretched out in friendship and never in want." He drank and extended his to Shorty who grasped it as if he was drowning and the hand would keep him alive. "Lad, you've naught to fear. You're a kind man who loves a woman, and Al's the sweet lass who loves you back. What's to fear?"

Abby heard her da's words and shuffled her feet.

What's to fear? Everything. Nobody really knows anyone.

Her stomach tightened, and her face paled as she recalled her own marriage. But he hadn't been invited, so she forced him from her thoughts and away from Shorty's wedding.

"What's wrong. You see a ghost?" Shorty asked.

"Nothing. No. I need to go get dressed. So do you. I'll see you down there."

He pulled her into an embrace, and she wrapped both arms around him, snuggled into his strength and drew a deep breath.

"I love you, Shorty."

"You too, Red."

"It's not red. Auburn. How many years have I been telling you? If you were anybody else, you could have a black eye right now. But I wouldn't want to mess up your pretty face on your big day." Abby lifted her chin and left the room, eyes snapping.

She didn't resemble their own Strange Al in the least. The white chiffon gown Mildred made snugged her body and flowed off hips no one knew she had. Her regal walk down the center aisle of the pavilion misted eyes, and not a few people wondered how the ragamuffin Tatum girl had turned into such an imposing beauty.

She walked with determined dignity like she had the whole afternoon to get there, eyes on Shorty's as he watched her. Either the whiskey had calmed him or the sight of Al had turned his thoughts to love because he ambled toward her with outstretched hand.

Pastor Jenkins cleared his throat to get Shorty's attention, and when that didn't work, he spoke up quietly.

"You're supposed to wait for her here, son."

"I'm done waiting."

Those in the front rows put a bawdy spin on his words, and tittered.

"Me, too," she said. "Let's get married."

Everyone heard her, and applause broke out. Shouts of agreement accompanied them to the altar.

"It appears they'd like to see you two hitched." Reverend Jenkins held a brief service which celebrated the bride and groom, and they were married. "You may kiss the bride. But don't hurt her." He couldn't help it.

After toasts and food, the band set up and the first strains of the bride and groom waltz skimmed across the lake, all the way to the island where vacationers sat in front of the *dog houses* – the small cabins built in the early years of the resort. Betty and Benjamin joined the newlyweds on the dance floor, followed by Samuel and Abby, Jesse and Edna, Patrick and Sue, and Gus and Sally. Bear lifted Daisy and danced with her in his arms while she played with the roadmap in his beard.

Abby lengthened her stride to match Samuel's broad step, afraid to tread on his toes. She feared her big feet weren't meant to waltz but would do a great job of mashing grapes in Italy. She'd seen that in a magazine once and thought she'd missed her calling.

"What do you think about inviting the Island people?" Her words stuttered as she tried to talk and move her feet at the same time – without stumbling.

"Island people? Invite them to do what?" Samuel teased. He danced as easily as he walked but knew she was hesitant. She actually glided in his arms, as light as a dragon fly when it lands on your hand, but she didn't know it.

"To come join us, Samuel. For music and dancing."

"Guess you'd have to ask Shorty and Al about it."

"I will . . . oops . . . sorry. Darn."

He tightened his arm around her, pulling her closer to his chest. "Relax," he whispered, and she forgot her feet as his breath whispered across her temple.

"Nice. Let's dance all night."

"I think you have others on your dance card, miss."

"I don't have a dance card, sir, and I'm not a miss."

Shorty thought it a fine idea, and Gus agreed to make the walk over the footbridge to deliver the invitation.

"I'll walk with you, Gus. Make sure you don't lose your way," Sally said.

He threaded her hand under his arm and patted it while they walked, an exceptional looking couple, to be sure. Long, slender Sally, always majestic and erect. Tall, broad Gus whose skin resembled a moonless night.

"Happy for your company, Sally. You sure do look fine and shiny in your red dress. Nobody wears a dress better than you."

"Don't say that in front of Sue, Gus."

"Think I'm stupid?"

The entrance to the footbridge lay near the front of Joe Foster's store. Gus ignored the group of men who loitered watching the activities going on at the pavilion. He knew Joe by his nasty reputation and recognized two others in the group, Terry Adams and the old *friend* called Yancy.

His arm muscles flexed in unconscious preparation for a fight, and Sally glanced down and then sideways.

"What's wrong?"

"Nothing, yet, sweetheart."

He brushed the long fingers wrapped around his thick forearm, moved forward at an idle but deliberate pace and looked around as if he had not a worry in the world.

A smile quirked the corners of her lips and traveled to her eyes. Beside her was a real man, and it felt good walking by his side. He said what he meant, did what he said, and made her feel treasured and safe. Every man should be like Gus, and every woman would cherish him. She looked up as his face stiffened.

"What?" she asked.

"Nothing."

"Don't lie to me, Gus."

"Just heard the good farmer Terry Adams express disappointment in the number of Negroes at the pavilion."

"He's a dope."

"You got that right. Way I hear it, all Adams men are dopes and then some."

"You have special powers of hearing or something?"

"It's practice. I own a bar and need to know what's going on in every corner. And behind my head."

Gus grinned at her. "You wouldn't believe some of the stuff I hear eavesdropping on conversations they don't know I'm privy to . . ."

His words jammed to a stop and his feet kicked up dust as he spun toward the group of men. "That's enough," he said, and took a long stride their way.

Sally caught his arm and dragged him around. "What are you doing? What's wrong?"

"They said something they shouldn't have."

"What? Tell me." She watched his eyes narrow and continued. "It was about me, wasn't it? But I don't care. Leave it alone. I fight my own battles, Gus."

"Nobody brown sugars you, Sally. You're a class act."

She pulled him in the direction they needed to go, listened to his breath return to normal and felt his arm relax under her hand.

"You're something, Gus. You really are, but I *am* a woman of the night. Let me rephrase that. Prostitution is what I do for a living. I don't hate it, and I don't love it, but it's what I do, and I do it well. I'm not embarrassed by my work, and it doesn't own me or reflect who I am. Get that? It's important you do."

He glanced back to the men and tried to stay centered on the footbridge without falling off and into the water.

"Sorry. I didn't mean . . . I can't stand those men, and they have no right to say anything about you. Nothing at all, even good stuff. Not off their black hearted tongues."

"People will say things, honey. It's great I'm so tall because I can look down my nose at most folks. You can, too." She squeezed his arm and they stepped off the other end of the bridge and made the rounds of cabins, with invitations to join the wedding party.

Several couples followed them back to the pavilion, and others said they'd be along. They packed the dance floor and hindered graceful movement.

After a long line of dance partners, Abby headed for the makeshift bar to quench her thirst, but arms snaked around her middle and squeezed the air from her lungs. She tried to free herself, but the arms gripping her couldn't be pried loose. When she twisted around, her nose smacked into his grinning face.

"You. Let me go, Yancy. I can't breathe."

"No. It's my turn. You been busy dancing all night long." His words slurred, and spittle dampened her cheek.

She wiped it with her sleeve. "You're drunk. Let go and go away."

"You're always saying bad things about me. I'm not drunk; just had a few is all. Come on. Dance with ole Yancy. You'll like it better than dancing with all those coloreds."

His hands moved across her in an effort to caress and hold her still at the same time, and Abby's stomach turned.

She lifted a foot to ram it on top of his, but he caught her movement and side stepped.

"Figured you out this time, Abigail. Not gonna let you hurt me tonight. We're gonna dance."

His smile was a leer. Abby could see it when she turned and caught a glimpse. They were packed in the middle of the dense crowd, and she didn't want to make a fuss but didn't know what to do about the obnoxious man. She didn't know him anymore.

"I need a break, Yancy. Let's go to the bar and get a drink. Move your hands, please, so I can walk and breathe."

She struggled to keep her feet as his arms tightened and then abruptly fell away. Samuel stepped between them, black eyes glaring.

"The lady asked you nicely. A gentleman would comply."

"You're not her keeper," Yancy said.

"And you're no gentleman."

Samuel put a hand on Abby's arm to lead her away, and Yancy stepped in front of them, bobbling as he moved.

"In the south, you'd be lynched for insulting a white man and touching a white woman. You know that, mister? You couldn't even take a drink of water at a fountain or take a piss in a restroom. What kind of gennelman does that make you?"

Laced with hate and slurred with drink, his words stopped nearby dancers who formed a wall around them.

"That's absolutely right, Yancy. Once again, what you say is true."

Yancy took a fighter's stance and waved his fists around in the air, goading Samuel to take a punch. He wanted him to so he could land a fist in his smug, perfect face. So he could see blood run from his perfect nose down his perfect, damned, white shirt – the arrogant, self-righteous bastard. Abby wouldn't want her lips on his face if it was battered and bloodied, and he was the man to do it.

His feet moved in a pathetic attempt at a boxing shuffle, and he blamed the crowd when he stumbled. He hadn't yet recovered his footing when a heavy hand clamped his shoulder and propelled him through the mass of people watching and wondering. His efforts to stand still and halt their progress were fruitless, and, because he didn't want to fall on his face, he kept his feet moving.

Bear shoved him down the road, pushing with one hand and hauling him up with the other when he fell forward. When they neared Joe's store, Bear stopped.

"You're no longer welcome here. Get your things from the stable in the morning. That's where I'll leave them. Don't come into the hotel. Don't speak to Abby."

"Tha's for Abby to say, not you."

"I'm saying it, Yancy."

"But listen, Bear. I'm jus' trying to make her see what she's doing is wrong. Being with all the coloreds all the time. You unnerstand?"

Bear glared and left, listening to Yancy babbling at his back. He didn't know where Yancy had been staying lately, but, for his sake, he hoped he was still welcome there. He'd worn his out with him.

Shorty met him halfway back, and Bear filled him in, apologizing for letting it go on as long as he had.

"Samuel was there," Shorty said.

"He shouldn't have to deal with Yancy."

"Right about that. Thanks for taking care of it."

"Go back to your bride."

Bear watched from outside the pavilion, taking a stroll around it every now and then, looking for interlopers who wanted trouble, who *were* trouble.

He didn't know the origin of Yancy's words and ideas but thought he hadn't invented the sentiments and figured they'd come from someone else. Maybe Joe or Terry Adams.

Or possibly further up the Klan ladder. Yancy didn't think beyond his own immediate desires, which made him a perfect Klan mouth piece.

Joe pulled his dirty trousers on and hitched the suspenders over a gray shirt, shouting obscenities at whoever banged a fist on his door.

"Closed. We're closed. Can't you see the dammed sign? Can't you read?"

He yanked the ragged curtain aside, sending up spirals of dust, to see Yancy leaning against the door, ready to thump on it again.

"Hold your damned horses, ya fool. I'm coming."

He fell into the room as the door swung in, and Joe stepped back and let him hit the floor.

"Damned idiot. Whadaya want?"

"I need a bed."

"Hotel's that way." Joe pointed a crooked finger out the open door and growled invectives at the still prone body of Yancy who was rubbing a red bump on his forehead.

"Why'd you hit me in the head?"

"You hit yourself."

"That's stupid. Why would I do that?"

Joe nudged him with his bare foot. "Less you want another knot on the head, you won't be calling me stupid."

"I didn't mean you. I meant . . . I don't know what I meant. I need a bed."

"Told ya. Go to the hotel."

"I can't. They won't let me."

"What'd you do now?"

"Nothing. I didn't do nothing."

Joe slammed the door shut and turned his back on Yancy, mumbling and heading for his own bed. "Take the couch in the back room. All I got."

After Bear left with Yancy in tow, Abby spun toward Samuel, sputtering her confusion, arms waving in frustration. Dancers moved to get out of her way as Samuel guided her through and around them. She pulled her arm from his hand and planted herself in front of him.

"What do you mean saying he's right? What kind of balderdash are you spouting? Why do you always agree with him?"

"Settle down, Abby. What he says is . . ."

"Nonsense. Yancy speaks drunken nonsense. That's all."

He grinned at the fire in her eyes. Times like this, when she got fired up and pink, he loved how she looked. But it wasn't the time or place for a debate. Maybe never, with him. "Most of what he said isn't . . ."

"It damned well is too, Samuel. Don't tell me it isn't." Abby was getting angry. And afraid.

She crossed her arms and clutched them. Yancy's hateful words turned to ice in her veins and held her stiff with frustration. They didn't live in the south. They didn't even have drinking fountains or restrooms here in Idlewild.

She stuck a finger in her mouth and gnawed at the nail, chewed until her teeth clamped on a ragged sliver and tore it away, leaving a raw wound.

"Will you listen for a minute, Abby? Can I order a drink for you? For us both?"

She nodded and started in on her thumb nail. Samuel pulled the hand from her mouth, put the glass in it, and clinked his own against it.

"Try the whiskey instead of the finger."

A smile wavered on her lips. "Thanks." She sipped. "I'm still mad."

He sipped, too, and watched her over the edge of his glass. "Okay, be mad."

"How can you say he's right? Tell me that, Samuel."

"I didn't say Jim Crow was right. I said he's accurate in saying those things happen every day because they do. All of the time."

"Words. Harrumph. You're playing with words. I wish you weren't a lawyer."

"But I am, Abby. And, what's more, I *am* colored." He moved closer and lay his hand on her shoulder. "And *you* aren't. You can't change who we are, Abby, not with all the wishes and fairy dust in the world."

"I don't want to change you, Samuel." She peered up, forced him to see her sincerity. "I . . . You're perfect."

He pulled a face at her. "Perfect? Since when?"

"Since . . . Okay, you're not perfect, but I'm used to who you are. You're like an *as is* purchase."

Her eyes slanted in attempted fun to wash away the filth of Yancy's bias; she filled her chest with blossom and herb-scented night air and listened for the cry of her loon over the chatter of guests and the music.

The world tilted off kilter. More than anything, she wanted to take Samuel's hand and leave the pavilion, walk Cassandra's nighttime trail, and look at the moon bouncing on Lake Idlewild. She wanted his hand resting on her hip as they walked and to feel the warmth of his body close to hers.

He heard her sigh and knew without asking where she'd been. He'd spent way too much time in her company and in her brain, and this night birthed the obvious child of their association, the battered product of their relationship. What had he been thinking?

"Want to risk your toes again?" she said. "I promise to tread lightly, and I won't yell at you."

Samuel pulled the gold watch from its pocket and flipped it open, knowing the action irritated her.

"I have an early morning, Abby. Sorry."

"It's the weekend, Samuel."

"I know. I have to say goodnight to Shorty and Al and be off. I'm sorry."

He left her standing there watching him walk away. It was the right thing to do, but he trudged with a heavy heart, his footfall bereft of the old Samuel arrogance.

He cursed the color of her skin, and she wouldn't care if she was a rainbow.

Chapter Eight

Al giggled when Shorty lifted her in his arms and carried her over the threshold to the farm house. He didn't put her down right away, and she didn't fuss about it. She relaxed in his arms, a small bundle that snuggled deeper into him, and let her gaze wander the room.

In the middle of the table, fresh flowers overflowed a vase: orange tiger lilies, white peonies, and purple dahlias, a combination that could only be Betty's work. Lavender filled her nostrils, and candles occupied every nook and cranny. Betty had spent some time making it perfect for her and Shorty, and Al smiled visualizing her at work.

She rubbed her cheek against Shorty's late day bristle and wondered at the dream that was her life. How had this happened?

"Happy, Al?" Shorty asked, his blue eyes squinting to see her face so close.

"Very."

"How much?"

"My love is even bigger than you." Her cheeks dimpled in fun, and he squeezed.

She squealed, and he immediately released her and set her down, fearing he'd hurt her.

"Shorty, you have to stop being afraid of me."

"I can't. Don't ask that."

"You must. I'm tough. Think about it."

She poured champagne from an icing bucket someone had left and held a glass out to him.

"To us, Shorty."

"Yes, to us for always. Thank you for loving me, for completing my life. I hope you know you do."

"I do."

"You said that at the church, and it's too late to take it back. Ever."

The cat Bear had given to Al wound around Shorty's ankles, vying with his orange nurse cat for attention.

"King and Nurse want milk," Al said. "Or loving."

"We all want love." Shorty picked up Nurse and scratched his neck as Al poured milk in their saucers. "King is kind of an odd name for a cat. How'd you pick it?"

"It's actually King George. Like the English king. A bit better than Al and Dog, right?"

"Al suits you. You're special."

"I need to milk and feed the chickens. It's late."

"I'll milk. You do your hens."

They ambled hand in hand toward the barn as if they'd been doing it for years. Shorty didn't use Al's milk stool. He was afraid he'd break it. He knelt instead, which worked just fine, and listened to the music of Al's clucking to her chickens and their responses.

The sun displayed the first streaks of a red sunset, and its daytime heat radiated from the ground, augmenting the farm perfume; feed and manure mixed with straw and sweet peonies growing by the door. He liked the way it smelled and the warmth created by the idea of her small farm. It worked on his insides where it tilted the corners of his lips in a smile of contentment.

"Want a goat?" he asked as Al came through the door with the empty chicken feed bucket.

"Why?"

Shorty shrugged, but he visualized Al with a Billy goat, and it turned his quirking lips into a full-fledged grin.

"Maybe just to look at," he said.

"That's it? Like a picture you have to feed and hear?"

He laughed at the words that were totally Al. "I think you can pet them, too. Like King George."

"Could be good. You about done?" Al peered in the milk bucket and raised an eyebrow. "Have you milked before?"

"It's been a while. Guess I didn't do so well?"

"Let me."

Al pulled her stool over and shoved the bucket back under the heifer. Squirts splashed the inside of the pail, and Shorty ran his hands down the silk of Al's long, nearly white hair. He loved it hanging down her back and swinging in the breeze, haloing her head and hiding her eyes when she bent sideways. He loved his fingers threaded through it and longed for the sun to finish setting, yet feared it, too.

He wondered if she did.

When the heifer said she had no more milk, he carried the pail in one hand and held hers in the other, feeling like a young boy with his first crush.

Their meal over, he washed and she dried to the sound of crickets and owls and nothing else. No words at all. He hung the dishrag and glanced her way.

"You want me to clean up at the outside pump? You can go on upstairs?"

"We'll both go up."

"Sure?"

"Yes, husband."

He scooped her in his arms and ran up the steps. He slid the dress from her shoulders, and she unbuttoned his shirt. He raised her shift and drew it over her head, and she unbuttoned his trousers and let them drop at his feet.

Shorty knew no other woman on the entire planet could compare with his Al.

The grand opening of the Oakmere Hotel captured the newspapers' attention and brought throngs of new people to Idlewild. The sign read *No Vacancy* and hung from the porch railing long before the actual day of celebration. Abby watched it swing in the light breeze each night from the new chairs on the new wooden porch.

Bear sat with her, but the rest of the nighttime rockers sat in chairs worn to their particular bottom shapes on the old porch. She peered at them across the lake, wondered what they talked about and if they missed her as much as they were missed.

"It's a footbridge walk away, Abby. Go for a visit. I'm betting they'd like to see you."

"Why? I'm fine right here. It's a great porch. Great chairs. Great company.

"Lots of 'greating' going on." He stroked Phantom and patted a shoulder in invitation to Cleo. Her tail flicked at the tip, and she teetered in indecision before leaping to Abby's lap.

"Thanks, girl. At least *you* choose me. I love you, too." Abby eyed Bear. "Did you mean to say I was grating on you? Not that I'm great?"

"Sounds right." He flinched when Abby backhanded his shoulder.

Her chair halted, but she didn't bother to look at him. "You give any thought to doing maintenance for us here? The job comes with room and board."

"I'll do your repair work, but on my terms."

"And what are those, my friend?"

"Later."

Abby, distracted by the long gait she recognized across the lake, stroked Cleo and let silence wrap around them. She watched his long legs lope up the steps, a hand drag his chair closer to the group, and saw Patrick go inside and return with a nightcap for Samuel.

Damned man.

She blamed missing her da for the knot in her stomach each night as she watched them doing what they'd done for a long time – telling tales, bantering with each other and telling lies when they had nothing else to say. They were her friends, and she missed rocking with them. And, of course, Samuel visited there.

At first, she'd thought it was a good idea for Patrick to continue work at the old hotel while she ran the new one. Eventually, other arrangements would be made, and they'd be together again. Betty already managed the rooms over there, Al the kitchen, and Jackson the bar, and they were capable. But someone had to be in charge overall, someone who lived there and would be available in case of trouble.

Maybe she should have stayed at the old place and let her da start up the Oakmere with Bear. Then she'd be sitting on the porch with all their friends – and Samuel.

She'd hired a cook named Alma Cross for the Oakmere, a nice woman with three sons. Abby didn't know if a mister Cross existed because she didn't talk about him and Abby didn't ask. She was a sturdy, attractive woman who did her job and left.

Except tonight, she'd stayed on to work the kitchen for the big weekend. Abby still needed to hire a waiter and upstairs help. Things were moving in the right direction, but she missed the old place.

The Oakmere Hotel would open whether she was ready or not, and she wondered what she'd gotten herself into. Patrick and Alma cooked night and day, and Charity did double duty at both hotels.

The night of the festivities, Sue and Sally glided through the doors draped on Gus and looking like movie stars in green satin gowns split up the sides and down the front.

"Ladies, I'm jealous. I can't pull off what you two can. You look stunning."

"It's an art form, Abby. You have to think it, be the dress, not just pull it over your head and button it up." Sue tugged at her tight bodice and revealed more skin.

Eyes around the bar opened wide, some with hope and some in fear the scant covering might reveal more than she intended. Sally stopped her cousin with a glare and climbed on a stool. Gus helped Sue up on hers.

When the strains of Benjamin's piano music got her attention, Sue spun on her stool and slid off, arms spread wide for balance. Her smile grew when she stabilized without tumbling.

"Gotta go see the piano man. He'll want me to sing with him." And she did, a sultry ballad that had couples holding hands and thinking about love.

The whole gang showed up for the opening revelries since they'd closed the bar at the old place for the night.

Both Jackson and Charity waited tables, Al and the new woman helped Patrick in the kitchen, Bear kept an eye out for trouble, and Shorty carried heavy things.

In between fixing drinks, Abby eyed the door. Anger and heartbreak simmered, a strange but potent brew, and, along with cursing his name in quiet but audible murmurs, her eyes glistened in defiance of her resolve.

When he strolled in and stood at the bar next to Sally, Abby ignored him. She had other customers to serve, drink orders to fill, and glasses to wash. He could wait.

She had.

Samuel turned to lean against the bar and watched the crowd. Sally's hand came to rest on his shoulder as she whispered in his ear, and Abby's skin prickled in thwarted frustration. "Damn it all," she muttered to herself.

"Oh, hello, Samuel. Nice of you to come by," she said in a deliberate corpse voice. "What can I get for you?"

He stroked his mustache and raised an eyebrow. "The usual, Abby. You're busy tonight."

"Sorry, did you have a usual?"

"Guess you've forgotten. Ale, please."

She drew the ale and slid it to him. "Refill ladies?"

Sally's eyes followed the brief conversation, and Sue's mouth hung open.

"What's wrong with you two?" she said.

"Not your business, Sue." Sally reached across Gus to poke her cousin.

"Nothing's wrong. I'm simply busy and haven't seen Mr. Moore since moving to the Oakmere. I have better things on my mind than to remember every customer's favorite drink." Her voice dripped melting ice.

"I'm sure you do, Abigail. It's good to see you." Samuel patted the watch pocket but didn't bring it out. White cuffs shot from his jacket sleeves as he lifted the ale.

"You must have been very busy. Away a lot?" she asked with hope.

"A bit," he said.

She spun off, again muttering to herself.

He can bang his knuckles on the bar if he wants a refill. I'm busy.

She didn't understand what she'd done that he stayed away so long, and it hurt.

Patrick shoved through the swinging kitchen doors carrying a huge pot of stew. He was going to start them out right – expect Irish food. Alma followed with a tray of soda bread and slabs of yellow butter.

Al moved the buffet dishes into some kind of order and herself out of the way as Samuel barreled around the table in un-Samuel-like fashion. He grabbed Alma around the waist from behind and planted his lips on her cheek.

Alma screeched and twirled to see who had attacked her. When she saw him, she gave a second, even louder wail that included his name. Both faces lit with joy.

Abby, watching and trying her best not to, blanched whiter than her normal pasty pale. Could this be the reason for Samuel's absence – Alma? And she'd hired the darned woman – even liked her. Something clogged the back of her throat, and she swallowed.

Bear saw and fought for serenity. Gus and Sally's eyes darted from Abby, to Samuel, to Alma and back, concern the dominant feature on their faces. They watched Patrick shuffle over, and then Alma removed her apron and followed Samuel to a small table in the back corner.

Charity got to the table first, chatted with the couple, and raced back to the bar with their orders, her face exploding with news she couldn't wait to tell.

"Well, don't you want to know?" she said to Abby.

"No. I mean, yes. Of course. How can I fix it if you don't tell me?" She flipped the bar towel over her shoulder and glared. "So what do Samuel and Alma want to drink?"

"Ale, of course, and Alma wants a whiskey, neat. Isn't that funny? Who'd look at her and think whiskey?"

"It's not so unusual. I've enjoyed a glass of whiskey myself from time to time."

"Aren't you going to ask me why Patrick let her off work?"

"No. It's none of my business, Charity, or yours. Here are the drinks. Get on with it. You have other customers to bother."

Charity smirked and wiggled a suggestive eyebrow.

Abby didn't comprehend how she could move just one, but she could, and she wiggled it well, too, almost up to her blonde hairline. Abby tried it on her own face and came up with a pained expression, like she was sick.

"Hmmm, needs work, Abby."

"Go on, girl. Go do your job."

Abby grinned as gratitude replaced the jealousy in her heart. Whatever else Charity did or didn't do, she engendered smiles, and Abby would pay her a salary just for that. Especially tonight.

Uncharacteristically, Charles Chesnutt turned on his stool and sat staring at Samuel and Alma, a quizzical wrinkle on his brow. Jesse thumped his arm to gain attention.

"Something wrong?" he asked.

"No. Thought I knew her is all."

"But you don't?"

"I do. Good woman who wouldn't mind you knowing she's mixed race. Don't see that much around here, not at her age, anyway. Comes from a big family."

"She doesn't look it."

Charles gave him a slow, meaningful half-smile. "Doesn't look like she came from a big family?"

"Wise guy. I meant it doesn't look like she's mixed."

"Neither do I. Do I?"

Jesse held his hands out palms down. "Now, this is colored. You two don't know how to be Negro."

"I'm sure she'd agree with you. We don't. Or how to be white. Ever think about that?"

Jesse shrugged and shook his head, a measured, distressed movement as if he'd said something he shouldn't have but wasn't sure what it had been. His eyes moved to Alma and Samuel again, and, when he turned back, Abby stood in front of him tapping his empty glass.

"Sure, Abby. Thanks. How about you, Charles?"

"Why not?"

Edwin sidled into the packed room and found standing space at the end of the bar. Abby saw him from the corner of her eye and slid a tall glass of beer his way.

"Glad you came, Edwin. All good at the old homestead?"

"Found a key in the kitchen and locked it up good afore I left."

Abby nodded, his words not sinking in, while she filled an order for Jackson. She put the last glass on the tray and dipped her head at Charity who passed a drink slip to her and sped off to another table of new guests.

"Bear," she shouted. "I need help."

He pushed Phantom further around his neck, feet hanging to one side, arms the other, and glided around the bar.

"I'll take Jackson," he said, and waved the young man his way.

With help, she had moments to look around the room. Many faces she knew from the old hotel and town, but many more were new, likely here for tonight's grand opening on Lake Idlewild Island.

It was a handsome crowd, the men dressed in summer lightweight, three-piece suits and the women in straight flapper shifts of all lengths – from ankles to above the knees. Pearls glowed, and diamonds sparkled on fingers and ears and in crisp white cuffs.

Abby's eyes widened, and she wondered where these people lived, what they did to earn such nice things. And then she noticed Alma still head to head with Samuel. She dropped her gaze and moved to the end of the bar where she couldn't see them.

"Sit for a minute, Abby," Bear said. "While we have a breather." Edwin climbed off the stool he'd managed to snare and held it for her so he wouldn't lose control of it.

"Thanks, Edwin. I could use a break. You said all was quiet back home?"

He nodded and moved to her other side so his back was to the wall. Edwin didn't like not knowing who might be coming up on him. He squinted a grin at Abby and told her his little quirk.

"I'll remember that," she said. "It's probably safer."

"You never know," he said. "Ever hear from Frank?"

"No. I don't expect I ever will."

Edwin rubbed his scruffy beard and thought of the picture she'd shown him of her and a handsome man, a man he knew as Jesse James who sold him a horse belonging to Al's murdered pa.

He pinched his nose, pulled at an ear lobe, and wondered how to say what he wanted to or even if he should. She sure got herself into a peck of trouble, this young woman did.

He cleared his throat and said, "Mister Yancy was around tonight. Him and old Joe. I told em we were closed and shooed em off."

Abby's back straightened, and her ears perked.

"They come around after Da left?"

"A mite after. I was sitting on the porch watching things when they came up."

"What'd they want?"

"A drink."

Abby worried her lip and Edwin watched.

"I sent em off, Abigail, and watched em go. I'm thinking you already know young Yancy's a scoundrel, and now he's hanging out with old Joe."

"Is he the reason you found a key and locked it up? We never had to do that before."

"Yep. You never left it empty afore, either. Thought you should know." He drained his glass and plopped a battered felt hat on his head. "I ought a be getting back."

Abby squeezed his neck in a one-armed hug, inhaled the scent of straw and horse flesh wafting from his flannel shirt, and murmured a thank you for his care.

His gaze landed on her face and stayed a second too long before he grunted goodbye and maneuvered his way through the crowd of revelers.

The little hairs at the back of her neck itched. Abby had never known what to make of the strange drifter who lived in the horse stable and did odd jobs for them. She still didn't. He had an uncanny ability to know things he had no actual business knowing. She watched him walk by Samuel and Alma and forgot all about Edwin's mysterious ways.

Damn Samuel.

Chapter Nine

"You should see them over there. Diamond rings, fancy suits and shiny shoes, all dressed up like they were going to an opera house in New York City. I mean, where'd they get that kinda money?"

Yancy whined, and Terry scowled. He couldn't stand whining. It reminded him of his little brother, George, and he didn't want to think about him for a whole lot of reasons.

"You don't know they're for real. Probably fake glass," Joe said. He picked up the whiskey bottle and slopped some in his empty glass, spilling as much outside as in. "What do the women look like? You only look at the men? Are you a girly kinda boy?"

Yancy puffed up and pushed his chest out. "Shut your mouth, Joe, or I'll shut it for you. And can't be fake glass. That's stupid. It'd be a fake diamond. Glass is glass."

"Knock it off, you two." Longstreet, the fourth man in the room, held a hand in the air for silence. "We're here to talk to you about joining our little assemblage, Yancy."

He nodded to a fifth person and sat back down.

Darnell Rumford stood and pulled on his fingers, making each knuckle crack individually. He was tall and the thinnest man Yancy had ever seen. And the palest. His cloud-white eyes had the merest tinge of blue, and one ticked so rhythmically his own eyes stared at it without volition, waiting for the next tic.

Darnell ran down the list of Klan business activities and glossed over the not so professional. He bragged about the number of Klansmen in Michigan and highlighted the men in counties close to Idlewild. It flattered Yancy when he explained how much they needed men like him who lived here but were not born to the area.

"You know what I mean," Darnell said. "We need white men with good heads on their shoulders to keep an eye on things and report back, men who aren't swayed by the philosophical hogwash they preach in their Chautauqua and church. Strong men who can stand up to pressure, to influences, and to the women."

"I sure know that," Yancy said, swaying toward the whiskey bottle for a refill. "That's egg . . . zactly right. If Abby's stupid husband had been half a man, she wouldn't be doing the stupid things she's doing. Damned shtupid Frank."

Terry stood and hiked his pants. "What are you saying, mister?"

"Stupid Frank is gone, and she's running around with that colored man. Frank wasn't good enough for her. I told her so, and see? I was right."

"Stupid Frank is my big brother, you ass. Watch what you say. And Frank wasn't dumb. Abby is. She's a loose piece of change, a . . ."

Yancy's fist met his chin, but it was a glancing blow since Terry had nearly a foot on the shorter, well-oiled man. When he stumbled against the counter, Terry's elbow went through the glass. Blood spurted everywhere, sending Yancy outside to heave his supper into the dust beside the store. Rumford and Longstreet found towels to wrap around the arm and tried to stem the bleeding, but the cloth continued to turn red.

Darnell's pale face glowed white in the lamp light.

"We need a doctor or the man's going to bleed to death."

"Doc Williams lives here now. Know his place?" Longstreet wrapped the towel tighter and closed his eyes. He would have prayed if he believed in a higher power.

He didn't.

"He's a negro," Joe said.

"So? Think Terry wants to bleed out because the man's colored?" Longstreet said.

Longstreet and Rumford stared at each other, neither willing to say what they were thinking. Would they rather die than have a colored doctor touch their blood? If not, what about all the brave words of the Klan? What about the hoods and the burning crosses and the lynching events they'd sworn never to talk about?

What about their strong beliefs?

Terry listened to them argue, turning paler by the moment, and yanked his cloth-wrapped arm away.

"Fools. Doc Williams isn't doing too well himself. Get the witch woman before I'm dead."

Darnell knew where to find both, and he took off on a run. The Williams home was closer, so he banged on his door first even if he was sick, but no one answered. He cursed, took off on a lope and soon headed down Cassandra's path. She met him in the middle with her medicine bag in hand and left him behind even though it appeared she ambled without haste.

Terry lay groaning on another counter that wasn't smashed while she dried the blood and poured whiskey on his multiple wounds, cleaning the flesh. Cassandra hadn't spoken a word, and he had positioned his head so he wouldn't have to look at the woman working on his arm.

Joe gasped when she brought out a needle and thread, causing Terry to glance at it and turn away with a curse.

"What you doing," Joe said. "Making a quilt outta his skin? Gonna do some voodoo along with it and cast a spell? Damned witch woman. You're crazy letting her work on you, Adams. She'll put some of her black blood in you. You watch."

"What *are* you doing?" Terry asked, eyeing the long needle.

"Nothing unless you turn your head back where it was. I'd be more than content to let your wounds put you in six feet of dirt where you belong. I'm here out of regard for your mama, and that's all. Miss Emily deserves to keep at least one son, even if he is an arrogant cave dweller."

She held the needle in the air and waited, the dark thread dangling back and forth in the draft of her warm breath. Terry turned toward the wall. His words were muffled but she understood them, stabbed the point hard into his flesh, and drew it through. Over and over, she stabbed, pulled, and stabbed again.

She crafted a nice herringbone pattern with the stitches where the skin came together, an intricate design her mother had tried hard to teach her to embroider on pillowcase hems. She'd finally gotten it right, and Terry's arm would forever be a work of art.

Cassandra smiled, thanked him for the opportunity to practice her embroidery, and drifted out the door.

His treehouse spanned the tops of several ancient oaks and rested securely in the upper crotches, nailed fast to the largest limbs. A ladder, its bottom wedged into the ground, slanted up to a balcony that wrapped around three sides of the structure.

A system of ropes and pulleys were attached to buckets and baskets which he loaded with items before climbing to his aerial home. From the balcony, he pulled on the ropes, and the containers carried up the goods.

Once inside, he did his usual check to make sure everything was as he'd left it. The door had locks, which he used, but he didn't trust people wouldn't find a way in if they wanted to.

The single, small but rambling room was snug with rugs, a handmade table, and a hammock on which lay a sleeping mat with neatly folded quilts. A mix of bowls, plates and utensils occupied a crude shelf.

He poured a cup of cold coffee and took it out to the balcony where he sat with his legs hanging over the edge. A half-dead tree stood adjacent, and he watched a pileated woodpecker widen the holes for his nest. The giant bird's bright red head turned his way periodically, his beady, gold rimmed eyes glaring and alert to possible danger. He was unused to the threat of man this high up in the trees.

"Don't be worrying about me," he told the bird. "You just do what you gotta do – like me. My nest is near done. You get on with yours."

He sipped and smacked his lips, enjoying the coffee brewed that morning over his campfire. Everything tasted better in the woods. He was in the middle of the forest and a healthy hike from civilization, but it was worth it.

Some days, he brought one of the horses but couldn't do it too often because they were easier to track. And he couldn't let that happen.

The snap of a branch made his head spin, and he stilled, watchful and waiting to see what had made the noise. When the doe stepped from behind the brush, his muscles relaxed, and he leaned into the railing that kept him from stepping off the balcony in the dark and plummeting to the ground.

"Where's your kids, Sally? Know you got two cuz I saw em last time you were here."

The whitetail glanced behind her, scuffed the ground a couple of times with a hoof, and two spotted fawns crept out.

"There you are. Knew you were there. Watch em close, Sally, cuz you never know what they'll do or when they're gonna up and be gone. Somehow. Some way."

He hummed a tune he'd created for the fawns and sipped coffee in between verses. It had no words, not even a real melody. It was more like air moving between the leaves or a thought he couldn't express coming from his throat in an attempt to comfort.

Squirrels dropped acorns onto the roof, and they rolled to land on the balcony next to him. Before long, the squirrels ignored his presence and used his treehouse as if it had grown from the trees for their sole use. His voice as he hummed and talked to them became part of the forest.

His forehead furrowed when he thought about the old camp he'd made on his own property, nearer the farm. He'd liked it but had turned it into a decoy camp after believing someone had followed him one day, though he still went there periodically to confuse nosy people.

He needed to keep folks away from the treehouse. Had to. It was his and his alone.

Only Sally the doe knew about this spot, she and the pileated woodpecker and the two squirrels perched next to him. He cackled and they looked up from munching on their acorns.

"Wife says I should've hugged my boys when they were little, should've let em cry sometimes and be little boys. Mebbe. But I don't know. Seems kind a weak and baby-like, boys crying."

He leaned his back against the front of the house and surveyed the forest. High above the ground, the world trembled with life as he knew it would. Here, he was king. No one judged.

"You don't need kids, anyway, squirrel. They think they know everything. They don't. I'm telling you, they're a whole lot smarter when they're just little brats. They get old and think they know more'n you do. That's when trouble starts. Best bet is don't have any. I'm telling you."

He went silent and twirled the empty cup in his hands. The squirrels stopped chomping and held the acorns steady in their hand-like paws. They scampered up the tree behind his back, and he felt their tiny claws grip his shoulder as they sprang from it. He smiled.

"They're not afraid of me. And look how little they are. I can be friendly."

Shorty curled around her, awake and watching as she slept, his favorite time of day. A little gurgle came from her throat, and he had told her she snored, but she didn't. Al was too flawless to snore.

Moonlight made shadows on the wall, and leaves flickered in the breeze coming through the open window.

His lids closed in an attempt to sleep and slammed open at the sound of the screen door banging. He slid his arm from under Al's head, grabbed his trousers, and crept to the stairs, damning the heft that made them creek under each of his footfalls.

"It's me," he heard and stopped dead still. A burglar wouldn't announce himself.

Something landed on the floor, and the intruder stepped further into the kitchen making no attempt at quiet.

"Get up, Al. It's me. I'm home. I'm hungry. Get down here and cook me something."

Shorty finished the stairsteps two at a time and shoved through the door.

"Who are you and what in hell do you think you're doing barging in here, hollering for Al?"

Marcus backed up a couple of steps and his eyes widened when he remember the big man standing in front of him. He was one reason the Tatum boys all went to jail, and Bear was the other. They'd patrolled the island looking for troublemakers and found them.

He threw his shoulders back in bravado and took a step further into the room. He knew Shorty didn't recognize him with his long hair as wild as the red beard covering his face, but he knew Shorty. What was he doing at his farm? Upstairs?

"Where's Al?" He growled in a belligerent snarl.

"Not telling you anything, mister, until you give your name. And if you don't do exactly that in two seconds, you'll be leaving this house by the seat of your pants."

"Al!" Marcus screamed, and, like a two-year old, his lips contorted in a distortion of fear and demand.

She showed up in seconds, and Shorty understood when she cried Marcus's name, flew to her brother, and wrapped her arms around him. He didn't respond, didn't take his angry eyes from Shorty until Al tugged him by the arm and led him to the table.

"I'm so glad to see you. Are you okay? You hungry?" she asked.

"Told you I was."

Al took the leftover ham from the icebox and hacked several thick slices from it, brought bread and silverware to the table and helped him assemble sandwiches.

"You want milk, Marcus?"

"Beer or whiskey. I've been dry a long time." He glared at Shorty as he bit into the food.

Al scrambled to pour a hefty glass of whiskey and put it in front of him. He grabbed it and sucked half down, slamming the glass on the table when he was done.

"Thank your sister," Shorty said.

"Drop dead, big man." He turned to Al. "What's he doing here? You turn whore?"

Shorty's arm shot through the air like lightning, and his hand gripped Marcus by the throat. He lifted from his chair to keep his head connected to his shoulders and quit struggling when stars in a black sky blinked on and off behind his eyes.

"Put him down Shorty."

"He's looking to die, Al."

"Put him down. Please."

Shorty dropped him back on the chair which flipped sideways, and Marcus fell to the floor gasping and clutching his throat.

"He didn't mean anything," she said.

"He called you a whore."

Her eyes reflected pain but lit with joy when a thought registered.

"He doesn't know." She knelt beside him and held her left hand in front of his face. "I'm married, Marcus. Shorty and I are married."

Marcus groaned, sat up and glared at her.

"You married the bastard that put me in prison? What's wrong with you? Wait until Skunk gets wind of this. Hell, wait until all your brothers get home."

He stared hard at Shorty, trying to intimidate and gain leverage from the numerous absent men. "Think you can take four of us?"

"Stop, Marcus. Shorty didn't do anything to you. The law did, and you earned it."

Marcus swept an arm through the air like he could wave away her accusation. "I need sleep. I'm going to bed."

"On the couch," Shorty said, stepping in front of him. "Get a blanket and pillow, Al."

He waited for her to return and, taking them from her, nodded at the stairs indicating she should head there. "I'll be up in a minute," he said. He flipped the blanket on the sofa, threw the pillow down and pointed to Marcus. "Sleep. In the morning, we'll talk."

Shorty lay awake with his eyes open and listened for footsteps as he watched the moon make its way across the sky from the nearest window. He didn't think Marcus a bad man, at least, he hadn't been evil before he'd been arrested.

He wasn't like the other three Tatums who'd beaten and raped Betty. Marcus had gotten involved in burning the cabins on the island, but Shorty believed he'd been pressed into it by his brothers. The youngest of the four boys, he'd hero worshipped his older siblings, and they'd used that. Used him.

But he couldn't be sure, so he listened and waited for daylight. He'd find out more in the morning.

He left Al sprawled with one arm flung over her eyes and inched as quietly as possible down the stairs. When the coffee appeared brown in the pot, he kicked Marcus's leg and suggested he rise.

"We're gonna talk," he said.

Marcus groaned. With mumbled curses, he knuckled his eyes and got up.

"Where's my sister?"

"Sleeping. It's her day off, and you interrupted her sleep last night."

Marcus grunted and reached for the cup of coffee Shorty put in front of him. He sipped, glared and swallowed.

"Pretty nice deal you got, big man. My sister and a farm all wrapped up in a neat package, and all you had to do was make a little sweet talk."

Shorty breathed in through his nostrils and rubbed his scalp. Determined not to make things worse for Al, he let the air out slowly, counting as it flowed from his lungs.

"Listen to me, Marcus. First off, my name is Shorty, not big man. Second, Al is my wife, and I won't let anyone, not even her brothers, give her grief or harm her."

"Speak up. Don't know why you have to whisper. Think it scares people? It only makes us mad."

Shorty hunched his shoulders and rolled his head to release the knots forming.

"Third, I can help if you know what you want to do now you're home. Have you given it any thought?"

"Hell, no. I just got here. And by the way, this is my house you're squatted in. My farm."

Shorty nodded and wondered what to say. What *could* he say? The man was right. It was the Tatum farm.

He had to agree, partly. "It's Al's farm, too. She kept it going. Fixed it up. It was pretty run down when you left."

"You think you can just say it's hers and now it's yours? Think again, big man."

He hadn't heard her footsteps, didn't know she was behind him until she spoke.

"We can all live here. There were six of us before."

Shorty watched the sneer grow on Marcus's face and wished he knew how to turn back time to when he was a sweet boy who loved animals and took care of his sister.

"We won't be sharing a bedroom with your brother, Al. If he wants to sleep on the couch, well – for a time, we'll see how it works."

Around the house, Shorty tried to stay out of his way, but Marcus's angry eyes followed him. Al tried to let her brother help by feeding the chickens, but it wasn't the same pleasurable morning activity it had been with her gentle conversation and the hen's sweet clucking. They squawked and tried to fly away from his grumbling and the feed he flung at them.

Hearing the noise, Shorty peered out the window, ran out and grabbed the feed bucket from him. But he'd already emptied it, and the chickens had scattered for cover.

"What's the matter with you?" Shorty said. "Al loves those hens."

"They're fowl. Should be Sunday dinner. Maybe they will be."

"If you touch a single feather on even one of those birds, you'll regret it." Shorty moved in close and poked a finger into his chest. "Count on it, Marcus. I don't make idle threats. They're promises."

Shorty found Al on the milk stool, her head pressed into the heifer, her hands stilled. The full bucket sat off to the side. He stroked her silky hair and waited.

"You hear the hens squawking? And what I said?"

She nodded, and when she looked up, unshed tears filled eyes that held too much bad history.

"I'm afraid he'll hurt them," she said, and Shorty had to lean down to hear her choked words.

"I don't think he will, but give this some thought."

She nuzzled into the calloused hand stroking her hair. Its warmth gave her comfort, and its gentleness gave her hope.

"What?"

"We could move cow, hens, Dog, Nurse and King George to the old hotel. Abby's been asking me to run it. We could live there and leave Marcus to the farm."

"Where would the animals stay?"

"Dog and the cats can live wherever they want. Hens, old Bessie and your mare can share the stable. Not using it much, anyway, with all the automobiles nowadays."

Al didn't say yes or no, and he waited for her to process.

"Can I think about it? And her name isn't Bessie."

"Sure thing. Take your time, and I'm thinking right now this cow wants to move out of this old barn. She's done milking for the day. What's her name?"

"I know she's too old to be a heifer, but she likes to be called that."

Shorty gave a short snort. "Alright, *Heifer* wants to be done here. You're sweet, Al."

"So are you, husband."

On the way to the house, she said, "Let's do it."

"When?"

"Morning. I need to talk with Marcus."

He wrapped an arm around her and squeezed. She didn't squeal when her breath left because she didn't want to scare him. She was working on his confidence concerning his extraordinary size and her extraordinary lack of it.

Shorty always quit holding her tight before she needed air. She expected he always would.

"I'll grease up the hay wagon wheels tonight. They haven't turned in a while. And scrounge up the chicken crates. It's a good decision, Al. Marcus will be fine. We'll be fine. Abby and old Irish will be happier than two pigs in mud."

Chapter Ten

The loon's wail, louder from Abby's position on the island, told her the nest lay closer, but the coyote yips, bat wing flutters and owl hoots hadn't changed. Twilight here was alive with northwest Michigan wildlife, satisfying her need for connection to them.

The wooden porch chairs gradually filled with late evening rockers making Abby began to feel like she'd come home – or the others had.

Building the Oakmere Hotel hadn't been her idea. Actually, it had been the Branch brothers, founders of the Idlewild resort, but she understood her father's need to own it. After all, somebody would, and they'd take all the business created by the novelty of being on an island in the middle of Lake Idlewild.

He figured it should be him finding that pot of gold, and she would stand by his side even if the idea of moving again made her want to punch somebody.

She still missed working daily with Betty, Jackson, Charity and Al, but on evenings like this, she was thankful to have friends around her, rocking with her on the porch.

Phantom and Cleo perched like guard cats on the new rail posts, eyes glowing in the moonlight, and the footbridge provided entertainment in the moon's white glimmer as people and critters strolled from the mainland to the island and back.

What more could she ask?

Cassandra and her clowder made periodic excursions across the bridge and poked in the mud of the island shoreline to fill her bag. Abby wondered if island mud provided different fare than across the lake. One day she'd ask. She hadn't been to tea with Cassandra in a while, and she missed that pleasure, too.

You're whining. What's wrong with you?

Patrick took command of the rocking chair tempo like he'd been on the Oakmere porch since day one.

"Shorty runs the old place like he's been an innkeeper all his life. He's one surprise after another," he said. "And Strange Al never needed me in the kitchen at all. Just let me think she did. Smart girl."

"It's still a good idea not to offer suppers there. Let folks come here for late meals. Jackson can handle the bar at night without help if there's no food to worry over."

"You still need help here, lass. When you gonna hire some?"

"Don't know. When I find some, I guess."

She let her eyes follow the footbridge and recognized Edwin's hunched saunter. He'd gotten into the habit of checking in with Patrick and Abby each evening since the night of the Oakmere opening when he'd turned Yancy and Terry away from the old place.

Abby indicated a spare chair, but he chose the step, squatted there and looked at the dark sky. Patrick continued to speculate with Edwin over possible workers they could hire.

"What about Marcus?" Abby said after bringing out a nightcap for Edwin. "I haven't seen much of him since he got home, but he seemed like a nice young man before – before jail."

Edwin twisted to look at Patrick. "Was gonna tell you. Marcus is farming for the Adams family since Terry's accident. And Yancy is staying at the Tatum farm."

"What? How do you know everything, Edwin?" Abby said.

"I just sorter listen."

"I hate to think of Al and Betty's work on the farm house going to waste. I mean, I'm not saying they'll wreck things, but . . . you know."

"How are Al's chickens and the cow getting along with the horses? No major battles?" Patrick asked.

"Animals are good. Dog and cats, too. They're never a problem. Told you on the day we met. I appreciate animals. They got sense."

"See much of Samuel?" Abby leaned toward Edwin, in a half-hearted attempt to keep the question between them without being obvious about it.

"Now and then. Not every night."

She nodded, not happy she'd asked. Certainly not happy she'd spilled her thoughts onto the porch floor for everyone to see and step on.

"And Yancy or Terry? See much of them?" Patrick asked.

"Seen Terry at Joe's. Arm looks like somebody embroidered on it. Downright pretty." Edwin's smirk told everything. He enjoyed Cassandra's little joke.

"Come on," Patrick said. "Pretty? I hear he got cut up good by all the broken glass."

"You'll have to see it. All crisscrosses and patterns like his momma stitched him together in the womb and he came out like a fancy doily."

His face showed no emotion as if he reported only the facts, and that's all, but his deep chuckle rumbled.

Samuel loped up the steps of the old hotel porch, and Al went inside to get him a nightcap. He sat in the chair next to Charles and stared across the lake at the Oakmere.

"Getting to be quite a group over there."

He thanked Al and sipped from the glass she handed him without looking at it.

"They're keeping busy," Shorty said, waiting for the questions he expected would come.

"Patrick settled in?"

"Yup."

"Abby hire help?"

"Just Alma so far."

"How are they managing?"

"You know Abby."

"Yes. Yes, I do."

"How do you know Alma?" Charles asked, interrupting the exchange.

"Through my mother and her father. Long time ago, when we first came north."

Charles let the silence fall while he thought it over. He remembered Alma's family, too, living in a small settlement not far from Stanwood. He'd talked with her mother and father when he was writing about ethnic relationships in his novels and short stories. He remembered the children – the healthy and the ones who suffered severe disabilities. He recalled the parents as folks who worked hard and weathered their trials without complaint.

"They're a good family," Charles said.

Samuel sat back and gave him a long look.

"You know them?"

"I do."

"Then you know Alma's father is a colored man."

"Yes. That's why I know them."

"You're gonna have to explain that later. First, let me make it clear I wouldn't have brought up her heritage," Samuel said, "but she makes it well known, herself. She's proud of her ancestry. Race was never an issue for anyone in her family, and both her parents went about the business of living life." He chuckled, but it didn't hold much humor. "Maybe they had too damned much work to do raising all those kids to bother with such a trifle."

"Or maybe it isn't as big a deal as you think." Shorty leaned into the conversation, surprising the other two.

"Said from a white perspective," Samuel glanced at his friend to see if he had tweaked a nerve.

"I heard your biased statement. I'm choosing to ignore your bad behavior. I hope Abby can." Shorty chose to keep it light, but he wasn't sure he wanted to. Abby hurt, and her pain was his.

"It's *for* her," Samuel said.

"I'll be sure and explain that to Abby."

"Alma's married, Shorty, and has three children."

"Then I'll be sure and explain the ramifications of *adultery* to *you*."

Samuel pulled the gold watch from its pocket and flipped it open, stared at the face and closed it.

"Thanks for the drink, Al. I'll catch up on my tab this week." He stepped with heavy feet as he left the porch, not knowing why he felt a knife jammed in his chest, but he did. And it twisted with each step.

I'm doing the right thing.

He yanked hard on the white cuffs sticking out of his suit coat sleeves, smoothed his mustache with a thumb and finger, and straightened his spine.

His shiny model T waited in the back of the hotel. He cranked it up, slid in and ran a hand over the leather. He told himself lies, that this made him happy. His automobile was all he needed, and it demanded nothing from him but gas in the tank and a foot on the pedal.

He said hello to Edwin who stepped off the footbridge as he backed into the road.

"Things going well over there?" Samuel asked to be polite, but Edwin didn't buy the casual interest.

"Sure. Friends stopping by. You might could, too."

Edwin spit in the dusty road, and a cloud spiraled from it. Samuel wondered if he'd made a statement with the act.

"I'll do that, Edwin."

"You just do that, Samuel." He ambled off without a backward glance, leaving Samuel feeling like a two-year-old who'd been spanked.

"Damn. Whole lot of people scolding me tonight. Maybe I should stay home. Have a nightcap by myself or get a cat. Maybe a dog. Hell, maybe both."

Al's dog made itself at home in the stable with Edwin. When she came out each morning, both Edwin and Dog met her; one with a slanted grin, and the other with sad, brown hound dog eyes. Edwin was the one with the sad eyes. The mare knew him from before when *Mr. James* sold the horse to him. So they were all one big, contented family.

"I can milk the cow, Miss Al."

"I know you can, Edwin. I enjoy it, and Heifer knows me."

Edwin nodded. He understood love of animals.

"Just so you know. Your brother's working at the Adams farm cuz a Terry's arm."

"I'm glad." Al got to her chores, Dog nudging her knee with his old, gray head and Edwin admiring her milking skills.

She's smooth with the heifer, he thought, and gentle handed. He watched and remembered his own farm – long ago when he still had a wife and a son. He didn't let memories in most of the time, but Al was easy to be around, and his recollections intruded without him realizing they'd slipped in – took hold before he could shut them down.

"I'll get the chicken feed."

He shuffled off to the other side of the makeshift barn, cleaned Heifer's stall, and grabbed a bucket of grain mixture for the hens. He smiled thinking how spoiled Al's hens were. On his farm, they scratched the ground for food, ate worms and grubs when they could find them and grass when they couldn't.

He opened the door to the chicken pen and the hens raced out into the sunlight. They squawked, screeched and flapped their wings as if they could fly off, and some did get into the air, but their flights ended with an awkward extension of wings and embarrassing, tilted landings.

You could see the chagrin in their beady little eyes, more so if you laughed at their antics.

Their clamor filled the air and Al's heart. Heifer and hens were good companions to start the day with. King George tried to stick his nose into the milk pail, and Al hissed to get his attention.

"Not the pail, King." She squirted a stream at the cat who opened his mouth, eager for the warm, fresh milk.

"Clean your face," Al said.

Edwin, leaning in the open doorway, chuckled, held a hand out for the milk bucket when Al stood, and exchanged it for the feed pail. They were a team.

He stood in the middle of the pecking, clucking flock and enjoyed the sunshine, watching people come and go at Foster's store.

It was busier than ever with all the new residents and vacationers in Idlewild, and, before they knew better, they stocked up at his dingy general store and paid the high dime. When they'd had enough of Joe's surly temper and ridiculous prices, they went into Baldwin for supplies.

He watched Frank Adams lumber in and slip out with a small parcel. Edwin saw him in town every other day, it seemed. He didn't spend much time in the store or linger to chat with folks. It was get in and get out kind of shopping. What could the old man need badly enough he'd ride from the farm so frequently?

Edwin's curiosity tickled. He'd heard a few things, and could be it wasn't all gossip.

Cecily and her son Bailey milked the herd every morning, and the younger boy, Chunk, fed the calves and chickens. Frank either left early in the morning or hadn't come home the night before, but none of the family expected him to help with the chores. Not anymore. He was absent even when he was there, with a vacant stare and possibly purposeful, senseless jabbering.

Terry supervised his wife and kids and did a one-armed point at what he wanted done. Marcus worked the fields, cutting and collecting alfalfa, and didn't need direction, having done it often enough as a boy before going to jail. He'd promised to help him out while his arm healed but was glad the season was about over.

"Abby wants me to try waiting tables at the Oakmere," Marcus told Terry.

Terry thought of all the reasons Marcus shouldn't work for Abby, but before he could spit them out, his mother shot through the door to the barn and demanded to know where his father was. She asked every few days and got the same answer every time.

"I don't know, Ma."

"I think you do, and if you don't, you should. Find him, Terry."

He saw tears glistening in the corners of her eyes and softened. He put his good arm around her shoulders and led her into the sunshine.

"He's okay, Ma. He goes into the woods and camps. He likes it there. The solitude, you know?"

"I don't think he knows what he's doing. He should be here. With us."

"Give him some time. He's struggling with – I don't know what – some things. He's a little crazy right now. Leave him be. I'll keep an eye out."

Truth was, he liked life without his old man around to criticize the way he did everything and treat him like he was too dumb to make a simple decision.

He was a man, for God's sake. He had a family and sons of his own and didn't need his father telling him what to do every second of every day and making him feel like a no-good weakling. He got angry just thinking about it. But he couldn't say that to his ma.

He patted her shoulder and headed her in the direction of the house.

"Go on in, Ma. Get out of the sun. It's hot today."

Chapter Eleven

Marcus shoved his chair back in an explosion of movement and stood glaring at her. Abby crossed her arms and tilted her head to glare back at him. She'd learned a bit since first coming to Idlewild. Yes, she'd like to yell at him and stomp off, but throwing a fit wouldn't solve anything.

"If you want to keep your job, Marcus, you'll learn to control your temper, and you'll wait on everyone with civility and treat them with respect. If you can't, you can leave now because you'll no longer have a job."

"He called me a boy," he said in a low growl. "I'm not colored."

"If you were, would it be alright, then, to call you a boy?"

"Well . . ." He slouched and made a tentative plea with his arms. "But I'm not."

"I asked a question. Would that make it alright?"

Abby saw his fists unclench and a foot shuffle. He didn't have an answer, not one she'd consider satisfactory, and he knew it. He looked like a ten-year old in his confusion, and she took pity on him.

"Sit back down, Marcus. When I hired you, I said you needed to do something with the chip on your shoulder. You were a sweet young man once. I want who you used to be working at this hotel, not the one who flares up at the least imagined offense."

"But . . . It was a colored man calling me boy."

"Maybe he thought of you as a young man – like he called you *son*. Doesn't matter. More than half of our guests are colored. You're not. I'm not. They are."

"So, I just have to take whatever anyone says no matter what?"

"No. You deserve respect, too. But give folks the benefit of the doubt, Marcus, and make sure they're really misbehaving before you react. And when you do react, be civil. Got that?" She smiled and stood, letting him know the meeting was done, and he could go back to work.

He nodded and felt foolish. Jackson, over at the old place, had told him about the time he'd made a big deal about waiting on white people. His little fit of temper hadn't gone over well, either. Marcus thought maybe color really didn't matter to his boss. He could learn to live with that odd idea, if it was the truth, but he didn't trust it was. Not yet. Prison had taught him a few things about the reality of truth and the different shades of both reality *and* truth.

"Sorry," he said, and Abby punched his arm.

"Apologize to Mr. Mason."

"Really?"

"Want your job?"

He ducked his head, and Abby's heart did a little lurch. When she walked away, she saw an imaginary little boy in her mind, one who looked a lot like Samuel, but had her big feet and teeth and red tints in his curly, black hair.

"Knock on my door when you see any of the Chautauqua planning committee, please."

"Yes, ma'am."

I'm a ma'am? When did that happen?

Like she had at the old hotel, Abby lived in the corner room facing the water. Wide windows and a door opened onto a balcony big enough for two chairs. Two more windows and a cushioned bench took up most of another wall. Her father had planned it for her so it might make living in a hotel seem more home-like. She'd decorated the room in white and yellow to match the afghan her mother had made. It lay over the window seat, now, inviting her.

Phantom and Cleo stretched and purred when she entered, looking forward to her gentle hands.

"Let's go sit on the balcony. I need some sunshine and fresh air."

She patted her leg and put her feet on the railing to make room for both cats on her lap.

"Don't get any bigger, babies. I guess you could tell me that, too, right?"

The day was warm, but she felt the familiar trace of cool in the breeze particular to the beginning of Michigan autumn. A few leaves showed yellow edges, and, while pretty, she couldn't appreciate them, not even the brilliant reds and golds soon to come. They heralded winter cold.

She wasn't ready for snow. And she didn't want fall. She didn't want . . . She didn't know what she didn't want. Or she did.

"You sound really stupid, Abby."

She cursed, and Cleo opened her green eyes wider than usual and waited.

"Don't look at me like I'm crazy. I'm not a happy person right now, and I can't figure out what to do about it."

"I can," a voice said from one floor below.

Abby stood, sliding the cats to the balcony floor, and peered over the railing.

"What are you two doing? Eavesdropping on my cat chat?"

Edna snorted and Sally slapped her leg.

"We're here for the meeting," Edna said. "Get on down here and we'll tell you why you're not happy. Everybody in Idlewild knows."

"Be nice, Edna. She's a gentle, silly soul."

Sally moved toward the door, and Abby would have fallen off the balcony had she leaned over the rail any further to watch.

"Gotta go, babies. Want to come down with me?"

In the bar, she wrapped arms around both women, happy to see them.

"Coffee, ladies?"

Edna scrunched her forehead in thought and glanced at the clock over the bar.

"I guess. A little early for a wine."

"Tea for me," Sally said. "Cassandra has converted me."

Abby turned to Marcus who stared with wide eyes at Sally. His mouth hung open, and nothing came out of it.

"Marcus. I'm talking to you." Abby tapped his arm and waited.

Looking as if he'd awakened from a trance, he turned a light shade of red, said "coffee and tea" and walked off to the kitchen. He was alert enough to bring coffee for his boss even though he'd forgotten to ask what she wanted, but the shock of seeing Sally with her arms around Abby had been too much. What was a prostitute doing at the hotel?

"Coffee, Mrs. Falmouth and Abby. Tea, uh, I don't know your name. Sorry."

"It's alright, Marcus. I know yours. My name is Sally." She couldn't help but tease, just a little, and her eyes lit with humor.

She'd seen the color creep from his neck to his cheeks and knew he'd recognized her. She remembered him, too. Sally recalled most all the young men in town and the surrounding area, in Reed City and Big Rapids, Luther and Ludington.

Marcus backed away from the table as if fearing to turn his back on it because something horrid would happen. Maybe she would put a curse on him, turn him to salt, or . . . tell his boss. He'd heard she could cast spells, or was that Cassandra, the cat woman, not the prostitute? Why in the name of God would that woman visit here with Abby and Edna Falmouth?

Jesse Falmouth came in with Charles Chesnutt, Micah Chambers and Ratty Branch, and Marcus got too busy to worry about Sally. But he saw them sit at her table and greet her with the same respect as the others. They called her Miss Sally and shook her hand.

"What the . . ." He caught himself before the curse word came out. He didn't need more trouble with Abby.

"Hicks coming?" Jesse asked.

"Said he'd be here," Ratty said.

"You remembered to tell him here? The new place?"

Jesse liked needling him to make him grin. Ratty had the famous Branch brothers smile – all teeth. He wasn't disappointed.

"Not so old I forget things. Not yet," Ratty said. "Where's Maggie, Micah? Thought I might get to see her pretty face."

"Couldn't get her away from Benji. She's crazy about our grandbaby. She's got him at the cabin. Probably sitting there staring at him, maybe waking him up to see if he's sleepy."

Micah laughed at his own little joke and shook his head in pretended disgust, but his eyes warmed with affection.

"Benjamin should be in soon," Abby said. "He plays here most afternoons. Don't know what I'd do without his music. I'm spoiled."

"Let's get to business," Jesse said. "I've gotta get back within the hour."

"I don't think it'll take even that long. Let's recreate the first Chautauqua. Buddy Black and his band, Florence Mills, Charles Chesnutt," Micah said.

"Hey. I'm right here. Let's talk about that last part."

"You're perfect, Charles," Abby said. "You know where Idlewild has been and where it's going, and you can include your literature."

The door opened and Sheriff Hicks sauntered in.

"Pretty fancy, Abby. Getting a bit too fancy for my pockets."

Abby heard a sharp gasp and turned to see Marcus turning red for the second time that day.

"Good to see you, Sheriff.," she said. "I'd know you and your pipe tobacco in the dark, but it's been too long if you haven't seen the new place."

"True and it's a good day when you don't need the law coming by." Hicks swiveled his head to look at Marcus behind the bar. "Glad you're home and employed, boy."

Abby could see Marcus's jaw clench and his body tighten and waited with interest to see his response.

Sheriff Hicks called any male under thirty boy, white and colored alike. It wasn't a slur, and Marcus would have to get over his irritation.

A slow smile worked its way onto her face when Marcus reached a tentative hand to the sheriff and asked what he wanted to drink. He didn't smile, and maybe being glad to see Hicks asked too much of him, but he didn't punch the man who'd arrested him and put him in jail, either.

"Coffee, son," he said as he took the hand. "Lots of cream." He rubbed his chest. "Heartburn. It's the job."

Son . . . Had Abby been right?

Marcus nodded, took his hand back and went to get the coffee. Hicks twirled a chair around, straddled it and propped his chin on the high back.

"Don't know what I'm doing here. Want to fill me in?"

Abby told him they expected high numbers for the fall Chautauqua and thought a shiny star presence might stop trouble before it happened.

"Having it here on the island?"

"Everywhere: the pavilion, the old hotel and the island. And a bonfire," Jesse said. "A large area to cover."

"Can I have Bear and Shorty again? Maybe deputize them?" He turned to Abby.

"Guess you'd have to ask them. Bear's outside working on a tool barn. Shorty's at the . . . well, you know where to find him."

When they finished, the sheriff left to find Bear, and Jesse to find his office. Micah and Charles found seats in the shade of the porch, leaving Edna and Sally to say what they wanted to Abby.

Never one to mince words, Edna got right to it.

"What's going on with Samuel and you, Abby?"

"Samuel and me?"

"You're pretty sharp today, woman. You can repeat like a parrot. Yes. You and Samuel. What's going on?"

Sally scooted her chair back and strolled with a queen's perfect posture over to Marcus with double intent

– to set the kid's mind at ease and to order drinks. They were going to need it.

"Three small glasses of white wine, please, Marcus."

As hard as he tried to make it stop, his face flushed hot and pink, and it infuriated him and came out in his voice.

"You don't need to be troubled, Marcus. I don't kiss and tell. You shouldn't either, but the way you're acting is significantly communicative. Cease, please."

"Why are you here?" He whispered in case Abby was listening.

"Here, as in out and about with regular people?"

"Uh . . . You know." His hands flailed, searching for the words that refused to come out of his mouth.

"Yes. I think I do. Abby, Edna and I are friends. Sue, too. Remember her?"

A deeper pink crept into his face, and his neck flared ruby red.

Abby glanced their way and smiled to see them in conversation. She knew Marcus had struggled seeing Sally in the bar. Leave it to Sally to take care of a ticklish situation in a direct and professional manner.

Edna leaned into Abby, lowered her head like a ramming sheep, and lifted her eyebrows. Abby swallowed and sat back.

"What did you want to know?" she asked.

"What happened between you and Samuel? Why is he avoiding you? What'd you do?"

Abby huffed an irritated puff of air.

"Why did *I* have to do something? Why not *him*? And . . ." She crossed her arms over her chest and squeezed her lips in a tight line. "Why are you asking me this stuff? Ask him."

"I will because he's acting like a whiny boy just like you. I don't mean you're acting like a boy, but . . . You know what I mean."

Sally came back with a tray of stemmed glasses and a decanter of wine.

"Marcus said to take this out of his pay. Said he owed it for some reason."

She poured, lifted her glass to clink against the others, and sat on the edge of her seat as proper. Ladies never let their spines rest against the back of a chair.

"To Abby being happy again. Now, how can we make that happen?" Sally said.

Abby sipped, but it sputtered when she tried to swallow. She stared at the door, hoping it would open and a mass of people come in so work would force her to leave the conversation. She blinked a couple of times before turning back to her friends.

"Nothing. Nothing happened. Well, sometimes it did, and it made me mad, but nothing. Really."

"That's perfectly clear," Edna said. "You make a better parrot than a storyteller, Abby."

"Thanks."

"You need to be nice, Edna. I keep telling you, and Sue, too. Let me try," Sally said, and put a hand on Abby's.

"When you were out and about with Samuel, people said disparaging things, you couldn't go into some places, and they wouldn't let you sit where you wanted to sit even when you were allowed in. Does that about sum it up?"

Abby clamped her teeth together and managed to bite the edge of her tongue nodding at Sally's words. She swore, but lightly, a whispered oath.

"And Samuel has pushed you away?"

"I don't know," came out like a squawk. "I need to get to work."

"What don't you know?" Edna said.

"I don't know what's going on. He hasn't told me. He simply doesn't come around unless he's here to see Alma. I think I hate her."

Abby put her face in her hands and giggled, a sad rather than joyful sound. "Isn't that appalling? I'm a rotten teenager all over again. I didn't like it the first time!"

It could have been a laugh punctuating the end of the sentence, but it wasn't. The sound took the words from Edna's brain, and she didn't have a response even though she knew what Abby had gone through at Samuel's side. Every colored man, woman and child knew from memory –

and way too much experience. Now Abby did, too, and she wasn't used to it, hadn't been born to it.

Satisfaction slithered into her mind. She tried to shove it aside because Abby was her friend, but Edna was honest and kind enough to recognize it for what it was and be sorry it existed. She patted Abby's shoulder.

"Look at me, girl."

"No."

"I said, look at me. I've seen your sad face before. Why don't you just come out and ask him what he's up to? Put it out on the table like three aces?"

Abby twirled the stem of her glass and watched the sun come and go in the light gold of the wine.

"Because I might not want to know. I'm afraid he'll be truthful."

"So, you're a chicken and you'd rather live life in a dream?" Edna said.

"Yes. And because I don't want him to know I'm miserable." Abby lifted her chin in defiance.

Edna relaxed and slouched in her chair. She had no scruples about her spine touching the chair back, and she'd never wanted to be a lady, anyway.

"Let's see if I have this right. You're a chicken full of the sin of pride?" She giggled. "You're an egocentric fowl."

Sally laughed and Abby choked on a sip of wine.

"Give the lady a red balloon. She hit the rusty nail on its head because I am all of those things."

"Where is that determined young girl who asked to look at the inside of my lip to see if it was black or pink? That took guts and respect for me to be so honest with your curiosity. Where's the courageous woman who punched that white-sheet-wearing Longstreet? I don't know you anymore."

Edna was right, but the words didn't feel good. Sally put a hand on hers, and the contrast of dark and light slapped Abby in the face.

She never saw the differences; maybe because she was used to them, maybe because she didn't care about them, or maybe because the difference in their colors hadn't directly impacted her and boy was that selfish. She hadn't given full consideration to what her friends dealt with on a daily basis and, in her ignorance, had gotten angry when bigotry impacted *her*, like at the theatre.

Like anywhere she'd been with Samuel.

But today it was clear. "I've been blind."

Edna snorted. "You're not gonna say you're color blind, are you? It's ridiculous and doesn't exist."

"No. I see colors just fine, but I've been blind to your deeply personal experiences. . . to the things that happen daily, to the words people say . . . and, God, the looks in their eyes. Cruel. Demeaning. I'm sorry."

Patrick leaned his scruffy head through the kitchen doors to see if the dinner crowd had straggled in and saw Edna and Sally as they stood to leave.

"Ye can't scoot out without a hug for the leprechaun. Not my two favorite lasses." He shuffled over and wrapped his arms around their waists.

His head came just above Sally's shoulders, and she kissed the top of it.

"I would have searched for you, Patrick, before leaving. And don't tell Sue she's not on your favorites list."

"Oh, she'll be on it when she's here. For sure. Are ye leaving? Can ye not stay for a wee drink with me?"

Edna unwrapped from his arm and said she needed to get back to her daughter Daisy.

"And we already had a wee drink while trying to talk some sense into your daughter."

"She's a hard head, that one," Patrick said. "Did ye do it?"

"You'll have to ask her."

Edna sent a smile Abby's way and left a six-foot-tall Sally wrapped in the arms of a red-headed Irish elf.

"What a sight," she said and walked away grinning.

The coyotes yipped like they were mad at the world, their rant waking the moon and sending night creatures into hiding.

"Listen to them," Bear said, talking around the tail encircling his neck. He stroked the cat on his shoulder. "Stay close tonight, Phantom. Coyotes like kitty dinners."

"I'd howl, too, if I could," Abby said, pushing back in the rocker.

The moon, a big orange orb, hung in the sky like it owned it and glazed the lake with streaks of red. She scratched Cleo's chin and waited for the purr.

"Why would you be howling, lass? You got some property to protect or just want to wail at the moon?"

"Both."

"Have a go. Set up a howl. You might like it."

"I'm feeling foolish for even thinking it, Da. I can see myself squatting like a dog on the front lawn, my snout tilted up toward the sky and emitting mad yip-howls."

Abby grinned at him, a movement of lips disconnected from the eyes but trying for something positive.

"Times like this I wish your Ma was here. She'd know what to say to your sad face."

"I'm fine, Da. Really."

The click of their rockers blended with the night chirps and flutters until they were indecipherable from one another – until Bear stood and interrupted the flow. He held an arm to Abby and asked her to take a walk.

"Where we going?"

"Down the footbridge."

"Why?"

"It's a nice night."

Bear grabbed her hand and pulled.

She didn't resist, but she also didn't take her eyes from the porch full of rockers across the lake.

"Good idea, Bear," Patrick said.

"Want to join us?" Bear asked.

"Nae. Old legs are too tired tonight. Another time."

Cleo and Phantom ran ahead, and George and Nurse met them mid-footbridge. It was a feline party of sniffing noses and raised tails – just in case. The clowder of four led the way to the old hotel as if they were the welcome wagon.

Chair shuffling and the shifting of bottoms occurred upon their arrival to make sure the guests had positions of honor. Shorty found Abby's old chair and drew her to it.

"Sit," he said. "Can I get you a nightcap? We already poured ours."

"I know," she said, wiggling her bottom around in the chair and feeling the comfort of an old, well-worn shoe on her backside. "It's like you're on a stage sometimes when the moon is right. I can see who's here and who's sitting with whom. Just can't hear what you're all talking about."

She glanced Samuel's way, not exactly at him, but close enough she could see his eyes were directed at her.

"Maybe that's a good thing," Shorty said. "I'll get you your drink."

"Thanks, my friend."

Bear followed him into the bar. He'd done his part getting her over the bridge.

Al watched her boss but didn't question why she was there. Samuel, as well. Charles jumped in.

"Are you simply getting some exercise, Abby?"

"Yes. And I miss you all. Don't get much of a chance to chat with you anymore."

"We'll have to remedy the situation."

"Has everyone been busy?" she asked the group.

One by one, they answered. Except for Samuel who stared.

"Busy, but good," Al said.

"Me, too. I need more help. Any ideas?"

"No. We're looking, too."

"Where is Alma? Not here tonight?" Abby said and bit her tongue.

She hadn't wanted to ask, didn't want to mention the woman or even acknowledge her existence at the moment. Bad enough she had to work with her day after day. Well, actually, her father did, and he liked her a lot. Motherly, he said. Hard working. Had a tough life and dealt with it like a soldier.

Well, goody for her . . . Stop it, Abby.

The screen door opened, and Shorty handed her a good-sized nightcap. She lifted it between her face and Shorty's to view the liquid's line and raised an eyebrow.

"Thought you might want it."

"You mean need it?"

"No. Pretty sure it's about wanting. Not needing. You don't *need* anything, and you know it's true, my friend."

Abby sipped at the warm whiskey and let her back settle into her favorite chair with her favorite people.

Not all of them, but most. Charity was missing. She'd become a favorite. Gus, too, and Sue and Sally. Edna and Jesse. And, of course, one of her first favorites – Betty, along with Benjamin and now Benji. So many friends.

"I'm pretty lucky," she whispered to Bear.

He let a hand lay on her arm, and Abby felt a prick of longing she didn't want to acknowledge. Samuel used to do that. Now he sat across the porch, silent and watching, distant.

George and Nurse flanked Phantom and Cleo along the bottom step and stared into the dark distance, ears tilting toward sound, whiskers twitching.

When Cassandra and her cats came out of the shadows, the four on the steps grew taller as their spines straightened and hunched in anticipation. She turned and pointed her walking stick at them, telling them to be aware of strangers you know.

"Explain what you mean, please," Abby asked.

"Almost a clowder of your own," Cassandra said. "War council?"

She walked off without waiting for a response, and only Samuel understood the war reference.

"Damn busybody," he growled.

"What's she talking about?" Charles asked.

"Cats. She was talking about the cats."

"You fibbing?"

"Possibly."

Chapter Twelve

Town crawled with strangers, more than Abby ever remembered seeing in Idlewild, and it gave her an odd feeling. They came for the Chautauqua, and, while she loved all the Chautauqua events, for an unknown reason the number of outsiders, this time, unsettled her. A peculiar shadow tainted her joy, and she struggled to throw off the unfamiliar sense of a dark kismet.

Guests packed the Oakmere, as well as The Old Place, the new name given to the old hotel one evening after small amounts of nightcap whiskey. Someone, no one could remember who, started the conversation by saying they'd gotten tired of referring to it as the old hotel because it didn't have a name.

"How would it help if it had one?" Abby asked Charles who had voiced agreement.

"Because everything needs a name, not just something you call it because it doesn't have one. Imagine if we had to call you the red-haired Irish girl all the time?"

"Auburn-haired, Charles. How many times do I . . ."

"My apologies," he said with a grin.

"Like Dog and Heifer and Horse," Al spoke up, surprising everyone by offering an opinion. She had them, but she didn't often share them.

"Yes. Like that."

"They like their names, though," Al added. "The words have capital letters."

In the end, they all agreed and formally named the hotel, The Old Place. Shorty offered to paint a sign, and they made it official by spilling a drop of their drinks on the porch floor.

"Don't want to break a perfectly good bottle of whiskey," offered Charity who had joined their nightcap evening social.

She tilted her head at Charles, continuing the flirt she'd begun when they first met and had asked if it wouldn't be better for him if he'd chosen to be white.

"What do you mean?" he asked.

"Like on a ship. You know how they break a bottle on the bow or some such thing."

Every head nodded at her as she spun hers from face to face, blond bob swinging, giving smiles and affection and asking for approval.

At the Oakmere, Benjamin's fingers flew over the keys as he played the jazz everyone kept requesting. He liked the new style of music but would prefer something a little more peaceful in between the more discordant sounds.

It was only Thursday, and the Chautauqua didn't officially begin until Friday night; even so, Abby welcomed a steady stream of guests. Bear toted their bags upstairs, and the line in front of the registration desk continued to grow. She swiped a damp lock of hair from her cheek and turned the book toward the guest to sign.

"Enjoy yourself, Mr. . . . Oh, my gosh. Mr. Black. I didn't even look up to see who was here. Welcome back. I'm so looking forward to your music."

"Buddy, Miss Abby. You know that."

"I do. I'm so happy to see you."

When she called for Bear, Buddy stopped him with a hand in the air.

"No need, Bear. I've been hauling my equipment around for years. It's my exercise. Just tell me where to go."

Abby danced with excitement and turned to the next person in line, glad Benjamin's music kept them entertained and their feet tapping while they waited.

When the line ended, Abby saw Alma walk toward her with a young man by her side. He hung back, but she took his arm and propelled him forward.

"This is Carl, my son, and he's here to help."

Abby's mouth opened, but no sound came out.

"He's a good worker. All you have to do is say where you want him and tell him what to do."

She looked at Abby and waited.

"Uh. . . I wasn't expecting you back today, Alma."

"You're really busy. You need help, right?"

"Yes. I do. Give me a minute to think, please."

"He knows how to wash dishes, make a bed, even cook. I taught all three of my sons how to work."

"I'm sure you did, but . . . I'm too busy to train this week."

Alma crossed her arms and stared, waiting for Abby to say what she actually meant. When she got tired of waiting, she asked.

"Do you not like me, Abby?"

"I . . . of course I like you. That's silly, Alma."

"Then what's the problem? If you don't have time to train Carl, I do. Where can you use him the most? Tell me and I'll show him how. He's smart, and it won't be any time at all before he'll do it on his own."

Abby's shoulders drooped, and to herself, at least, she admitted to being foolish and green-eyed – which she was. In a fleeting moment, she wondered if jealousy came with green eyes. Blue and brown eyed people were too sane to participate in such nonsensical, malicious behavior.

Weren't they?

"Thank you, Alma. I appreciate your thoughtfulness. "You can start in on the mound of dishes left from lunch, Carl. When you're done there, come on out to the bar. I'll try you on clearing tables."

Abby looked up at the tall boy standing mute next to her, a head taller than herself. His shoulders were broad, but he still had the lanky body of a boy not yet a man. His dark, curly hair and tanned skin added to his beauty, and

Abby's mind went to his ancestry even as she tried to corral her errant thoughts.

He reminds me of a young Charles Chesnutt.

"Come on, Carl. I'll show you the kitchen."

"I'll do it," Alma said as she strode away with her son by her side.

"Well . . ." Abby's hands flew into the air, and for a wicked moment she wondered if Alma was trying to take over her life. First Samuel and now the hotel.

"Wonder if she's after Da, too," she muttered, not liking Alma or herself. "If she makes a move on Bear or Shorty, I'm calling a halt to this – this whatever it is."

She looked over her shoulder to see if anyone was near enough to hear her mumbling and spotted Bear entering with a broom, about to clean up the floor in front of the registration desk after the flood of boots and shoes.

"Have you seen Alma?" he asked and ducked as the pencil in her hand flew at him. He considered making a dive for the protection of the sign-in desk, but checked her hands for other projectiles, instead.

"Abby! What's going on?"

She stomped a foot and growled like a wounded animal. "Nothing. Nothing at all."

"You tried to spear me with a pencil."

"I know, and I'm sorry. Alma's in the kitchen with her son, Carl."

"Good."

"Why good?"

"Good she decided it was okay for him to work here."

Abby looked at the registration desk, and Bear decided to move her away from temptation by grabbing her arm and walking toward the exit door.

"You knew?"

"Yes, that she might."

"Nobody thought to tell me?" Hands went to her hips, and her chest thrust forward. "Why?"

"I . . . You'll figure it out."

Bear went back inside, picked up the broom and swept, mostly to keep from scratching his head. Abby perplexed him lately. He didn't know how to help lighten her load or her sorrows.

But he'd see the glow back in her eyes later that day.

Betty pulled the massive baby carriage up the steps and onto the porch of the Oakmere. She blew out a breath and lowered herself into one of the rockers.

"Either you're getting fat, Benji or I'm getting weak."

Abby, glancing out the window, spotted the carriage and raced out the door.

"I'm so happy to see you two. Can I take him out and hold him?"

"He'd be delighted. Wouldn't you, Benji?"

Abby picked up the gurgling baby and peered into his wide, brown eyes. She kissed his forehead while he twisted a fist in her long hair.

"I forgot. He likes to pull out hair by the roots."

"You're on your own, Auntie Abby. He doesn't let me untangle his fingers until he's ready." Betty laughed at her painful predicament, patted her own short curls, and didn't rise to help.

Abby didn't mind. Benji could pull out every last strand as far as she was concerned. He could have it all, and she'd grow it back and let him rip it out again.

She rocked back and forth as she held him, like every mother since the beginning of time. A tiny murmur cooed from her throat, a sound of contentment to him and for her. Betty watched and wondered what was in her friend's mind with the half-waltzing and half-singing.

"Hear you're pretty busy," Betty said, interrupting the slow dance.

"We are. Over at The Old Place, too, I'm told. Alma's son is working for me now. Still need one more." Serene moments passed. "Are you waiting for Benjamin? He doesn't have to stay if you need to get home."

"No. I thought I'd say hello and walk on over to the store. We need a couple of things before we go home."

Betty took Benji from her and put him in his carriage where he drifted off. She ran in for a quick kiss from her husband, maneuvered the carriage down the steps and wheeled it across the footbridge to Foster's.

On the way, folks stopped her to peer at the sleeping baby and tease about the next one. Betty accepted all the accolades and agreed a more perfect, beautiful boy did not exist.

She took her time, enjoyed the sunshine and throngs of people crowding the island and footbridge.

Each year, so many folks came to play at Idlewild, she could hardly recall the sleepy place it had once been. She liked the activity, the hustle and excitement folks from the big cities brought to their small town.

With the carriage bonnet partially pulled to shade the sleeping baby's face, she parked it under the tree and scooted into the store. It was Benjamin's birthday, and she was making his favorite - devil's food cake. She needed butter and cocoa and prayed Foster had both.

The store was packed with people she didn't know, and she tried to slip around them and get to Foster, but he ignored her in favor of the moneyed tourists buying big quantities of groceries for the weekend. She checked the carriage through the dusty window and was satisfied not to see fists flailing.

"Would you mind if I went ahead," she said to several people in line. "My baby is outside asleep in his carriage. I don't want to leave him too long."

"Go ahead, sweetie. We know how it is."

Foster grumbled when she asked for a single tin of cocoa and a pound of butter.

"Folks in line before you."

"Sorry. I need to hurry."

"What you need is manners, girl."

Betty finally made it through the door with her purchases, stowed them in the back pocket of the carriage, designed with that in mind, and pushed the hood back.

A scream came from deep in her gut, echoed across the lake, split the air around them, and rent the bowels of the earth and the heavens. People raced from the store and down the footbridge, eyes wide with fear. They came from The Old Place, leaping over the steps as if they weren't there.

The wail was so fierce in its intensity, listeners thought it feral, from the jaws of a savage animal. They surrounded her and stared but didn't get close. She was obviously deranged, and her ferocity frightened them. They whispered together, tossing out possible reasons for her display, wondering who would brave the distance between them and do something with the crazed woman.

Shorty got there first. He pushed the gawkers aside and gruffly sent them away. Not all left, but enough to satisfy him, and he put his arms around Betty and pulled her to his chest.

"What is it? What's wrong, Betty?" he whispered, but as he looked over her shoulder, he saw the empty carriage and deduced her pain.

"Where is Benji?" He shook her. "Betty, tell me where Benji is?"

When she didn't respond, he turned to the nearest man and sent him running to the hotel to get Al.

"The Old Place," he reminded him. "Not on the island. Tell Al to come fast."

He held Betty tight, sent another person for Benjamin, and went into search mode. He eyed each face for information, for knowledge or guilt, and looked into the distance for anyone hurrying away, or even walking or ambling while holding a bundle, doing anything he didn't like. There were too many people. Too many strangers.

Al was there in minutes, but it didn't feel like it. She pulled at one of his arms and wedged herself into the circle that was the three of them. Then he told her the horrible news.

Benji was missing.

Betty still hadn't spoken a word, but kidnapping was the only reasonable possibility with an empty carriage and a distraught mother. Al took over.

"You must talk, Betty. Tell us what happened."

Betty's eyes were black pools of anguish, and her face glistened with the flood of her tears. Al grabbed her chin.

"Look at me, Betty. Talk to me."

Her mouth opened and nothing came out but a guttural groan. Her lips pulled back in an unrecognizable shape, and her eyes squinted tight, shutting out the world.

Al shook her friend's shoulder.

"Stop! Now! You want your baby back?" Al knew it was cruel, but they needed information. "We need the sheriff, Shorty."

Betty's head nodded, and she hiccupped.

"Talk, Betty," Al said.

"I was inside. People all over. Benji . . ."

She sobbed the name, and Al yanked on her arm. "Benji was sleeping so I pulled up the – pulled the shade cover – and left him." She sobbed even harder. "Oh, my God, I left him. I left Benji. I left my son."

The crowd around them understood now what they hadn't when they'd thought her deranged. A mother would sound unbalanced learning she'd lost a child, would likely become unhinged. Sympathy flowed around Al and Betty.

Shorty sent someone for Hicks. He wasn't leaving Al to deal with this alone.

"Come on back to the hotel, Betty," Al said. "We can wait for Benjamin and Sheriff Hicks there."

Betty started to follow but turned back to get the carriage. She didn't want to leave Benji's riding bed. He loved it. He'd need it later. When she glanced up, she saw Foster standing in the open doorway, eyes squinting, lips parted in a brown-toothed smirk.

"Lose something, girl?"

Al strode to Betty and took her arm to make her come along. Betty's fingers were claws around the carriage handle, but she let Al lead her away. She glared at Foster and didn't dignify his words with a response, but Al did.

"Someone's gonna kill you someday, Foster. Hope it's me."

"Didja hear, folks? That scrawny Al Tatum threatened to kill me."

His head rotated to peer at all the faces staring at him, some of whom would like to see him, if not dead, at least beaten. Maybe they'd even like to be the one to do it.

"If I come up dead, you'll know who did it. She's did it before, you know. Killed that Adams boy right after he did the dirty with that skinny black girl. Probably that baby's pa."

Shorty wheeled the carriage up the steps and onto the porch. He wanted to take Betty into the dark hotel bar, but she refused, saying she would sit on the porch and watch Foster's store – see who went in and out.

He parked the carriage next to her and asked Al to sit while he got them both a brandy.

She took a seat and immediately saw something missing, the matching bag which carried the day's supplies when Betty brought Benji to work with her: diapers, bottles, clothing changes. Al had teased her it held everything a baby needed for a month.

"Where's the bag?" Al said, as much to get her talking as wanting to know.

Betty jerked forward, grabbed the carriage and ripped at the sides, felt under the mattress and blankets, digging for the bag.

"It was here. You know it was. I changed him more than once today and fed him his bottle."

"Could it have fallen off?"

Betty deflated. Her head fell forward, shoulders slumped, and a moan built in her chest and spilled from her throat.

"Noooo! They took it. And they took Benji. Oh, God!"

"But that's good, Betty. They mean to take care of him. Don't you see?"

Shorty came with four glasses on a tray in time to see Benjamin racing down the footbridge. He sprinted across the grass, leaped up the steps and spun the carriage around to peer into it as if they had simply missed his baby boy lying inside. Seeing it empty, he shoved hard, and it crashed against the railing, bringing another wail from Betty and a guttural groan from him.

He fell to his knees and took Betty's arms, one in each hand, squeezing but unaware of the strength of his grip. Betty didn't feel it, either.

"What the hell happened?" he asked, his voice too soft for anger, too controlled for the rage inside. Shorty heard and moved to him, put an arm around his shoulder, and forcibly made him stand and move toward the door.

"Let me," he said, and Betty nodded, unstoppable tears flowing again.

Inside and after Shorty explained what he knew, Benjamin threw out a dozen possible explanations for the kidnapping, none of which seemed plausible to either of them. There wasn't a good reason to steal Benji. There wasn't any money for ransom. He didn't think he had enemies - not in this country - and, if so, they were all soldiers he'd fought against in WWI.

"Think this could be revenge for what my friends did to George and the Tatums? I did bring them here. I was responsible."

Shorty shook his head. "No. Nobody knew. Pretty sure nobody connected you to the reckoning payment."

Benjamin banged a fist on the registration desk, and a hand pulled at his hair, frustration making him want to pull it out by the roots. "I'm not so sure of that. Maybe somebody saw."

"You weren't there to see, Benjamin."

"I know. Jesus help us. What now?"

"Sheriff Hicks is on his way . . . No, he's here now. That's the county automobile pulling up out front."

Hicks dragged a chair over to Al and Betty and sat, wondering what to say. What does somebody say at a time like this? He never knew, and these things got harder and harder with the years. He nodded to Shorty and Benjamin as they came through the door and patted his chest, the pain taking over.

Al saw and asked, "Can I get you something, Sheriff?"

"No. I'm fine but thanks. Want to tell me what happened?"

Betty drew in a long, slow breath, seeking courage, hoping the words would come and the tears would stop. Her boy needed strength from her, not a weak, sobbing wreck. She blew air out between tightly pursed lips, taking her time and watching a pair of trumpeter swans fly over the lake. She told her story when her lungs filled.

And he asked questions.

"See anybody you know at the store besides Foster?"

She shook her head. "Just a lot of strangers here for the Chautauqua. Didn't see anybody else."

"You see anybody near the carriage?"

"On the footbridge lots of people stopped to peek at him. He was asleep even before we left the Oakmere."

"Doesn't give us much to go on, does it?"

"You gotta get him back, Sheriff. Find my baby. Please."

Betty's black eyes begged, and he felt the sharp edge of her pain deep in his belly. It twisted and turned, lodging itself deeper inside him with each troubled breath she managed to take.

He knew it was only the monumental effort to control sorrow and rage that kept her from falling apart. The strain of it took a toll on him as well. He patted her hand, and she latched on, gripping with force, telling him what she couldn't voice with words.

"I'll find him, Betty."

He bent to rise from his chair and felt like an old man. He took Benjamin's hand and tried to look him in the eyes, but it wasn't easy. These things didn't usually end well, and he couldn't tell them that reality.

"Ask that nasty old man what he knows."

"Foster? He do something?"

"Smirked," Betty said. "Asked if I lost something. Made him real happy."

She controlled the sob working its way from her chest with swallows of bile.

Chapter Thirteen

Edwin and Dog appeared on the porch shortly after the sheriff left. "Real sorry," he mumbled to Betty.

Benjamin's head lifted, and his eyes narrowed. "How'd you hear. What do you know?"

"I just hear things, is all." He glanced at Shorty. "Want I should let Miss Abigail and Irish know?"

Benjamin took a fighter's stance inches from Edwin. "What else did you just happen to hear? You always seem to be in the middle of trouble. Like buying a dead man's stolen horse."

He barked the words, anger taking over his brain where innate civility had lived and making him hang onto Edwin's shadowy past.

"Those things is true. You know it, Al, right?"

"I know they are, Edwin. I have to get back to the kitchen now," she said and left.

Shorty moved to the steps, pulling Edwin with him.

"I'd appreciate it if you'd let Abby and Patrick know. And can you stop at the Chambers' cottage and then ride the mare out to Betty's parents? They'll need to know, too, but I'll take care of what details we know when they get here."

"I can do that," Edwin said, and left the footbridge with Dog.

"I'm going to look around Foster's" Betty said, already walking away. "Coming Benjamin?"

They left for the first of many searches, looking for a single, meaningful set of footsteps in the dust along with the hundreds of prints tormenting them.

Word had spread. Eyes stared at them as they neared the store, and whispers followed. A few people coming from Foster's asked to join them, and Benjamin eagerly accepted their help.

"The sheriff is in there now asking questions," a man named Jasper said. "He seems like a good man."

"He's okay, but he's one man, so if you want to help, we'll take your offer."

Three men and four women moved to join in, and Benjamin acknowledged them with a nod.

"Should we wait for Sheriff Hicks?" Jasper asked. "He's grilling that surly owner but should be out soon."

"Nope. He'll have others to talk with. Stay or go." He ignored Jasper and pointed to the trees. "If we walk in a line making a circle around the store, we'll cover all the near ground."

They walked, eyes alternately on the ground looking for clues and in the distance as if they'd see somebody skulking behind a tree. They raised their faces and sniffed the air like they'd catch the scent of the kidnapper because his smell was pungent and evil.

She listened for the squall Benji could be making. He wouldn't go quietly. Would he? Not if her son was alive, and she wouldn't, couldn't contemplate the alternative.

Benjamin stopped, stilled and intent, positive he heard a twig snap in the distance and bent to look at a footprint, sure it belonged to the man who took his son, and tried to follow it with his eyes.

A whitetail watched, and an eagle followed, soaring above the branches, visible for a moment through the leaves and then gone.

"I wish I could fly. I could find him if I could fly," Betty said.

Benjamin took her hand and squeezed it.

"We will find him, Betty. I promise."

"Don't make promises you can't keep." Her lips were hard, tightly pressed and gray, her anger palpable.

He turned her to him and the others walked on, leaving them alone. He pressed her against his chest, and she let her head fall into the crook between neck and shoulder and let go.

"Please, Benjamin. I want my baby. Please."

"I'll find him, sweetheart. Believe in me." He moved her away from him, so he could look into her eyes. "Believe me."

"It's all my fault. I let this happen. I'm so sorry, Benjamin."

"It isn't your fault, honey. You did nothing wrong. Some son of a bitch did, not you. And I will find him."

In Foster's, Sheriff Hicks had Joe backed up to the glass counter, wanting to shove him through it like Yancy had done to Terry Adams. The satisfaction on Joe's face infuriated him.

"What do you have against that girl and her baby, Joe? Why are you being such an ass?"

"Nothing. I got nothing against her cept she ain't white. That's plenty enough. Baby's black, too, course. Blacks are everywhere. Can't move without stepping on one."

"You ignorant, foul mouthed bigot."

He spun away and faced the milling customers. Hearing something terrible had happened, they gathered to watch and listen, taste the anguish hovering in the air like a thick, gray cloud.

Hicks looked each one in the eyes before asking any questions. He'd learned over the years prefacing questions with a stare garnered better answers, but not this time.

"See anybody by the baby carriage outside today?"

Every head moved from side to side and a few mouths muttered "No."

"See anybody eyeing that pretty, young, colored woman who was here?" He hung his head, and it bobbed a couple of times. "Yeah. I know. Lots of pretty ladies around today. Sorry. Let me help you. Betty is tall for a girl, around five ten or more, and really thin. Short black hair. Real short. That help?"

Again, heads shook and said, "Nope. Don't remember her. Uh uh. Can't say as I recall her."

Dust motes swirled in the stream of light forcing its way through the dirty window glass, flickered on the scarred wood floor and danced over shoes and up legs like millions of fairy flies. Sheriff Hicks pointed at the window.

"The carriage was right out there. Nobody noticed it from inside the store or when you were coming in?"

A woman stepped from behind her husband and shrugged off the hand on her arm trying to pull her back.

"I did. And several people peeked in the buggy. Couldn't see much because the sun shade covered his face, but you know how folks are about babies." She glanced at the man by her side. "Most folks, anyways."

Hicks' eyelids closed in silent thanksgiving. A start. The woman was a start.

"Could you describe who was there?"

"My two friends and me." She pointed behind her to the friends. "And an older white man. He was still there when we came in the store."

"Did you see him from this window?"

"No. He was gone by the time I noticed we could see the buggy through the window."

"What did he look like?"

"Old. White. Kinda scruffy-like."

"Hat?"

"Oh. Right. He did wear one. The kind I've seen on a lot of men around here."

"What was he wearing besides the hat?"

She twisted her lips as she thought back to the man at the carriage, and her forehead wrinkled. "Dungarees? A dark shirt? I don't think they were too clean."

She spoke in questions, so Hicks didn't have a lot of faith in her words, but something was better than nothing.

"Sounds like you're not too sure," he said. "But Thanks. Anybody else other than the white man and your friends here? How about you, ladies? Can you add anything to what Miss Theresa told me?"

He went to the door, opened it, and invited Joe's customers to leave. "Come back later, please. Sorry, folks."

"You're costing me money! You can't send my customers away." Joe's face purpled and the smirk left.

"I just did. Now, do your best, Joe, and have a real conversation with me." He crossed his arms and waited. "Who all was here while Betty was in the store?"

"Customers."

"Funny boy."

"I ain't no boy."

Hicks slapped his hand on the counter, rattling the glass that hadn't been caulked in place since Terry had replaced it.

"Answer me. Who was here?"

"All strangers coming for that damned Chataukie thing. Nobody I know," he said, but his face shut down. Hicks knew he was lying, and the lie meant one thing. Someone Foster knew had been around, and he'd guess that someone had taken Benji. Foster smiled.

"Let's try this again. Who was the old white man at the carriage?" Hicks asked.

"Didn't see."

"No one matching his description was in the store today?"

"Guess not."

"God help me, it's a wonder someone hasn't shot you, Joe."

"Only the second threat I've had today. Slow day." His rotten teeth showed in a grin only the devil could make, and his sour breath hovered in the air between them.

The sheriff backed up a step and his shoulders drooped.

"Wasn't a threat, just an observation with a little surprise thrown in. I'll be back in case you suddenly remember something you think I should know."

At the Oakmere, Abby wiped her eyes and cast about for a way to leave the hotel and go to her friend.

"Put Bear behind the bar with Carl waiting tables and Marcus at the registration desk. I'll give up Alma to help upstairs. Ye know I can cook alone, and she catches on quick. It'll be slow, anyway, with everyone going off to help with the search."

Patrick had an arm around her back and was shoving her toward the door.

"I'll explain to them, lass. You go."

"Are you sure, Da?"

She kept seeing Benji with a fistful of her hair in his fat, little hands and Betty with proud, happy eyes. Rage flared her nostrils and the side of her fisted hand hit the door frame on her way out.

"How could this happen?"

"Go on. Be gone with ye. Find the wee laddie," he shouted at her back.

From the footbridge, she saw a line of people moving through the woods at the other side of Fosters and ran toward them, praying they'd found Benji alive and well and not a silent body. When she walked closer, it became obvious they hadn't found anything.

Betty's feet drove her forward, but she moved like a dead woman, and tears were rivers on her cheeks. She had no ability or resolve to stop them. Abby moved to her side, took her hand and, without a word, walked with her. They searched for hours in ever increasing circles.

The sheriff had joined them and reorganized the search party. "We'll stop at eight," he said. "I can't have you mucking up clues in the dark."

"But – Night – Dark. We can't quit," Betty cried.

Hope died, leaving despair as dark as a starless night, and her eyes flickered back and forth from Hicks to Abby to Benjamin to strangers who might help her. Complete strangers who might hand her baby to her and tell her it was over. It was a mistake.

Abby pulled Betty into her arms.

"We'll find him," Hicks said and clutched his chest. But he had no reason to believe they would.

Samuel took a group of men further into the woods, designated by the sheriff to lead his party. Shorty took another group along the lake's edge. Over a hundred people, many of them Chautauqua vacationers, moved through fields and forests looking for Benji and his abductor. Some searched in the lake, not wanting to peer into the water, not wanting to see anything except what belonged there.

They met back at The Old Place after night claimed the earth, their tread heavy with mud caked shoes, and deep disappointment in their hearts. Al had kettles of colcannon and soda bread ready to put on the buffet, free for all the volunteers. Shorty helped haul the heavy containers, and Abby went behind the bar to help Jackson serve drinks.

"On the house," she said.

"Somber group," Charity said, and Abby raised an eyebrow at her.

"Didn't mean anything. I'm sad, too. Benji was a beautiful baby."

"Is."

Charles dragged himself onto a stool next to Sally who had been part of the search with Shorty's group.

"Where's Sue?" he asked.

"Holding down our little tavern. She's not built for walking in the woods."

Charles dug up a half-smile as he pictured Sue climbing over logs and wading in streams and ran a hand over his smudged face.

"Me either. Not anymore. Too old."

"Never, Mr. Chesnutt. You're at a supremely delicious age."

His sorrowful smile widened.

Samuel and the sheriff took chairs on his other side.

"Have you questioned everyone in the room?" Samuel asked Hicks.

"Hell, no. Not in this room. Talked with Foster, all the folks at the store and people close to Betty and Benjamin. It's some white, old man. That's what they say. Don't know what to believe, yet."

"Why? Why would an old man take a baby – a black baby, to boot?"

"I don't like to think why. But who knows what people will do? I gave up trying to figure them out long ago."

"How could no one see him take Benji? How did he just walk away with a kid in his arms?" Samuel pulled the gold watch from its pocket and rolled it in his palm, feeling the smooth warmth. He flipped it open, glanced at it and shoved it angrily back in its nest.

"A kid *and* a giant bag with baby things in it. That's what Al told me," Hicks said.

"Could Benji have been in the bag? Might explain why no one saw him walking away carrying a baby."

"Oh my God, Samuel. That's it. It would look like he'd just bought stuff at the store and was carrying it off. Damn. I've got to ask these people if they saw anything like that." He banged his glass on the bar and stood.

The murmuring stopped as they stared at the sheriff, wondering what they'd gotten themselves into. They were here for music, dancing and a little enjoyment – not this. But they would help; they'd see it through.

"Before you start, Sheriff, can I speak to these folks for a minute?" Abby said.

"You taking over?" His grin was tired but etched in the lines on his face. He'd known Abby for a long while and had gone through some tough times – with her always in the midst of it. "Sure, my friend. Take over."

"Thanks," she said and came out from behind the bar. "Jesse Falmouth says the music will start at nine under the pavilion, with dancing if your feet can take it. We so appreciate your help, today. Colcannon and drinks are on the house. Thank you, again. Here's the sheriff."

"Short and sweet, just like Abby."

"I'm neither one, Sheriff Hicks."

He rolled his shoulders, easing the painful muscles in his back, and held his hand up for quiet, sorry to quell the happy chatter Abby's words had produced.

"Hate to bring you down, folks, but I have a question to ask. Did anyone see a man – an old, white man, or anyone, for that matter – carrying a very large dark blue bag? It would have been heavy enough to carry a baby inside."

He let his words settle and listened to throats clear and chair legs scrape as a restless need to leave overcame them.

"I could have," someone said. "I'm not sure."

Hicks nodded. "Anyone else?" When no one else spoke up, he told them they could finish their meals in peace and leave if they chose and headed to the voice.

"Hicks," he said, shaking her hand and trying to smile.

"Fannie, and I just saw the bag from a distance."

She couldn't describe the bag, other than blue and big, so Hicks drew her over to the carriage.

"Could it have been this color, Fannie?" he asked.

"Could be."

Betty was by their side in an instant with questions.

"I don't know," Fannie kept answering. "I told you what I saw, an old man with a bag kind of this color."

"Why didn't you stop him?" Betty shouted. "Why didn't you do something? Why'd you let him just walk off with my Benji?"

She gripped the woman's shoulder, her fingers rigid and her voice rising to a mindless shriek. Fear absorbed her like a child in the throes of a nightmare she was unable to wake from.

Hicks pried Betty's hands loose and gave Fannie a thank you nod, his eyes pleading with Benjamin for help with his wife.

"Get Cassandra," Al said to Shorty. "Betty needs something."

Shorty took off at a run through the hotel and met Cassandra coming up the steps to the porch.

"Damn, Cassandra. You scared me."

"I do that, don't I?"

"Betty needs you."

"I know. I have tincture of poppy in my bag, seeds and leaves."

He shook his head. "Will it calm her?"

Cassandra looked up at the big man and two lines formed between her eyes. At the same time, one eyebrow rose.

"Sorry," he whispered.

"Well, you should be, young man."

Al met them at the door and led Cassandra up to the room Shorty had given to Betty and Benjamin.

"Until they find Benji," he'd said.

It was the one at the far end of the hallway from their own, the one Patrick used to stay in. It even had a rainbow painted across the ceiling and a pot of gold near the floor on one wall. Abby had surprised him with it for one of his birthdays, and they hadn't wanted to repaint the room when he moved to the Oakmere. Guests seemed to like it.

"I don't want to lie down, Benjamin. I want to look for my baby. I have to."

She stood near the pot of gold and slapped his hands away as he tried to move her to sit on the bed, getting angrier and more fearful by the moment.

"You want him alone in the woods all night? Who's gonna feed him? Change him? Stop it, Benjamin. Leave me be."

They heard her shrieks downstairs, and Cassandra hustled her footsteps.

"Bring hot water," she said to Shorty who stood motionless at the bottom of the stairs, eyes closed and listening to the painful wails.

He bobbed his head and left. Cassandra rapped a knuckle on the door and walked in to see Betty facing her husband with fists on her hips and fury on her face. The room crackled with torment and crawled up her spine.

"Come sit at the table and talk to me, Betty. We'll have tea. Remember when you spent time at my house? It was peaceful there, wasn't it? Peaceful and pleasant. You watched the warblers outside the window and whitetails nibbling leaves. And when it rained, even the raindrops were tranquil in their rhythmic patter on the panes. Uh-hum. Uh-hum. We rested. We relaxed. Uh-hum. Uh-hum."

Cassandra's hypnotic voice crooned on until Betty's hands relaxed and she ambled toward the table.

Shorty brushed his knuckles on the open door to let them know he was there and set a teapot on the table. He started to ask a question and stopped when Cassandra moved her head slowly from side to side. She poured seeds and leaves from an envelope into the pot and put the lid back on.

"Sit, Betty. Talk to me while we wait for our tea."

Betty sat, rigid and fragile, like the wings of a dragonfly, delicate, beautiful and breakable. The scent of heartache, musky and dank, followed her to the table and hovered over them.

Cassandra put her hands on the table palms up, and Betty lay her own in them. She felt the warmth of the older woman's power. Or maybe it wasn't power, she thought. It might be wisdom or love or even witchcraft, like everyone said. Regardless, Betty left her hands folded in Cassandra's and took her first easy breath in hours.

She sipped at the warm, nut scented, poppy tea after Cassandra poured, and her eyes began to soften. A tear formed a crystal bubble at the corner of her eye. Cassandra watched it glide down her cheek and rest in a salty pool on her upper lip.

"Do you know where Benji is?" Betty whispered, hope a stormy sunrise on her face.

"No, girl."

"But you know things. Things other people don't."

"Some things, yes. For others I must look and listen."

Betty stared into her cup, disappointment etching her heart once again. "You sure?"

"I'm sure you'll get him back, my dear. Be patient. Drink your tea and get into your night clothes. I'll wait with you until you fall asleep."

Chapter Fourteen

"I'll walk you over," Samuel said, when Abby appeared ready to head back to the Oakmere. He stood next to her as she removed her apron and hung it on its hook at the end of the bar.

She unconsciously leaned into him and sniffed the male, woodsy scent surrounding him before stiffening and lifting her chin. She wanted to walk next to him in the dark, take his hand in hers or wrap an arm around his back, more than anything, but she wasn't going to look for his company anymore or let it happen accidentally.

"I can get across the bridge by myself, Samuel. Thank you."

He'd hurt her and made the platonic nature of their relationship clear. Besides, it occurred to her he only wanted to go to the Oakmere to see if Alma happened to be there. Well, he could do that on his own without pretending to be doing something kind for her.

"It's dark, Abby. Don't be stubborn."

She flipped her long braid and, as it lay on her chest, noticed a leaf woven into it along with small pieces of twig and debris from her trek in the woods.

"Jeez, I'm a walking forest." She picked at the fragments, irrationally irritated at her hair. "This hasn't been a good day. I'm going, Samuel. Thank you for the offer."

She left without looking back, her head held high as sturdy shoes clomped on the wooden floor. She paused at the pavilion to suck in the sound of Buddy Black's guitar string bending a note, and the mellow wail of a cornet filled the night sky. The music captured her.

She watched dancers moving across the pavilion floor as if they glided on ice, cheek to cheek, holding each other without space for a breath between them. Her heart constricted, and she swallowed sudden moisture gathering at the back of her throat.

She swayed back and forth as if dancing out there in the middle of them all, and her eyes closed halfway in the dream. The song ended, and she sighed.

"You're a silly woman, Abby," she murmured. "What's wrong with you?"

"Not a thing."

She whirled around to see Samuel behind her and buried the smile leaping to her eyes.

"What are you doing?"

"Walking you back. I thought I'd made that clear."

"I told you I didn't need you. I thought *I'd* made *that* clear."

He tried hard to keep the smile from his lips, but his own eyes betrayed him. "I didn't hear you."

"Yes, you did. You ignored me like you've been doing for the past months, so I'll be on my way. By myself."

She strode off toward the footbridge, head down in stubborn determination, eyes on her feet as they stomped in the grass until she bumped into something solid. She bounced off Yancy with a sharp yelp and looked up into his smiling face.

"This day just keeps on getting better," she said, her anger at Samuel, fear for Benji, and her rotten mood transferred to the man in front of her.

"I saw you, Abby, and I came to get you." His words muddled together without spaces in between them so she struggled to understand.

"I'm heading home, Yancy. Enjoy the music."

"No. I'm here to walk you."

He swayed, and for a moment Abby grew concerned. All she'd have to do is push against his chest with a single finger and he'd fall over. But . . . A drunk is a story all its own. Being raised in a home where the dining room was a bar, she'd seen over indulgence a few times, but other people had always been nearby to take care of belligerent drinkers. This time, she was on her own.

"No, Yancy." She scoffed at the bothersome man and walked off toward the footbridge. The urge to look behind her plagued each step, and she forced herself to face forward as if she wasn't troubled. But it wasn't true.

Yancy bothered her.

Anger boiled in him, and she wasn't sure how to deal with it or him.

She kept her feet moving and tried not to run, listening for footsteps on the planks. Hair stood erect at the base of her neck, and she kept walking until a hand clawed at her shoulder.

She twisted around with a hand tightly fisted and ready to fly into Yancy's face, when he sailed sideways into the water, and Samuel's eyes met hers.

"You still going to use that?" he said.

Confusion wrinkled her brow, and she cocked her head.

"The fist," he said. "You want to punch me?"

"Maybe I do."

She shook her hand, releasing the pent-up force meant for Yancy's chin and looked for the intended recipient. He thrashed in the water a few feet away, and Abby wondered how it happened she hadn't heard either of them behind her. Yancy certainly filled the air with audible howls and splashing, now.

"Damned interfering, stupid idiot," he sputtered in between dipping below the water line and sucking in part of Lake Idlewild.

Samuel took Abby's arm to propel her down the bridge, and she planted her feet.

"Aren't you going to help him out?"

"Why would I? I put him in there."

"He's drunk. He might drown."

"Good. Do the world a service."

Abby crossed her arms and watched both men. As he flailed backwards toward the shore, Yancy's hard eyes glared at Samuel. He stood upright, once in the shallows, and turned to face them, eyes blazing with fury.

"You ever hear of the Black Legion, black boy?" Yancy's screech penetrated the night.

Samuel flinched and went cold. In fact, his entire body froze, and his breath became still as a corpse.

"It ain't a glorious colored unit in the United States army," Yancy said. "It ain't a unit in the army at all, but it *is* glorious. It's damned fine. That it is." He sloshed up the bank while still talking, and Abby heard ". . . so you better watch your back, black boy."

Their eyes followed him as he mumbled his way into the dark. In the absence of his voice, quiet settled around them, a bubble of silence tempered by the music a short distance away. Their world had separated from the rest with Yancy's vile threats and the tempest of their thoughts.

Abby put a hand on Samuel's shoulder.

"What did he mean? What's the Black Legion?"

"Doesn't matter. Let's go."

"Samuel! I'm not moving a step unless you talk to me. Who are they? What is it?"

Frustrated, he faced her. "A nice little assembly of men in Michigan and Ohio. Keepers of the peace."

That made no sense, she thought, and wrinkled her brow. Why would Yancy holler about keepers of the peace?

"You're lying."

"They're nobody. Come on, Abby. Let's go."

"If you can't be candid with me Samuel, go on back to the music. Leave me alone!" She strode off.

His head drooped, and he closed his eyes, wanting the peace darkness brought in the moments before sleep. Not while *in* sleep, not in the dreams he battled in the middle of the night. Just the peace of darkness when he sat on his own small porch at the edge of town, no lights except the stars to interfere with his thoughts. He wasn't black then, and Abby wasn't white. They simply were.

He jogged to catch up. He'd see her safely to the Oakmere whether she liked it or not.

She didn't look his way when he came abreast or acknowledge his presence. Nor did he, her.

It was a silent, uncomfortable kind of quiet with Buddy's music drifting over the water as if it slid to them on glass, bumping over the star reflections and fish-feeding circles in time to the rhythm. It was a syncopated tune that in a better moment would make either of them tap their toes with an urge to dance. This night, it irritated and mocked their churlish attitudes.

They were glad to leave it outside when they entered the Oakmere.

"Thinking about closing up, Abs," Bear said. "Really slow."

"Pour us a wee nightcap and let's call it a night, Bear," Patrick said. "How's our lass holding up?"

"Tell you on the porch," Abby said, and headed back out.

Bear and Patrick found their favorite chairs next to her, and Marcus brought the tray of drinks: one for everyone, including Samuel and Alma. Carl was too young.

Abby let out an explosion of air loud enough to raise Bear's eyebrows when Alma sat, becoming part of the *porch rockers.*

"Thanks for helping out, Alma. You, too, Carl," Abby said, thinking the words came out stiff and insincere. She did mean it, right?

Patrick saved her from opening her mouth again.

"So, tell us. How's the lass and lad? Any word on the babe?"

"Cassandra is with Betty, trying to get her to sleep. Benjamin, too. No word on Benji. He disappeared. Was in his carriage one minute and gone the next."

Abby sipped the hefty drink and hoped it would help her sleep, too. Maybe she needed Cassandra. Her mind was a battle of conflicting, contemptible thoughts, and the target sat on her porch. It was hard not to bite her lips.

"They think somebody might have carried him off in the giant diaper bag." Samuel mused the words, sifting them through his trained legal mind.

"You don't believe it?" Alma asked.

"I don't believe or disbelieve. And I don't know."

"Pffft. Lawyer talk," Abby said, and all eyes turned her way.

"Then what do you think, Abby?" Marcus said on his way down the steps to head home.

She hedged. "Well, could be that's what happened. Then again, maybe not. I guess I don't know."

Samuel slapped his knee, and Alma snickered. Bear's chest rose and fell in silent laughter, and Patrick rocked back in his chair. She praised the dark night for hiding the embarrassing blush spreading from her neck to her hot face.

"Pffft," Samuel said. "Abby talk. I'd know it anywhere."

"No, you wouldn't. You wouldn't know Abby talk if it smacked you in the face," she said and turned to Bear. "Samuel pushed Yancy in the lake tonight."

Bear's laugh became audible. Patrick actually stopped rocking, and Samuel shook his head.

"You sound like a three-year-old tattling on her big brother," Samuel said, his mustache wiggling in visible glee.

"Well, you did. You threw him in."

"Children, don't bicker," Alma said and received a scowl from Abby. "Sorry," she added. "I'm a mother first and last, and, uh, I was teasing. That's all." She set her unfinished drink on the floor by her chair and clasped her hands together. "I'd better go."

Samuel stood. "I'll give you a ride. It's late."

Young Carl's eyes lit with the thought of riding in an automobile. He dreamed of having his own someday.

"Our mare is at The Old Place. We'll take her," Alma said, not wanting to impose on a friend. "We ride double all the time."

"Nonsense. Come on Carl."

Samuel saw Abby's hands clench, and her rocker stuttered on the wooden porch.

God, her eyes.

What he'd just done didn't feel good. He hated hurting her, but he needed to. It was the right thing to do, and he knew it. Every time he listened to some ignorant fool like Yancy, every time he read the news or listened to it on the radio, someone told him hurting Abby was the right thing to do – before someone else hurt her beyond repair.

It felt wrong, though, completely and horribly wrong, and he didn't seem to be able to simply stay away. Idlewild was a small town.

Fewer people volunteered for search parties on the second day, and fewer yet on the third and fourth. By the end of the week, the Chautauqua closed, and the tourists went home leaving fewer searchers to walk the fields and forest looking for signs of the missing baby.

Abby temporarily closed the bar at The Old Place and sent Jackson to work at the Oakmere. Between Al and Charity, the hotel limped along, so Shorty, Bear and Abby could be part of the hunt for Benji.

The sheriff had other business to tackle and sent his deputy to organize the search party, but Betty could tell the deputy wasn't interested and the law was done looking.

Hicks sent out descriptions of Benji and the old, white man to surrounding law enforcement agencies in case they'd left the area, but everyone knew he didn't hold out much hope. Oh, he didn't say so, but it was clear the heart had gone out of the search. He believed Benji dead.

"Bet if a white child went missing, they'd still be here looking," she said to Benjamin. "Bet they wouldn't quit until they found him."

Benjamin's head spun to see if anyone had overheard. "That isn't so, Betty. Everybody's doing all they can. You know it."

"No, I don't know it."

"Look around you."

She looked where his finger pointed and saw her friends; Bear, Shorty and Abby plodding in a line with her parents and Benjamin's father. Every single day they walked the fields and forests with her.

She would have felt shame, but there wasn't room in her for humiliation. Rage and sorrow sat next to her broken heart leaving no space for appreciation, no space for any other emotion except fury and pain. Every part of her wanted to scream and keep on screaming until someone handed her baby to her. She couldn't be grateful. Not right now. Not to anyone.

Benji grabbed the man's beard and gurgled. He'd gotten over the upset stomach from the cows' milk and didn't fight the bottle anymore. Hunger made for easy adaptation.

Because his mother had taken him to work with her since the beginning of his life, he was used to being outside and away from his own home, so that didn't bother him. The sling across her back as she carried him around and the carriage he slept in while she worked had both lulled him to sleep much like the swaying bed *the beard* put him in now.

"Time for sleep," he said. "I'm off to get milk for morning, but I won't be long. Don't run off." He chuckled at his wry humor as he watched Benji's eyes close.

The baby couldn't resist slumber as soon as he was placed in the hanging bed. It swayed back and forth like he was in the womb. A thumb went to his full lips which suckled in contentment.

Used to night travel, *the beard* slipped quickly around trees and brush in the shadowed forest. Even though he chose different paths each time, his eyes adjusted to the darkness, and he didn't worry about becoming lost. The moon-painted shadows on the sides of trees used to startle him, make him hide to watch and listen for breaking twigs and footsteps, but not anymore. He was confident and needed speed.

He didn't want the child to wake up while he got supplies. He was safe; animals couldn't reach him, and he couldn't fall from his bed, but still . . . If the kid screamed it could bring trouble.

He knew where to find the milk but tiptoed first into the house and headed for the larder to stock up on provisions. He stuffed leftover roast, pie, cheese, eggs and bread into the bag he carried for that purpose and prepared to slip out through the kitchen door he'd left open.

The dog stood in the doorway with his head cocked to one side. He had only one eye, and it stared at the bearded man. He ambled further into the kitchen, sniffed at the pant legs and looked up.

"Move, Butch." He pushed him with the toe of his boot, and the dog ambled back outside, unconcerned. The old man followed.

In the milk house, he filled the jug with milk from the cool water trough, screwed the cap back on, and wedged it between the roast beef and cheese. He didn't want to crush eggs, and especially the pie. He salivated thinking about it.

His stomach growled and he silently cursed. Taking care of a baby took energy and time, a lot of it. He'd missed more than one meal because of the child, but he didn't mind. Every time he looked into those black eyes, he saw George. Poor dead George.

At least, he thought he did. He couldn't be certain, but he wasn't taking a chance, in case. He picked his way back through the woods, unconcerned with noise. He was alone and knew it.

With a rope tied to the neck of the milk jug, he lowered it into a deep pool where a finger of the Manistee River curved and carved out the bottom before meandering south and west. The glass jug sunk to the bottom and nestled itself in the sand.

He checked on Benji and pulled the thumb from his mouth, slowly so he wouldn't wake, and sat on his own bed to eat.

He engulfed the pie first, wild raspberry, one of his favorites if it weren't for the seeds that stuck between his teeth. Pulling the folding knife from his pants pocket, he opened it, wiped the blade on his shirt sleeve, picked the seeds from his teeth, and cut slabs of beef and cheese. He ripped a large chunk of crusty bread for the night's dinner and sunk his teeth into it with satisfaction.

It was fresh and yeasty, and the scent of Monday filled his nostrils, the day she covered every counter and table with trays and bins of rising bread. Breads of all kinds, sweet and savory, cinnamon and poppy seed. Memories of Monday carved his lips into a smile as he chewed.

"What about Tuesday, Benji? What does Tuesday smell like? Bleach and sun dried sheets. That's Tuesday's scent. You'll know it someday. Don't know about Wednesday. She probably sat around on Wednesdays and didn't make any smells. Don't be lazy, Benji. Gotta stay busy and work hard."

He chewed, savoring the mellow beef and sharp cheese, and held it on his tongue before swallowing to make the pleasure last. It occurred to him food hadn't tasted so good before the kid and he wondered why. He always ate to fill his belly as fast as possible and couldn't recall what he'd had for supper the moment the last bite had been swallowed. That was before him, before Benji.

"Pretty strange. You gave me taste buds, baby George. Beef tastes like autumn. Someday you'll see what I mean, child. You'll see."

Benji woke before light and squalled for a diaper change and a bottle. The old man rolled off his hammock, lifted the baby over his shoulder, and made his way down to the hot ashes of the campfire to stoke them into flame. He lowered Benji into a makeshift cradle and added kindling and small pieces of wood to the red ashes.

He retrieved the milk from the cold stream and prepared the bottle. When the water in the pan over the campfire was warm, he placed the bottle in it, changed Benji's wet diaper, bundled him again, and put him back in the cradle, a crevasse between two logs.

It had become routine, and he no longer had to think about what he should do. He knew babies liked their milk warm, and he didn't mind doing these little things for this child. It was even close to a pleasure, something like a fulfillment, he mused.

"Gotta wash some more diapers tomorrow. Hope it doesn't rain so they'll dry." He checked the night sky for signs of clouds but saw the glow of yellow-white stars instead. Like candles, thousands of them.

"Shouldn't be long, son. Look around at the stars while you wait. Really bright right now. You should learn about stars, about lots of things. I'll teach you."

He tested the milk on the inside of his wrist like he knew how to do but not *how* he knew. The milk felt no different than his skin so he picked Benji up, sat himself on a stump chair, and found a secure way to lie the babe on his lap.

Benji suckled like his mother's breast had always been a rubber nipple. He kneaded the gnarled hand holding the bottle with his own and stared up at the bearded face, trying to focus both eyes at the same time.

He recognized the beard, now, and liked to wiggle his fingers in it. It was a comforting face, one he expected to provide for his needs, to soothe him when he was angry over nothing, and to entertain him when he was bored.

He liked the bearded man.

Chapter Fifteen

With The Old Place bar closed, all their old friends had gathered at the Oakmere, and Abby jealously thought she liked it this way. Maybe she'd leave the other bar closed permanently. They didn't need two, did they?

She filled glasses and gazed around the room and down the long counter at familiar faces, faces she cared about and missed when they weren't there.

"Where'd you search today?" Sue asked. "Seems like you coulda covered the entire county by now."

"There's a lot of ground to walk. A lot of places to hide a baby – if he's even still out there. Can't imagine he is, but we don't know what else to do." Abby rubbed at the nape of her neck where a crick plagued her.

"It's nerves," Sally said. "You need to relax. You could get something from Cassandra."

"What's nerves?" Abby asked, confused by Sally's thread of thought.

"Your neck problem." Sally's beautiful face broke into a grin. "You're not paying attention, either."

She wasn't. She was still walking over fields of tall, dry grass and scrub brush and between trees, through creeks and stubbled acres of tree stumps and young pines.

"Who owns all that land?" Abby looked at several faces for the answer, but it was Samuel who gave it.

"The government for back taxes. Originally, most of it was deeded land, but it's no good for farming even with the trees gone so they sold the logs and left their land to whoever could use it. They were done with it."

"Why can't it be farmed?"

"Dirt doesn't go down very far before it becomes rock. Acres of it burned near the end of the lumber boom in the late 1800's, same year much of the whole country tried to go up in flames. We destroy things. Wonderful, beautiful things. It's in our nature."

Abby watched Samuel's eyes grow hard and hurt and created double meaning out of his imageries, but they didn't quite fit. She did her best to ignore what she saw in his eyes and tried to concentrate on her own words.

"Anyway. We're searching through acres and acres of nothing. Betty is distraught. I'm concerned about her. Benjamin, too."

"Many of us are," Charles said. He shook his head, pondering more than the sorrow of his friends. "I keep thinking the world is getting better, and the worst of our viciousness is over, but . . ."

"We have Idlewild, our paradise, my friend," Sally said, putting an arm over his shoulder, not thinking about Benji being stolen in Idlewild. She didn't want to. No one did.

"Speaking of the best and worst." Abby dove into the thick sludge silence had created. "I have a question for you. What's a black legion? I have a suspicion it's in the 'worst' category, but don't know what it is."

"Why?" Charles said, alert and on guard.

"Somebody sort of mentioned it the other day."

"Exactly how was it *sort of* mentioned?"

"Maybe in a threatening way? That's why I suspect it's part of the worst category."

Samuel ran a hand over his face and groaned. Charles stiffened, Jesse swore, and Edna glared at him. Bear and Shorty eyed each other, saying 'not again' without the actual words. For long moments, no one spoke, and fear prickled Abby's spine.

Edna tapped Abby on the hand and pointed to her empty wine glass. "I think a second one tonight, please. Did this person *sort of* threaten you, Abby? Here in Idlewild?"

"No. Not me. And I don't think it was really a threat. More of an unsettling observation." Abby peered at Samuel who had removed the hand from his eyes but left it over his mouth and watched her. He shook his head.

Charity bounced on her red cushioned stool. "Just spill it. Who said it, and what's a black legend?"

"Legion. Black Legion." Charles rubbed his clean-shaven face as if he could feel bristles growing there and moved his tongue around what to say, how to say it to this diverse group of folks. Some of these friends were, if not accustomed, at least acquainted with accounts of the atrocities inflicted upon coloreds. Yet, some would think it an impossibility. To them, it was clearly exaggerated talk. Others . . .

He gave a tired sigh and let it spill from his tongue like lye into a wash tub full of clothes of different colors.

"The Black Legion is a small group of men, an offshoot of the Klan, who are more violent, deliberate, and determined than the KKK ever thought of being. A specialized group protects Klan leaders. Mostly in Michigan and . . .."

"No!" Charity said, interrupting and sounding offended he would say her very own state had committed KKK atrocities.

"And Ohio," Charles continued, raising his voice mildly to talk over the Charity prattle. "The Midwest. Guy called Shepard formed the Black Guard. They're the worst."

"I've heard they're nearby," Jesse said. "But never thought they'd come to Idlewild."

"This wasn't a member," Abby said, wanting to reassure them. She hadn't meant to stir up trouble. "He wasn't part of the Black Legion. He was talking about it because he was angry. That's all."

"Just who ye talking about, lass? You might wanta tell us so we all know." Patrick wanted people soothed. This home of his should be a happy place.

"Da," she said, hoping to quash his question, but he was a stubborn Irishman.

"Your da asked you a question, lass. Who is this man. Ye did say it was a lad, yes?"

She blew out a puff of exasperated air, and Yancy's name came out with it.

"The wee lumberjack? He's running on about Black Legion nonsense?"

Abby nodded and Samuel jumped in. "But it was only after I threw him in the lake."

Heads swung his way, eager to hear more.

"Every time I hear this story, I like it better," Shorty said. "Not sure about the Black Legion part of it, though. You left that out last time."

"How many people are going to throw that boy in the water?" Bear asked, soothing Cleo who perched on his shoulder.

"He isn't a boy," Abby said. "He's supposed to be a mature man."

"But he isn't," Shorty said. "His mother spoiled him, and this is the result."

"It's kind of fun watching him flail about in shallow water as if he was drowning," Samuel said.

"What'd he do to earn this particular dunking?" Shorty asked.

"I felt like throwing somebody in the lake, and Yancy was, unfortunately for him, right there. I made kind of a spur of the moment decision."

"And you happened to be there, too, Abby?" Edna asked.

"I was. And I was about to take care of everything myself, but Samuel interfered like he had a right to."

"Take care of *everything*? What's everything?" Edna's black eyes bored into Abby's.

"Edna, never mind," she said. "Yancy was being his obnoxious self and needed to cool off. The lake, where I was about to put him, did the job, but not before he spouted off about the Legion. I'm sure he doesn't have anything to do with that awful group of men. He's all talk – mostly."

Shorty and Bear weren't so sure, but they weren't inclined to say anything. They'd watch him, though, because Yancy wasn't the man they remembered from back in the lumber camp. Or maybe he was, and they'd not known him at all.

Edna said she had to get home to Daisy, grabbed her husband's hand and pulled him off the stool. He gave her a wicked grin that said she had more on her mind than her daughter who happened to be spending the night with her grandmother.

"You're a wanton woman, wife," Jesse said with approval and admiration.

"Well, I'm following you down the footbridge," Shorty said, "so behave until you get home."

"Me, too. I'm right behind you. Watching." Samuel said.

Abby turned out the bar lights and the remnants of their group found rockers on the porch. Night folded around them and dampened their words, letting the rhythm of their rockers speak for them. It was the loon's turn to talk, and the crickets and owls. Bats owned the night, too, not human voices unless they were whispers.

Abby followed one as it zigzagged across the yard, heading for the next insect, dinner on the fly. She didn't like it that anything had to die to provide food, but she did it, too, and recognized the fact.

In the moment, she felt like a hypocrite. A dissembler like she had been much of the night.

Liar. You didn't want Samuel to leave you alone on the bridge.

She restarted her rocker and smiled at the wisdom of rocker rhythm.

It was warm for Michigan autumn, but gold edged leaves told the story they all well knew. Winter was on its way, and thoughts ran to Benji, praying he wasn't in the outdoors when snow happened.

Beside Samuel, Shorty slowed his step letting Jesse and Edna move ahead.

"Tired, old man?" Samuel matched his pace to Shorty's.

"Guess it's been a long day. Humor me."

Samuel listened to what was left unspoken and made sense of it. He had something to say and was working at the words.

"Why don't you just take a stab at it, Shorty?"

The big man rolled his shoulders like they needed loosening and took the stab, and Samuel leaned in to hear Shorty's whisper.

"If you're playing with Abby, I'll throw you in the lake with Yancy. Nobody gets to hurt her. What's going on?"

"Dying Grass Moon," he said, looking at the reflection as it made its way across the lake.

Shorty's step faltered as he tried to connect Samuel's words to the question he'd asked, but he couldn't put the pieces of the puzzle together.

"What the hell does that mean? Dying Grass Moon?"

"It's October's full moon, also known as Blood Moon and Hunter's Moon."

"Samuel, why're you talking about the damned moon? Why not just answer the question I asked?"

"It came to me when I looked at its image in the water. It's a time to reflect on death. Winter is coming. Vegetation dying. My Potawatomi grandmother taught me to praise our ancestors and all the worldly gifts we've given up to the *other* world – always, but especially during the month of Dying Grass Moon."

Shorty's head throbbed trying to follow his friend's line of thought, and he shoved his hands deep into his pockets in frustration and quickened his step. He longed for Al's simplicity and clarity, her purposeful sentences. God, he loved who she was.

Samuel kept up with his quickened step.

"Sorry, Shorty, if I wasn't clear. I'm not playing with Abby. I never have. I'm trying to keep her from being hurt. I'm giving her up to another world like I was taught. Sometimes I'm not very good at it."

"Look, it took me a long time to like you, Samuel. I thought you were arrogant and irritating. And now . . . I'm starting to not like you again. You're confusing the hell out of me."

Samuel's mustache twitched as he held back a smile he didn't think Shorty would appreciate.

"I know, and I understand, believe me. But you haven't seen the horrendous things that happen when a black man goes around with a white woman. You don't know."

"I don't think Abby cares about bad things happening, and they won't stop her from caring about you."

He stared at Samuel's Blood Moon, angry he couldn't make it right for Abby. And Samuel.

"Damn it, man. While I'm at it, what's with you and this Alma woman? What are you doing? I ought to pitch you in the lake right now."

This time, Samuel let the laugh out. He couldn't help it, but it didn't last because none of this was a laughing matter. Nothing about it was funny or fun.

"Abby needs to find a nice white boy to love. That's her world. She doesn't need threats from the Black Legion or gray-haired old biddies who shoot arrows with their eyes because she's at the theatre with me, or ushers who want us to sit on separate floors of the theatre just to watch a damned show. And I'm only beginning. We live in the country. In the boondocks. Imagine if she wanted to take a trip to Ohio, or Alabama, or Florida? Think, man."

Dead stillness captured the night and Jesse and Edna had long since stepped off the footbridge. Samuel rubbed the gold watch through the fabric of its pocket, wanting to bring it out, smooth the cool metal, hear the soft tick as he opened and closed it. But he didn't.

"And babies," Samuel said when Shorty didn't respond. "Think about the babies."

"She's already thought about it. I know her, and she doesn't want a nice white boy. She wants *you*. I'd say she loves you."

"When I'm done, she won't like me at all."

"And how are you going to accomplish that feat?"

"Once she thought I was an arrogant SOB. I can be that again."

"Once you were," Shorty said. "Dying Grass . . ." Shorty mumbled, done with talk and ready to see Al.

Betty watched night crawl by in the crack between the curtains and waited. She knew enough to keep still until moonlight sharpened shadows on the walls and for Benjamin's breath to settle into deep sleep. His hand on her belly lay like lead, telling her enough time had passed.

She slipped from under the hand and covers, snatched her dress and coat from the hook, the lantern from the dresser, and tiptoed out.

The door closed with a quiet snick, and her eyes flickered down the hallway, looking for a guest to be up and about while she drew the dress over the top of her nightgown. She flipped on the battery-operated lantern, checking to make sure it worked, and quickly shut it off. Outside, a chill breeze slapped her cheeks and tears formed. She didn't care about the cold, but Benji was a baby, and he needed warmth. All the way to the wooded area north of Fosters, she sent up prayers begging for him to be bundled up warm and well fed.

She turned on the lantern and headed deep into the woods where the tallest trees stood. Once far enough from town, she began calling his name, pleading with the ghostly image of his abductor to return him. She tried to imagine the man, to see him as kind and loving to her son. Prayed he was.

"Benji," she wailed. "Cry for your mama. Let me hear you, please. Tell me where you are. It's okay to cry. Do it, please. I know you're here, so cry loud, I'm begging you. Benji!" she screamed.

The name went on and on, echoing from the small circle of light out to the deep forest, Betty in the middle of the yellow halo, an aura in a land of darkness and agony. She keened her pain, one hand clutching the baby blanket she'd brought to wrap him in.

She passed the lantern over the ground in front of her, looking for something they'd missed the last time through

– a bootie, a scrap of blanket stuck to a bramble, a footprint where it hadn't been before, as if she knew every track in the forest. And she cried out to the man, to the specter who stole her baby, her life.

"I'm begging you, mister. Give me my baby, please. God, listen to me. I'll give you my life. I'll trade. Let me take Benji to his daddy and you can have me. Take me to the Promised Land. Let my boy live. I'm begging."

She fell to her knees and let the sobs have control of her body. Her shoulders heaved, and she clutched her belly as her insides twisted in birthing pains too great to bear.

She vomited sour bile and sat back on her heels, her face to the dark sky, and the scream that came from her, came from a savage place hidden deep inside. Wolves answered, calling to one another across the woods, from forest edge to forest edge, recognizing the primal howl she'd voiced.

Betty listened to their responses, blessed the wolves for listening, and pushed herself upright. The wolves understood. She picked up the lantern and trudged on. One step at a time and calling his name with each footfall.

"What do you mean, Benjamin? How do you know she's gone all night if you're asleep?"

"I'm telling you, Abby. She goes out all night, every night. She pretends to be asleep and waits until I am. I try to stay awake, but fail. She slips out and is back before morning when I'm still out."

"But when does Betty get any sleep? She has to be half dead."

"I don't know." He rubbed his head and closed his eyes. "I don't know how she keeps going all day. Walking through the woods all night long, going to every barn and abandoned home in the county. She says she's been there."

"Where is she now?" Abby asked.

"Cleaning. Shorty told her she had to work with Charity and do her job."

Abby stepped back, shock widening her eyes. "I don't believe he said that."

"I did," Shorty said, rounding the registration desk and coming through the bar doors. "She needs to work."

"But . . . That's just . . . I don't think . . ."

He picked Abby up and placed her on the bar so he could look into her eyes.

"Am I running this hotel?"

Abby nodded. "But . . ."

"Then let me run it. She needs to work. She needs to think about something other than Benji."

"He's right, Abby. Just look at her. Really look. She's a skeleton. She doesn't eat."

Benjamin rubbed his eyes as if he'd looked again and found the sight too painful. "She's killing herself, and that's killing me." He shook his head. "Sounds selfish, doesn't it?"

Upstairs, Charity ran a steady dialogue with her cleaning partner, trying to find her friend in this silent stick of a woman. She threw a sheet in the air and let it land on her head like she used to do to get a rise out of her. She dumped dirty water into the wash stand pitcher. She put Al's orange cat in the armoire, and that's when Betty emerged.

"How in tarnation have you been cleaning these rooms all by yourself? You can't do anything right. Never could. Exactly what do you know how to do, preacher's daughter?"

"Nothing. That's what the preacher's wife tells me."

"The preacher's wife is your mama. Call her what she is." Betty's voice was clipped and irritated, but her eyes weren't.

Charity grinned the Cheshire grin.

"Oh, you wouldn't want me to do that. Anyway, I don't think you'd understand the words I'd be calling her."

"Stop it. Give me that sheet. I'll show you one more time how to make a bed. Clean the pitcher and put in fresh water this time." She mumbled as she tucked corners and flipped down the top sheet.

Charity watched and ran the dust mop, glad a little bit of old Betty seeped out around the edges of her sorrow. She chattered at her friend, controlling her with nonsense and noise, and when the shade began to pull down as [illegible] enji took hold, she chattered louder and [illegible] her forward and held on to the reins of Betty's emotions.

Chapter Sixteen

Yancy rode in as dawn fell over the land and washed it in gold. Puffs of cumulus clouds dotted the sky and turned the fields to a patchwork shadow quilt.

Since Marcus no longer worked as the hired hand, and two of the three sons were gone, and their old man was gone in a whole lot of other ways, the Adams' farm was short of male workers.

He'd made up with Terry after shoving him into Foster's glass display counter and found himself working for him at the farm. He didn't mind, since he needed money, and the work was easy – easier than lumberjacking, anyway, and they needed him.

Besides, being needed sweetened a few bitter pieces of Yancy's heart, and he'd found ways to make the work more tolerable.

He took the saddle from his mare, slapped her into the near pasture to graze, and stretched.

Cecily stood on the porch watching. She tied her long, dark hair back in a yellow ribbon and gave him a welcoming smile.

"Morning, Yancy. It'll be real nice today. Look at the pretty sky."

"But *I'm* real nice every day, Miss Cecily. Think you'd know that by now." He winked along with his grin, and Cecily blushed.

He liked flirting with Terry's wife and could tell she enjoyed it, too. Yancy knew how to play with the ladies; knew they wanted to be admired and loved; that's all, and he was the man to do both better than most. He had no doubts about those talents. They were his birthright.

Black eyes peered up at her through long, dark eyelashes.

"And you're looking just as pretty as the sky this morning, Cecily."

She blushed again and moved down the steps toward her chores. She'd taken over feeding the calves and chickens since Yancy came to do the milking. She enjoyed it, leaving Emily to the housework, and, truthfully, she liked working with Yancy.

He told her stories while he milked, and she prolonged feeding the calves and cleaning their pens so she could linger nearby. Yancy bordered on risqué in the tales he told, deliberately, so he could glance away from the milk cow's belly to watch her flush. If her husband came in on his way to the fields, she'd turn all business, grab the chicken feed or the wheel barrow and exit the barn. Terry put a damper on his fun.

Yancy finished a tale that ended in him defeating three giant men who were taking advantage of a beautiful young woman.

"It was me against three. Big men, they were, but nobody takes advantage of a lady while Yancy is around. Don't care how big they are or how many. That's for damned sure."

The cow in front of him lowed, wanting out of the milk stanchion and into the sunshine of the pasture. Cecily glanced at the cow, awakened from being engrossed in his story.

"Tessie wants loose," she said.

He nodded. "We all do. But we want some ties, too. You know? I could never be tied to one person, cuz I'm a loose kind of man."

He shrugged his shoulders as if he couldn't be faulted for it, and it couldn't be helped. He didn't believe it for a moment, but it sounded good, and he wanted her to believe it. Women liked a vagabond kind of man, didn't they? A bad boy?

Cecily flipped her head toward the door. "I meant the cow. She's done and wants loose."

He led her to the back door and took the rope from around her neck. She kicked a back hoof up and pranced like a bronco, flinging mud his way. He scampered sideways and twisted his head to see if Cecily had seen his close meeting with manure. But she was busy.

With the lead rope around its neck, she led the next one to the stanchion. It bawled to be relieved of its milk burden while Yancy put his narrow bottom on the stool, took his time washing the teats, and began his next tale.

He timed the stories to end as the cow finished giving up the last of her milk, and in this one, bad lumberjacks took advantage of sweet young ladies.

"You don't know about most lumberjacks," he said. "Cept for me, you don't want a trust em." He checked to see if she was still there, still listening, and saw her standing next to the pitch fork, her chin resting on the handle top, her eyes somewhere far away.

"Done with this one," he said. "Want to bring me another?" He stood, emptied the bucket into a milk can cooling in a water trough, and led the heifer out. "Hey," he said, seeing her still mesmerized by the fly on the wall - or so it seemed. "Where you at?"

Cecily started and dragged her thoughts back into the barn. She'd never tell where she'd been, ever, and leaned her pitchfork into the corner to bring him another bawling heifer.

"Thanks, sweetheart. You're a good woman - pretty as a picture, too. That Terry is a lucky man." He winked and glanced at the door to make sure they were still alone.

Cecily followed his glance, her heart beat quickened, and she wondered if he had read her thoughts on her face. Had they been written there for him to see?

She stepped back and he sat.

"Wait," he said when she skipped to the wheelbarrow, anxious to get out of the barn and away from Yancy. Yancy who made her breath do funny things, Yancy who made her blush, Yancy who made her fantasize the unmentionable. She paused near the door but outside, well into the sunshine.

He twisted around and grinned. "Ever see the old man anymore? I mean, where does he live?"

"Don't know. None of us do. He just isn't here."

"Hmmmm. Think somebody'd know. Maybe he's dead in the woods somewhere."

Cecily shook her head. "No. He steals stuff from the pantry and larder, and people see him at Foster's once in a while."

"Strange."

Cecily maneuvered her full wheelbarrow behind the feed lot and emptied it, loosening the manure with a shovel to let it compost into next year's garden fertilizer. The sun beat on her shoulders, warm in the autumn chill. She wondered if her father-in-law would come back home when snow fell and dreaded the thought. He frightened her because he controlled everything and everyone. Even her sons. He always had. And Terry acted nicer to her without his father around.

She needed to go back to the barn for another load, but hesitated. Yancy both thrilled and bothered her. When she was away from him, like now, some of his magnetism melted away and she could take a reasonable breath without it twisting up in her chest.

But she was always pulled back, the thread of the thrill drawing her in like a fish on a fly line. She told herself she'd go back in, finish cleaning the pens and be done with him for the day.

Yancy brought in the last of the cows and watched Cecily deliberately ignoring him. It brought a smile to his lips. He knew what she was doing.

"Hey," he said, wanting to fill the empty space with words. "What do you think about that black woman's kid that was stolen? Do you think it really was? Maybe she killed it, you know, and then said somebody took it."

"Betty wouldn't do that. I know her."

"She's a friend of Abby's, isn't she? Abby has all colored friends."

His words made her straighten. "No, she doesn't. I'm her friend."

"Well, you kinda have to be. You're her sister-in-law."

He twisted on his stool so he could watch her.

"Say, isn't she the same colored girl Terry's brother liked to toss around? Could be it's his baby. Wouldn't that be something?"

Cecily grabbed the chicken feed bucket and headed toward the door as Terry walked in. She gulped, wondering if he'd heard and knowing he'd believe she'd been talking about George. He'd be mad.

"Go on in the house, Cecily, and take care of Ma. She's fit to be tied. Wants me to go traipsing through the woods, find Pa and make him come home."

He kicked at the straw strewn over the dirt floor. Dust motes shone in the sunlight, tiny earthbound stars twinkling briefly and falling to the ground.

"What do you want me to do?"

"Keep her busy. Damned fool old man. He's lost his sense. What little he ever had."

"Any idea where he is?" Yancy asked.

Terry nodded. "Had a camp in the woods but hasn't been there in a while, last I checked. Maybe made another one. Who knows. He isn't hurting anybody, and it's a lot better around here without him."

Sheriff Hicks rode his mare instead of taking the county's automobile. He wanted to amble slowly through the woods surrounding Idlewild one more time in a search for missed clues, anything that might help him discover what happened to Benji. The forests had been tramped through so many times, though, anything he found could be a clue to who had searched for the baby rather than stolen him.

Hicks didn't believe they'd ever find him. He'd been gone too long, and they didn't have a single bit of evidence to go on. They were searching in circles. He delayed today's meeting with Betty and Benjamin because he'd rather eat nails than tell them what he thought.

They were upstairs in The Old Place cleaning rooms. Abby had sent Charity to the Oakmere to clean so she could spend more time with Betty. Over the years, they had weathered many storms together and supported each other – become closer than what she thought sisters might be.

Her da had said being around a female friend might help Betty deal with her pain, but nothing did. She was short tempered, and Abby didn't blame her.

"It's okay. I'll clean it up," Abby said when Betty knocked over the dirty water bucket and the contents spread over the wooden floor they'd just cleaned.

"Stop it, Abby. I spilled it. I'll do it."

"You're tired, Betty. Why don't you sit a minute?"

Betty glared, chin thrust high, lips flattened. Her breath didn't sound like her own. It rasped like air through a screen door.

"Will you just leave me alone? I'll get the mop and clean it up."

She *was* tired. Searching for her son half the night, every night, while other people slept did that to a body. She snorted, a vocal comment on her thoughts and strode from the room.

Abby stood staring at the mess on the floor, biting her cheek and rubbing her arms like she was cold. She heard Betty's returning footsteps and managed to get back to polishing the dresser before she came through the door.

The reoccurring tune playing in her head was they were friends – or had been. She didn't know what they were anymore but recognized it was complicated, and she wasn't about to give up.

"Want to talk?" Abby asked.

"What about?"

"Anything at all, whatever might help. Things seem to be a bit tougher for you today, even more than usual. Maybe talking about it could ease things a bit?"

Betty dragged the mop head through dirty water and soaked it up. She twisted the gray strands until they gave up their fluids to the bucket and repeated it until the floor was almost dry. When she was finished, she glowered at Abby, her black eyes granite hard and brows drawn in anger.

"How do you think I should be, boss? Telling you jokes? Laughing? Singing you a tune?"

"N-no. Of course not. I know all this is terribly hard. It's just . . . Never mind, Betty. I understand."

Betty threw the mop handle and it thwacked the floor several times before lying still. She moved to stand at the window, her rigid body an ancient, porcelain statue likely to crack if touched with even a gentle hand. Her sightline made a direct path to Foster's store, like it always did whether she meant it to or not. She had no control over her eyes. She had to stare, look for the old man.

It stood where it always had, it's leaves gold tipped in the sun, the tree under which she had parked his buggy. And she saw the filthy, dust covered window she'd glanced through to keep an eye on the carriage, until she couldn't. Until she didn't. And the people went in and came out of the same damned door she'd gone through when she abandoned her son.

The voice in her brain screamed, *you didn't deserve him*!

She had spent hours looking at the scene from the window in her own room down the hall. Some superstitious part of her brain believed if she looked long enough, she could generate Benji with the sheer power of wishing and needing. She could turn back the clock. But nothing filled the buggy. It stood in the corner of their room, empty and accusing.

"You don't understand," she whispered, "because you can't. Nobody can." Silence spent long moments coloring the air with disquiet.

Abby moved to the window by Betty and stared at the same picture, wishing the window framed another scene, one without the nightmare.

But this is what they had. The past couldn't dissolve like salt in the rain, and the present would continue to hold them immobile and tied to the scene until they had a different perspective – maybe a hopeful future from the same window.

"Except for Emily Adams," Betty whispered. "She might understand."

Frown lines formed on Abby's brow as she tried to follow the line of thought. Emily Adams? "Why her, Betty?"

"You don't lose a son and just get over it."

Betty's voice scratched like angry cats' claws on a wooden post, and Abby felt stupid for having had to ask. She wished she could put an arm around her like they used to, wished they could cry together. They had before, more than once. But that was before.

She heard Betty gasp as they watched Sheriff Hicks round the corner of the hotel, dismount and tie his mare to the rail. She started to shake and sob and backed away from the window.

"What's wrong, Betty?" Abby asked.

"I don't want to talk to him. Make him go away," she sobbed.

In moments, Benjamin's voice called to his wife, and Betty backed into the corner and slid down to the floor, shaking her head. Abby knelt beside her and took her hand.

"I don't know what's going on, but you don't have to talk to the sheriff if you don't want to. Can you tell me why, though?"

She shook her head.

They were tucked in the corner together when Benjamin found them. He picked his wife up and nodded for Abby to leave them alone. She found the sheriff in the dim bar and learned what Betty didn't want to know.

They were giving up.

With nothing to go on, no new people to question, no evidence to guide them, they couldn't keep men walking the same woods, talking to the same people. They didn't know anything more today than on the day he was taken. It was exactly what Betty had feared. They were done looking. They thought him dead. Or sold like a prize hog.

Hicks' heavy feet moved up the stairs when Benjamin called to him. He walked with bent shoulders to the room at the end of the hall where Betty sat curled in the window seat.

He explained what he'd just told Abby. The case was open, he emphasized, but the current search was over.

"You wouldn't quit if Benji was white," she screamed at Hicks when he explained. "You'd still be out there looking not standing in a hotel room talking to me!"

The sheriff backed up a step, slapped by the force of her rage and saddened by the bias she thought he harbored. Benji's skin color had never been an issue. He was a baby, an innocent, and that's all. And that's everything.

He tried to console her with a touch on her hand, and she recoiled as from a flame. He rubbed his chest instead and felt the thrust of that old toxic knife inside. He understood, but it didn't feel good, and he wondered briefly if one could die from an imagined poison blade.

He ran into Abby where she'd waited for him downstairs. She had questions, he knew, but he didn't have any answers, just theories, long shot guesses.

"Could be black marketers. Men, women too, I guess, who find children for couples looking to adopt. In big cities, mostly. They pay good money for babies, and we had a lot of city people here the weekend Benji went missing, people we don't know."

"But that's so . . . I don't know. Rotten. Absurd. How can you simply steal a person, somebody's child? And for money? It's a vicious act, worse than murder." Abby's eyes blazed. She couldn't come up with appropriate words for something so heinous.

Hicks squeezed his temples with a thick hand. He agreed. Nothing compared to kidnapping in his mind.

"Head okay, Sheriff?"

"Throbbing. Not my best day."

"Can I get you something? A cold drink?"

"Water would be good. I gotta get back out there, make one more tour of the island and talk with people. Best I can do."

Betty's words echoed, knocking against the walls of his heart and brain. Were they accurate? Did they try as hard as they could to find this black child?

"Hell, yes," he muttered. He knew he had; they all had, but the words she'd spoken had left their mark on him. An indelible stain that felt visible, like the mark of Cain.

Abby went back to the room they'd been cleaning, finished up there, and went on to the next. Her feet dragged as if weighted with concrete, and her back bent.

She splashed water as she filled the wash stand bowls and didn't bother to wipe it from the floor. She jammed the dust mop under the bed and furniture, and the cats flew out of the room, not bothering to look back at her.

She stripped the bed and flipped the clean sheet in the air, trying to do it as perfectly as Betty, but no one could. She flipped it again, and it landed in a tangled ball in the middle of the bed. Again, she tried, and again and again, until she whipped the white linen in the air in violent waves.

Abby flailed each sheet, anger and grief lashing at the air, her breath ragged and her mumbled words reviling. Damning the man who'd taken what didn't belong to him. Damning the forest trees for hiding them. Damning everyone, the world and maybe even God for letting His world be corrupt and wicked.

She worked the rooms as if they were possessed with evil she could exorcise by cursing every hateful person plaguing the world.

In the last room, absorbed by exhaustion and worry, she glanced in the mirror she'd been washing. Smudges of dirt covered her face, her hair stuck out like a shock of autumn leaves, and her eyes were red rimmed and swollen. She hadn't realized she'd been crying. Anger had ridden in the saddle on her back, had held the reins while she worked and driven her hands, feet and tongue.

When she recalled her scandalous words, she glanced out the door to see if guests might have listened in on her theatrics. None were in the hallway, but that didn't mean anything. If they'd heard, they most likely fled from her ranting, and she couldn't help the crazed chuckle that came from her throat as she pictured them in quick retreat.

Betty needed help; Benjamin, too. She'd talk with him about how to keep Betty home at night.

She stood at the window but refused to give the view its power. It was only a tree and a small, grubby store. They held no authority.

Chapter Seventeen

"I hate coming here," Sue said. "We need to get Abby to take us shopping in Baldwin. Bet she could use a break anyway."

Sally held open the door to Foster's and waited for her cousin to climb the two steps. She huffed her way in, bouncing off the door frame and complaining.

"They're making doorways too darn narrow these days. A body can't even get in."

"These days?" Sally said with a raised eyebrow. "This store is as old as we are, Sue. You're just getting wider."

Her cousin wasn't being mean. She knew Sue liked her width. It made her special because she was the widest person in town. "And I think Abby's a bit busy what with trying to run two hotels and helping out Betty. But maybe. We can ask."

Sue nodded at a couple of men she recognized, brushed by them and watched them blush. It was a favorite pastime of hers.

"Haven't seen you around lately, Frank. The farm keeping you too busy to visit?"

Sue flirted, knowing he'd never, ever visit their establishment. They were colored. Most didn't care the color of their occasional bedmates, but Frank did.

He kept his head down and continued talking with Foster.

"What you gonna do with a portable stove?" Joe asked.

"It's for heating, not just cooking. Can't take the cold barn anymore. Getting old."

Joe showed him the catalog, and Frank picked the Perfection kerosene heater. It was small and safe, perfect for his needs.

"Take a day or two to get here. You want it dropped out at your place?"

"No. No need. I'll pick it up."

"Saw your wife this morning. Her and that Gerard woman. Don't know why she goes around with the colored gals. Looking for trouble, if you ask me. A man should put a stop to his wife misbehaving and such."

"She's just going to church." Frank slipped over to the window to peer out. He didn't need her coming in here and making a scene.

He couldn't remember the last time he'd seen her because he went home at night when she and everyone else was asleep. He didn't know why, but he didn't want to see her – or her him.

She used to look up to him, believe in him. Even when he wasn't totally sure of himself, she was. That all changed on the day George died. Since then, her eyes accused. It was obvious he disgusted her, and he'd rather not see it in his wife's eyes. He didn't know why and couldn't figure it out, but, for the first time in his life, doubt plagued him. About him.

James Gerard pulled the Adams buggy under a tree near the pavilion and flipped the reins around a low branch. He helped his wife and Emily from their seats and turned to help Cecilia, but she'd gone out the other side and was corralling her sons. They'd gotten used to attending the mixed church service and had made friends with a few boys their own ages. They ran off to play with them before they were forced to sit still and listen to the boring preacher.

Several hobbled mares grazed nearby, and a few buggies had been tied to other trees to take advantage of the shade. More automobiles than horses lined the road in front of the hotel now, mostly belonging to tourists taking advantage of their last vacation days.

It was warm for Michigan autumn, and the sun was going to be high in the sky before Pastor Jenkins released them with a final amen.

Mildred scanned the crowd for her daughter's face, worry etching her own.

"She needs to be in church. She needs it." She pulled at Emily's arm. "I'm going to the hotel to get her. Save me a chair."

"Want me to go with you?"

"Nope. You and James get some seats. Looks like a big crowd."

She found Benjamin sitting at the piano, not playing, but staring at the black and white keys, his fingers poised, heels of his hands resting on the wooden front. He twitched when she put a hand on his shoulder.

"Where's Betty?" she asked when he turned to look at her.

"I wish I knew."

"What does that mean, Benjamin?"

"I don't know where she goes. Out there, somewhere." A hand waved in the air without direction. "I can't keep her here. She sneaks out in the night and comes back in time to clean. She won't quit."

"But Sheriff Hicks said Benji's gone. Long since gone. Probably far away by now."

"I know, but she won't accept it. She's . . . I don't know what to say."

"Come on to church, Benjamin. Come sit with us. The Lord can help when no one else can."

Abby took her time crossing the footbridge from the Oakmere and soaked up the sun. Few things caused her to smile these days, but sunshine came close. She lifted her shoulders, turned her face to the east and took a long breath.

You need to get outside more, Abby. It's good for you.

Two harmonic meows came from behind her, and she twirled to see Phantom and Cleo following.

"Coming to church, babies? It's good for your soul."

Cleo raised an eyebrow and twitched her whiskers.

'So, finally someone believes we have souls.'

"Of course, you do, and I intend to find you in heaven, too. It will be glorious with all the animals looking for their masters."

'Masters? Who do you think is master of whom? Phantom, help me out here. Don't simply plod on like a senseless canine.'

Cleo fixed a contemptuous sneer on her shiny black face, and Phantom hissed a response.

"I didn't mean that, Cleo. You own me, and you both know it."

"Really?" came from behind her. How he caught up so fast, she didn't know, but Bear tugged her arm, pulled it through his and grinned.

"Talking to the animals, huh?"

"Uh . . . Caught in the act. I do. They make more sense than many people."

"I understand. It's one reason they have places on my shoulder whenever they wish."

"You *are* the cat man. Going to church?"

Bear nodded. "Thought I'd keep you company. Don't get to see you enough since you're at The Old Place so much."

"Too much change. I don't like it."

He nodded and scooped up Cleo who hung herself around his neck and purred. Phantom ran ahead to show he didn't care.

"Can I do anything?"

"I wish you could. Bring back Benji. Fix Betty. Close the Oakmere so we can all be together at The Old Place. Make Samuel nice again." The last was a whispered plea.

"You sure he ever was?"

"Nice?" Her eyes misted and she searched for his face in her memories. "Yes. He is. Was." Then she searched for his face among the congregation about to be seated and found him at the back.

"We'd better hustle," Bear said and pulled her to stand with the men under the pavilion, at the back.

She rolled her eyes Samuel's way without turning her head so he couldn't tell she was looking at him, and he made a serious attempt to show he hadn't noticed. Abby flared her nostrils and straightened her spine, Samuel fingered his pocket watch, and Bear shook his head.

As Reverend Jenkins named the song they were to sing, Benjamin, sitting next to his mother-in-law, saw her round the corner of Foster's store and stand under the tree where she'd parked the buggy the day he was taken.

Betty stood with one hand on the oak's trunk and felt the rough textured bark, sniffed the musky scent of autumn and pungent odor of the rushes and cattails growing at the edge of the lake. She let herself live in the sensations, moving through the here and now to another time, unaware of the crowd gathered under and around the pavilion.

She was in the space where he'd last been and didn't want to leave it. She wanted to live under Benji's tree.

Benjamin watched and waited for her to walk his direction. When she didn't, he left his seat and went to her. He picked twigs from her hair and brushed at dark smudges on her cheek with his handkerchief.

"Come to church with me," he said. "Please. You can pray for Benji with me."

Her feet moved because he pulled her. She didn't tell them to.

"It won't help. He doesn't listen. Nobody listens. Not even God."

Betty's black eyes were hollow pools of pain. Her agony pierced his heart as much as the loss of his son. How much could she bear? How much could he?

She was a constant ache in Benjamin's heart and mind, but he didn't exist in hers because she couldn't see beyond Benji. Betty couldn't see any face except her missing son's.

They sat, and he held her hand to remind her he was there. She wasn't paying attention to the reverend. She was in the woods, searching and calling. Benjamin gasped and jerked at Betty's screech.

"No! Damn it! No! You can't pray for that . . . that monster. Don't you dare!" Her finger stabbed at the reverend, and her mouth twisted in torment.

Reverend Jenkins had asked them to pray for Benji's safety *and* for the soul of the unhappy creature who had stolen him.

All eyes turned to stare at her, but only for quick seconds, trying not to embarrass her by gawking. They understood but hadn't worn her mud-soaked shoes, hadn't walked the woods and roads searching for their lost hearts.

His prayer was brief, and he held his arms out to her when it was over. She sleepwalked to him, and he folded her in his arms.

"Take it to Him, my child, and leave it with Jesus. Let Him be your comfort."

Betty pulled back and peered up at Pastor Jenkins' peaceful face.

"I can't. You don't believe me. Nobody does. But Benji is out there. Alive. I know it, and I have to find him."

She twisted gently from his arms and moved toward her mother who stood among a group of animated people.

"I'm saying Frank. Your husband," Sue told Emily looking her straight in the eyes. "He was there, and he bought some kind of heater thing. Out of a catalog."

"But why would he do that? We don't need a heater."

Emily's gaze flickered to Foster's store, to the crowd standing around the potluck tables, and back to Sue's wide face. She frowned, irritated and confused.

"Don't know. He didn't say."

"Yes, he did, Sue," Sally said. "He told Joe it was cold in the barn, and he was getting old. That's what he said."

Sue leaned into Emily to whisper. "Don't think I believed him, though. He didn't sound real convincing." She poked a pudgy finger at her temple and squinted her eyes. "Truth to tell, I think he was lying. I can tell."

At the edge of the group, Cecily held Chunk's collar in one hand and Bailey's in another, having corralled them from a game of marbles for the luncheon. They listened to the talk about their grandfather, rolled their eyes and made faces at each other. They liked it a lot better at the farm since he wasn't there bossing them around all the time and being ornery.

"He doesn't need a heater for the barn. He's never in it," Chunk said, sticking his skinny chest out to make his words matter.

"He isn't anywhere, not at home, anyway. He's a ghost." Bailey waved his arms around and made eerie sounds until Cecily jerked his collar and choked him.

"Stop, boys. That's Grandpa you're talking about."

"But he isn't, Ma. He only comes at night to steal food, and you know it."

Bailey's face reddened, embarrassed they hadn't found his little joke funny, and he wasn't sad to leave the group when Cecily dragged them off to the food tables.

Mildred listened to the words whirl around her. The events had no meaning. She didn't care about Frank Adams or Joe Foster. She didn't need to know about any stove or heater or the fact that Frank didn't come home except to steal food. Her face crumpled, and she backed away. Emily saw and followed.

"How can I help?" she asked, drawing her arm through the crook of Mildred's.

"It's so strange." She left it there, unclear in her own mind what was strange, but knowing something was.

"Explain it to me, my friend."

"We all go on like nothing is wrong. We eat breakfast and work. We go to sleep and get up and do it again, and I wonder why. I just left church, and I wonder why I went. Where is Benji? Where is God?"

"Nothing easy about this life. That's for sure." Emily patted the arm she held.

"You'd know. You surely know loss." Mildred's eyes misted in memory.

"Yes. I lost more than a son when George died. I lost the man I've loved since I was sixteen."

"I don't understand. How so?"

Emily let the sound of birds and insects fill the silence while she thought about her friend's simple but difficult question. Mildred didn't push her to respond, and she waited to answer, gathering her feelings.

Gold and red drifted to the ground and fluttered around their feet. Overhead, geese said goodbye with raucous, blaring honks. They filled the autumn sky, their black necks stretched long and pointed south.

Emily kicked at a stone in the road and huffed.

"I wish I knew. I mean . . . I'm not sure about much, but I see Frank clearer than before, and I don't worship him anymore. He can't understand why. We ruined our boys, and I blame me for George. Frank didn't do it alone. I should have opened my eyes sooner. I don't think he knows any of that. Or understands it at all."

"I don't think I do either, but it's okay."

"Yes. It is. I'm here for you, Mildred. I'm happy to be here."

Chapter Eighteen

"You know something you're not saying," she said, her eyes firm and challenging. "I'm not messing around anymore, Terry. What do you know about your father? Where is he?"

He and his mother stood outside the barn doors, near enough Yancy could hear them talking. Silence followed her words and hung between them, a dark fog weighted with uncertainty.

Yancy figured Terry knew and didn't want to say, but he didn't know why – other than the man treated his son like he had no brains. He glanced at Cecily who did her best not to meet his eyes during the argument between her husband and his mother. She forked pungent bedding straw into the wheelbarrow and kept her head down.

"What do you think?" he said, watching her from the milk stool on which he squatted, his head pushed sideways into the cow's warm hide so he could see Cecily's face.

She ignored him and shoved the pitchfork into the pile of damp, manure filled straw. She dumped the fork's load onto the steaming heap in the barrow and watched vapor rise as it met cooler air.

"About what?" she mumbled.

"Where your father-in-law might be."

"I don't know. He isn't here. That's all I know."

Outside, something hit the side of the barn, and both of them straightened, startled by the loud thump.

"Stop that!" Terry bellowed. "Don't be pushing me, Ma, or I'll push right back. You know I will."

Yancy and Cecily moved to the open doorway to see Emily with her fists planted on her hips, her chin jutted out and her eyes blazing.

"I should've pushed you while you were growing up, turned your backside up to meet the flat of my hand. All you boys."

Terry straightened and tightened his own fists, but Emily didn't back off. She moved forward to put her face a foot from his. If he was going to hit her, he'd have to look into her eyes as they stared at his.

"I deserve some respect," Emily added, "whether you like it or not, and it's high time I got it." She poked a broken nailed forefinger into his chest. "I asked you a question. Do you know where your father is?"

"No." He glared and edged around her, rolled his shoulders and strode off without looking back.

Emily deflated like the air keeping her upright had leaked out. She turned and left without acknowledging the audience viewing her humiliation. She couldn't think what else to do and couldn't understand why her son didn't want his father to come back home. Well, that wasn't quite true. She could imagine why, but it wasn't right.

Something troubled her husband, and he needed help. He needed his family. She cared about him, even if she no longer worshipped him.

"You're a man, Frank, not a god," she mumbled as she went into the kitchen. "Just a man, a husband and father, and as soon as you accept those simple things, we'll be fine. What's left of us will be fine."

Bailey and Chunk hung onto opposite sides of the doorway between the kitchen and dining room, eyes wide and knowing. They'd seen and heard and scrambled back when they saw her head their way.

"Come on, boys. Get your garden shoes and you can help me bring in the last of the beets and winter squash. Bring your baseball mitts, too."

Their lips opened in wide grins, and they ran off. This was a new grandma, and they liked her much better than the old one.

He hung Benji in his hammock and pushed it back and forth, a gentle movement the baby loved, one that soothed like he was still in the womb. The old man watched, and when the dark eyes closed, he touched the soft cheek with his finger, traced a line from the tightly curled hair around the curve of his ear to the dimpled chin.

A smile grew under the scruffy beard and stayed there while he watched his baby drift into a peaceful doze. He hummed a lullaby and wondered how it had come into his mind and down to his lips and tongue. Had his mother sung it to him? It had a German sound, so he figured she had. He tried out a word or two and saw Benji's eyes settle further into slumber as the flicker of dreamland moved his lids.

When he was sure the child was in deep sleep, he settled himself on the front porch high in the trees, observed the bats as they darted about looking for dinner, and listened for Benji to waken and need him.

He pondered their home nestled in the branches. It was good for now, but winter was coming soon, and, while the cold would keep their food cool, how long could he steal it from the farm? He'd need to plug up the holes in the walls, too, to keep them warm, and Benji would need bigger clothes soon and a bigger bed. He had a lot to think about.

Those needs didn't disturb him. He turned them into plans and let them fill his heart and mind. It was good to plan for yourself and your son.

Benji's needs defined him. He could feel them take hold like a sanctification, a meaning for his life – the voice directly from God. And he didn't know anything about God, but he knew that to be truth.

He pondered the child's color and didn't remember liking dark skin much before, but he did now. He surely did. Benji's skin glowed with health, was as smooth as a river-washed pebble, and caused him to wonder what he hadn't liked about dark skin.

He wasn't certain it would remain so deeply brown and perfect. He'd heard it sometimes faded, and lighter skin would probably be a good thing. People might accept them together more easily if the boy's color was more like his own, but . . .

The moon hung high in the sky, a half-moon cocked at a crooked angle that caused stark shadows behind the trees. It shined on a racoon digging for crawdads in the mud bank of the shallow pool where he kept Benji's milk cool. He leaned against the wall and pondered what it would be like in a month – in three – or when his son was a toddler. He had a big job ahead, and he looked forward to it, but first things first.

He didn't sleep much at night because his schedule was erratic, foraging in the dark for food and staying out of sight during the day. He liked it, and the baby didn't seem to care since his schedule was erratic, too.

As dawn broke, Benji cooed waking sounds, and the old man pulled in his legs and bent to stand, knees creaking and fingers aching when he tested his hands in several stretches.

"Hell of a thing, getting old. Don't do it, son."

Benji eyed him with expectation and the beginnings of a smile. His small hand reached for the long gray beard, and the old man let him take it in his fist. He bent to nuzzle his nose on Benji's, and the baby gurgled.

"Come on, son. Let's get that wet diaper off and heat a bottle on this fancy stove. Nice not to have to stir up that old campfire."

He set the bottle in the heating pan of water and changed the diaper. When he had a dry Benji in his arms, the bottle was ready, and they sat together on the little deck at the top of the trees.

"Got a surprise for you," he said and watched Benji's eyes focus on his face. "Dang. You're getting good, son. Big, too."

When the bottle emptied, he tipped Benji over his shoulder and patted his back. He belched and the old man grinned.

"Good job, my boy. Here's the surprise. We got some work to do, and you're going with me. I'll sling you right here." He patted his chest. "Kinda like the Indian women did. Leastways, I think they did. You'll like it."

He lay Benji on a long piece of cloth, pulled it partially together, and tied the ends around his own neck. The baby swung as if he lay in another hammock.

"You good in there?" He peeked at a contented face and smiled again. He couldn't remember ever smiling so much and began to think it might be Benji who brought it to his lips. This child was made for him.

Certainty moved with him as his feet found the ladder rungs and then the ground.

For two hours, he strung twine around their home and tied pieces of tin together like wind chimes to hang from the string. If they were wiggled by an intruder, their noise would wake him in time to load his shotgun or rifle. He walked in a circle around the tree house, inspected his handiwork, and nodded satisfaction. "We're safe, my boy."

He folded the fabric of his sling back and peeked into the bundle hanging against his chest. Benji lay content and comfortable in his nest. Intent on the world around him, his eyes left the old man's face every few moments to follow the flight of a blue jay or the sound of a chattering squirrel.

"Couldn't get any better than this, could it, my boy? You're gonna have the *real* mother, the best of all of 'em. Can't beat mother nature to teach you what you need to know about life. And me – your old man."

The tin chimes didn't clatter unless a whitetail moved through and broke the twine. More than once, the sound of tin clanging together woke him as intended. He had bolted from his hammock, grabbed his rifle and pushed the safety lever so fast he surprised himself. He'd decided to keep it loaded, and he was glad he had.

When it happened, he'd been terrified they were there to take his baby, and he knew he couldn't have loaded the gun. He'd broken into a sweat, and his hands shook as he aimed toward the offending noise.

It seemed the makeshift security measures worked, however, and the old man slept sounder and felt safer most nights. He hung new twine when it broke and replaced the chimes when needed.

They took walks in the woods, Benji slung across his chest, his rifle across his back. He pointed out plants and named them. He described the different birds zipping from tree to tree and tried to imitate their calls. He stood motionless when they came upon a doe with a spotted yearling, pointed them out to Benji and grinned, convinced the baby understood his words as well as saw the beauty of Michigan's whitetails.

They came within view of the tree house, and, before he moved further into the area, he walked around it to check for broken twine indicating intruders might have visited. He was vigilant. He couldn't be too protective when the safety of his son was concerned.

He sniffed the air and smelled pine, moss, and the river. Good, normal scents. He listened for the snap of a twig and heard only the continuing chatter of wildlife. Good. They weren't afraid. He turned in a full circle to look for movement. Nothing. They were alone.

Life was perfect. Almost.

The more he dwelled on Benji's skin, the more it worried him. He didn't want the color to fade but had to know if it would wash away or remain its beautiful deep brown. He needed certainty.

"You gotta know things, son. You gotta be sure when you put your shoes on the ground what they're gonna step on or into."

Some ways away, dark eyes scanned the night as she cocked her head to listen, moved on into the murky woods with stealth, and stopped to listen again. She squished with each footstep on the damp forest ground and walked into a swamp before she knew it was there.

Words she didn't know she could utter came out of her mouth, her frustration fueled by the water above her ankles, and the curses clarified exactly what she'd been feeling for a long time. They were unforgiving and brutal and said what she thought about herself for abandoning her son to the clutches of some kidnapping maniac.

She walked longer than usual this night, following the quarter moon as if it guided her like the Star of Bethlehem had the wise men.

A raccoon's furtive movements startled her, and she pressed the flat of her hand against her heart to stop its thunderous beating. The nocturnal creature's careful footfall had led her to believe something human followed her, a different kind of predator. It was stealthy, deliberate. But the bandit peered around a tree and glared through his perfect black mask, waiting for her to leave or fight.

"I'm going. Just looking for my son. You go on and do your business, coon. I'll do mine."

Sitting in the dark on his tiny aerial home balcony, he talked to the trees and whatever nocturnal critters foraged nearby and would listen.

"But how could it fade?" he murmured. "They must lie. If that was true, there wouldn't be any grown up colored folks, and they're all over the place. At least in Idlewild, anyhow."

Stewing over the issue didn't resolve it, so he decided to find out for sure. When Benji woke, he'd give him his bottle, and they'd head out to a spot he knew of where it was out of the current and calm. He'd give him a wash and see if the color came off a little. He could use a scrub himself, anyway.

He tiptoed inside and gathered supplies: the extra towel he'd taken from his old home, a bar of soap, clean clothes for both of them, and the sling he'd gotten used to using.

Water heated and bottle prepared, he waited. Benji would be awake soon, and they'd get their bath. He couldn't remember ever being so excited to get clean, but everything was new and wonderful with his son.

Not bothering to dress either himself or Benji after removing the wet diaper, he fed him, burped him and put him in the sling. Jaybird naked and trekking to the meander part of the river, words to a made-up song tumbled from his mouth, and he marveled at the pink slivers of dawn peeking through the leaves.

He dropped the towel with the bundle of clean clothes on a large rock and waded in. As soon as Benji felt the freezing cold water on his back, he filled the dawn with a sharp howl of displeasure.

"Shhh. Hush now, boy. Won't be long, son. Just hang on. We're gonna scrub up, is all."

He removed the baby from his sling and, holding his head in one hand and body in the other, dunked him under the water like a baptizing preacher bringing a baby to the Lord. Benji choked and gasped for air, grabbed for the gray beard, screamed and flailed.

"Shhh, now. We'll be done soon."

Pulling him close to his chest, he ran the soap over Benji's body and worked up a good lather, staring at the froth to see if it contained any black residue. Again and again, he worked it into a lather and peered at it. Nothing. His son was still beautifully dark, and the old man's lips parted in a wide grin.

He wrapped the still wailing Benji in the towel, placed him on the grassy bank, and waded back in to lather himself.

"It is cold, Benji. I grant you that, but when you kinda get used to it, it feels good. You'll see when you grow a little bigger. You'll see."

He watched the bundle on the bank and listened. Benji's sobs had quieted to hiccupping gasps, and he hastened to rinse in his need to check on him. With the baby in his arms, he sat on the flat rock where he'd placed their supplies, wrapped him in fresh diapers and warm clothes.

Yes, he was naked as a newborn possum wearing goose flesh, but he didn't care. Benji was warm and quiet and contented.

He braced his feet on the rock, making a nest of his body, and snuggled the child into the cradle between legs, chest and arms. His wrinkled lips grazed a clean, chilly forehead and glanced off the end of his nose.

Benji's happy sigh filled him with bliss he'd never known, a painful bliss that simultaneously cleaved and clenched his heart and head and parts he hadn't known could hurt with loving. But they did, and he wondered briefly if he was dying now, right this minute. Was this what the end felt like? But he couldn't die . . .

He had a son to raise, a son who needed him.

And Benji smiled. He grabbed a fistful of gray beard and smiled.

Red hints of dawn began to slip through the branches, when all the forest creatures immobilized as the shriek rent the air and rendered movement impossible. Even the crickets and tree toads went silent recognizing the wail didn't belong to a scavenged animal being killed for food, and it continued long after it began like death was slow to complete.

The single night creature who understood the sound spun in a circle trying to discern the direction from which it came. But it echoed off the trees and sky, bouncing from one to another. She ran to where she thought it should be, tripped over a fallen log, jumped up to listen, and turned to run in the other direction.

Tears streamed from her eyes, a rushing torrent of salty water that burned and created more. She swiped at her face, marking it with the black loam crusting her hands. She stopped again to listen to the cries.

"I'm coming, Benji. I'm coming. Keep crying. I can't figure out where you are. Keep crying, please."

She pleaded, begged for him to cry louder and prayed nothing would hurt him to make him cry at all. She sobbed with the contradiction, fell, got up, and changed directions again. Over and over, she made circles in the forest, treading on her own footprints and falling on the same log. Her own sobs kept the forest animals silent.

And then the screams quit.

She froze and listened to the heavy, hateful sound of nothing, more terrifying than any noise could ever be. Why had her baby quit yelling? What made him stop?

Betty fell to the earth, held her face in her hands, and begged God. She pounded the ground and berated God. She grasped mounds of damp leaves and crushed them, squeezed until they were pulpy globs and traded her life to God . . . if he'd give Benji breath to scream again.

She slumped in defeat.

When she could move, she headed in the general direction of the hotel.

"Benjamin," she whispered. "He'll believe me, now. He has to."

He dropped his shoe when she slammed the door open, and it crashed against the wall. He might not have known her, so much dirt and debris covered her clothes and body. Her hair stuck out like black straw with twigs and leaves embedded in the mess.

Benjamin struggled not to be angry. She'd gone out again – sneaked out to search while he slept, after he'd begged her not to and after the sheriff had told her it was futile. His head fell forward and shoulders slumped as he struggled to find compassion. But it was nearly gone, along with his son and the wife he'd known.

"Quick. You have to come. Put your shoes on, and hurry."

"I'm not going out there again. It's crazy. You know it, Betty. Deep down, you know it."

She grabbed his hand and pulled, but he tugged it back and she stumbled to the floor and knelt there, gazing up at her husband.

"I heard him, Benjamin. I heard him crying, and I couldn't figure out the direction, and I couldn't find him, but he's out there. I'm telling you, he's out there! I heard him." Her words grew louder as she begged to be believed.

"No. You didn't hear him, sweetheart."

"Are you saying I'm lying?"

Her eyes bore into him, daring him to say it. She'd been suspicious all along that he placated her, going to the woods to search with her when he knew better. He thought she was a fool for believing Benji was nearby and alive.

"I'm not saying you lie. You're just . . . I think you're confused, is all. You think things that aren't real."

Her lips drew back in an ugly, harsh line and her nostrils flared.

"You need help, Betty. Let me get Cassandra. She'll give you something."

She collapsed and lay on the multi-colored rug, unrecognizable as the person she had once been, as the woman Abby trusted to run the cleaning of the hotel, as Benjamin's wife, Benji's mother. And she knew it, knew she looked ludicrous, crazy even, but they had to believe her this time. Her life depended on it. His did.

She crossed her arms and moaned, a low rumble at first that soon grew in volume until it reverberated into the hallway and brought Shorty and Al to the door.

Benjamin sat next to her on the floor, his hands clasped together under his chin as if beseeching a higher power to help the disheveled woman by his side. He didn't know what to say or do and shook his head in response to the question in Shorty's eyes.

"What happened?" Al asked and knelt by her friend. She took her hand and held it, letting her know she was there for her.

Betty mumbled. "He's out there. I heard him. I really did."

"Where?"

"In the woods. He cried."

"You're sure?"

Betty nodded.

"Let's go."

Al's belief in her stemmed the wave of sobs threatening to drown her. She uncurled and sat up, ready to move forward.

Chapter Nineteen

Betty showed them the log she'd tripped over and the matted ground where she'd sat waiting for his cries to begin again, and her tangible grief found new ways to wound them all, new blades to penetrate their hearts.

"Point to where the sounds came from," Al said.

Betty extended her arm but turned in a complete circle, anguish drawing new lines on her face because she knew it wasn't possible. The cries couldn't have come from everywhere at once. But it had seemed that way, deliberately confusing her, spinning her around and around in a gruesome game of Ring around the Rosie.

"It's okay, Betty." Al took her hand, and they moved deeper into the woods, away from the tracks she'd made in the dark confusion of dawn.

Benjamin held her other hand like she was a child needing to be coddled and kept safe.

"We'll get Sheriff Hicks back out here," Al said.

Betty's eyes widened in surprise. "Yes. He needs to know." She dropped her husband's hand and grasped Al's shoulders, her face vibrant with anticipation. "Thank you, Al. We need to go get him."

She glanced at Benjamin, worried what his response might be, afraid he'd say they were done looking, and he wrapped an arm around her shoulder, pulling her close.

"We will," he whispered. "Let's go home for now."

She had hope again.

Sheriff Hicks brought two deputies, and Benjamin and Betty took them to the place she'd last heard the cries.

Doubt tinted his rugged face, settled in his pale blue eyes, and betrayed his eagerness to be finished with it. He'd been here before and figured nothing good could come from a return to the case with little new to go on except Betty's nighttime cries.

He agreed to take another look, but made it clear the sounds could have been any of a variety of different animals – from peacock to fox to bobcat to a rabbit in distress.

"Northwest Michigan has all of them," he said. "And they all make human sounds. I've heard em."

"This was a baby, Sheriff. You think I don't know my own baby's cry? Do I look stupid?"

Hicks glanced at Benjamin with a look she'd learned to hate. It said, *Your wife's crazy. You know that, right?*

Benjamin suspected it was true, but that was for him to think, not Hicks. He wanted to punch him but knew using his fist would earn him a stint in jail or worse – all for the satisfaction of hitting a decent man. Coloreds didn't hit white men, let alone white sheriffs. And he liked Sheriff Hicks – but he shouldn't be looking at him that way.

"You go on back to the hotel and let us get started. My deputies and I will make a wide circle from here."

"I'll be walking with you," Betty said.

"Go on, now, Betty. Go on back and let us do our work."

She pounded hard fists on her thighs and glared, black eyes blazing in fury. She was brittle, a long-dead stick to be cracked in two with the snap of a finger. He saw her fragility and looked to Benjamin for help.

"I'm walking," she said, her screeching voice prompting wings to flutter in fear, dart through the overhead branches and soar to safety. "Either with you or next to you or behind you, but I'm walking and I'm watching you do your damned job. Don't think I won't follow."

Benjamin held out a hand, but she thought he meant to haul her off to the hotel and whirled away from him.

"I'm not leaving, Benjamin. Just forget it!"

He moved behind her and whispered in her ear. "Together, my love. We'll follow them together. Take my hand, please."

Her shoulders collapsed and she flung herself at him. "Thank you," came out a wet, raspy mumble against his chest. "He's out there, Benjamin. He really is."

They walked the woods for two more days and found no trace of Benji. Again Sheriff Hicks gave up, and again he described all the critters that could make crying sounds like babies and women, make them so real people constantly reported brutal beatings and murders going on in forests at night.

He crossed the footbridge and headed to the Oakmere to update Abby and Patrick, and to soothe his injured heart with a shot of Patrick's Irish. Nothing else would help. He needed out of this job. It was killing him.

All heads looked his way when he entered; all eyes pleaded for good news. He almost turned around to leave so he didn't have to disappoint everyone but shook his head instead.

Patrick shuffled around the end of the bar, poured a hefty shot of his best and slid it toward him.

"Figured you could use one," he said. "Nothing, huh?"

"Not a trace. Cept her own tracks." He took a stool next to Samuel, glad for the presence of his logical, legal mind. He'd heard a bunch of bad stuff in his career, too, and knew how to deal with it.

Abby joined the three of them. "I'm assuming you're done looking. Does Betty understand?"

The sheriff's head drooped remembering her recriminations. "That boy is gone. What she heard could have been any animal or in her mind. She just doesn't get it or refuses to believe it."

"It's her child, Sheriff," Abby said. "How do you think she should react?"

"I know, damn it. I really do. But she's not thinking right. It's like she has information none of the rest of us know about but can't say what it is or why she knows it. She just does. That's a little bit irrational, don't you think?"

He implored her understanding. He liked these folks and had been through a lot with them.

Samuel crossed his arms and contemplated his glass. He fingered the watch pocket and thought about Betty bloodied and beaten – more than once. And raped. Used as if she was a rag doll and tossed aside when they were finished playing with her.

"Betty went through hell and came back, but this particular abyss she can't climb up and over. The others each had an end. She healed and moved on, but this hell has no end. She has a right to some senselessness."

No one spoke because they couldn't. They all knew the hell Samuel meant. They all remembered. Hicks tossed back his whiskey, and Patrick filled it again.

"On a horse?" he asked.

Hicks nodded.

"Can't go on one leg."

He came in, surprising the small group. Dog followed, and Shorty pointed to the rug in front of the hearth. He gazed up with drooping hound-dog eyes and begged to stay near, but Shorty shook his head, and Dog ambled over, turned in a circle and flopped down.

Phantom glided over to sniff his head and waited for Cleo's nod of approval. Dog didn't even open an eye when the two cats curled next to his saggy belly, bringing welcome smiles to sad faces.

"Where's Al?" Abby asked.

"With Betty and Cassandra. Thought I'd join you for a bit and do a porch sit."

He took the stool by his old buddy Bear and nudged his shoulder, the equivalent of hello along with a bunch of other words he didn't need to say.

Bear nudged back.

All the regular porch friends arrived and gathered around the hearth, and Abby wondered to what she owed the rare pleasure. Celebration of the first few flakes of snow? It was too warm to pile up, and the grass showed green as they fell. Winter couldn't make up its mind.

A few geese still made Lake Idlewild their home, reluctant to make the hard trip south. Beaver dams had long since been constructed under the moon named for their work, but winter delayed. It was as if fall hadn't finished, and winter lay in wait, lurking around the corner.

The longstanding group resumed their rhythmic rocking as if there had been no break in nightly gatherings: Shorty, Bear, Charles, Patrick, Abby . . . and Samuel.

Earlier, when he crossed the threshold to the bar and ordered his *usual*, Abby's breath had caught. Embarrassed to be seen gawking, she didn't even bother to pretend she couldn't remember what the usual was.

Now, sitting next to her in their rockers as if time hadn't passed and things hadn't changed, he said, "Good to see you, Abby. I stopped by The Old Place to see how Betty's doing, but they're buttoned up tight."

Pain closed her eyes.

So that's why he's here. Nobody's there.

"I'm glad you came," she said, and meant it. Once again, she wanted to fight for him, for them, but didn't know how. She put a hand on his arm like yesterday had been the last time she'd done so, and he pretended not to notice.

"Thank you for reminding the sheriff what Betty's been through, Samuel."

"This time, it may be more than she can take. She's tough, but . . ."

Worry tainted the room at the end of the hall, the one that used to be Patrick's, and sucked all the breathable air out of it.

Betty's mother had tried to make it a cheery space for her daughter with a yellow print tablecloth she'd brought from home. She covered the small, round table near the window in an attempt to give the room a bright, uplifted feel. But ten tablecloths couldn't help the room tonight, and the painted rainbow on the wall mocked them. Despair had taken over and the pot of gold didn't exist.

Cassandra put her satchel on the window bench and opened it wide. She removed a small tea pot, filled it with hot water Al had brought from the kitchen and pulled several herb packets from her pocket. She added their contents to the pot, and the scent of lemon balm, passion flower and chamomile filled the air.

Betty paced from window to door and back again, her back rigid, her face granite. Grooves had been etched between her heavy eyebrows, and her beautiful silk skin wore blotches. Benji's disappearance had carved age from youth.

"It needs to steep a few minutes." Cassandra stood erect in her flowing, gold gown, regal and serene. "Cease pacing, please. Sit."

Betty did. They'd had a relationship ever since she spent several days at Cassandra's house recuperating from the attack by the Tatum boys and George Adams. Because rape frequently became the fault of the victim, and not wanting Idlewild to examine her shame, she had stayed there until the physical wounds were no longer visible.

The internal wounds, her anger and fear, had long before been hidden from the world, and she thought her need for the healer had ended with the Tatums in prison and George dead.

Cassandra arranged three flowered cups and matching saucers on the table and stood back to soundlessly contemplate.

"I can leave," Al said, thinking Cassandra looked like she wanted to say something to Betty.

"Must you?" Cassandra asked.

"No."

"Then sit, young woman."

She smoothed the brightly colored headwrap holding in wiry, gray hair and her hands disappeared into the long folds of her sleeves.

The atmosphere throbbed with unspoken thoughts and questions, and only Betty appeared to be distressed. She noted the silent serenity emanating from the other two and briefly wondered if their hearts pulsed blood through their veins like normal people. She glanced back and forth from one living statue to the other.

The healer – tall, with eyes as black as onyx stone and robes of textured silk. Regal as the queen of Ashanti.

Strange Al - pint sized and nearly albino, with white-blonde hair, ivory skin and pale blue eyes. Tough as the hide on a cranky old bull.

They're Phantom and Cleo, she mused. She'd once told Abby her cats hadn't mated because they were different in color, like people, but Abby had scoffed.

"They will," Abby had said, "as soon as they know each other well enough."

"Hah! Animals know better," Betty said, responding out loud to the memory and startling both of the statues.

"Animals know better than what?" Cassandra asked.

Betty glanced at Al and twisted her wedding band before threading her hands together on the table.

"Nothing. I didn't mean anything. I don't know what I was saying."

Cassandra put her nose over the tea pot and sniffed.

"Ready." She filled the cups and handed them to the other two women. "The time has not yet come."

"Time for what, Cassandra? You said it was ready." Confusion radiated from Betty's eyes. She hung onto a short string of composure these days, and any contradiction or misunderstanding upset her.

"The tea is ready. The time for your child is not."

Betty's chair tipped and crashed to the floor as she leaped from it.

"Of course, he was ready! I birthed him. Remember? Don't talk riddles to me, Cassandra! Do you know something I don't?"

Al pressed her back against the chair slats, willed herself away from Betty's instant rage and tried to disappear.

"I know, girl. Be seated." She placed her hands in her lap and waited for Betty to pick up her chair and sit.

It took every ounce of resolve in Betty's body, every bit of respect she had for this woman, and the desperate yearning to find her son to make her obey. She wanted to pick up the chair and smash it against the wall or through the glass window. But she didn't.

"Sip your tea," Cassandra said. And they all did.

They warmed their hands around the cups, inhaled the lemony scent of her herbs, and let the musky taste of centuries of knowledge slide over their tongues. They were quiet as they drank.

Betty leaned her back against the chair and took the first deep, healing breath she'd had since . . . When she calmed, Cassandra spoke.

"You've said your son is alive and near."

Betty nodded.

"It isn't simply a wish. It is reality." Cassandra said the words slowly, enunciating with precision to be sure they were understood.

Betty's eyes were black embers glowering at the woman though her head remained poised over her teacup.

"What are you saying?"

"I have seen him alive. Happy."

"Where? When did you see him? Take me there." Betty's words were weighted with need, but she was coherent and quiet, not screaming her need as she had in the past.

"I don't know *where* he is. I just know he *is*. It isn't time." Cassandra sipped her own tea and watched Betty absorb her words.

"He lives?"

"He does."

"Why can't I have him back?"

"He is serving a purpose. That's all I know. And if I could find him, I would. Take comfort in knowing he is healthy and happy."

"Why did I hear him screaming?" Remembering the anguish in Benji's screams, Betty leaned forward at the waist, chin jutted forward and hands clamped on her narrow hips in a demand for answers. "He didn't sound at all happy then."

"You must listen to me, Betty. He is happy and will come home."

"Do you promise?"

"I don't make guarantees. I can only tell you what I see."

Betty sat back and let her shoulders relax and breath calm, but she stared at Cassandra and searched her face for lies. She tried to peer into the woman's soul to see any trace of malicious deceit but didn't find any and should've known better because the healer couldn't lie.

Al's head nodded imperceptibly, and Betty grasped the slight movement as agreement. Al believed.

Cassandra opened the door when Benjamin tapped, and he took a step into the still room. He regarded his wife's tranquility and slumped against the doorframe in relief. Her eyes locked with his and he beamed.

She looked calm, untroubled, nothing like she'd been when Hicks told them Benji was gone and they needed to get used to the facts. She'd been a mess, and he'd sent Al to get Cassandra.

"You feeling okay now, sweetheart? What's in that tea, Cassandra?" he asked when Betty slowly nodded.

"A few special herbs."

"We could both use a good night's sleep, especially my wife. Can you leave some with us?"

"It simply calms. News of your son has made the dramatic difference in our Betty."

Benjamin left the doorway and reached Cassandra in two long strides. He grabbed her arm, eyes blazing.

"What news? I've heard nothing. Hicks said he was done looking. Where'd you get information?"

"Not from Hicks." Cassandra smoothed the folds of her dress with her free hand and went silent, avoiding the scorn she'd see in Benjamin's eyes. And she would.

He wouldn't believe.

"Cassandra. What news?" he repeated, yanking her toward him.

"Leave her be," Betty said, standing to come between them. "She saw Benji alive and well."

He dropped her arm and headed for the door. "Let's go! You lead."

He ran from the room and stood at the head of the stairs, waiting for the rest to follow. "Come on!" he shouted and strode back to the doorway confused. Why weren't they on their way to get his son?

Three pairs of eyes stared at him when he entered.

"What's going on?"

"She saw him in a dream," Betty said.

His head fell forward. His back bent.

"She really did, Benjamin. And Benji is fine. It's just not time, and she doesn't know why, but he's safe."

"You are kidding, right?" Benjamin's voice hissed at them and held weeks of built up bitterness, weeks of sleepless nights and days of watching his wife fall apart to become one irrational step away from an insane asylum.

And she believed another crazy woman's dream. His world kept disintegrating into slivers of reality like the pieces of a broken mirror, and there wasn't a damned thing he could do about it.

He grasped the doorframe and leaned into it, pushed his forehead against the wood until it hurt and bruised his skin. His knuckles turned white, and he couldn't let go.

Not even getting shot in France had hurt this much. He'd laid in muck outside the trenches with dead American brothers scattered around him like broken toys, and even that hadn't produced the desolation filling him on this day.

He'd lost them both and had not even been able to fight for them. He shoved away, spun and left.

Chapter Twenty

The chickens squawked and flapped their wings as they scrambled to get the feed Al scattered on the ground. It was her favorite time of day, watching the sun slide up into the horizon and her chickens do their happy dance around her feet. She hadn't seen the man slumped against the back wall of the stable when she went in the small barn for the feed bucket.

He tried to sit up but fell back, grabbed his pounding head, and moaned. The bottle perched between his straw covered legs tipped, but it was empty so no whiskey spilled.

Hearing the groan, Al peered around the open door, afraid Edwin, who still made his home in the back room, had hurt himself. When she didn't find anyone, she tiptoed further into the dark room.

Benjamin inched away, not wanting to be seen. He hadn't been back since Cassandra's revelation, and he'd spent his days with a whiskey bottle and his nights curled up wherever he dropped.

Last night, it had been the hotel stable.

"Benjamin?" Al whispered. "Are you alright?"

He couldn't look at her and didn't want her to see him in his current, disheveled state. He put both hands over his face and dropped his head.

"Go away, Al."

She turned to leave, but he called her back.

"Wait. How's Betty?"

"Better than you."

Dog ambled in, stuck his nose in Benjamin's face and backed away.

"I stink."

"You must. You've seen what he'll chew on."

Al waited. The next move was his, but he hadn't realized it, so she walked off toward the morning sunlight streaking through the doorway. A chickadee's fee-bee song was calling her outside, but Benjamin's moan halted her feet, and she shook her head.

"What?" Al gave him a few seconds and a view of her back. "Get up. Take a bath," she said and went outside with Dog on her heel.

"Heifer," she called and turned to see the cow lumber her way attached to a rope in Shorty's hand. A smile lit the animal's eyes, and Al smiled back. "You're the best, Heifer. And you, Dog."

"Better than me?" Shorty said.

"Close." She reached for Heifer's lead rope and stood on her toes to nuzzle Shorty's neck with her lips.

He picked her up with one arm and dislodged the two cats he wore. They leaped off and went to investigate as Benjamin stumbled through the door.

"Abby's looking for you," Shorty told him. "She wants a trip to Nirvana someday soon. With you."

Benjamin, a sheepish half-grin on his face, nodded without asking why. He knew. He'd been a dope the last few days and had no excuse. Well, he did, but he should have been man enough to be there for his wife – with his wife.

"I've neglected their Nirvana home. Tell her I'm here. No. I'll tell her, after I get cleaned up, see Betty, and drink some coffee."

"Food will be ready before long," Shorty said. "Everything's on the stove."

Benjamin turned a decayed shade of green and ran around the stable. When he returned, the green was rosier but green, nevertheless.

"Maybe Betty and I'll move back, away from . . ." He pointed in Foster's direction. "Things were good there."

They watched him trudge off wearing lead shoes and heavy weights hanging from his shoulders.

"He's a strong man," Shorty said. "He'll come back. Milk your sweet cow, and I'll go finish breakfast."

Betty was pulling a dress over her head when Benjamin opened the door. She screeched, not knowing who might be walking in with her in a state of half dress.

"It's okay. It's me just passing through."

He'd bathed in the downstairs tub so he wouldn't wake her, and now he held her close, head still encased in the dress she hadn't had time to pull down.

She snickered. "Charles. You shouldn't be here."

Benjamin stiffened. "Charles?"

He pulled the dress off instead of down over her body, and Betty crossed her arms over her breasts.

"Oh. It's my dear Benjamin. You finally came home."

"Who's Charles? And why would you expect him in your – *our* bedroom?"

"Charles Chesnutt. Don't you remember how he introduced himself to Patrick when he first came to Idlewild, and we called him *Just Passing* for a long time after? He thought it was pretty funny because of the books he wrote on coloreds passing for whites."

"You're babbling. Why did you think I was Charles?" Jealousy ate at his sour belly, and he wanted to punch the wall. He clenched a fist in preparation.

Betty put her arms around him and pulled him close, knowing her giggles were more than he wanted to hear at the moment. He was green-eyed, and she was glad.

"Let me explain . . . again. You said you were just passing through – like Charles did. I was having fun with you."

Benjamin pulled his head back to peer at her face. Her skin was clear, her brow smooth, and she looked rested. A smile and twinkle had replaced lines of anxiety and told him she'd been sleeping at night instead of wandering the forest.

"Having fun?"

He stepped back for a better view and wondered the reason. Was it because of a concoction from Cassandra or the healer's dreamt-up news? Betty looked good and grinned at him, so he really didn't care why.

Samuel and Jesse walked in together and took stools at the bar next to Bear who had just finished hauling suitcases upstairs for the many Chautauqua guests. The place was buzzing, with all rooms full and the bar nearly so. Patrick trudged out of the kitchen carrying a tray full of soda bread, and Bear slid from his seat to help with the heavy load.

"Why don't you call out, Irish? You don't need to be handling everything alone."

"Didn't need ye, Bear. I'm not so ancient the Faeries are looking for a resting spot for my old bones."

"Didn't say that, but . . . Never mind. Any more to be hauled out?"

"Just the stew pot. Thought I'd save meself some shoe leather and set it here. Let folks help themselves."

Bear pushed through the kitchen doors and returned with the huge kettle filling his nostrils with the rich scent of bay leaves, thyme, and, of course, cabbage.

"Go sit yourself," he told Patrick. "Have your tot of whiskey."

Patrick's grin ignored the number of years he'd spent on the planet and settled in his eyes.

"Thank ye, lad. You're a good one."

He made his way to the stool held in reserve for him and climbed on. A small glass filled with dark amber liquid waited for him. "And ye, too, lass."

Abby eyed her da, and worry found a home. He'd aged since they opened the Oakmere, though he'd never admit it. Running two hotels was too much, and even though she took as much on herself as she could, his tired step showed the strain.

He tipped and sipped, closed his eyes and savored the whiskey scent in his nostrils as he held the glass close to his lips for a second sip.

"I need to pick up Cab Calloway at the station tomorrow, Da. Around four. Remember?" Abby said. "Bear is going to tend to the bar and take care of any stray guests checking in."

"Riding double on old Marie?" Patrick chuckled and elicited snickers from others at the bar.

Abby's head tilted, and she raised her eyebrows.

"Thought about it but changed my mind. I recalled Samuel and his fine automobile." She tapped a finger on the slender, manicured hand resting on the wooden bar and grinned. "What do you say, Mr. Moore? You up to giving me a ride to Baldwin to pick up the famous Mr. Calloway? It's the least we could do, wouldn't you say?"

Abby waited as his hand moved to the pocket, paused and landed back on the bar. Something in his eyes told her he'd had a fight with himself and had settled it.

His mustache twitched, a sure sign of a looming grin. "So, I guess your buggy's broken?"

"No. Buggy's fine, but not as fine as your beautiful Model T, and I knew you'd be happy for my company." She tossed her head to emphasize the words, and he couldn't keep the grin hidden under his mustache.

"Of course. I'll gladly do my part for the Chautauqua after all your hard work."

Abby knew she was pushing societal boundaries with Samuel but didn't care. Men fought wars for good causes, and so would she – finally. And the battle she'd wage would be for something worthy, too . . . him.

Next to Samuel, Jesse snorted and gave him a sideways glance. "She worked you that time, brother. I declare Abby the winner of that little skirmish."

"Thank you, Jesse," Samuel said. "I didn't know it was a combat."

"You didn't? Where've you been?"

The front door crashed against the wall, rebounded, and stayed halfway open when Yancy walked in. He couldn't simply open a door; that was too commonplace. He had to make an entrance, make sure all heads turned to him and all eyes stared.

"Shut the door, ye wee fool. You're heating the outside." Patrick shook his head. He wasn't angry at him; in fact, he still harbored affection for the wiry ex-lumberjack. But he acted the buffoon so many times it frustrated the Irishman.

He'd been allowed back into the Oakmere, provisionally, providing he exhibited good behavior. No one had faith in his ability to accomplish it with any consistency, and many eyes noted his entry.

Yancy took his time strolling back to close the big oak door, smoothing back his black hair and making sure the metal taps on the heels of his shiny shoes landed with a sharp click on the wooden floor. His entrance had been spoiled by Patrick's words of reprimand. He'd been called a fool, and on top of that affront - a small one, and it rankled.

All stools near Abby were taken, so he found one at the other end next to a stranger. He nodded a greeting toward her and climbed up to wait for her to come his way. She had to, right? She was the bartender.

It had taken him a long time to return to the hotel bar and his old friends, and he hadn't been sure they would let him back into their fold. He hoped memories had faded, and they'd forgotten or forgiven his churlish behavior.

Now he needed to convince Abby of the sincerity of his affections and his maturity. He gazed at her, an enthralled patron of the arts in front of the Mona Lisa. And, to him, she was.

Abby saw him sit tall on his seat, clean hands folded in front of him, lips smiling on his clean-shaven face, and she searched his eyes for signs of inebriation and belligerence. She'd decided to toss him out if he'd already been drinking. Chautauqua folks who came to Idlewild for a weekend of good music and pleasure didn't need the likes of Yancy interfering in their good time.

Neither did she.

"You look beautiful. As always, an Irish goddess," he said as she drew near. "Apologies again for my past bad conduct, Abby. Will you accept, please? I beg you."

"I already did, Yancy, king of blarney, or you wouldn't be here. Will the childish behavior be repeated?" Her words were clipped but with friendly overtones. She didn't want to crush him, just put him on notice.

He reached for her hand, unable to stop himself, but she pulled it out of reach.

"Sorry, Abby. I'm really sorry about what I've done. I don't know what's been wrong with me, but I know I acted badly."

His words were full of sorrow and remorse, and Abby felt the ice of her anger melt.

"I'm glad you see that, Yancy."

He tried not to grin. "Do you think I could have a short ale?"

"Good choice, my friend. And yes, you may." She put it in front of him with a warning twitch of her brow.

His head hung, aiding in the sad repentant image.

"You're on probation, you know. Limited drinks and a short leash on your manners."

"If I behave, will you step out with me tomorrow? Maybe for a drive to take in the beautiful crisp weather . . . for old time's sake?"

"Sorry. Samuel is driving me to Baldwin to pick up Cab Calloway. And I'm not sure a second ride with you is a good idea."

He couldn't help the stiffening of his spine and the whitening of his fingers around the glass. He glanced down the bar and Samuel's eyes drilled his. He'd been watching them, and Yancy's frustration flared, an instant intense flame. He rubbed his chin in an effort to hide the anger from Abby.

"I'd be happy to take you."

"Plans are already made but thank you for the offer. I hear you're working at the Adams farm."

She didn't want to stay for a long chat but Yancy needed diverting. He was trying, but she couldn't forget the way their last drive ended or his rampage at Samuel.

Both were inexcusable.

She kept glancing Samuel's way but tried not to. She didn't want him to leave, not without confirming the Baldwin trip, and not without a goodnight. Fighting for a relationship with him depended on proximity. She couldn't do it from a distance.

"Yes. Milking cows." Yancy tried to sound happy, but the words came out like he'd been forced to split rails in the hot sun. In seconds, though, he pulled on the mask and his voice turned silky. "It's honest work, Abigail."

"And I need to get back to mine," she said, tapped his arm, and headed toward Samuel, stopping to fill a glass or two on the way.

"I'll be right here, Abby," Yancy called after her.

She wondered if he'd meant to sound ominous or if she was simply hearing threats where none were meant. She tilted her head at him and tried to smile.

Samuel moved like he was readying to leave, and she scooted down to halt him.

"You have a curfew, Samuel?" she teased. "Poppa going to take you out to the woodshed?"

"Might be."

"I'd like to see that. The great Samuel Moore getting switched on his backside."

Abby's eyes sparkled with fun, but Samuel didn't appear to find pleasure in the memory. His eyes darkened as he thought about the father he had adored, the one who had been more than singed by the flames of racism. He hadn't visited his mother in a while, either, and needed to. Alma reminded him constantly.

"Sorry. Did I say something wrong?" she asked.

"Course not. Just have to go," he said, his immobile face unreadable, much like the facade he'd worn when they first met. "Early day tomorrow."

She didn't believe him but let it slide when her foot itched to be stomped and her heart wanted to know where Samuel had gone. *Her Samuel.* She tried a different track.

"Can we take Cab Calloway to Gus's place for a quick drink tomorrow?"

"Why would we want to do that?"

"Uh. Because I promised Gus?"

It was Samuel's turn to doubt. Green eyes can't lie – not hers, anyway.

"What's the real reason, Abby?"

"I miss Gus, and he wants to meet Cab."

"Does Gus know he wants to do that?"

Not likely, she thought. Probably doesn't even know Mr. Calloway's coming to Idlewild, but this was a chance to show Samuel how she fit in. He'd see. They accepted her at the colored bar.

Maybe they hadn't originally but . . .

She'd been terrified when she dropped the cousins off and went on to buy linens for the hotel. She had come back early, stood in the open doorway and peered into the dark room while every eye in the dingy little bar stared at her white face. Her heart thumped a crazy beat as she shoved her chin in the air and strolled with bravado to the bar. The man behind it, Gus, he'd said, stood close to seven feet, even bigger than Shorty, and Abby bit her tongue trying to ask for a glass of water.

"What do you want?" he'd growled.

She lifted her hands in confusion and squeaked out "Uh, whisky?"

"What you doing in here, white girl?"

"Picking up some friends,"

He looked her up and down. "You don't look the type and shouldn't be in this bar picking up um – *friends*."

Flustered, skin turning a vivid sunset, sweat making a stream down her back, she'd stammered out their names.

"They're in the back. They're beating the pants off all the men." He paused and wiggled a knowing eyebrow. "Playing poker."

She'd thought they were . . . plying their trade, and he'd played her for a fool and loved every minute of it. Gus had been expecting her because Sue had told him to.

They'd both laughed about it over a glass of whiskey. Since that day, she continued to be at home in the dark little bar on the wrong side of town.

Gus would help show Samuel he had nothing to worry about, and he could love her. People would come to accept them together. Eventually. He'd see.

Chapter Twenty-one

Samuel pulled up to The Old Place porch and grimaced. He never should have agreed to this trip to Baldwin with Abby, and Yancy was only one of the many reasons why.

He got out to stretch, leaned against the side of his automobile, and nodded a brief hello to the man propped against the porch. One leg was cocked with attitude, like he had nothing better to do than stand and wait for Abby.

"Fine day for a ride," Samuel said.

"Wouldn't mind it, myself," Yancy grumbled.

Samuel pulled at his earlobe and wished Abby would hurry. He hadn't spoken with Yancy since giving him a well-earned swim, and he wasn't looking to renew the acquaintance. Something about the man made him uncomfortable. Irritable.

"I'll bet," Samuel said, and opened the passenger door for something to do.

"Want me to go get her?"

Her smiling face appeared in the hotel door as Samuel shook his head, and he couldn't help the answering grin on his. He tried out severe expressions, but Abby made him smile whether he wanted to or not.

She sprinted across the porch without noticing Yancy, gave a one-armed hug to Samuel and slid into her seat, filling her chest with a deep, satisfied breath as he closed the door. From her leather cocoon, she noticed Yancy and waved to him with happiness glazing her face.

He waved back and made a half-hearted salute before hiding a tightly clenched fist in a pocket. He couldn't help the sneer his lips made and hoped it came off as a smile.

"Indecent bullshit," he murmured. "Somebody needs to put a stop to that obscenity."

Dog and Edwin rounded the corner, both shuffling like broken down cowboys. They even emphasized their crooked hobbles because it worked. Much wasn't expected of either of them.

"Which obscenity should cease?" Edwin asked. He'd forgotten to use the hillbilly jargon he normally spoke and swore Dog did a double take to glare at him.

Yancy pointed to Samuel's vehicle as it pulled from the hotel driveway and out onto the road.

"Now, I'd think you'd think an automobile would be anything but obscene. It's a thing of beauty, it is." He rubbed his hand over the beard sprouting in honor of the coming frigid winter air and squinted his eyes.

Edwin had a long beaked nose he was exceedingly proud of. He thought it marked his Indian heritage even though neither of his parents claimed Native American ancestry. He looked down that nose now and eyed Yancy.

"Where you staying these days?" he asked.

Yancy let his eyes scan the lake and avoided the old man, not wanting to give up any information. Who did he think he was asking questions, anyway?

Dog took a rest on Edwin's shoe, closed his eyes and emitted a deep, contented rumble.

"Wake up, Dog. We got work to do. Gotta make our rounds."

Yancy harrumphed, a contemptuous sound causing Edwin to smile and hide it.

"And what work do you do, old man?" Yancy said.

"We go looking for scalawags and skunks that might be skulking around the hotel, looking to prey on innocent folks. Maybe hiding under the porch or maybe even next to it. Never know." He snapped his suspenders. "That's right, whippersnapper. We secure the grounds to keep it safe for honest folks. Don't we Dog?"

Edwin didn't bother to look Yancy's way when he spit. He'd tweaked the young man because he didn't like him – and that was reason enough to poke at him. His chuckle wafted back to the porch as he trudged across the leaf strewn grass and headed back to the stable.

She leaned against the door so she could watch Samuel as he drove. His attention was on the road, and his hands were on the steering wheel. She tucked one leg under her and got comfortable.

His window was down a couple of inches, and Abby contemplated the autumn sounds and scents wafting in: damp leaves all raked and ready for burning, the last of the geese honking farewell, and the sweet, spicy scent of cloves and bay leaves . . .

Wait, that's not autumn. It's Samuel.

"I like your smell," she said.

"I smell?" His lips twitched, but he didn't turn her way.

"Yes, you do. Of Bay Rum. Nice. You don't smell in a bad way."

"Good to know. Are you going to watch me all the way to Baldwin?"

"I might." She reached a hand to his shoulder and let it lie there. It felt good touching him, natural and normal and exciting, like it used to feel. "Unless you want to pull off the road and kiss me. Then I'd close my eyes."

"Pretty brazen words, Abigail Riley."

"You liked kissing me. I know you did." She leaned in to him, ran a finger up the back of his neck, and smiled as his head snapped to her. His eyebrows rose.

"Stop, Abby. Behave."

"I've decided not to. I'm done behaving, and I'm going to fight for you, Samuel. For us."

He touched his mustache, filled his lungs with air and let it out slowly through pursed lips.

"You know there is no us." The hurt in her eyes settled in his chest, a heavy, sodden mass that tried to choke him. His next words came out in whispers. "There can't ever be an us, Abby. You don't know how they'd treat you. You haven't been there."

"It's been done before, Samuel. Once people got used to us, they'd be fine. Why let others make your decisions for you? It's not like you at all."

"Nobody is messing with my mind. I do what I want. What I must."

Liquid formed in the corners of her eyes, but she refused to give way to sorrow. His words were lies, and that much she knew for certain.

"You'll see, Samuel. I'm not giving up, and one day, you'll see."

"There's our train. We're just in time."

As he pulled into the station parking lot, she leaned in and her lips brushed his cheek. His hand flew to the spot as if she lips had burned him.

"Damn it, Abby." He exited and went around to open her door. "Be good," he said.

She threaded her arm through his while they walked to the platform.

"You like me," she said with a girlish grin.

"I'd like to spank you, and I think you've lost your mind. And your Gus's bar privilege due to misconduct."

"My comportment is perfect, I'll have you know. Yours is questionable."

The train came to a slow stop and disgorged its passengers. Disheveled travelers flowed over the platform and into the station. Cab Calloway was one of the last, and Abby recognized him immediately: dark hair, slender mustache, fatally handsome. In fact, he could have been Samuel's brother.

She waved to him and called his name.

"Thanks for coming to get me," he said. "It's been a long, dusty trip."

"We're happy to do it, Mr. Calloway, and we'll remedy your thirst immediately, right Samuel?"

Samuel shook his head like a harassed parent dealing with a toddler, but agreed, and wished he could capture Abby's cat-who-ate-the-canary expression and keep it in a treasure chest.

"You win, girl."

Gus's voice thundered a greeting, and he showed his perfect white teeth when they walked in. Samuel's eyes widened as several tables full of men greeted Abby and vied for first hugs. When Gus picked her up in a bear hug, she peered over his shoulder and wide-eyed Samuel, showing him these men were her friends. They didn't care about her white skin.

After they introduced Cab Calloway, drinks were on the house.

"Just one, Gus," Abby said. "Mr. Calloway has had a long ride and probably wants to find his room and a rest."

"Call me Cab, please. And it might take two to get the dust out."

"How'd you hear about Idlewild?" Gus asked.

"Doing a tour of *Plantation Days* in Chicago. Idlewild comes up in conversation quite a bit there. Talk is the place is one of a kind. Negros entertaining, eating and sleeping – all in one place. Amazing concept," he said, with irony, "and I look forward to finally seeing it."

One eyebrow rose and he nodded at Abby. "Must admit, you were a surprise, Miss Abby. Didn't expect you."

"Why is that?"

He made a few starts and stops as he tried to put the ideas into words, and Samuel finally felt sorry for him and helped out.

"You mean because of Miss Abby's pale Irish face?" Samuel said.

Cab ducked like he was dodging a missile.

"Guess I wouldn't have put it quite so crassly, but yes. That's it, exactly. And it's apparent she's been in this place before – more than once." Cab's eyes roamed the bar and the dark faces. "Gutsy."

Samuel snorted and coughed to cover it. "Don't encourage her, Cab. She doesn't need help getting into trouble."

"I've missed the cousins," Gus said as he put drinks in front of them. "It's been a while since you brought them visiting, Abby." He tilted his head toward the back room and grinned. "Not sure the boys in the back would agree, though. The ladies stole every last dime of their paychecks the last time and sauntered outta here stuffing dollars down their bosoms all the way to the door."

His hearty laugh reverberated, making folks look up and Abby smile. Nobody could laugh like Gus, and it was infectious.

"Sue and Sally don't have to steal, Gus. They're better card players. And they're smart."

Abby explained to Cab who the cousins were, and Samuel filled in the missing pieces she didn't suppose appropriate to divulge.

"It's a profession," Cab said, shrugging his shoulders. "No better, no worse than others. Hope I get to meet them."

"They're particular friends of Abby's," Samuel said.

Cab sat back and gave Abby a once over, making the hair at the back of her neck tickle. Like Samuel, sometimes, she couldn't tell what he was thinking by his expression.

"What?" she said, feeling his scrutiny. "Do I have dirt on my nose?"

He tipped up his glass and swallowed the last of the whiskey before answering. "Nope. Nothing marking up your good looks, Miss Abby. Not a thing wrong with you. Guess I don't know many white women quite like you. It's refreshing. I'm gonna like Idlewild. And you."

Abby's skin tingled with blood flooding her face, and she sat straighter in her chair, determined to make the red go away.

"Have dinner with me some night while I'm here?"

The question took her by surprise, and she couldn't help glancing at Samuel as she formed a response. Her eyes said, *See? Nothing to it.*

"Am I overstepping boundaries?" Cab asked, feeling something reverberate back and forth across the table between his new friends. "If so, I . . . uh, apologize."

"Not at all," Samuel said. "Abby and I are friends. That's all. I'm sure she will enjoy having dinner with you."

She swallowed the hot lump rising in her throat as a result of his words and turned on a false but workable smile.

"Thank you, Cab. It would be lovely to dine with you – if I can find someone to work for me."

Take that, Samuel.

"Dine?" Samuel said like he'd never heard the word.

"Yes. I dine when I'm around people who view dinner as more than shoveling food in their mouths. Why? Don't you dine, Samuel?"

Abby tossed her hair like a flapper girl and winked at Cab. She was acting ridiculous and felt embarrassed, but couldn't stop. The scalawag in her danced in double time.

It was Samuel's fault. She was sure of it.

Cab Calloway's voice carried across the dusky purple, star-lit sky and drew people to the pavilion. Folks stood shoulder to shoulder and spilled out onto the lawn and over to the bonfire where they watched the flames and swayed to his smoky voice. His music sweetened their souls and crept into their hearts.

They shouted encore over and over to encourage more songs, and he capitulated and sang the extra tunes before leaving the pavilion. He spotted Abby standing next to two men, one draped in what appeared to be a shawl, and headed her way.

"Cab," he said and extended his hand to the cat covered man. Unaccustomed to the sight, his eyes lit with interest.

"Bear. I work for Abby and Patrick."

"You don't work for us, Bear. You're part of us." Abby was surprised. She never thought of their friend as an employee and didn't much care for it that he did.

Cab's hand moved toward the second man and hovered in the air long moments before the stranger took it.

"Yancy," the man finally said. "Old friend of Abby's."

"You're not that old," Abby said, trying to diffuse the awkwardness created by Yancy's subtle but rude behavior. "I enjoyed your music, Cab. Blues does something to me."

"And to me. This is an amazing place, your Idlewild. I've never seen so many of my people relaxed and having fun together. Whole families. It's rare."

He turned to take in the vast number of folks gathered for the Chautauqua festivities, a crowd of many dark faces sprinkled sporadically with white, and Abby's eyes followed.

She'd gotten used to this scene, so it didn't resonate like it used to in the early days of the Idlewild Resort. But seeing it fresh through Cab's eyes gave her a new appreciation and perspective that she needed and filled her with courage.

Abby looked again for Samuel's face and turned back to Cab.

"We are fortunate," she said. "We had a few years of trouble. You know, people not used to change and doing some horrid things because of ridiculous ideas about what the future should be. But for the most part, Idlewild is a peaceful place for all of us."

"Things changed for miles around. Not just right here." Yancy sounded disgruntled, like he'd been personally put out by the influx of negros to the community.

"Do you work at one of the hotels?" Cab asked, trying to put the obviously irritated man at ease.

"No. Helping out at a farm in need of a hand. White family. Just to be neighborly, you understand. I'm no farmer."

"I see. Considerate of you." He turned to Abby. "Did you find someone to work for you on Sunday?"

"That would be me," Bear said as he stroked Phantom's white fur. In the dark of night, the cat truly looked its name, a silvery cape on one of Bear's shoulders. Black Cleo opened her jade eyes and stared.

"And I appreciate it," Abby said and turned to Cab. "Bear is a man of many talents, and I don't know what we'd do if he and Shorty hadn't come back to us several years ago. They're family. We knew them both when we ran the Aishcum Hotel in Nirvana – before we came to Idlewild." She carefully hugged Bear, trying not to dislodge or disgruntle either feline.

"The three of us are old family friends," Yancy said, puffing up and moving in closer, needing attention and trying to demand it. "Bear, Shorty and me, three lumberjacks and the Rileys. It was just us in Nirvana. Wasn't it Abby? We were more family than friends."

"Yes. We were," she said, humoring him.

"Why do you need Bear on Sunday? Something I can help you with? You know I'm right here, ready to be of service." Yancy eyed her, judging her reaction. She didn't even flinch as she dismissed his offer.

"Cab and I are having dinner, so Bear said he'd tend bar for me."

Yancy scratched his head, and a puff of hot air escaped between his pursed lips. He chewed on the side of his cheek and tried to contain his temper, but it was hard. She was doing it again.

Another date with another colored man, but she wouldn't give him the time of day. What the hell was wrong with her? He clenched his hands and stuffed them into the pockets of his trousers. She showered everyone else with her favors – everyone but him.

He took a couple of long breaths to get a handle on his frustration and listened to the small talk before saying goodbye as politely as he could.

Bear watched him walk off, legs stiff, hands in his pockets, and knew Yancy was waging a war with his anger. They'd forgiven his bad behavior and allowed him back into the hotel bars, but Bear wouldn't mind seeing the backside of their old friend. The man made him itchy.

Chapter Twenty-two

The clock struck six, and Yancy groaned and rolled, tugging his dingy blanket tighter around his body. A sledge hammer banged on his brain, and he grabbed his head in both hands trying to stop the noise and pain.

On the other side of the curtain dividing the room in two, Marcus grinned. He'd heard Yancy stumble in last night and knew his boarder would have a tough morning.

"You're gonna be late, Yancy. Sun's coming on."

"I don't give a damn."

"You'll give one or two when Terry fires you."

Marcus heard feet hit the floor accompanied by a feral groan and wished once more he'd tried to get along with his sister's husband – then they'd be living here instead of Yancy. Al was easy to be around, quiet and sensible. And Shorty had turned out to be alright, after all; he even liked him, but hadn't known it at the time and had acted the fool.

Right out of jail, he'd been mad at the world and nasty tempered. He'd gotten over all that, but it was too late. Al and Shorty were settled at the hotel and liked living where they both worked. He missed Al – and her cooking and cleaning.

"I hate farms," Yancy said with a snarl. "They stink and stupid animals are always squawking at you, needing something."

He slammed his now booted feet on the plank floor, and belched, a loud, guttural sound, and Marcus hoped the man wouldn't vomit until he was outside.

"You drink too much, Yancy. It'll kill you someday or you'll do the killing to somebody else."

"Shut up. Who the hell are you telling me what I should do, jailbird. Some pious reverend? My sainted father? Hah!"

Yancy stood immobile, trying to get his innards to settle down and head to stop spinning. "Sides, some people need killing anyway, so just shut the hell up."

Marcus left him to his misery and went downstairs to the kitchen. After adding chunks of wood and stirring up a flame, he made coffee and set the pot on the hot spot of the wood stove. He threw some bacon on and waited for the sizzle and scent of smoky maple breakfast to rise from the pan. It was his favorite time of day, and he wished Al's chickens were still here. He missed the friendly noises they made.

He was sorry he'd ever said Yancy could stay at the farm with him and got sorrier every day. If he wasn't drunk, he was hungover, and Marcus was tired of it. He didn't plan on sharing his breakfast, either.

Yancy tripped down the last couple of steps and hit the wall with a thud. Marcus watched him stumble to the door, disgust in the set of his shoulders and the squint of his eyes at what he saw.

"This isn't gonna work, Yancy. You need to find another place to stay. I'll be locking the door tonight." He followed him to the porch and repeated the words, determined to have him gone and out of his life.

Yancy ignored him, used the outhouse, and went to the barn to saddle up his horse, hoping the mare would be there because he sure as hell didn't remember riding her home last night.

"Did you hear me?" Marcus said when Yancy came out with the mare saddled. Probably wore the gear all night long, he thought. Poor horse.

"I heard. I have other options, other friends," Yancy said with a sneer. "Don't need this pitiful shack."

Marcus felt like he should say more, like *good luck* or *see you soon* or *nice having you here*, anything most folks might say, but it would come out wrong. He knew it would be off the mark because he didn't mean any of it. Yancy wasn't all wicked or pure evil, but there wasn't much good, either, and what little there was had burrowed deep down inside, hidden under the man's resentful character.

He rode off without a backward glance, and Marcus shrugged and went back inside to finish cooking breakfast, his step lighter by a hundred and sixty-five pounds of discontent. Maybe he'd talk to his sister about coming back home. There was room for all three of them.

The chickens scrambled around, pecking at the ground and each other like they were toddlers wanting to eat the same cracker. He rode the mare through the middle of the flock and watched as they tried to fly out of the way. He knew the mare wouldn't step on them, but they didn't.

"Stupid birds."

Cecily, squatted on the milk stool, turned her head to watch as he dismounted and led the mare to an empty stall. She continued to pull at the udders, filling the bucket. She was glad to see him and wished she wasn't, but the flutters in her stomach made each morning brighter and gave her something to think about in the dark of night.

"Terry was looking for you."

"Well, I'm here now."

"He was mad, but I told him you had an early appointment and would be a little late. I made out as if I just forgot to tell him like you asked me to."

Yancy stroked her shoulder and arm. "Aren't you the helpful little woman, lying for me and keeping me out of trouble."

She jerked away from his hand.

"Stop. Go get the next one. Pearl is almost finished."

He did, and she turned the stool over to him. Cecily fed the calves and cleaned their pens while they ate, keeping an eye on Yancy.

"I need a new place to stay. Got a room I can rent? Right up close to yours." He whispered the last part, expecting the look of fear that crossed her face and left in an instant, relishing his control over her.

He held the power. It was all his and pulsed in the blood of his veins.

She shrugged, pretending ignorance. "Have to talk to Ma Adams and Terry. I don't know."

"Well, I'll just bed down here in the straw tonight and you'll know right where to find me." He winked, and Cecily blushed.

He heard the old man's footsteps in the creak of the porch boards and the door as it opened and closed. Rumor said old Frank came back to raid the Adams' larder at night and was out of sight long before morning. Most of the family, other than his wife, weren't inclined to put a stop to it or make him come home. They were likely glad he lived elsewhere and took his ornery belligerence with him.

Old Frank knew everything there was to know about everything and made sure the whole world understood that fact. Yancy was familiar with a man like that. He'd lived it. He snorted, tossed in his bedroll on the straw, and rolled his eyes, remembering *his Abby* had been married to the younger Frank.

Rumor said little Frankie boy killed old man Tatum and skedaddled. Went off to Wyoming or some other wilderness state. Some great husband he turned out to be. And the youngest Adams son got shot whipping a woman. And a lunatic old man. Nice family.

His brain wouldn't let go of the Adams clan. They were all loco and pranced around in his head at night when he should be sleeping. And Abby Riley . . . How in hell could she snub him? Like she was better than him. It rankled, and he needed whiskey. She'd change her mind. He just needed to figure out how to make it happen.

Yancy pulled on his boots and slid back the barn doors a few inches, wide enough so he could watch and slip out if he wanted to see where Frank went when he left. Just for something to do.

Waiting a few seconds after Frank crossed the yard and disappeared into the black night, he stepped one foot outside to follow when the old geezer came back. He must have dropped his load because his arms were empty.

Three times he went into the house and came out with bundles.

Yancy didn't know what he was doing with the bounty, but he obviously had a way to haul the stuff. He gave it a good wait after the third trip and slipped out to follow when Frank didn't come back for a fourth load.

The clever old fool had a horse. She'd trampled and muddied the ground where she'd been standing, and it occurred to Yancy he'd taken one of the farm mares, but were they missing one? He wouldn't know, but why hadn't Terry or Cecily said anything? Then again, why would they?

The halfmoon highlighted his trail, and Yancy had spent enough time as a lumberjack in the woods he didn't have any trouble following it – until the moon went behind a dark cloud, and Yancy cursed.

He didn't even know if he could find his way back to the farm and his straw bed. Stupid old man.

In the morning, he awoke to the scraping of the barn doors sliding open as Cecily drew them back. He pulled up the blanket and hid from sunlight suddenly and brutally flashing over his face.

"Why do you have to start so early?" Yancy mumbled, his face stuck in a blanket that smelled like new straw and old manure. "It's not human."

"No. And neither are the cows. They expect to be milked every morning and evening whether you were out late or not."

"I wasn't. Well, I was but not like you're thinking." He let the blanket drop and squinted his eyes at her, a sly smile hinting he had something sinister and juicy to tell her and couldn't wait. "Guess where I was?"

Cecily cocked her head, dark pony tail swishing and jealousy making her heart race hot. "Hotel bar."

"Nope. Guess again. Here's a hint. Closer to home."

Cecily rolled her eyes and groaned. "You went to see the cousins, didn't you? You degenerate. Shame on you."

"The colored whores? Not on your life. I have some common sense even if nobody around here seems to understand what's right and what's wrong. I thought better of you, Cecily. Thought you did of me."

He watched the color crawl from her neck to her face, sat up and searched for his boots in the thick straw. He tipped each one and gave it a good shake to dislodge any critters who might have made a nest in the toes before shoving his feet in.

"Nope. I was right here, and then I was out in the woods tracking your father-in-law. Saw him sneaking into the house – three times he went in and came out with arm loads. Don't know what all he took, but it was a bunch."

He started to tell her about the horse, find out if they were missing one from their herd, but decided against it. He'd keep some things back, save some knowledge for himself. Never know when some little piece of information might be useful.

"We know. He comes a lot, and I keep hoping Ma Adams won't wake up while he's in the house and make him stay. Things are better with him gone. My boys are happier not having him around yelling at them or making them finish a fight. You know."

Cecily fidgeted, scuffed a boot through the straw dust and drew a house with her heel.

He did know. That was the hell of it. Yancy stood next to her, a head taller than she was, and he liked the way she had to look up at him. It made him feel big. He yanked his trousers higher and leaned out the open doors to spit.

"Yeah. Happy is good. Gotta use the outhouse. Grab a heifer for me, and I'll be right back."

Alma put the coffee on and stretched bacon slices across the flat griddle as she did most every morning in the Oakmere Hotel kitchen. Abby came through the swinging doors, nodded with a smile, and Alma instantly began prattling about her boys and what they'd done the day before. It was automatic. They were her life and what occupied her thoughts day and night, and it didn't occur to her others might not share the same enthusiasm she felt over her sons.

Abby grabbed the bowl of clean potatoes and started cutting thick slabs. "Sounds like you had a great evening," she said, knowing some kind of response was the polite thing to do.

"Someday you'll understand, when you have sons of your own. You love them like nothing else, and . . ." She gulped at the flash in Abby's eyes and backtracked. "But it's not all ice cream and flowers. Some days I want to give my boys away, send them off to an orphanage. You know? Can't put em back where they came from."

"I guess," Abby said, and the knife blade hit the counter with a heavy click. "Every mother must have those days. It's part of the contract."

She missed mornings with Al. She didn't talk much, but Abby knew her, understood her, and liked her. Al was her very own Strange Al.

Alma could cook, and she was pleasant, but she could be a New York City chef and it wouldn't matter. Abby couldn't get past being angry with her.

It was all Samuel's fault, she thought with an honest smirk at her blatant fraudulence.

She told herself she didn't have to like everyone. Said Alma probably had unforgivable faults, anyway, and murdered little old ladies in their sleep. She chuckled.

"It's been a busy week," Alma said. "Bet you'll be glad to see the end of it. You could use a break."

Abby shook her head. "No. I'm always sad when a Chautauqua ends."

See, the woman didn't understand her at all.

The parade of people and luggage would start after breakfast finished, folks heading back to their other lives in America's cities: Chicago, Cleveland, Detroit, Cincinnati, and all the way up to Medicine Hat, Canada. Ground trampled by feet and tents would show empty silhouettes in memory of the Chautauqua events.

To Abby, the sad vacant shapes told stories about Idlewild's recent past, a pictorial history to be pieced together with threads of recollection and imagination. She embroidered pictures that included Alma and Samuel way too often before sleep and couldn't seem to design a tapestry without Alma in it. Jealousy drew scenes she didn't want to believe existed.

Patrick shuffled into the kitchen rubbing his disheveled gray curls and yawning. He peered at the perking coffee pot and listened for the telltale blipping sound indicating a developed brewing process.

"Time?" he said.

"Give it another minute," Alma said. "You're early today."

"Aye. Have to make sure Abby lass has time for her big date today. Not every day she goes out on the town with a famous entertainer."

He reached to untie his daughter's apron as he did every single day, and she scooted out of reach.

"Sit yourself down, Da. You didn't need to get up early, and it's not a date. We're simply having dinner. Dining," she added with an inscrutable smile.

"Aye. Dining with Mr. Cab Calloway," he said, pride puffing his chest.

Alma's eyes grew round and her mouth popped open but sound didn't come out. She stepped back to ogle Abby.

"Wow. That's something I wouldn't mind doing. He's one good looking man, and he can surely sing. But you do realize he's colored, don't you?"

Abby dropped the potato mid-slice and stuck her finger with the knife as she grabbed for it.

"Damn," she said, wrapping the tail of her apron around the small, bleeding cut. "Course I know. So what? So is Samuel. And I've been made fully aware of the differences in our skin color. Have you?"

One of Alma's eyebrows rose as she gave Abby a quizzical stare. "Yes," came out like a question. She didn't know how Samuel got into the conversation, and, from the expression on Abby's face, she wasn't going to ask.

"Rinse your hand lass and let me put a wee bandage on it." Patrick scratched his three-day growth and did his best to figure out what had just happened.

She held her hand under the pump and watched the water turn pink and wash down the drain along with her irrational anger. With her finger squeezed in a towel, she held it out to her da and tried to hide her thoughts from him behind the bandaging process. She felt like a foolish child as he tended to her wound and knew she'd acted like one.

"I'm really sorry, Alma. I don't know what I'm saying these days."

"That's okay, Abby. You don't need to apologize." Alma had moved on, away from Cab Calloway, Samuel, and the color of skin. It was something she'd spent way too much time on in her youth, and she was finished with it. "You need a rest, a bit of a break. That's all."

No, it isn't what I need, not at all. I need some sanity.

Alma had the potatoes sliced and sizzling in the pan by the time Abby's finger was wrapped.

"Where you going on this not-a-date dinner?" Patrick kissed the bandaged finger to make it all better and wished it would work on his daughter's heart.

"I don't know. He said he'd borrowed an auto. Hope he knows how to drive it."

"I'm sure he does, but he can't know the area very well." He peered up into her face, and apprehension creased his brow, a look not compatible with his leprechaun image. "Be sure where he's taking ye, lass. You know where ye can be and where ye can't."

I do. It's been made all too clear to me. Almost nowhere outside of Idlewild.

She nodded and reassured him. "I'll find out when he picks me up." She sucked her chest full of optimistic oxygen, threw her shoulders back, and ignored a tiny tear welling in the corner of her eye.

Patrick saw it slide and heard the determined slap of her shoes on the floor as she left the kitchen. The sound told the tale she wouldn't.

No Irish pot of gold or blarney stone could make it better for her.

She skipped down the footbridge well before she was due to meet Cab, hoping to spend some time with her old friends. Shorty stood at the desk helping a guest and looking like he belonged there. She smiled and waved at him, mouthed *Al* and sprinted up the stairs after his nod in that direction.

Betty's laugh exploded down the hallway and Abby's heart expanded. She hadn't heard that laugh since Benji's disappearance and hoped it would stick around. Prayed it would.

She rapped on the frame since the door was ajar and walked in with Betty's call to enter. She and Al sat at the small table by the window drinking aromatic tea. The scent of mixed herbs wafted across the room.

"Cassandra's concoction?" she asked.

"Course," Al said. "She drops it off every day."

"Says it has to be picked fresh daily or it doesn't work as well as it could." Betty closed her eyes to take a gulp, wrinkled her nose and shuddered as she swallowed.

"Why are you drinking it if it tastes so bad?" Abby asked. "You should see your face . . . but you look great. You must be sleeping better."

"Hibiscus tea with lavender for the third chakra. You know, the center for clairvoyance. Uh . . . for prophecy. It's something we all need to improve. Oh, and a bunch of other stuff, too."

Betty threw out the explanation as if everyone should know about chakras and looked at Abby with wide eyes, daring her to dispute the need for clairvoyance.

"Sure thing. Everyone needs it." Wondering if Betty had been given something calming for her nerves, Abby peered at her eyes as discreetly as possible. Her pupils looked normal, and she seemed serene but alert.

"Wish I had some. Clairvoyance, not lavender and hibiscus tea. Doesn't smell all that good, but I could use a little prophetic ability."

"What are you doing here?" Betty asked, never one to couch a personal question in niceties.

She told them and listened to their snickers and dating prophecies.

"It's just a dinner." It seemed to Abby she'd been saying the same words way too often.

"They have dancing at the Rooster," Betty said. "Get him to take you there." She gave Abby *the look* with lots of white eyeball making a big nest for her brown irises. "Not that I'm approving. I'm not. But we've had that discussion – back when you went riding over to Nirvana. With my husband, I seem to recall."

"Benjamin wasn't your husband when we went, and there was nothing wrong with what we did."

"Except your husband left you over it." Betty snickered and had a smile on her face, but she wasn't joking.

Abby stomped a foot and grinned. "That wasn't why he left, and you know it."

"Maybe, but I told you then you could be getting Benjamin in some real hot water. You haven't seen what some people do to colored men who mess with white women. It's what I told you then, and I'm still saying it. I'm reminding you, Abby; racism hasn't changed. The Klan still lives even though folks deny it, and Idlewild is more accepting, but not so much you'd notice."

Betty scrunched her face and sipped again. Al's tea was gone, and Abby wondered if she'd dumped it out the window when they weren't looking.

"Why do you want to tell the future?" Betty asked.

"No real reason. I was mostly kidding." Abby blushed and lifted her shoulders a couple of times, shrugging off the question. She'd never hear the end of it if Betty knew.

"Mostly? What's beyond mostly?"

"Nothing, Betty. I was kidding all the way. Why do you?"

"We want to see Benji like Cassandra did. Well, I do, and Al is nice enough to go along with me."

"Cassandra saw him?" Abby was stunned, and her head spun looking for the child lying asleep in the room somewhere and felt foolish and confused for looking. "I didn't know. When? Where?"

When Betty explained, Abby tried hard not to sound incredulous, but she didn't want to encourage her friend in this – fanciful line of thinking. She could only lose him again in her mind and heart.

"I don't know exactly when or where. Cassandra didn't know either, or we'd just go get him. It was like this. As you probably know, when I was out searching in the forest one night, I heard him crying, screaming and screaming, and then he quit. I called to him, begged him to make noise again so I could follow it to him, and I waited, but I heard nothing more. I came to get Benjamin, and he and I went to where I was when I heard him cry, but . . . nothing. Then Cassandra told me her dream."

Abby watched hope light Betty's face, belief in Cassandra's dream had given her life, a reason to continue life. No wonder she looked better. Because of Cassandra and the forest cries, she believed Benji lived.

"Has she seen him in her dreams since then?" Abby asked.

"No, but she will. I know it. She said it wasn't time. Al heard Cassandra. She was there."

Abby glanced at Al who nodded and said, "She said it. I was there."

"That's, uh . . . Maybe her dream doesn't mean what you think it does, Betty, but I understand your desire for clairvoyance. You know, could be it only works for Cassandra."

Abby was at a loss for the right words and didn't know what to think. It seemed ridiculous, but she'd seen Cassandra's work before and trusted her. Who knew what the woman could do or see?

"That's what I told her," Al said, and Abby knew she was protecting Betty, trying to shelter her from pain.

Al had been protecting her friend for a long time, beginning with killing George Adams, and she wasn't about to stop now. She was certain the loss of her baby boy hurt ten times more than being beaten and raped. But Betty didn't deserve any of those things. Not then. And not now.

So, Al drank disgusting tea with her friend and listened to stories about Benji, the same ones over and over. But Betty needed to make him live every day through the stories she told, through recollections as threads of hope no matter how fragile the strand, and Al let her. Friends did those things.

Benjamin couldn't listen anymore. He dealt with Benji's disappearance differently, by leaving the room, by setting his grief aside. He buried it along with continual memories and took Benji out of his metaphorical coffin when he was alone. It was how Benjamin survived his loss.

She saw his automobile gleaming in front of the hotel and Samuel relaxing in one of the rockers on the porch, watching ducks act like foolish fowl on the lake. She savored his image for a moment through the window before joining him.

"Where's your date?" he said.

"What are you doing here?"

"Your chariot awaits, all shined and pretty."

"This isn't a date."

"And this isn't a conversation. Typically, the way dialogue works is one answers questions with answers – not questions, especially ones not related to any prior words or thoughts."

She smirked. "Thank you for the lesson in conversational etiquette. So, it was your auto he borrowed. I didn't realize."

Samuel leaned back in his chair, smoothed his mustache and studied her.

"You look nice."

"It feels odd, going with Cab in your vehicle. I hope you don't mind."

"Why should I? He's a responsible man. I trust him."

"With your Model T or me?"

"You're not mine to entrust."

Abby wished she'd worn a different dress, something more flattering or revealing, something to make Samuel wish the two of them were going out to dinner. She wanted to make him reconsider his . . . trust.

"I think we might dance at the Rooster tonight. Doesn't that sound like fun? A little tango, a little lindy hop. Maybe a snuggly waltz or two."

"We should have practiced more."

Samuel rebounded from every barb she poked him with until Cab planted his feet on the porch. He took her hand and bowed over it like some English knight, and Abby wanted to wipe the grin from Samuel's face as he watched.

They threaded their way through the packed room and were led to a small table at the back of the Red Rooster. Saliva moistened her mouth at the scent of charred steak, briny shrimp and fried chicken. She peered at the plates on the tables they passed and came close to grabbing a crispy leg on the way by.

"I'm hungry, Cab."

He wrapped an arm around her back, and leaned in to whisper in her ear. "Me, too."

What did he mean by that?

Abby's head spun, and their noses met since he hadn't backed away quickly enough.

"Sorry," she said with a self-conscious giggle. She wondered, seeing his surprise, if she'd misread his tone.

She had. Cab Calloway was a gentleman, a debonair escort, and when they pushed the tables back to make space for a dance floor, Abby decided not to worry about being tired in the morning. She left behind anything and anyone who might cause her anxiety, the hotels, Benji, Betty, Samuel, Alma – all of them.

She needed someone to flirt with her, to think she was special, or act like it even if they didn't think so. And Cab did all of that. He danced like a dream, and she followed his lead, a nymph in his arms. He kissed the back of her hand at the end of each dance, and his dark eyes sparkled.

Abby quit thinking and let herself live in the moment and revel in pleasure. In the Red Rooster, no one looked at them with daggers in their eyes or made them sit at separate tables. If anyone even noticed they were not of the same race, they didn't care enough to make a point of it.

I love you, Cab. Okay, I don't. This feels good, but I don't really love you. I merely wish I did.

"Do you dance here a lot?" he asked in the middle of a close waltz.

"Never."

He pulled back to look at her. "Never?"

"Correct. My husband would never have brought me here, and Samuel won't take me anywhere."

"And those are your only options? Where is said husband?"

"Gone, gone, gone." She sang the words and waved her hand in the air like he had drifted into the sky and disappeared. "He's an ex. Scandalous, right? Are you embarrassed to be seen with me? A divorcee? I think we are considered evil women on the socially acceptable scale."

Cab pulled her tighter and nuzzled her hair with his chin. "Not in the least. And what about Samuel. Why won't he take you dancing?"

He felt her deep sigh and regretted his question. "He'd have to be a fool not to bring you here," Cab said. "I'm betting he'd be jealous if he saw us right now."

"He wouldn't."

Cab drew back to look in her eyes.

"I don't think he likes me anymore."

She sounded like a five-year old and looked like it. Her eyes widened like she questioned the world and didn't understand any of it.

Cab's lips turned up in a grin he couldn't help.

"I'm sure you're mistaken. How could he not like you? Thick auburn curls, bright green eyes. Smart, too. You're a beautiful, exceptional woman, Abigail."

She swallowed, trying to set her feelings aside and not care what Samuel thought – about anything.

"He likes Alma better now. Or somebody else. Who knows?"

"Doesn't explain why he threatened me when I asked to borrow his auto."

Abby pushed back to check his eyes for lies. She squinted and stared, turned sideways for a better view.

"He threatened? How? What did he say?"

Cab twirled her in circles, one hand held over her head, and she spun like a ballerina before coming back into his arms.

"Suffice it to say he cares about you, Miss Abigail Riley. He likely has reasons to do what he does."

"Well, of course. He thinks he has an excellent reason for every single thing he does, and his current one is that he is colored, and I am not."

"Yes. I can see you are not."

She pushed back to stare at him again.

"I apologize. All of that was uncalled for. I'm having a wonderful time, Cab."

A deep chuckle rumbled from his chest and Abby could tell he was having a good time, too.

Chapter Twenty-three

Shorty added a couple logs to the fire and sank into a rocker next to Al to watch the flames and soak in the heat. He touched her hand, and she smiled as two orange cats leapt instantly to his lap. They'd been waiting. King bumped his chest with the top of his head several times and curled into a ball in the depression where his legs met. Nurse stretched across his shoulder and rumbled in his ear. Shorty was content.

Betty and Benjamin sat across from them, and Samuel felt like an intruder when he walked into the bar and noted the tranquil scene. No one spoke beyond hello, but a pleasing air existed. Words weren't necessary and would have been an intrusion into the harmony.

"Don't get up. I'll pour my own." He drew a short whiskey, left money on the bar and pulled up one of the vacant rockers brought in from the porch for the approaching winter.

Flames danced an orange tango on the walls and polished floor, and all eyes studied its mystery. It had a rhythm. It flickered and grew tall before shrinking to a blue marble at the bottom and threatening extinction before rising to gulp oxygen and turn bright red again.

"Abby get off on her date okay?" Betty asked.

"It isn't a date." Samuel hid behind a sip from his glass.

"She told me dinner and some dancing," Betty said. "Sounds like a date to me."

"It isn't."

"Why're you poking the bear, Betty?" Benjamin said. "He's our friend."

"That's why. He needs it."

Her words caused a sharp ache in Samuel's gut, and he tried to ignore it, put it away and stuff it in his watch pocket so he could look at it later. What the hell was he doing?

He scrutinized his friend and noted she looked well, better than in a long while. He cared about this woman. They cared about each other, but sometimes you wouldn't know it.

"You good, Betty? Cassandra taking care of you?"

"I am, Sam. And she is."

"Samuel, to you, Mrs. Chambers." He emptied his glass and rose. "I'll leave you lovebirds to your fire."

He didn't know where he was headed but watching two happy couples gazing at the flames was not what he needed at the moment.

Samuel walked the footbridge to the Oakmere, thinking he'd get some dinner and relief from being enslaved by his own lurid thoughts.

"Date," he mumbled. "She said it wasn't a date."

Two seconds after he offered to loan Cab his vehicle, he'd regretted it, but it had been three seconds too late. He didn't know why he'd made the damned magnanimous gesture in the first place. But he had and was now paying the price.

He did that, sometimes . . . gained a strange kind of supremacy with a noble attitude he wished he felt, especially when he didn't like what was going on right in front of him. And he definitely didn't like Cab Calloway going out to dinner with Abby.

But he'd helped make it happen. His mouth and ego had gotten the better of him.

His long legs ate up the length of the bridge and he found himself on a stool at the Oakmere bar next to Jesse and Edna Falmouth. Edna glared at him and Jesse slapped his shoulder.

"Saw your automobile and your woman, Samuel. Both of them out with another man."

Jesse's smirk put him on edge, and he wanted to punch something. Him.

"Only one of those belongs to me, Falmouth."

Bear lifted an ale glass and jiggled it, questioning Samuel who nodded. He filled it and, after wiping the drips from the bottom, placed it in front of him.

The action reminded Samuel of Abby. When she was miffed, she let it drip just to aggravate him.

"Use your sleeve like everyone else," she'd say and trot away before he could complain. Her pique always made him laugh.

The last time had been after their failed attempt to go to the theatre, and he frowned with the memory.

"I don't think Abby agrees with your verdict, Mr. Lawyer," Edna said, bring him to the present. "And a while back, you didn't either."

"That was then. This is now."

"You're an ass, Samuel."

"So I've been told. In fact, I've said it myself. What's on the menu tonight, Bear?"

"Patrick's branching out. He made Hungarian instead of Irish stew tonight."

Bear's face didn't show humor, his lips didn't turn up, but his eyes gleamed, and Samuel understood and appreciated the stoic man with the scarred beard. His manner matched Samuel's in feigned indifference, though false in both cases. Neither was apathetic about anything.

"Sounds good to me," Samuel said.

Sally slipped up behind him and wrapped her arms around his neck. He heard the shuffle of Sue's feet and her voice in song as she followed.

"Will you be having some humble pie with your stew, tonight, Samuel?" Sally asked.

He spun around, almost knocking into her.

"I have no reason for humility."

Sue snorted, coming up in time to hear his words.

"I like a man who thinks a lot of himself, and that's certainly you, Sam."

"Nobody calls me Sam . . ."

"Except for me. I do. And I will." Sue said and tried to climb onto the seat next to him.

He stood to assist, glad for something to do besides talk about himself and Abby . . . and Cab Calloway.

"We ate at the Rooster tonight. Guess who we saw?" Sue said, a grin on her chubby, cherubic face.

"I'm not feeling like guessing games tonight, ladies. If I buy you both a drink, can we talk about something more interesting?"

Sally kissed his cheek and checked out his eyes. He wasn't happy, and she didn't want to add to his sorrow. She liked him. Even more than that.

"I ain't had a better offer," Sue said.

"I *never* had a better offer, Sue."

"Me, too. That's what I said."

Sally hung her head, and Samuel chuckled. She had tried for years to fix Sue's language, but it only got worse, and Samuel saw the twinkle in the large woman's eyes as she tweaked her cousin. The night ladies were just what he needed, and he ordered three drinks.

It would be a long walk home if Abby stayed out late.

He was getting sick of sleeping in a barn on straw instead of a clean mattress. Dust clogged his nostrils and made his head hurt, and the odor of old manure was constant, saturating his clothes. He tossed the half-full bottle at the wall and winced at the thud.

The only thing making this tolerable was Cecily's blush when he teased her, when he let his hand slide down her arm or his fingers slip under her braid at the back of her neck. She'd squirm and goose bumps popped on her exposed skin, while her eyes begged and threatened simultaneously.

Yancy knew some night soon she'd slip out of her husband's bed to join him in the straw. He could tell by the way she licked her upper lip, by the way her voice got husky when it was him she was talking to, and mostly by the way she smelled when he came near. Like salt and clean sweat and woman.

But he didn't think he really wanted her in his straw bed. The chase was the fun part, watching her want him more than her ignorant husband, Terry. Watching her wait for him. Cecily looked good, but he knew what he wanted, and it wasn't her.

Someday, Abby would wait for him, would know his worth. He just had to show her he could wait, too.

Yancy lifted his head from the bedroll and held his breath. The footsteps weren't Cecily's, and they weren't heading toward the barn. He left the warmth of his blankets and crawled to the door. He'd left it open enough to peer out or for Cecily to sneak in when she made up her mind or found the courage.

It was the old man heading to the house on his regular forage for goods. Yancy watched and waited, considered following him when he left – closer this time so he didn't lose him in the dark. He dug around on the floor where he'd tossed the whiskey bottle and grunted with satisfaction when his hand bumped into it.

He uncorked it, swigged a couple of times, and sat back on his heels to wait. It took longer than usual, and Yancy began to wonder if he'd imagined seeing the old fool. He held the bottle up to the moon's haze to see how much he'd had and cursed. Just as he was about to crawl back to his bed, he saw the old man steal across the porch and back to the other side of the yard where he'd left his horse the last time.

When Frank went back into the house, Yancy yanked on his boots, cursing as he packed a pile of straw in the toes, and slipped out of the barn. He heard the mare knicker before he saw her, patted her behind to settle her, and backed up a few steps to hide behind a tree.

Frank must have gone into the barn for feed because when he got back to the mare, he put a bucket in front of her and spoke love words while he hung a bag from the saddle horn. Old fool. He didn't even bother with stealth as he loaded the saddlebags and spoke in a normal tone of voice, unconcerned about being overheard.

Yancy almost chuckled out loud. The codger had no idea someone shared the darkness with him.

Once again, he made three trips into the house and came out with loads he packed on his mare before climbing into the saddle and riding back into the woods. He whistled a tune as he left, a jaunty one that said he hadn't a care in the world. The whole planet belonged to him.

Yancy shook his head and was about to step out from behind his tree when he heard a noise by the barn and lurched back into the shadows. A heavily cloaked figure came around the corner and watched until Frank couldn't be seen. It slipped into the woods, following close behind him.

He'd almost been caught. But doing what? Following a crazy old man? Yancy didn't know why he felt the need to be secretive about it, like he was up to no good, but he did. Habit, he guessed.

He waited until the beating of his heart stilled before poking his head around the tree to see if whoever had been lurking in the dark fooled him and still hid there. Did someone else want to know where Frank went?

Or did someone think it was *him* stealing from the house and slinking off into the woods? Did they think they were following him, not Frank?

He edged back toward the barn, careful not to step on twigs or dry leaves that could crackle and give his position away. He needed to think about what the hell was going on at this so-called family farm. Something was off and it didn't feel to him like it was just the old man.

People sneaking around in the night. Frank stealing his own food and living in the woods or who knows where. Who'd followed the old man? Terry? Frank's wife? Maybe Cecily. Could be she has the hots for more than himself. Maybe she likes decrepit old men.

He snorted and looked around, suddenly skittish at his own noise. He found the whiskey bottle with the toe of his boot, grabbed it and flopped down in the straw to think.

He needed to ponder. He pulled off his boots, propped himself against the wall and took a swig.

The bottle, held upright wedged between his thighs, was almost empty when Cecily nudged his leg. Without opening his eyes, he grabbed her foot and tugged until she fell on him. He rolled on top of her and ran a hand over her breast, tugging at her clothes to get at bare skin.

"Stop it, Yancy. Quit it!" She pushed at his chest, breathing hard as tears formed at the corners of her eyes. She was angry that he believed he could inappropriately touch her, and she was afraid and angry when it excited her.

"You want this, Cecily. You know you do, else why are you out here?" He tugged at her hair to gain access to her throat and nibbled the tender skin at the edge of her night dress. Her resistance thrilled him more than if she'd thrown herself at him.

He liked a challenge, liked being in control.

"Stop, Yancy. I'm looking for Ma Adams."

He flew into the air above her, stood and glowered, his head spinning to peer into the corners of the barn like the woman would be hiding in the darkness.

"Here? In the barn? What the hell?"

Cecily rose and brushed off the bits of straw clinging to her nightdress and hair.

"Bailey has an earache. I looked everywhere for the hot water bottle and couldn't find it. Eventually I went to Ma's room to ask her. He was crying so hard. It really hurts him. It's so awful when your babies get sick and you can't help them."

Cecily sniffed back tears thinking of her son in pain and crossed her arms over her chest.

"Yeah. Okay. He hurts. What about the old lady? Why were you looking for her out here? She have the hots for me, too?"

Cecily glared. "She wasn't in her room. She wasn't anywhere. I looked in the whole house and finally came to the barn."

Yancy rubbed an arm over his mouth, wiping at the dust and saliva, and reached for the now nearly empty bottle. He took a long swig while he plotted his best angle.

It was the old lady who startled him and took off after the old man. Have to hand it to her, going out in the middle of the night to trail the old geezer. Should he say anything to Cecily or go find her himself? Must be some kind of a path by now as much as he came and went, so it'd be easy to find in the daylight unless he went a different way every time. That would make it harder, but he could be a hero if he brought her back. Abby would like that. She'd see him in a whole new way and wouldn't be pushing him away all the time.

He sipped again and felt Cecily's hand on his arm.

"What are you thinking, Yancy. What's going on?"

He gave her his best 'I'm your friend' smile and pulled her close enough to plant his lips on her forehead – the good uncle kiss – and patted her back.

"Just thinking. Sun will come up soon. If she doesn't show up by then, I'll find her. Don't you worry about it. You can tell folks in town, but say I'm on it. It's all taken care of." He paused in thought. "You say anything to Terry, yet?"

She shook her head. "I thought I'd find her outside so I didn't wake him up. He doesn't like it when I do."

"Don't. When he's up, tell him I'm getting his ma. You'll have to milk this morning cuz I'll leave at first light."

He'd have heard someone following if he hadn't been singing happy jingles all the way back to his new home. But he didn't notice twigs snapping or branches slapping, and his merry tunes led the hunter without a single misstep all the way through the dark woods.

He heard Benji whimpering when he neared their aerial nest, and his heart contracted wondering how long he'd been awake and needing him. He flung the reins around a branch and took the ladder rungs two at a time.

"I'm right here, boy. You should know by now I wouldn't leave you. Not for long, leastways."

He lit the lantern and turned it down low so it gave enough light to move around comfortably without banging into anything. It hung from the roof peak, out of the way. "See? Here's your old man."

Benji gurgled his delight in hearing the craggy voice and pulled his lips back in a smile that tore the curmudgeon's heart out and cut it up in pieces. It wasn't 'til Benji he knew he had a heart – or even wanted one, and now it lay smashed to bits and pieces because of a smile.

"See what you do to me? It's all you. Let's get you changed, son, and I'll let you swing while I take care of all our things."

It was comfortable in the room, and he was glad he'd bought the heater. It helped with heating up food, too. He fixed a bottle and put it in water to warm while he unloaded his mare.

Wrapped in a blanket, Benji hung from his small swing on the porch and watched him take bags from the mare and put them in a bushel basket on the ground, climb the ladder, and haul it up by a rope. He unloaded, lowered the basket, crawled back down, loaded it and climbed the ladder to haul it up again. When he finished, he sat wheezing and holding his chest, concern wrinkling his brow.

"Need to take my time just a little. Too old to go running around and up and down like a young fool."

He checked the bottle warmth on his wrist, picked up the baby and went to sit sideways in the porch hammock, Benji lying in his arms. He could hold his own bottle now, and he sucked greedily while the old man watched and rested, his breath taking its time to settle. He pulled a heavy blanket over them both and hummed a wordless lullaby.

Benji's eyes roamed the whiskered face above him and opened and closed in sleepy content. When the bottle dropped and he was lifted to a shoulder, one hand grasped the beard he'd come to know as his security, his happiness.

The old man sat for a time, resting and rocking back and forth in the hammock, and Benji fell asleep on his chest.

He had cut the brush back from the trees holding his house so he could see whatever approached in the small clearing he'd made. He didn't want any surprises. Now, he could watch raccoons slink by on silent feet as they headed for the river's edge to dig crayfish. Tonight, a possum joined him, and they did their best to ignore each other.

He wondered which would win in a battle over territory and chuckled, visualizing the wily raccoon trying to outmaneuver the actor.

"You're a big one, raccoon, but I'm thinking ole possum will just go to sleep 'til you get tired of watching him and leave. I'd show you, Benji, if you were awake. Creatures are cleverer than us. Don't forget it. Mother nature made em smarter. They hear better and smell better and some of em even see better, too."

The raccoon chattered, stood high on his back legs and went perfectly still, staring out at the black forest. The possum fell to his side, dead, and the old man sat up. He hadn't heard a thing, not a flutter or a snap, but they had.

He crept inside, laid Benji in his swinging bed, and stepped out. He stood pressed against the wall and scanned the trees for movement, checked for the coon who was gone like an apparition, silent and ethereal. The possum lay still as if death had really claimed him.

He waited, scanned again and, seeing nothing, slipped with deadly quiet down the ladder, his heart thumping and banging against his rib cage. He pulled his Winchester 30-30 from the saddle sling he'd made to tote it, cursed at the noise it made when he racked the lever, and squatted behind the mare to peer under her belly. She gave a nervous nicker and her ears twitched forward.

He crouched for half an hour and watched the clearing, the creek and the woods until his knees ached and back spasmed. Nothing except the possum moved. It stretched as if waking from a night's sleep and slouched off. He stood and stretched, too, spoke to the mare as he removed her saddle, and gave her a handful of oats from the bag hanging on the saddle horn.

"Don't know what spooked you all. Got me spooked just watching you." He scratched between her ears, threw a warm blanket over her back, and let her burrow her velvety muzzle into his hand. "Going up, now. Gotta get some sleep. You just give me a good whinny if you hear anything at all."

He climbed the ladder, checked on Benji, turned down the lantern so it left a soft glow for him, and lay down on the inside hammock. He'd prefer to be outside so he could hear better, but it was too cold. And he was tired. Morning would be here soon.

"Night, Son."

Chapter Twenty-four

She didn't know how she ended up on the wrong side of the creek. She'd followed his songs all the way and didn't even have to get too close because his froggy singing voice led the way. She almost stepped into the water before she knew it was there. A raccoon chattered, startling her, and she chuckled when a possum fell down to play dead. Nighttime was full of natural delights.

She moved quickly down the river, looking for a place to cross and found a thick fallen tree that nearly reached from bank to bank. Her sturdy shoes navigated over the water as she sidestepped on the bark covered trunk and only collected mud when she slipped climbing up the other side. She stopped to settle her breath and looked around. She didn't want to lose him now.

She spied a light – up high, like it was in a tree – and figured it had to be him.

Up in a tree?

She shook her head and moved in slowly, not wanting to alert him to her presence but needing to know what was going on. She settled in to wait and then saw him. From behind the shelter of tall brush, she watched as he climbed down from a tree house.

Of all things – Lord, a tree house!

She saw his mare, heard the lever action of a rifle, and watched him crouch and wait. She did, too, and wondered what her husband was doing living in the forest in a tree house. Half of her smiled at the idea, and the other half worried. She moved deeper into the brush and saw him stretch, climb the ladder, go into the shelter and turn down the light.

What now? She had found him but didn't really know who she'd found and wondered if she ever had.

She knew she had to be done thinking about next steps, about them and the life she no longer wanted. She was determined it would change, but that was for later. Right now, she was standing in the woods pondering.

Enough! Do something. That's your husband up there playing in the trees like a boy.

She moved her feet in his direction but heard a strange, tinny clanging to her left and jumped, startled by the odd sound. She ran in the other direction and heard clanging to her right. Then she heard the racking of his rifle.

Frank didn't speak, just stood stock-still plastered against the structure, praying Benji didn't wake and cry out. He didn't know what was out there, but he . . . Well that was just it. He didn't know. Probably a whitetail buck chasing a doe crashed through the woods, hit a line and hit another on the way out. His grip on the rifle relaxed but held sure against his shoulder. He'd wait on the porch to be safe.

In what little light the moon gave, she could make out his shape in the shadow of the wall behind him – and the barrel of a rifle pointed in her direction.

Inch by tortuous inch, she backed up to a thick tree, hid behind it and waited. Would he really shoot her? Would it be better if she called to him or would the noise get her killed if she spoke and the sound told him where to shoot? She didn't know him anymore, and he frightened her.

She put another foot behind her and heard the crack of a branch, saw the barrel follow the sound, and sucked in a ragged breath. She wanted to back further into the dark woods but was afraid to make any more noise and didn't want to take her eyes from the gun to look at the ground where her feet would step.

She dropped to her knees, feeling for twigs that might snap, and turned around slowly. For several feet, she ran her hands over the damp ground, moved small branches out of the way and crawled over the large ones. When total darkness encased her, she sat back against a large oak and let mute tears fall.

Night sounds had ceased with the uneasiness her presence caused. The coyotes held their yips, and tree frogs fell silent. Even the owls didn't ask *Hoo* was there. But as her eyes adapted to the dark, she saw a whitetail crawl on his belly deeper into the woods right in front of her.

She forgot Frank and his rifle in her awe. The buck slithered like a snake until he was out of sight, and, shortly afterwards, the refrains of a nighttime symphony restarted with the erratic flight of a bat followed by the songs of a nearby tree frogs.

She dried her face on a sleeve and peered around the shield of her tree. Through tangled branches she saw him. He stood sentry still but leaned against the wall like he needed to sit.

You're an old man, Frank. What in heaven's name are you doing wearing yourself out living in a tree house?

Her heart softened, and she saw the man she'd married. He'd been strong and handsome, without the fears of mortal men. The power of his will cut Frank's path through life, never the easier ones others took. He made his own, and damned anyone who got in his way, even his family . . . when he noticed them.

Would he really shoot her?

Without another thought to dissuade her, she called his name and heard the sharp scuffle of his feet and the tick of the rifle's safety.

Had he clicked it on or off?

"Don't shoot, Frank. I want to talk to you."

He didn't answer. She pressed her back against the damp moss growing up her side of the tree and scenting the air with musky vanilla. She sniffed and wondered how she'd spent sixty years on this earth and not known tree moss smelled like earthy pudding.

"Frank. Talk to me. Please."

Silence.

"Frank?"

Nothing.

She stood still behind her tree and spoke to him – gently wooing him with a tranquil voice.

"I'm going to walk toward you, Frank. Please don't shoot me. I won't make you do anything you don't want to do. Honest."

She moved slowly, trying to keep a tree between her and his gun, but knowing he could shoot her if he wanted.

Frank knew it, too, and had considered it. If he let her come up, she'd see Benji and take him. If he sent her away, she'd tell everyone where he was. She'd bring Terry and make him go home. Take his son. There was no way to win. He'd have to kill her or make her stay.

Before he could make up his mind, she was climbing the ladder and then standing in front of him, pushing the barrel of his rifle down toward the ground.

"Click the safety on, please, Frank."

Her words were whispers and her fear great. She felt the thump of heartbeats in her throat and swallowed them away, determined to speak to her husband with composure. He wouldn't appreciate an emotional plea, would, in fact, be disgusted by it and likely do the opposite of whatever she asked. At least old Frank would.

She wasn't sure about this one.

"What you doing here? Following me?" He didn't put the rifle down, but didn't point it at her, either. "I don't like being followed."

The first rays of sun lightened the small clearing around the tree house. They weren't really streaks of sunlight, more like pale yellow fog creeping in and changing the color of dark. He could see her eyes now. They looked perplexed and pleading, but he didn't know what she pled for, what she wanted. He'd never known.

When Benji whimpered, the eyes widened in shock, and Frank was torn, destroyed in a single moment. She had ruined everything.

He shoved her toward the door and she went.

"Sit on the floor in the corner." He pointed to the furthest spot. "If you try to leave, I'll shoot you. I mean what I say. You know I do."

"Yes. I know that, Frank. You always mean what you say." She went to the corner, pressed her body into the space, sat and watched.

He hung the rifle next to the shotgun over the door where he could get to it in a second and gave her a hard look. Taking the few steps to the baby's bed, he picked him up and murmured unknown words.

Good God. So, this is what happened to Betty's boy. Frank is the old, white man in a hat.

Benji stopped crying as soon as he saw Frank. In fact, he gurgled in happiness, and Emily was stunned. He put him over his shoulder, and the baby pulled at his beard and tried to put it in his smiling mouth. Frank patted his back and mumbled to him.

"Getcha cleaned up in a minute, son. You just be patient." He glared a warning at Emily and went back to taking care of Benji.

With one hand, he got the bottle ready, put it in a pot of water on the stove, and grabbed a dry diaper. He changed the wiggling baby with a grin on his face, and Emily tried to remember a single time he'd changed one of his sons' diapers. Just one. She couldn't.

What was happening here? Who is this man?

He tilted the bottle so it dripped on his wrist and grunted. "Another minute, boy." He rocked back and forth from heel to heel with the baby over his shoulder. He nuzzled Benji's soft black curls with his beard, and the child cooed his delight.

Emily couldn't believe what her eyes told her.

When the milk tested ready, he sat in the hammock sideways and leaned his back against the wall. The baby held his bottle like he'd been doing it for a while and hummed contented sounds while he suckled. Emily's mouth hung open, her brain unable to process all she'd seen.

"Why did you take Betty and Benjamin's baby, Frank? Why'd you do that? And keep him? Do you know how they've grieved? How they're still grieving?" Her words were soft, begging to understand.

"He's not theirs. This is my son. Always was. Don't know what they were doing with him in the first place. You need to quit saying he's theirs."

Emily didn't know how to approach him. He couldn't be lucid, and she was afraid to say the wrong thing and set him off, make him do something rash. She slumped against the wall and looked around the room.

It had everything they needed: hammocks to sleep in, a stove for heat and cooking, a porch for sitting and watching the forest around them. Frank had thought of everything, even a small table and chair.

Hearing the gurgle of the bottle going dry, he flipped Benji over his shoulder and patted his back. The baby gave a healthy belch, and Frank smiled.

"Good un, son. You're a chip off the old block, aren't you?"

Frank hung a long piece of fabric around his neck, crossed it at his stomach and knotted it behind his back. Emily watched, wondering what he'd do with it. When he tucked Benji into the front fold, she understood, even admired his ingenuity. He was a clever man. But she'd always known that about him.

Benji pounded his fists against Frank's chest in happy anticipation. He like to ride in the nest as the man moved about the forest and liked feeling the rumble of his voice as he talked.

Frank pulled a ball of thick twine from a shelf, patted his trouser pocket until he felt his jackknife and headed to the door. There, he looked back at his wife, lifted the rifle from its perch and pointed it at her.

"Come on. You first."

She was about to die. Tears gathered, and she breathed them away. She could do nothing about the coming end of her life and knew she should have started changing things a long, long time ago.

Now, Frank would do what he would do, but he always had. And she had always let him.

She stood, took resolute steps to the door and went out ahead of him. Her feet found each narrow rung of the ladder with dread, and it occurred to her to run.

Now. If you're running, now's the time.

But she didn't. She saw the rifle, remembered his deadly aim, and her boots stayed put on the ground, waiting for him to climb down.

"Where are we going, Frank? What are we doing?"

"Fixing the lines you broke. Head over there."

He pointed with the rifle, and she moved in the direction indicated where a pile of tin cans lay crumpled on the ground. When he picked up a line, the pile came with it, and she understood the strange noises she'd heard last night and couldn't help admiring his imagination.

He cut a length from the ball of twine, repaired the broken one with a splice, and told her where he wanted her to go next. As they walked, she listened to him talk to the baby about whatever they came across. Once he stopped to point at a red squirrel poised on the side of a tree.

"Don't let em jump on you. They'll do that, and they bite bad. Listen to me, son. Pay attention. Your old man wants you safe and smart."

She shook her head in wonder and slowed her step as he pointed to a crab apple tree still full of the red ripe fruit, plucked one, nibbled and puckered his lips.

"Tart but good in a jam with lots of sugar. You'll figure it out. Up there is a black walnut. Nuts come out sometime in the fall but no good 'til about now. Use em in cakes and stuff."

Emily moved slower and slower until she walked beside him instead of in front. She watched his face soften, the muscles relax and lines smooth out as he talked to Benji.

And the care in his voice? The love? Where had all of this been with his own sons?

The thought left a bitter taste on her tongue, and acid burned in her stomach. She wanted to lash out at him.

Frank Jr. banished forever. George dead.

Her booted foot nearly buried itself in the loam so heavy was her step, but detestable knowledge rushed in.

You can't give all your blame to him. Wear your own.

They curved around and came out the other side of the small clearing where a second pile of tin hung from a broken line which he spliced and rehung. Benji fell asleep in his sling, and Frank walked a circle around the trees that braced up his new home. He kept an eye on his wife and pointed to the ladder when he was satisfied they were safe from intruders.

"I need a necessary, Frank." She grew embarrassed at the words and felt the glow of a blush creep to her cheeks.

"Got the whole woods. You just stay where I can see you."

"Frank. No."

"You can go behind a tree. You only have to make sure I can see parts of you. I'll be sitting on the porch. Aim is real accurate from there."

Emily did what he said and, afterwards, climbed the ladder, exhaustion dragging at her legs. She'd had no sleep all night and was feeling the strain. Her stomach grumbled, too, and she knew Frank had to be hungry. He'd had no food yet this morning.

She sat next to him on the pine planks of the narrow porch, dangled her legs over the edge and leaned her forehead on the wooden rail until her feet prickled with numbness. Her view was of green and brown and red and purple, the vivid colors of an autumn she hadn't realized existed before today.

She hadn't paid enough attention until now.

Benji grasped one of Frank's fingers as he slept, and Frank glanced from his face to the trees beyond and back again. Blue jays screeched, and tiny chickadees chased them, fluttering from branch to branch. For the first time, she heard the ripple of the small arm of the river she'd crossed in the dark and glimpsed its silver sparkle through naked autumn limbs.

It was peaceful in Frank's treehouse, and she felt her breath come slow and deep, a healing kind of breath. She tried to remember the two of them sitting quietly together and couldn't, but the moment touched her.

"Hungry?" he asked.

"I am, but I'm more tired."

"Stay put." He stood. "I mean it. Don't think about moving."

He put Benji in his bed and brought out food he'd pilfered from their larder the night before. She recognized the half ham she'd cooked yesterday and the late apple pie. Was it only yesterday? He cut slices of both and handed them to her.

"With my fingers?"

He shrugged and stuffed the pie in first like he had always wanted to do. "Fingers work just fine."

And they did. She licked the gooey sweet from them before wiping the fingers on her skirt and ate her fill and more before scooting back and collapsing against the wall.

"What now, Frank? I need to sleep, and so do you."

"Gonna have to tie your hands and tie you to me 'til I figure it out."

He gave her the hammock and threw a blanket on the floor for himself. The hard wood bore into his back and hips, but . . .

The air in their small space smothered her with its stillness. It slid over her face, filled her nostrils with fear and love and the life she knew they should have lived.

"Are you going to kill me, Frank?"

Years of hearing him breathe told her he was still awake, and her words came on a whisper because the answer was horrific and pretty much assured.

What else could he do?

Chapter Twenty-five

He'd tried to catch some sleep after Emily followed the old man into the dark night, but his imagination ran circles in his head as he thought about the two of them out there in the woods.

They're both crazy, Yancy told himself, but the whole thing worked to his benefit. He would drag them back home, be a hero, and make sure Abby heard all about his selfless, generous efforts.

The little left in the bottle went down his throat. He coughed, dumped the straw out of his boots and went outside to wait for morning light. It lit the clouds before sliding over the horizon, a hint of daybreak waiting to spread.

Yancy led his horse from the stall, saddled her, and rode in the direction he'd watched Emily go. He heard the rooster, whose neck he'd wring someday, crowing at his back, and warm, whiskey breath misted in front of his face.

The mare's tracks, some old and some new, split off in different directions several times, and Yancy smirked at the old geezer's clever ploy. He wasn't making it easy for anyone to find him.

He slid from the saddle and eyed the tracks, trying to gauge which ones were made last night. He hoped the woman hadn't lost her husband in the dark or he'd play hell finding and hauling her back. He looked for her lighter prints in the leafy earth, but spotting one was rare. The horse hooves, on the other hand, were obvious.

But which trail?

"Probably doesn't matter," he said to himself. "They'll all lead to his campsite at some point. Pretty sure about that."

He settled himself in the saddle and enjoyed the morning. The tracks crisscrossed themselves several times, and once, Yancy thought he'd circled back around to the farm, but he kept on.

Around midmorning, he came upon what looked like a small clearing. Not sure what it was, he reined in the mare and looked around.

He didn't see a campsite. There was nothing but the remnants of an old, unused campfire and an area of whacked brush. He stared at it for several seconds before he looked up.

His eyes widened in surprise, and he chuckled out loud before checking himself and backing further away from the cleared area and into the woods. Dismounting his horse, he tied her off and crept forward to watch for any movement from the house in the trees. On a damp log seat, he listened and waited.

Where in hell were they? Had she dragged him home already? This had to be the place. Didn't it?

Silence choked the forest with his presence, but after he sat motionless for a time, the forest inhabitants went about their daily occupations. A squirrel scampered nearby, rustling the leaves and causing Yancy to lurch aside, heartrate thumping in answer to his nerves. A stray bird called to a mate, and some hidden predator flushed a covey of quail making him grab his heart in fear for his life.

"Damned stupid birds."

Minutes later, he heard their voices.

Okay. That's it then. Should I just saunter up to the crazy house and tell them to come on down?

Hell. He hadn't planned that far ahead. But they were old and he wasn't. He could whip the old man, but he didn't really want to knock him around. How would he get him home if he was out cold? Throw him over the horse? Should have brought a gun.

And then a baby's cry split the air.

What the hell?

He listened to make sure it wasn't an animal, maybe a rabbit being taken by a coyote. No, it was human. And it was up in the tree tops.

Yancy froze on his log seat and tried to make sense of the information. This was a totally different situation than he'd expected. He backed behind a tree, desperate to remain invisible while he considered what the old man was doing with a baby and where it came from. He figured the geezer had to be too old to make one of his own.

Wasn't he? But maybe that's why he left the farm. He had a woman on the side and . . . and a baby.

His incomplete thoughts rambled on and on, but he came up with no answers to what he'd heard. And none to what he should do. Minutes later, when Frank Adams came out to the narrow porch, it figured itself out.

The baby was colored.

And the old man had a rifle hanging from one hand.

Yancy wasn't going up against a gun, not even for Abby. Frank surveyed the woods, his hard eyes seeking and searching, and Yancy felt his skin prickle with goose bumps. He was afraid of Frank with a rifle. Old men can still shoot.

Damn, damn, damn. This was bad. Hmmm. Or good.

He hoped he hadn't said the words out loud as he turned and backtracked to the mare. He was leaving, and he needed to hurry. He'd think it out on the way.

Hoping the noise his mare made would be confused with a large whitetail, he prodded her as fast as he dared and tried not to think about being shot in the back. He followed tracks he hoped would take him back to the farm but skirted it when he got near and headed straight to the old hotel. He threw the reins to Edwin, said he had to run, and sprinted down the footbridge.

The plan was taking shape.

Before going in, he ran hands through his hair, considered what words would work to his best advantage, and entered the hotel on a run yelling Abby's name.

She was at the registration desk when the door crashed open and looked up in stunned amazement.

"What on earth, Yancy? What's wrong?"

He took an exaggerated gasp. "Betty's baby. I've been working on this day and night, and I finally found him. I knew I could do it."

Abby stepped back, eyebrows lifting. "You found Benji? Really?"

Her 'really' didn't sound curious and astonished but skeptical, and the tone troubled him. This wasn't going well . . . but it would. He'd see to that.

"You need to tell Betty, Abby. Uh . . . I would've but she knows you. The shock, you know. You should be there for her."

She closed the registration book and pointed the guests she'd been registering toward the stairs. They took their key and went, looking backwards at the curious conversation they were leaving.

"Where is Benji, Yancy? Where did you find him and how do you know it's him? Where is he now?" Her arms crossed in front of her, and her eyes expressed doubt.

This wasn't going as expected, nothing like his imagination had produced on the way here. Why weren't her arms around his neck, hugging him? Why wasn't she kissing him in appreciation, looking at him with adoration instead of misgiving?

"He's in the woods. Old man Adams has him."

Abby chewed the inside of her cheek. She didn't believe him, but could she risk ignoring him if he was telling the truth? She leaned forward to see if she could smell whiskey on his breath.

"Where in the woods? How do we find him?"

"A long, long way into the forest. There's tracks leading from the Adams farm to where he lives. They crisscross, but eventually they get there. He rides a horse to and from the farm."

"Wait just a minute. Frank Adams lives in the woods? This sounds more far-fetched by the minute."

"I know it's unbelievable, but it's true. He built some strange house up in the trees." Yancy reached a hand to touch her like an old, trusted friend who cared. "He has a gun, Abby, or I would have grabbed Benji. I was afraid he'd hurt Mrs. Adams and the baby."

She ran her fingers through her hair and held the top of her head like it was about to explode. "Stop! Emily Adams? What was she doing out there?"

"I don't know, but the old man's a menace, shouting, screaming obscenities. He's crazy, Abby. Betty needs to bring help. Get Samuel and Charles, maybe Jesse and the sheriff. Don't wait for the sheriff, though. Send for him. You never know when he'll go all the way insane and hurt the baby and Mrs. Adams."

"Thank you, Yancy. I . . . It seems I've misjudged you. I'll tell Da I'm leaving and go see Betty right now."

She left without asking where Yancy was going and what he was going to do. She didn't even think about him.

He retrieved his horse from the stable, rode to the Adams farm and found Terry and Cecily in the house. In between gasps, he explained what he saw in the woods and warned Terry about the mob they were collecting in town to get the baby back.

"Bunch of colored men are going in armed and mad," he said.

"Pa isn't gonna shoot anybody," Terry said and turned to Cecily. "Why didn't you tell me Ma was trailing after Pa first thing? Why in hell didn't you wake me up; I could've stopped all this nonsense."

Yancy stepped in. "She didn't want to bother you, and I told her I'd bring your ma home, save you the trouble. And we didn't know about the baby. But there's gonna be bloodshed, I'm telling you. If you want your ma and pa back alive, we better get the Legion. Your pa is Klan. You, too, for that matter."

Terry swiped a hand over his face and considered Yancy's words. He didn't believe everything the man said, but his words had some ring of truth. He knew his old man had been crazy for a while, living out in the woods, sneaking in to raid the larder and slinking around at night.

"Damn it all. This shit stinks. I'll go on out to find Ma and Pa and try to talk them out of this business, get em to come home. You go get some of the Legion, just in case."

"Sure thing, Terry. Just follow my trail. Easy to spot alongside his. They crisscross a lot, but they all get there – eventually."

Daniel Longstreet lived between Idlewild and Chase, a couple miles from town. He'd been to his house before when he'd first heard about the Black Legion, and Daniel had been recruiting members, namely him. It had sounded too dangerous to Yancy, too violent, and he wasn't gung-ho about any philosophical ideal so much he needed to fight for it. He didn't care all that much about anything except a good meal, a bottle of whiskey, a soft bed – and Abby. Ideals were highfalutin, meant for folks who could afford them, and he couldn't.

Today he was glad to know Longstreet and his friends. He banged hard on the door, in a hurry to get them to the woods and eager to put his plan in motion.

"You know Frank Adams and his wife Emily, right?" he said without preamble when Longstreet came to the door.

"Hello, Yancy, and of course I do. Longtime resident of the area, a farmer." He yanked his vest down, irritated he'd left his meal for a man who didn't give their invitation the time of day when it had been offered. "What about them?"

"They're cornered in the woods by a bunch of coloreds. Frank has a rifle, but he's way outnumbered. It'll be murder for sure if you and the boys don't get out there."

Leaning against the door frame, Longstreet studied Yancy until he squirmed under the dark scrutiny.

"Look, if you don't want to help, I'll see who else I can find. Some great Black Legion you got if it won't do what it was meant to do. Frank is Klan, and you know it."

"Hold on. I didn't say we won't go. Didn't say anything. Come on in for a minute. You interrupted my meal."

Longstreet threw a saddle on a tall sorrel, jammed a rifle in the scabbard and looked for Yancy's gun.

Yancy turned red under the man's inspection. "I didn't have time to get it."

"Stay put," Longstreet said. He went inside and came out with a replica of the one he'd hung on his own saddle. "Winchester lever action 1894, 30-30. Good little firearm. Not too bulky and it's quick. A straight shooter."

Yancy held it awkwardly since his saddle didn't have a place to hang it, and the odd thought came to him that it looked a lot like the one the old man had up in the tree. Must be a popular rifle, he thought, but he didn't really know one from the other.

Wake up, Yancy. What in hell are you going to do with a gun? Shoot somebody? You know better. You want somebody else to do that little piece of work for you. And then you get to console her . . .

They rode off toward the edge of the Adams property, stopping along the way to get Darnell Rumford, Joe Foster and two others. Longstreet filled them in along the way, and Yancy was interested to hear his version of the growing story. It had altered, as untruths tend to do, and Yancy didn't clarify when he heard him say a bunch of colored men had taken Frank and his wife and were holding them in the woods. Betty and her baby weren't mentioned.

"We need the Klan to protect white families all across America. If the Legion doesn't stand up to protect our Klan leaders, we'll be taken over because we won't have any Klan. I'm telling you the truth!" Rumford's high voice screeched to be sure all the men heard his harangue. "We won't have any jobs, and coloreds will be in our schools and neighborhoods. Hell, they'll be marrying our white women, our daughters. You want that?"

He was a weaselly little man who tried to make up for his lack of breadth with his mouth. When Yancy looked around at his companions, he had the good sense to realize they were a questionable lot. Each one had something to say about why they didn't like negros, some real or imagined insult or injury they'd suffered because of a colored person.

Yancy couldn't think of anything he'd suffered, but then he thought of Samuel, the one person who couldn't fare well on this day. He'd been suffering plenty because of him. If it weren't for Samuel, Abby would be his, and he couldn't stand the sight of his smug face.

Maybe you can shoot somebody, Yancy. Just maybe.

Benjamin sat at the piano, his fingers searching for new ways to turn the air to magic. A few people, their voices muted to match the melody, sat at scattered tables around the bar.

The scent of cinnamon from Al's apple pies hit Abby's senses with a hidden longing to come home to The Old Place. She missed it, missed spending every day with her friends.

Having run the entire way, she stopped once inside the door to catch her breath before tracking down Betty. She could hear where Benjamin was.

"You're out of shape, boss," Betty said, leaning over the banister. "You're gonna give yourself a conniption fit if you keep that up. You're not a spring chick anymore."

Abby bent over at the waist and sucked in air before standing erect. "I've missed you, too. Conniption fit? Is that a new medical term?"

"Just made it up." Betty stretched her long frame and yawned. "I was taking a nap. What're you doing here?"

"Need to talk to you. I'll grab Benjamin and we'll be right up."

Her mouth opened and shut, the gravity in Abby's tone gripping her, and she walked to their room like she didn't have legs. She couldn't feel them and didn't know how her body got here. She raised her hand in the air and wiggled the fingers. She saw them move but couldn't feel them, either. Nothing was working right because she knew something was wrong, and it concerned her son.

That . . . she felt, no, she *knew. It grew* deep in the pit of her stomach, and it ached, burned with acid and poison and flames. Benji was in trouble.

The piano music quit. Footsteps moved up the stairs and entered the room. Abby explained in quick terms what she'd learned from Yancy.

She watched Betty's eyes harden, fill with liquid and then fire. She moved from where she sat on the bed to the window and stood stiff and erect staring out at the brown wintery landscape, the gray-blue water reflecting a pale sun. Abby moved to her side.

"I don't know how much of what he said is true, Betty. You know Yancy; he's a dissembler. I don't completely trust him."

"It's true. I know it is. Cassandra saw him, and I believe every word she says." She looked hard at Abby, then at her husband, and pointed at her own chest. "And I heard him. We have to go. Now."

Benjamin put an arm around his wife and drew her away from the window. "We'll check it out, sweetheart, but we need to get the sheriff. If what Yancy said is even half true, that old man is crazy. And he has a gun."

"I'm not waiting for someone to call for Sheriff Hicks just hoping he's available. I'm going now. Like you said, he has a gun. And our son. Get your boots, and saddle up a couple of horses. We can use Al's. She'll want that."

Benjamin dropped to a chair, ran hands through his hair, and covered his face. The groan he emitted spoke of too much hope dead and buried.

"I'm going, Benjamin. With you or without. I'm not waiting for Hicks."

Benjamin looked up, his glance going from his wife to Abby who watched the dark menace of skepticism grow in his eyes and knowledge mixed with suspicion tighten his jawline.

"Did Yancy say who else he told about Benji and your father-in-law?"

Abby shook her head, not sure the direction of his thoughts, but realizing she should have gotten more information. She hadn't asked him any questions about where he'd been, where he was going or who he'd talked to on the way. From the look on Benjamin's face, the knowledge was significant.

"I don't know. I'm sorry. I was anxious to get here. I . . . I should have asked, but I didn't."

"What else did he say, Abby? Think."

She dropped her chin to her chest for a moment and closed her eyes, trying to bring back all of Yancy's words.

"He said to bring help, to bring Samuel, Charles, Jesse. Oh, and maybe he said Shorty, too."

Benjamin rubbed his temples like a pounding headache raged there.

"Think. Did he say Shorty?"

"I'm not sure."

"All black men – oh, and possibly our token white guy, Shorty. You see what's happening here? This might not be about Benji at all. Something about this stinks. If we're going out there with guns to get my son from a crazy old white man . . ." He touched his wife's cheek to get her to look at him. "You know how this could turn?"

Betty stiffened, sparks of anger flashing up the middle of her back. "I've been colored all my life, Benjamin Chambers. You're not giving me new information." She snorted, a sound that would normally embarrass her, but not today, and she quieted thinking how he might feel about her harsh words.

"Course I know, Benjamin. Somebody could die out there, even you or me, but I'm going after my son, and I'm going now. You go get the others and send somebody for the Sheriff. I'll meet you out there. I'm not waiting."

She sat on the edge of the bed to remove her shoes and pulled a heavy pair of boots from under it. She yanked them on, pulling harder than necessary and revealing angst she didn't want to speak.

Benjamin breathed out a heavy sigh of defeat. He wasn't letting her go without him. He'd be by his wife's side even though he wished they had the sheriff's knowledge and expertise.

"Go on, now." Betty stood and grabbed a coat from a hook on the wall. "Go get help, Benjamin. Abby'll go out to the woods with me."

"Can't do that. I'll be going with you. Shorty can bring the men and send for the sheriff."

He found Shorty in the kitchen with Al and explained what he knew. Shorty drew himself up to his six-foot five height and tightened his fists, ready to do battle. Fury tangled with affection on his face and emanated from his thick, coiled body.

Benjamin put a hand on his shoulder and asked him to get the others, send for the sheriff and catch up.

"Start behind the Adams farm, behind the barn, and follow the trail," he said. "It should be clear, according to Yancy, but it's apparently a long, long way into the deep part of the forest. We'll be there getting our son back. It may be over by the time you all arrive. But . . . I doubt it."

Benjamin's eyes clouded with uncertainty and fear. His war experience added to his understanding of gun play and its consequences, and it had no connection at all to play and plenty to do with horror and grief and loss. And that was only the beginning. He wished the day over.

"I'm going, now."

Shorty squeezed his friend's hand and gave him the only advice that came to mind. "Don't be brave," he said. The words seemed stupid, but they were all he had, and he hoped Benjamin took them in the way they were meant.

He nodded like he did and turned away.

"Taking your horse, Al, if that's alright." He didn't wait for the answer because he knew it. He knew Al.

Shorty followed close on his heels all the way to the stable, saddled his tall gelding and left for Samuel's house without more than a nod in his direction.

Benjamin saddled the two mares, and he, Betty and Abby galloped out toward the Adams farm with early afternoon sun in their eyes, the day not yet cooled by autumn's evening chill.

Anxiety rode with them in weighty silence, dread an invisible companion. They wore foreboding like a shroud they couldn't throw off and discard, and all three worked at trying not to foreshadow trouble.

Chapter Twenty-six

Benji's whimper woke her, and she had no idea where she was when her eyes opened. Just a few feet away, a window framed a pale sky and showed dark branches right up next to the pane, close enough to slap at the glass. Emily's brain couldn't adjust to that picture, her surroundings – or to a baby's cry.

She turned her head as heavy feet hit the floor and saw her husband untie the rope binding them together. Now, she remembered. A house in the trees, Frank, and Benji. Her head began to throb and she held it between her still bound hands.

Benji gave a happy warble when Frank picked him up and attended to the necessaries. He brought the bottle in from the porch where it stayed cool and put the pan of water on the stove to warm the bottle. He changed a wet diaper, all the while telling Benji what he was doing and about their lives together.

He ignored Emily, and she wondered if, in his mind, she wasn't there. He turned in a circle, a frown on his face as if he wanted her out of his hammock and out of his life but didn't say a word.

"Need to sit here?" she asked.

"Usually do, I guess."

"Can I hold him for you. Maybe feed him?"

Frank's glare, twisted with suspicion and anger, shot through her.

"You shouldn't be here. House wasn't meant for three."

A flicker of hope sparked.

Would he let her leave? Had sleep brought him some clarity?

"Then I'll go, Frank. I don't want to be in the way."

His head jerked toward her, and his eyes settled on her face. "You can't leave. You know that."

Frank's voice held no animosity or sorrow. He uttered effortless facts, and their simplicity held more threat than if they'd been filled with passion, even anger. *That* she understood and could deal with.

A shiver ran down her spine, and Emily prayed for help. Would her son come for her? She hadn't told him where she was going, but surely, he'd notice her absence and go looking. Wouldn't he? And when he found her, what then? Would Frank shoot his own son to keep Benji and throw her off the porch to her death?

The hammering in her head made her sick to her stomach, and she thought she might throw up. She dropped her head until her chin touched her chest and tried to gather strength, to settle her breathing, to pray.

When she could, she held up her bound hands. "Will you untie me, please, Frank?"

"Not now," he said. "But Benji can lay on your lap with his bottle while I do a couple of things." He held the baby to her but stopped halfway and glared into her eyes. "Don't do anything stupid, and don't you hurt my son, or . . . Just don't."

He tucked Benji on her lap, tapped his chin in affection, grabbed a bucket and left. When he came back, he hung clean, wet diapers on the porch rail and filled clean bottles with milk. He performed his parental duties expertly, and Emily chewed her lip in thought as she watched and tried to understand how Frank had come to this place.

What had happened to make him a real father to a false son, and not merely a father but a good one? His affection was tangible, his care of the child faultless. This man was not the Frank she knew.

When his chores were finished, he untied her hands and took Benji from her. He bundled him in a blanket, shuffled into his old coat, grabbed his rifle, and went outside.

"You can sit out here if you want," he said. "Benji needs fresh air."

He held the baby, his back against his stomach, so he could look out at the woods and groaned as he sat with his legs hanging over the deck. Emily sat next to him where he'd pointed – away from the ladder and away from his rifle which lay next to his thigh and available.

"See the pileated out there?"

She didn't know if his question was directed at her or Benji so she remained silent until he stared at her with a keen question in his eyes.

"I don't, Frank. Point, please."

He did, and she aimed her sight along his arm and finger until she spotted bright red plumage and gasped. The bird was gigantic. She'd heard about them all her life but had never seen one. And there it was, sitting not thirty feet from her nose.

"Oh, good Lord. He's almost two feet long." She whispered the words in veneration for the spectacular creature and because she didn't want it to fly away. "Look at his coloring. He's amazing."

"Insectivorous and second in size only to the ivory billed woodpecker."

She turned away from the bird to stare at her husband. "Insecti . . . what?"

"Eats insects. Mostly ants, but it's a lie that's all he eats. He likes berries, too. And some nuts."

"I didn't realize you knew this kind of stuff, Frank."

She had supposed he didn't care to spend his time learning anything that didn't directly impact him. Especially any kind of knowledge not having to do with farming. He knew that well enough.

He lowered his head to speak with Benji and pointed out the bird. He used a lot of multisyllable words and made no effort to adjust them because he was talking to a baby. Emily approved his teaching methods. Once again, she reconsidered the man by her side. Was it possible she had never known him? Not at all?

He told Benji about the creek, how it was spring fed which kept it cold all year round and also free of ice because it bubbled where it came from the ground. It was an icebox and water well all in one. Perfect for their needs living here in the forest.

"It's pushed from the ground, you see, instead of being pulled by gravity like most creeks and rivers. It's called an aquifer, son, and the water's as pure as it gets. None better. Cold for a bath, though. We know cold, don't we? Pretty darned near freezing."

"You took Benji into the creek for a bath?" Emily was horrified and curious at the same time.

He chuckled and nuzzled the top of Benji's head. "We both took a little bath. Was washing off the black, but it didn't go. I was really happy to see that. He's perfect just like he is."

Frank's words were natural, as if everyone had a perfectly legitimate desire to know if skin color rinsed away, and Emily stared open-mouthed - but shut it before he saw and pushed her off the porch.

"Probably need to bathe up here for the winter. Need to get a wash tub big enough for two."

Once more, Emily pondered sitting next to her husband and having a conversation, discussing the natural world and what they'd do during the winter for baths. She could have grown used to this man, could have grown used to a life with him. Could still.

Almost hoping no one sought her, she let her eyes roam between the trees as deep into the woods as she could see, looking for movement, listening for the snap of a twig to indicate human footfall. She sighed with relief. Not yet.

She - they were safe for the moment. She wasn't asking for the moon, merely to enjoy the unrealistic harmony they'd forged for a little while longer.

Shorty pushed his large gelding all the way to Samuel's house, hoping he was home and not in court saving some vagrant petty thief from a decade in prison in payment for a stolen loaf of bread. Those were his usual clients, in between the few who had money and paid for his services, providing food and shelter for Samuel.

His fist rattled the door for several moments before Samuel threw it open.

"Trying to take it off the hinges?" Samuel opened his mouth to give the big man some grief but closed it with a look at Shorty's fierce eyes. "Come on in. Pleasant though it is, why the visit?"

Shorty stood his ground when Samuel waved him in. "Still have a horse, I assume. The model T can't go everywhere."

"Course. Why?"

"Saddle up. I'll tell you on the way."

He followed Samuel to the small barn behind his house and helped ready the mare, sketching in the details of what he knew.

Samuel flung a leg over the saddle, patted her black neck and urged her forward.

"Hard to believe Emily and Frank have had Benji all this time and nobody knew it. Hard to think Emily would at all. Good Christian lady stealing a baby?" Samuel shook his head in disbelief. "Doesn't figure. Now, Frank . . ."

"I know, but keep in mind all this information comes from Yancy. He's the one who saw them."

"Damn. Truth isn't Yancy's strong suit. He'd embellish the Bible and find a way to put his name in it."

They repeated the sketchy bits of information for Jesse and sent Edna to get the Sheriff.

"Tell him to start behind the Adams' barn. It's the beginning of the trail that will supposedly take them there," Shorty said.

He hugged the woman and climbed onto his tall horse. Together, they looked mythological – *the giant and his steed.*

"Be safe," she said. With her daughter Daisy squeezed to her side, she climbed into their buggy, flicked the switch over the mare's head and took off at a faster pace than she'd ever driven before, praying they'd find the baby safe and that she and Daisy wouldn't crash into the ditch before getting the sheriff.

"Need to make one more stop at the Old Place for Charles," Shorty uttered. "Said he'd be ready to go when I got back."

The soft-spoken author of nonviolent literature sprinted across the porch to a saddled mare. He'd used the time while he waited to pray no violence would be committed this day, and as he mounted, he noticed the complexion of the men in their small group and wondered if they had noted it, as well.

"Do we have a plan?" he asked.

"Nope," Shorty told him. "Won't know until we see the lay of the land, but given Benjamin's experience, I'm guessing he'll have one."

"Expecting a standoff?" Jesse asked, looking down at the rifle scabbards filled with a variety of hunting guns. A trickle of sweat ran down his back, cooling in the afternoon winter chill. A shiver followed.

"Could be," Shorty said. "They've had Benji quite a spell. Guess they would've given him back by now if they'd been so inclined. Can't believe Emily has known where Benji's been all this time. It isn't like her. I don't see that at all."

"And she's been hauling Betty's parents to church every Sunday, pretending to be such a good white Christian," Jesse said.

His words shot from his tongue with hostility, and Charles wondered if he was the right man for this job. He liked Jesse, but today he was itchy and it made Charles nervous.

She waited at the end of the tree lined path that led to and hid her house from folks passing by, arms crossed, hands tucked inside long, wide sleeves and surrounded by her clowder. Worry flickered when she saw the harsh lines of their faces, eyes set with grim determination, and she held a hand up to halt them.

"Cassandra," Samuel said.

She knew him the best and treated him like a son, thought of him as her own.

"Don't push Frank. He loves the boy, and Benji has been teaching him many things he needed to understand in this changing world. Frank won't see him killed by a stray bullet, but he won't want to give up his son."

Jesse gave a harsh laugh. "Son? That's rich."

Cassandra scowled. "Go gently, not waving your rifles or your wagging tongues. Brute force isn't the way *this* time."

Samuel's eyebrow rose, remembering the time she had recommended ruthlessness, and he gave her words credence, more so than did the others in their small group who knew nothing of that horrific time.

"We'll do our best, Cassandra."

"It may be time. It may not." Her long robe swirled as she spun and floated back down the path, disappearing into the copse.

"What did she mean?" Jesse asked, irritated at the lost time and the vague words. Just plain irritated about the whole damned mess.

"Who knows," Shorty said.

"I can guess," Charles said. When three faces peered at him, he gave them what he thought. "She's saying, if Frank has learned enough from Benji, he may give him up. It may be time. If not, then . . . Well, the opposite is true and he may fight for him. Lives may be lost. Just a guess."

"Learned from a baby?" Jesse said. "That's damned nonsense, and the world has gone mad. Gone to hell. That's all I have to say. Let's go."

Shorty chuckled. Jesse was a good friend, a good man. He didn't mean anything by his crankiness, but he was nervous. They all were.

Men expressed fear in many ways.

Benjamin lifted Betty down first and slid from the saddle soundlessly. He wasn't sure they were in the right spot, but his military training had kicked in, and he sensed they were near the camp.

There was a hesitance in the bird and insect song, a change in the scent on the air. A savage kind of waiting surrounded them and stilled the audible forest heartbeat. It halted foliage movement and clenched his stomach and heart in fear. It was war again.

He put a finger over his lips for silence, motioned both women nearer and whispered.

"No noise. Look where your feet land so you make less sound than a snake moving through the grass. Follow me and put your feet where mine went."

He looked at their eyes for conformation they understood and were ready. Two heads nodded and sucked in breath from deep in their bellies.

They came in from the far side of the creek and, unknown to them, traveled the same log to cross it Emily had many hours earlier, long before dawn.

Once over the water and moving over dry ground, Benjamin stopped their forward movement with a hand and pulled them down to the forest floor. He pointed, and they all stared in awe at the house in the trees.

Diapers hung over a railing from which a rope dangled and was tied to a basket on the ground. A ladder slanted up to a narrow porch-type landing, and framed windows looked out at a small cleared area, a yard of sorts. The structure was alluring, charming, even homey.

"Back up," he whispered, pointing to a convenient place to watch and not be seen themselves.

They hunkered on their knees and sat with bottoms on their heels in the damp undergrowth, silent and scared. Betty couldn't breathe visualizing her son up in the small fortress. She swallowed the lump in her throat and twisted her fingers together until the knuckles screamed, desire to rush up that ladder tacked to the deck unbearable.

If this was Frank's fort, Benjamin thought, it was impenetrable. The man had chosen well. He looked around for cover should they need to rush the place, and the dire situation they were in overwhelmed him.

Frank could sit up there and shoot at them all day long, and they could do nothing but take a bullet. He'd cleared around it so they'd be spotted the moment they left the trees and killed before they made it to the ladder.

They whispered one plan after another, none seeming better than the last, and waited for something to change or reinforcements to show up.

"The sheriff will know what to do," Abby said, watching the desperation in Benjamin's eyes.

"Maybe."

"I want to shout his name," Betty said. "Maybe if I call to him. Tell him how much I want my baby, how much I love him."

Her tears had long since dried even before Yancy's revelation. And to be this close and not have him in her arms was agony greater than could produce weeping.

"Not now. Wait. Wait for Samuel and Shorty. Don't give it away that we're here. Please, Betty, we need to watch and learn. He may come down with Benji. Who knows? If he does, we'll ambush him and take our son. We've waited this long. Don't rush it now."

On the other side of Frank's home in the trees, six men slithered through the underbrush on their knees and elbows, rifles held out of the damp growth and ready. Joe Foster grunted and snorted, peevish and complaining that this wasn't what he'd had in mind.

"What *did* you have in mind, Joe?" Longstreet asked, the smirk on his face making it clear he was enjoying Joe's discomfort. "Walk on in and start killing?"

"Sure as hell not walking on my elbows like some animal."

"Shut up," Rumford hissed. "Shut your big mouth afore they hear us."

Yancy brought up the rear behind two men he didn't know, and his stomach churned acid, sending it up to his throat. He spit, trying to clear it as softly as he could. Talk on the way here had made him more than nervous.

The Black Legion killed people. They didn't send warnings. They were harsh in their lessons, and people died or wished for death.

Yancy began to think he shouldn't have brought them here and hadn't lied to them. They didn't know anything about the baby Frank had stolen – he'd left that little bit of information out. They believed it was a feud between a black family and a white one, and they were here to make sure the white one won. That's all. They didn't care who the people were or the reason for the quarrel. White was white.

Yancy felt like he was going to lose what little food was in his stomach and stopped creeping forward to let them get further ahead. When the last of the two strangers slithered out of sight, he let go of his stomach contents and sat back on his heels, sweat sliding down the back of his shirt and sticking black hair to his forehead.

The acrid smell of his perspiration clung to him like an aura proclaiming noxious guilt.

When he'd visualized this foray, the picture in his mind hadn't looked like this. He'd seen himself becoming a hero for finding the baby. And getting rid of Samuel. He didn't want a war, and he certainly didn't want to be part of one, but that's what it was becoming.

How many could die? And who?

He hadn't thought it through, and realized Abby was probably coming out to this ungodly place, too, with her friend, Betty. Damned stupid baby. Abby could get hurt.

Could he turn around? Crawl back the way they'd come, get his horse and skedaddle? He'd hear about everything later and didn't need to be here to see it all happening.

He was on his elbows and knees heading in the other direction when the twig snap behind him. He looked back and saw Longstreet's angry face.

"Did you get lost? Lose your sense of direction, Yancy? You think north is south now?"

He swallowed and slowly turned to follow the man back to the others who waited, their cold eyes boring into his. No words were needed. No explanations or excuses would have worked. They knew.

Foster spat and wiped his mouth, and the brown glob landed inches from Yancy's knee. He leaned back and crossed his arms, pinching his thin lips together like he was readying saliva for a second volley.

"Enough," Longstreet sputtered. "Move on."

The old man had made several different paths through the forest in order to confuse anyone who might want to track him, and it worked. Some led to his first campsite, the one he'd used before building a home in the trees. Some led to the back side of the new place, some to the front across the creek, and some miles off to the other side of the forest before heading back.

Luck would have it that no two parties took the same trail, so they failed to bumble across one another as they fumbled around the damp woodland looking for Frank, Emily, a baby, or a battle between coloreds and whites as described by Yancy.

Benjamin, Betty and Abby watched the front of Frank's cabin, the Black Legion came up from the rear and knelt to watch the back of the small clearing and listen for the gunfire they'd been told about.

Was it all done? Were they too late?

Common sense told the Legion to listen and wait.

Samuel, Shorty, Jesse and Charles were on their way and, according to recent tracks, would be coming up behind Benjamin's group. They left their mounts tethered near the two they recognized and went the last of the way on foot.

Chapter Twenty-seven

"You can't keep Benji here forever, Frank. You must see that."

Emily tried again to convince her husband to give the baby back to his parents, but Frank wasn't listening, or he heard her pleas and disregarded them as he always had.

"No. He's mine. He needs his father."

"But you're not his father. You know that. Benjamin Chambers is his father."

He glared, squinting his gray eyes at her with unmasked ferociousness that made her wary of continuing this line of argument.

"No," he repeated.

Emily sat in the corner on the floor where she'd been curled. She thumped her head against the wall, trying to think of some way to persuade him, something that would jog his memory to a time when he had three sons of his own.

"Remember Frank Junior?" she asked. He looks a lot like you. Stubborn like you, too."

"Course I remember him. He's off in some God-forsaken place like Wyoming cuz of that stupid wife of his. Think I'm demented?"

"No, I don't think you're crazy at all. You have a wonderful brain, and I've loved the time we've spent here in the woods together. You've been hiding from me all these years, and I've not really known you, but I like this Frank. We could do this kind of thing back at the farm. Together. Sit and talk. You could teach me some of the things you know about."

She crooned her words, waited and watched her husband's face, hoping an idea might penetrate, eager to see some change in his fixed expression.

"Your son Terry is tending the farm. You remember him, don't you?"

His jaw muscles twitched in irritation.

"What kind of fool do you take me for, wife?"

"I don't take you for any kind of fool, Frank. Why don't you tell me what's going on here, with Benji? Talk to me. Tell me what you're thinking."

He ignored her request and watched Benji wiggle in the throes of waking up for his bottle and a diaper change. He didn't wait for him to cry but picked him up. He kissed his nose, smiled and put him over his shoulder. Benji grabbed a fistful of beard and warbled his pleasure, and Emily's heart broke.

"Welcome to the afternoon, son. I've missed you," Frank said. He danced across the small room and serenaded the baby, repeating the lilting lines of the lullaby he'd added to since recalling it many days ago.

Emily fought the sting of tears flooding her eyes. It would kill her when she separated the two of them, but she had to. And it had to be soon, or she couldn't do it. She'd throw herself from the small balcony, hoping for instant death, and she knew that, too. Death would be easier than separating the two of them.

Benji tugged on the beard and let out a happy wail.

Hiding in the woods, Betty leaped to her feet and Benjamin yanked her back down.

"It's him!" she whispered. Her eyes beamed and lips opened in a wide grin. "It's Benji."

"Most likely is, but you can't go rushing up there."

Coming up behind them, Shorty heard the wail, too, and pointed ahead while looking back at the others.

"Need quiet," he whispered, and they crept forward.

Benjamin heard the nearly silent footsteps and stole back to intercept them before pointing to where his wife and Abby waited.

"Seen Benji or the Adams?" Shorty asked.

"No, and that's the first peep we've heard out of them."

"Don't suppose the Sheriff is here, yet." Samuel said, hunkering down between Benjamin and Abby.

Benjamin shook his head, discouraged and afraid.

"Don't know what he can do. Look at that place. It's positioned like a fortress on a hill."

Shorty looked and then cast his gaze around the clearing and into the trees near the edge of the open space, forming a plan.

"We need to circle the place and let Frank know we have guns and he's surrounded. There is no escape for him or his wife."

"What about Benji? He could be hit," Betty said, her dry, scratchy throat distorting the words. She repeated them and did her best to straighten her back. Blubbering wouldn't do Benji any good. Strength would.

"We won't shoot if hitting him is a risk. Hell, we likely won't shoot at all. We'll just let him think we will." Shorty patted her shoulder and pulled her against him. "Nobody's gonna hurt your Benji, girl."

Putting his military training to use, Benjamin pointed out semi-secluded spots in the wooded circle around the treehouse and then to the individual men. His plan was to scatter them evenly, and he told them to stay hidden several feet into the foliage and be ready to make their positions known when he gave the signal.

"What about us?" Abby said pointing to herself and Betty.

"Stay back," Benjamin said, pointing behind him, further into the woods.

"Really? We can make noise, too, let him think there are more men in the woods than we really have. You can't simply send us away." Abby's eyes accused. "Shame on you, Benjamin. Use us."

He inhaled and ran a hand over his face. "Stay back, please. You can make noise when I give the order but from behind a tree and a short distance from either side of me. Please."

Abby nodded, not wanting to cause him more angst.

"Do we have a plan after that?" Charles asked. "What are we to do when we get there?"

"Whistle when you're in your places, like a whippoorwill." He gave an example, and each man nodded. "When I hear four, I'll call out to Frank. Tell him he's surrounded and to give up."

"And if he doesn't?" Jesse said.

"We'll make noise and convince him of a heavy armed presence. Thrash around. Stomp branches. Sound big and like a lot of men."

Benjamin was tired and it showed in his eyes, in the slant of his shoulders. And he was afraid. What would he do if Frank said, 'Go to hell?'

"If he still balks, make more noise and shoot over his head, carefully. Don't hit them and don't hit each other. Listen for my shot and don't go ahead of it. Got that?"

Samuel left first since he had the furthest to go, to a copse straight across from where they knelt in the brush, and Shorty followed a few minutes later, slipping through the woods to his assigned place. Jesse headed off to the right toward the creek and Charles went left. Betty and Abby walked away from Benjamin, moving several yards to either side of him, and made sure to find trees wide enough to hide behind as they were told to do if shooting began.

Two whippoorwills whistled before the strange sound of tin cans clanging together stopped all movement, and the door to the cabin swung open.

Frank stepped out with Benji in a sling over his stomach and a rifle in his hand pointing toward the tin chimes. He racked the lever on his Winchester and swung it from side to side as he peered into the shadows between the trees.

Silence dropped over the forest.

Betty knelt on the soft ground. She struggled to take air into her lungs as she peered through the trees and saw her son hanging against the old man whose hand had settled on her baby's head.

Frank watched for movement in the woods and listened for the sound of an intruder, apprehensive and praying to spy a whitetail bounding away and provide a peaceful reason for the alarm.

No one inhaled for immeasurable seconds waiting for some response to the tin-can noise.

What the hell?

Benjamin gave a whippoorwill whistle. He had to know if the other two were in position.

Charles gave a response to Benjamin's encouraging birdsong and looked at the tangle of broken twine around his foot. He had to give credit to Frank's ingenuity and use of what he had available.

One whistle . . . Good, Benjamin thought. But where was the fourth whippoorwill?

Damn.

Setting his rifle in the grass, Charles tried to keep the tin from clanging again as he slid strands of twine from around his ankle and boot. He cursed, stood on one foot and nearly toppled into the pile of tin. Once unraveled, he grabbed the abandoned rifle, slipped into his assigned spot without further incident, and prepared to face the enemy.

What enemy? Charles thought, feeling stupid and anxious. An old man and a baby?

I'm too damned gray-haired for this. You too, Frank.

He hadn't heard a whistle from Samuel's area and concern wrinkled his brow. He should have given it by now.

Benjamin waited as long as he thought reasonable and hoped all the men were safely in place. Maybe the fourth call had sounded and he hadn't heard. His voice rang harsh in the forest stillness.

"This is Benjamin Chambers. I want my baby, Frank. Give him up and there won't be any trouble. We have men surrounding the place. Men with guns."

Frank's face reddened in fury. He stood back against the wall and wrapped a protective arm around Benji.

"You can't have my son. Period. What man would give up his child? Go the hell away. I mean it. I can pick you off one by one, and I will."

He stepped sideways until his shoulder felt the doorframe and sidled inside to the safety of the house.

Frank's strong voice carried through the woods and, hearing it, the sheriff urged his mount faster than he wanted or should, given the tangled undergrowth.

"I repeat," Benjamin said. "You're surrounded, Frank. Give up. We're not leaving here without Benji."

Emily moved to the open door, her eyes searching the woods. She crossed her arms over her chest and rubbed them, chilled by more than the early winter cold. Her head spun as she tried to spy people hiding behind trees, rifles pointed at them in their strange home.

"Frank," she whispered. "I'm afraid."

He yanked her away from the open door and slammed it shut in frustration, thought again, and opened it enough to stick the end of his rifle out.

"Watch from that window. Tell me if anybody steps into the clearing and moves toward the ladder."

Branches cracked off to the left, like somebody stomping through the woods without a care for silence, and then noise could be heard behind, to the right, and all along the front. He didn't see anyone, but the clatter encircled them. Frank's head twisted from one sound to the next, determination stiffening his spine, jaw clenched.

"Bastards. Take a man's son."

Emily moved the few steps to his side and wrapped an arm around his back. She kissed his cheek and wished for his lips, wanting more from him. She wanted the man she'd seen all day, the man who loved his son and showed it, the one who pointed out woodpeckers and squirrels and spoke to Benji as if he understood every word.

How could he have hidden inside the body of the man she'd slept next to for forty years? How could she not know him?

She couldn't tell him about these new feelings, and she couldn't tell him the baby wasn't his. Not anymore. It was too late for all that. But she couldn't let him hurt anyone, either.

Damn him.

An unfamiliar voice came from behind them, unseen from their positions at the window.

"There's more than coloreds in the woods, Frank. You have help you didn't know anything about. From the Black Legion. We protect Klan members like you, my friend. Keep what's yours and say thank you."

Frank didn't recognize the voice, but he was glad for whoever was there to help him and his son. Someone cared about his family and wouldn't let ambushers and liars murder him just to take what was his.

He held tight to Benji, who had begun to whimper, and nuzzled the top of his head. Moments later he heard movement, cursing, moans and grunts, the sound of fists meeting flesh and boots meeting bone. The picture it engendered sickened him, and it continued on forever. He understood someone was being beaten and prayed death didn't follow. He didn't want anyone to die – if they didn't have to.

Emily's face blanched and she put her hands over her ears to stifle the noise and stepped behind Frank. She wrapped her arms around him and cupped Benji's ears to keep him from the horror of what was going on.

Yancy put on the hood they'd given him and stayed well away from the action. He didn't know why, but it was where he preferred to be.

When the first fist struck Samuel's damned perfect face, it sounded good and felt right, like it was his own fist and filled with jealousy and anger. But as it continued, he took a step back, and another, until he could no longer see the bloody work the Legion was engaged in. He could hear it, though, and no longer wanted any part of what he'd set in motion.

What in God's name have I done? No. What in the devil's name have I done?

Yancy peered behind him to see how far away the horses grazed and wondered if he could make it to them without being seen, without being caught by the very men he'd conned into coming.

He decided to run and had turned when a heavy hand landed on his shoulder.

"Forget something, mister?"

The skull and crossbones on the man's mask leered at him, and tremors crawled down his spine.

"Just checking the mares. That's all."

"You'll want to get a punch in. That's for sure."

With a hand under Yancy's elbow, he propelled him to where Samuel was in the process of losing his life. He could no longer stand, let alone fight back, and two men lifted him so Yancy could throw his punch.

"All men participate – *all,*" Longstreet hissed. "We're waiting on you."

Yancy's Adam's apple jumped, and he yanked his arm from the hand holding it. He didn't know who it was, hadn't recognized the voice, but they all sounded different behind their masks. They acted different, too, with their faces covered, as if they were deities, pagan gods who ruled but were themselves never governed by anyone. The evil they embodied terrified him, and in the moment, he wasn't sure he'd survive this day any better than Samuel.

"Let's get it done, Nancy. That a more fitting name?"

He made a fist and shoved it into Samuel's weakened flesh. It sunk in like he had no muscle, no bone, and Yancy's stomach turned. He swallowed back the bile and turned to leave, but a hand stopped him.

"You call that a punch? This is a punch." Knuckles crunched against the side of Samuel's face, and they let him slide to the ground.

What hell have I created? If I die, I deserve it.

He watched them swing Samuel into the clearing like a lumpy sack of grain, heard him thump to the ground, and ran off. Without looking back, he mounted his mare and rode her into the gloom of the darkening woods. If they shot him in the back, he didn't care. He'd botched everything.

From a distance, he heard a shot, then another, but couldn't make himself turn around and do anything about it. He'd caused it. What could he do? They were right; Nancy was a fitting name.

At the side window, Frank had seen the hooded men carry a man by the arms and legs and swing him back and forth like girls with a jump rope before letting go. The body landed with a sickening thud, and the men quickly retreated to the safety of the trees.

He was a black man, of course, but so bloodied and bruised it would have been hard to tell if he hadn't known. But the men behind the treehouse had claimed Legion, and they would not slay a white man. Dark splotches seeped through his clothes, and he lay where he landed, a discarded heap.

Near the edge of the clearing, he lay as still as death.

Chapter Twenty-eight

Abby's horrified shriek ripped the air as she tore unrestrained through the brush and woods to the body, knowing it was Samuel the moment her mind let her believe it. Nothing could keep her from his side, not even fear of a bullet. It could take her with him.

"Abby! Get back here," Benjamin screamed. "Charles! Grab her before she gets shot."

She threw herself at the pulpy mass on the ground, collapsing over him to shield him from more harm.

Samuel's body had been tossed near where Charles hid, and it only took a few steps for him to reach her, but she would not be pulled away. He tugged, yanked and cajoled, but she wouldn't let go.

Giving in, yet not willing to leave her, he hunkered down next to them to make a smaller target should they decide to shoot and hoped, if it truly was Legion out there, they might think him a white man and let him live.

The smell of his false breath hung around him, and the odor of turncoat seeped from his pores. He had smelled it before. It wasn't the first time in his life he'd been content his black heritage stayed hidden beneath his pale skin. But he detested his failed courage.

"We need to get out of here, Abby," he begged. "You can't help him now."

"I'm not leaving him." Her nostrils flared in anger, and she glared at the woods where the men hid. "Cowards!" she screamed. "Damned monsters!"

Charles felt the anguish pour from her soul and reverberate through his body, forcing tears to well up in his own dark eyes. He wrapped them both in his arms, held tight, and prayed for some guardian angel to protect them.

Furious now, Benjamin bellowed. ""Frank! Give up! You can't win this."

A shot rang out and others followed, zinging through the branches and slamming into trees with solid thunks.

Sheriff Hicks leaped from his mount and threw the reins over a branch. He bent forward at the waist as bullets flew overhead and sped in the direction of the voices. He came up behind Benjamin and put a hand on his shoulder, startling him.

"Damn. I could've shot you, Hicks!"

"But you didn't. Give me details, Ben."

He explained how he'd sent four of his men to circle Frank's fortress and that they'd seen Benji and Emily up there with Frank.

"Emily?"

Benjamin nodded and pointed to Charles, Abby, and the body in the clearing. He figured it had to be Samuel.

"Damn it to hell. Are they alright? Who the hell is responsible for that? Not Frank."

"Don't know. Somebody over there, behind the fortress. I heard a voice but don't know it. Black Legion, they said."

"How in hell did they get involved?"

"Again, I don't know. I'd just be making guesses."

"Terry here?" Hicks asked, letting his gaze roam the circle of the trees.

"Haven't seen him."

"Odd, that. Edna told me Yancy's the one who spotted Frank and Emily with the baby out here sometime early this morning. Where's he now?"

"Haven't seen him either."

Hicks racked the lever on his rifle and pounded a fist over his heart like he was trying to help it beat or restart it. "Stay put," he said and moved out of the tree line so Frank could see him.

"Frank. This is Sheriff Hicks. I'm told you have Benji in there. Leave him inside with your wife and come on out and talk."

"Go to hell, Hicks." He shoved the end of his rifle through the crack in the partially opened door and fired a shot over the sheriff's head.

"Aw, Frank. You don't want to shoot at me." He lowered his head and it swung back and forth as if he was a disappointed father. "Just tell us how we can get Benji back to his momma and poppa without anyone getting hurt. Come on now, Frank."

"Next one won't be over your head, Hicks. Back off. This isn't your fight."

Hicks ambled back into the woods, unwilling to show fear by a quick retreat, and removed his hat, slapping it against his leg in frustration. For the moment, he was stymied. He squatted next to Benjamin and laid out different semi-plausible scenarios, none of which had much likelihood of success.

Benjamin pulled at his lip in thought.

"What about this? I slip through the woods until I'm at the back of the fortress, climb the tree and come up under the balcony. He won't see me if I come from behind. I can slip over the balcony and get in the door before he even knows I'm there."

"Couple things wrong with your plan. First, unless they lied, the Black Legion men have that area of the woods. They'll likely get you before you can get where you're going. You see what they did out there." He pointed to the man Abby and Charles were slowly dragging toward the cover of the woods. "Second, you'll die by Frank's gun as soon as you open the door. If you corner him, he'll shoot you."

Benjamin cursed and clenched his fist.

"Then somebody follows right behind me. They get to Frank before he can rack another bullet. They grab Benji and run like hell."

Hicks shook his head. "Ain't gonna work. Two dead men?" He pointed to the body in the clearing. "Maybe three. Not on my watch. Settle down and let's think this through. If Frank keeps wasting shots, maybe he'll run out of ammo. I don't think he really wants to shoot anybody or he would've by now. He's a crack shot, so he could. At least, that's the man I used to know."

Still squatting, Benjamin shifted and dropped his other knee to the ground. He was frustrated and didn't want to wait any longer. He wanted action. Needed it, now.

Dusk darkened the forest quicker than the sky, and waiting grew more difficult as the temperature dropped. A moan came from where Abby and Charles hid with Samuel, and heads lifted, eager to think he was alive. It prompted Hicks to call out.

"I'm going over to see to the wounded man, Frank. Hold your fire unless you want me to burn down your house."

Frank shot again and then set the rifle in a corner and pulled Benji from the sling. He handed the wailing baby to Emily, shrugged out of the fabric sling and picked up the rifle. He loaded several more bullets into it and shook the box to see how many he had left.

"Fix him a bottle. Might keep him quiet for a bit," he told Emily.

"Give him up, Frank. End this - this nonsense - before anybody else gets hurt. Please, do this for me."

"I'm not giving my son away. You do what I said."

Frank opened the door enough to duck his head out and be able to shoot if necessary. His eyes were glued on Sheriff Hicks as he walked toward the wounded man.

He stepped out and shot in front of the sheriff, and moss and damp dirt sprayed into the air and clung to Hicks' trousers. They eyed each other, motionless.

Inside, Emily had wrapped Benji in the sling and tied it around her neck. She didn't know exactly how it should work, but he hung safely against her belly and she only needed one free hand to steady her as she climbed down the ladder.

She thrust back her shoulders, said a prayer, and passed behind Frank without breathing. Her feet were on the first rung of the ladder before he bellowed and pointed the rifle at them. She tripped down several rungs, banged her shins and fumbled her grasp before her shoes grabbed a solid perch and a hand gripped the rung in front of her face. She squeezed Benji tight against her chest.

"You'll hit the baby, Frank. Don't shoot."

He roared his fury, and Emily expected to get a bullet in the middle of her forehead at any second. He was a marksman. He could do it, and his anger was such she believed he would if it wasn't for fear of hitting Benji.

"Damn you, you Jezebel, stealing my son!" he screamed, spittle flying from his lips. "Damn you to hell. Never trust a woman, son! Don't trust anybody!"

When her foot hit firm ground, she spun on it and ran as hard and fast as she could. She felt a hot, searing pain as the bullet bit into her back, and she went down. Frank, right behind her, tossed her off Benji like an enemy corpse, grabbed his son, still tucked into the fabric sling, and sat in the dirt, one hand on the baby and one on the rifle.

Unchecked tears streamed down his face and leaked from his chin, and his shoulders trembled with sobs. He murmured the foreign words of his lullaby over and over in between cursing Emily for her treachery and damning her for making him shoot her.

"It's all your fault. Damn you, woman! Why'd you make me do that?"

Hicks ran back to stop Betty from rushing headlong into Frank's bullet and shoved her over to her husband. "Hold on to her," he said.

Benji lay kicking and screaming on Frank's lap, right next to the rifle, Frank's hands on both.

"You just hang on for a minute. Don't need any more bullet holes," Hicks told Benjamin and Betty. "I mean it, Benjamin. You want your son alive, you do what I say."

Benjamin's look was murderous, but he obeyed.

Hicks quieted for a moment, watched Frank with the baby, and pondered the safest move. He sauntered out to where Abby and Charles sat with Samuel.

"When I'm ready, Abby, come out. I'm gonna need your help."

"With what? Samuel needs me . . ."

She hated the Black Legion with a fury she'd never before known and would put a bullet into them herself if she had a gun and the opportunity. Without hesitation, without sorrow, without regret – she'd kill them, and she ardently wished for the chance. At this very moment.

Hicks eyed her, hard, and both sets of eyes locked. Hicks broke it first.

"Frank isn't gonna let black folks near him, let alone help with that baby. And he still has his gun." He nodded his head to the woods behind the clearing. "Don't forget who's out there. Want Betty and Benjamin out here in the cleared area being Legion targets?"

The air went out of her, and she deflated. Too much was happening, and she needed to get help for Samuel, lie down next to him and keep him warm.

"You could just shoot him." She heard her own words, recoiled from them and wondered briefly who she had become.

He cocked his head and stared at her.

"Blood and fear changes people. When I give you the nod, walk my way, slowly." The Sheriff called to Frank, "I'm gonna come over and talk to you, Frank. And see to Emily's wound. See if you need help with your baby. Is he okay?"

"I swear to God I'll shoot you all," Frank sobbed, and squeezed Benji to his chest with one hand and held the rifle with the other, swinging it around him in a circle.

Hicks moved toward him like he had all day and murmured quiet words of comfort.

Blood poured from Emily's chest, but she was alive, for the moment, and Hicks turned her over so he could see where the bullet went in. He pushed his hands over both entry and exit wounds to staunch the massive flow of blood.

"I'm gonna get Abby out here to help me, Frank. Is that alright with you? Your wife needs help."

When Frank didn't scream obscenities at him, he dipped his head to Abby who mimicked the sheriff's easy stroll as she moved toward them. She knelt by Emily, blanched when she saw the amount of blood – and the sheriff's eyes.

"I need fabric, something to stuff in the holes and wrap around her. Got anything?"

She slid off her petticoat, ripped it into strips, and helped bind Emily's wounds, while keeping her eyes on Frank and his gun as well as watching Charles with Samuel. Benji's screams filled the clearing, and Frank grew more and more agitated.

After she'd done all she could for Emily, her efforts turned toward Frank. Intent on the squalling baby on his lap, he no longer seemed to be aware of his surroundings, and she didn't want to divert his attention to anyone else, especially with the rifle at his fingertips.

"Can I help you, Frank?" she asked, her voice buttery, like she had asked if he wanted sugar and cream with his coffee. She sat next to him, eyeing the rifle balanced on his legs.

He shook his head at her offer of help and tugged at the gown Benji wore.

"Benji's fine, Frank. You see there's no blood on him. He's just upset and cold. Why don't I wrap him up for you?"

Frank jerked the baby to his chest and glared at her, and the rifle wobbled and tipped to the ground. He didn't notice and let it lay.

"Don't think I don't know what you're doing. He's mine. You can't take him."

Benji settled down as soon as his flailing fists came into contact with Frank's beard, and his sobs soon turned into hiccups. Frank patted his back, chanted his alien song, and rocked back and forth, a strange drop of serenity in the middle of chaos.

His mind didn't comprehend his wounded wife or the beaten man. His eyes saw what he wanted to perceive and nothing else. He heard the baby's soft gurgle of contentment, felt him relax into his chest, and his fear ebbed.

Abby waited for Frank's eyes to show some of the same quietude as Benji while glancing furtively toward Samuel. Time crawled while his life force drained, and she couldn't wait any longer. She let her hand settle on his rifle, told him she wanted to see to the wounded man and stood holding the rifle as if it was hers.

She handed it to Hicks who smiled at her, and he left them in the middle of the clearing while he strolled over to Benjamin and Betty.

"Everybody stays put," he told them. "I'll let you know when it's safe to come out. I'm going to look for the Legion, see if they're still over there." He handed Frank's rifle to Benjamin.

"Just stand here and wait?" he asked. "Just watch him with our son?"

"You heard me. If the Legion is still around, they'll happily pick you off one by one."

Benjamin held the man's own rifle trained on him as he sat in the clearing and held their son. The whole scene was ludicrous, macabre, and he wouldn't hesitate to shoot, almost wishing Frank would give him a reason. He had put them through all kinds of hell for a long time, and from this close range, he wouldn't miss. Benjamin hid his grief down deep in his bones, but it lived.

Frank had no cognizance of what was going on around him, of the gun aimed at his back, of the men moving into the clearing after the sheriff's 'all clear' nod. Nothing registered but the baby.

"Let's get this done," Shorty said, in his throaty whisper. "I can take Samuel on my mount. The sheriff can take Mrs. Adams. You guys figure out how to deal with Frank and Benji."

"I'll walk," Charles said. "We don't have enough mounts, so they can take my mare. I'll get the horses."

An odd disquiet fell around them. The lack of angry shouting and hostile gunfire left a void that seemed to collapse in on itself. Their nerves jumped and they looked over their shoulders like they were unsure this new peace was real or that it would continue, and they couldn't help wondering if fresh misery lurked in the darkening forest.

In the woods across the clearing, the Black Legion had watched events unfold from behind the shelter of the trees and left well before Sheriff Hicks came looking.

"We seem to be short a man," Longstreet said.

"Not sure I'd call him that," Foster said.

Terry met up with them when they were astride their mounts and heading out the way they'd come in. They filled him in on what they'd witnessed and shrugged when he asked questions.

"We don't know much of anything," Rumford said. "Came to protect your pa is all. He's sitting out there in the dirt with a black baby. Don't know anything beyond that. Think he shot your ma, but she's alive for now."

"Damned old fool!"

"Oh, yeah. And Moore's a bit bad off."

"What happened to him?"

"He got in the way," Longstreet said.

The look on Longstreet's face turned Terry's stomach. His eyes closed, and he wished he could leave them shut and sleep for a long time. He was tired. Inside and out.

He'd followed the wrong trail all the way to the other side of the forest until the tracks finally curved around to this spot. But that wasn't what made him tired. He didn't understand what in hell was going on or what his old man was doing. Didn't think he wanted to.

"Get on out of here," he told the men with a groan and a wave of his hand like they were annoying gnats. "Take the back way to the west edge of the forest. We never talked."

When the men were well out of sight, he continued on the trail, leading his mare. Once in the clearing, he saw his mother lying motionless in the sheriff's arms, and tears stung his eyes. He swiped at his face, irritated at himself.

Hicks called him over, wanting to ask the man a bunch of questions, wanting to know where the hell he'd been and if he'd seen the Legion men since he came the back way through the woods. He supposed they were long gone. That was their way, hit and run; kill and vanish. Cowards.

He stared at Terry as if he could see the answers in his eyes. He understood now wasn't the time, but he'd damn well ask another day.

"About time you got here. Climb on your horse. I'm gonna put her into your arms. Get her to the doc. If Williams isn't around, take her to Cassandra's house and don't waste time. She's in bad shape."

Terry looked at his pa sitting on the ground holding a colored baby. He opened his mouth to ask a question and the sheriff shook his head and handed Emily up to him. She didn't weigh much now, not like she used to when she had three sons and a husband to cook and care for. A farm and grandchildren. Events had conspired to make her lose sleep and weight, and maybe life, itself.

"Come on, Ma," Terry whispered and he settled her on his lap. "We'll get you fixed up. Hang on." He headed toward the shortest route to a road, knowing where he was now. "We'll get you help, Ma. Don't die on me. Please?"

She groaned and tried to sit. The voice she heard was one of her son's, and she needed to speak with him. Tell him everything would be alright.

"Don't move, Ma. Hold still." His words croaked through moisture clogging the back of his throat, and he wondered when he'd become such a crybaby. When did he start wanting his momma?

"I need you to help me out, Ma. I'm gonna get you to the doc, and he'll fix you. But you gotta help me. Don't die."

Tears fell unchecked down his cheeks and fell onto his mother's hands where they lay clasped on her stomach. She reached for his face and tried to wipe away the tears as she'd been doing her entire life.

Back in the clearing, Sheriff Hicks and Charles lifted Samuel's long body as high as they could, trying to get him up on the tall gelding. In the saddle, Shorty ended it by grabbing him around the chest and dragging him into the cradle of his lap and arms. Samuel groaned with the painful effort.

"Sorry, old boy. Hurts like hell. Believe me, I know."

"I'm coming with you. Wait." Abby ran to her mare and threw a leg over the saddle.

"You're good here, right?" she asked Hicks.

Somehow, events had settled into a strange normalcy, and their relief made them want to laugh or tell a stupid joke. Lives still hung balanced between this world and the next, a baby was still wrapped in the arms of an old man who claimed to be his father, and Benjamin still pointed a gun at his back . . . but the safety had been flicked on. And that was everything.

"Between Benjamin, Betty, Charles, Jesse and me," Hicks said, "I think we can handle Frank with a baby instead of a gun in his hands."

She mimicked the smirk Hicks gave her, not feeling his levity through her worry, and prodded her nimble mare to catch up with Shorty and Samuel who followed a short way behind Terry.

The rising moon shed light on the blonde back end of Terry's sorrel, and they kept pace so they didn't lose their way in the shadowed woods. The back and forth swish of her tail called to them like a beacon for a ship on a dark sea.

"Must be why God made sorrels," Shorty said.

Abby nodded, even knowing he couldn't see her, but she couldn't respond with words. She was busy trying to stem the surge of tears.

When she tried to loosen her tight throat to speak, water rolled from her eyes, and she didn't have the energy or ability to stop the tide. She didn't need to. It was dark and she rode alone.

She licked her lips and tasted salt, inhaled and the scent of Samuel settled on her tongue, bay rum and blood. Abby choked and tried to pray.

They made the long trek back to town with their wounded, leaving the healthy to resolve the mess in the woods.

Chapter Twenty-nine

Charles and Jesse headed into the woods and found the mares where they'd been left to graze.

Betty moved to sit by Frank and her son, her eyes taking in every single inch of Benji and doing her best not to grab him and run. Hicks had explained – very clearly – what she needed to do, and how she needed to treat him. She twisted her fingers in her lap to keep them busy.

Eventually he quit glaring at her every time she mentioned Benji's name. He even let her touch him as long as he was the one who held him.

"I have a baby, too, Frank," she said. "A little boy."

He tilted his head to stare at her, engaged by the thought that she might understand him if she was a parent, too.

He squinted his eyes and noted the deep russet skin, much like his son's. The girl seemed especially dark in the low light of the deepening sky. He let his eyes roam to her lips, her nose, her tightly curled hair, and looked at the baby on his lap.

"You do?"

She nodded. "Surely do. Looks a lot like yours."

"I was gonna ask you that. Must be a beautiful boy, then."

"He is."

"Where is he right now?"

"At home. Want to go see my baby, Frank? Maybe they can be friends. Yours and mine."

He wiggled his bottom on the ground. "It is getting cold, now. We should go home."

Betty prayed he wouldn't look up and see his treehouse, prayed he had forgotten all about it.

"We can ride double, if you want. I'll ride in front and hold your baby for you. That way you'll know he's safe. Alright with you?"

He grunted when he stood up, stiff with cold and age, and his back bent.

She called to the others. "Benjamin, let's go home. I'll ride with Frank."

Sheriff Hicks moved fast before Frank changed his mind. Betty had been gaining his confidence, but he knew Frank's fragile mind could snap in a breath and was glad to see Charles and Jesse coming up with the rest of the horses.

He grabbed the reins of one, helped Betty and Frank on and handed Benji over, surprised Frank hadn't roared his displeasure. Was he tired out? Coming to his senses? He didn't know what would happen when they got back to town, but they were moving in the right direction and a little calm was good.

"Wait," Frank yelled, and everybody froze in fear. "Get Matilda. She's behind the house."

"Hope that's a horse, Frank," Hicks said, not quite joking.

"Course it is. Think I've got a woman hidden out there?"

Frank shook his head and wrinkled his forehead like Hicks had lost his mind, and it made them all chuckle at the incongruity of some truths.

Benjamin slid off the back of Jesse's mount and ran back to the clearing and into the woods behind it. He came out leading Frank's mare, climbed on, and the odd company ambled through the woods.

"Day couldn't get any stranger," Jesse said.

"That's a fact," Charles said. "I couldn't write it and be convincing."

"What do you think happened to Frank?"

Charles shrugged and stared at the old man a moment before he expressed an opinion in a hushed voice.

"In tragedies, a typical fatal flaw is the unrestrained need for power."

Jesse's eyes went blank. "Huh?"

"Haven't you read Macbeth?"

Jesse shook his head.

"Any of Shakespeare's other tragedies?"

Benjamin, riding next to them, said he had read them all and agreed it was possible. Power could be Frank's fatal flaw.

He'd relaxed enough to listen to their conversation but hadn't participated for fear of missing an opportunity to shoot Frank, except his wife and son were right there in front of the old man so that was out of the question. Eventually, even that desire dissipated, and, as he watched them, he began to feel a hint of something close to compassion. He couldn't go as far as empathy. Who could feel the common thread of empathy when your baby is the crown he craves?

The rifle he held was still pointed at Frank's back.

Hicks nudged his mare closer to Frank and Betty and let his mind deliberate. She'd been right all along; Benji was alive and in the woods. She'd told him.

Mothering was something else...

And what about Frank? What had he been doing up in a tree with a baby? He smiled at the whole idea because it was one of those tales nobody would believe, not even if you were completely sober when you told it.

Still, when he retired, he was gonna write a book. This day would take up at least two chapters. He shook his head and rubbed his chest

Al waited on the porch and ran down the steps to take Benji from Betty's hands. Frank didn't howl in anger, and Betty slid from the horse, hugged her friend, and retrieved her baby.

When they went inside, Cassandra met them with two steaming teapots. Hicks raised his eyebrows, but didn't bother to ask. Over the years, he'd gotten used to her merely showing up when she was needed.

Her clowder prowled the bar, lining it with feline mystery. She handed a cup of tea to Frank and watched him drink it down. From the second pot, she poured for the others. Shorty went behind the bar and added something stiffer to the teacups.

"Sheriff, show Mr. Adams to his room. He'll sleep for a good twelve hours." Cassandra waved to the stairs and called to her cats.

"I'll be back in the morning to figure this all out," Hicks said when he returned. "Keep Frank in his room, if you can. Samuel and Mrs. Adams are heading for your house, Cassandra. They need help, badly."

"Yes."

Hicks twisted his hat. Sometimes the woman got to him with her mysterious manner.

"Will you be there to help them?" he asked, trying to nudge her home.

"Of course."

Sometimes he wanted to shock her.

Some day he would.

Shorty and Abby turned down Cassandra's lane, while Terry went on down the road, probably headed to Doc's. Abby called to him, but he either didn't hear or didn't care.

Shorty slid from his horse with Samuel in his arms like he carried full grown men every day of the week, and Abby followed, glued to his side. Cassandra, having gotten there first, met them at the door and had beds already prepared in the back of her living area.

"Don't hurt him, Shorty," Abby said through the clog in her throat.

He placed Samuel on the bed and glanced up, wondering how in hell he could help *her*.

"We're tough. Lord gave us strong bodies, strong wills," he said, wrapping an arm around her.

She squeezed him back and bent to touch Samuel's face with feather-light fingers, trying to force the bruises to heal with her own strength and the ferocity of what she felt for him. Placing an obviously broken hand on the sheet beside him, she chewed her lip and cursed her lack of knowledge.

"Help me, Cassandra. What should I do?" Abby said, and looked for her, but she was pushing Shorty out the door.

"Go track down Emily."

Shorty didn't flinch, didn't ask the healer how she knew what she knew, just turned and went to do her bidding.

Terry hadn't gotten far down the road before he caught up to him.

"Why not bring her to Cassandra? Quicker," he said. "And you don't even know if the doc is in town."

Terry shrugged and turned his mare around. At Cassandra's door, Shorty dismounted, and Terry handed his mother to the big man who had every reason to dislike him and none to be kind. But he was, and Terry had the good sense to recognize it.

Cassandra's home was a long, single room that served as kitchen and living space and was filled with too many plants to count on a variety of shelves in front of huge windows. Like she was a baby, Shorty carried the wounded woman to a bed beside Samuel. A yellow and orange flowered screen separated the two patients.

"Cut her dress off, Abby, while I help Shorty with Samuel," Cassandra said. "Mr. Adams, pour hot water into the teapot on the table and more into the two basins. Bring them down here."

He obeyed without question and the room filled with the singular scent of lavender and an aromatic combination of Cassandra's herbs. He carried the teapot into the room, put it on the table at the end of his mother's bed, and went back for the basins.

When Samuel was ready, Shorty propped him on a pillow while Abby spooned tea between his lips. As much drizzled into the towel below his chin as went in, but, while he hadn't spoken or opened his eyes, he seemed to understand he needed whatever it was she was giving him and tried to swallow through the pain.

Cassandra sang as she worked and Terry raised his eyebrows at her words.

Bilberry for troubled immunity.

Comfrey for tissues and broken bones.

Burdock for liver, lungs and kidneys.

Lavender just because.

"I learned it as a song from my grandmama, Mr. Adams. I was very young and found it easier to remember as a song. Are you distressed by my methods?"

He shook his troubled head and raised his hands, palms out like he was warding off trouble. "How can I help."

"You can spoon the rest of the tea into Samuel while Abby helps me wash up your mother."

She knew she had asked him for the moon. She intended to because the room held more than wounded bodies; some suffered injury to their spirit. Terry would have to find the moon, reach for it, and give them all pieces. He owed it.

After he'd spooned the rest of the cup into Samuel, she handed him an oddly shaped object and pointed to a nine-inch square she'd laid on the table.

"Grind it up fine with the mortar and pestle, Mr. Adams, and spoon it onto this piece of linen. We'll soak it in a little hot water and make a poultice."

Terry didn't speak. Instead, he put all his angst into pulverizing the comfrey root. When the bowl was half filled with what looked like meal particles, he put it in front of Cassandra for approval and dumped it on the cloth she'd indicated. She handed him a piece of string to tie the bundle while she held the edges together.

"Good, Mr. Adams. You did fine. Soak it in the pan of hot water for one minute, please."

He didn't understand the strange woman, her bright turban, her outlandish flowing dress, or the voodoo herbs she used for medicine. But she was taking care of his mother, so what could he do but obey? And, truthfully, she went about it like she knew what she was doing.

Cassandra handed him a large piece of linen and told him to fold it several times and put the hot poultice in the middle.

"Lay it on your mothers front wound. When we have a second one made, we'll put it on the entry wound and bind them so they stay put."

Cassandra watched him deliberate, and their eyes locked for the space of a long breath. He'd barely spoken three words since handing his mother over to Cassandra's care, and she could see misgiving on his face and deep in his eyes, but he grabbed another piece of comfrey root, held it up for her approval, and began grinding.

She tried not to smile until he turned his back.

It was alright to question. One should, and Cassandra didn't mind that he gave second thoughts to her healing methods. A son should worry about the care of his mother, and she wondered if this was the first time he had. If so, it was well past time, and she could tell Terry was unused to how it felt or how he should go about it.

Emily moaned when he turned her onto her side so he could apply the poultice to her back. Cassandra appeared with several long strips of white cloth which she wrapped around Emily's chest and shoulder to keep the two poultices in place.

"Sorry, Ma," he whispered into her hair. "It'll just be for a minute." His head swiveled to Cassandra in fear. "She's got a fever! She's burning up!"

"I expect so, Mr. Adams."

"Terry, damn it. I'm just Terry."

"She's been shot in a vital place, Mr. Adams. Her body is working to repair itself. It is making heat."

Terry huffed out a frustrated breath and held his mother up while Cassandra wrapped and wrapped. It took forever, and his arms began to shake from the stress of holding her while trying not to cause her pain. She was white as the linen when they were finished and propped on her side against a pillow.

"What now?" he asked.

"Now you spoon some of this tea into her. It will help her sleep and boost her immune system." Cassandra shined a smile at him. "And it will do all of those other things I was singing about."

Terry pulled up a chair and tilted his mother's head so the liquid would find its way to her stomach. The spoon felt awkward not heading to his own mouth, and he couldn't remember ever doing it before this day – not even with his own boys when they were babies. Cecily always fed them.

He opened the towel wider to catch drips he made on the way to her mouth and sighed with relief when some of it went where he intended. He put the cup on the table and stretched, rubbed his neck and swiveled his head. His back cracked and snapped with the movement.

"How much should I give her?"

"The whole cup. More is best."

He sat back down in his chair and, before picking up the cup, brushed limp gray strands of her hair away from her face. He tucked it behind one ear and smoothed it back from her forehead.

"Frank," she murmured. "You're home." Her voice was a mere whisper, a sigh, a silent prayer.

Terry didn't correct her. Back and forth his hand went, growing more adept with each effort, spooning in the liquid he prayed would sustain his mother's life.

Cassandra peered at them as she moved between the two patients and thought Mr. Adams' whispered words may have been a good sign.

In the kitchen, Shorty was using the mortar and pestle to make poultices for Samuel while Abby spooned more tea into his mouth.

"Shorty," Cassandra said. "Let Abby finish making the poultice. I need you with Samuel and me."

Abby didn't like leaving him but did as she was told, and, when she was out of sight, Cassandra cut the clothes from Samuel, and her eyes widened when she saw the bruising all over his body. Shorty groaned and his fists clenched.

Deep purple marks covered Samuel's chest, stomach and back. His legs were spotted with bruises, and ugly lacerations ran along his shin bones where leather and buckles had met thin skin-covered bone.

"I'm going to use some pressure on his torso, Shorty, to determine internal injuries. Keep him secure, as he may likely fight."

Cassandra pressed fingers over his abdomen and ribs and felt for swollen internal organs, doing her best to keep her face immobile as she noted the damage they had done to her would-be son.

His kidneys were bruised and enlarged, ribs broken, and one hand crushed, and those were the highlights. She had no way of knowing what had been done to the inside of his head.

"We'll need cold poultices for his wounds, not hot. Abby," she called, pulling up the sheet over Samuel. "Bring water from the well. Cold as you can get."

Shorty went back to pounding the pestle.

"Don't break the bowl, Shorty," Cassandra said trying to get a small smile from the big man. "You've been where he is, and he'll survive, too."

But this time she wasn't sure, and she wished her spirit, her life-force, allowed for hatred.

They made cold compresses with the pulverized herbs, and when they were ready, Cassandra called Terry to help.

"He's too heavy for one, Mr. Adams."

He flinched at her formal address, confused by her persistence in using it, but he didn't correct her this time.

She drew the sheet down and watched Terry's eyes take in the damage. The three of them stood motionless, waiting for one of them to speak or move or do something.

Cassandra would have liked to preserve Samuel's dignity by partially covering him, but he was a lesson, and she would use what she had available.

"Shorty, Mr. Adams, lift him while I wrap this linen around his ribs, then turn him on his side, and we'll place the cold poultices. They'll need to be changed when they grow warm. Ready?"

They gathered in the kitchen when Cassandra called to them and gave specific instructions for each patient.

"Sleep in shifts. Keep the poultices either hot or cold depending on the patient, pour a cup of tea down them every hour or so."

"Are you leaving?" Abby asked, fear icing her words and perspiration beading her upper lip, as Cassandra glided to the door. "Where are you going?"

"Looking for my clowder. I miss my babies."

"Cassandra," Abby called as she stepped out the door following her. "Does Samuel have any family here? Somebody we should get in touch with?" She rubbed at her neck and tugged the long braid hanging over her shoulder. "I can't believe I never asked. What kind of friend doesn't ask about family?"

"We are his family, girl. It's everything he wanted us to know."

Cassandra went into the night, guided by the moon she'd asked Terry to give her. It had already stolen the sky and now trekked to the other side of the world, so she knew midnight had passed. Sleep didn't call to her, but the night creatures did, and she talked with them as she moved down her path to the edge of the lake where her clowder waited.

She picked up a long branch and began her own trek, digging at the mud with her walking stick, pulling roots and saving them in the sack hanging from her shoulder.

Her name was healer, but this is what she embodied – the night, the felines, the solitude, the communion with earth and sky and beyond. She raised her hands to the stars and her robed silhouette splashed an image on the still water. The twin form could have been witch or wayward spirit or angel with flowing sleeves as wings and stick as shepherd's crook.

She smiled at the image and took a cleansing breath of the coming winter air.

Chapter Thirty

Thick frost clung to individual blades of grass and twinkled like fallen stars in the early sunlight. The weak light of morning, when winter battled with fall for a hold on the earth, spent long moments turning rime to liquid.

Cecily slid her feet into tall boots and gazed out the window at the white that would soon be snow. She shivered, as much from her thoughts as the cold. Terry hadn't come home after traipsing off into the woods to find his mother and father, and she didn't know if Yancy had returned or not. She had no idea what was happening.

She closed her eyes and banged her forehead against the window pane until it rattled. She could have married the Baldwin hardware store owner's son. She could have been taking care of a mansion – well, maybe not a mansion, but a big house, one that didn't sit next to a barn full of cows and chickens, one that didn't house a bunch of crazy people.

She snorted and didn't bother to look around to see if anyone heard it. No one was here but her and her sons, and they were asleep. She grabbed a barn coat and shuffled out into the cold, her boots making shapes in the undisturbed frost.

She slid the door open and peered into the semi-darkness, hoping to see someone milking cows, but she knew better. Cecily dumped the entire bucket of chicken feed onto the ground outside and brought in the first heifer.

When she sat on her three-legged stool, she heard a man's groan and fell backwards into the straw. She lay frozen in irrational fear, telling herself to stop being a fool, but it wasn't working. Footsteps moved her way, and

Yancy's scruffy face appeared above her, shadowed by the feeble light from the open door.

"Hello. Waiting for me?" he said, his lips curved in a lecherous grin.

"Geez, Yancy. You scared me half to death. Why didn't you say something?"

"Who else you waiting for in the barn?"

"Nobody. I thought I was alone."

Yancy rubbed a hand through his straw littered hair and over his two-day beard.

"Haven't been here long. Took forever finding my way through the woods in the dark." He nodded at the empty horse stall. "Terry not back yet?"

"No. Didn't you meet up? Bring them home?"

He didn't know what to say. Didn't know how much to tell her about what had happened in the woods. He wasn't even sure how the whole thing had ended. He'd run off before then, before he'd been forced to take a stand one way or another.

"Didn't see him. You go on and do your calves. I'll milk."

"But, what about Frank and Emily? What's going on, Yancy? Tell me."

He righted the stool and sat. He didn't want to answer any questions, didn't even want to think about the night. It needed to go away. Maybe he needed to go away, too.

She pushed her hand at his shoulder to get him to look at her. She wanted answers, and he wasn't giving any.

"I don't know anything, Cecily."

"You serious?"

Cecily scrutinized him as she did her chores. He hadn't flirted with her since his first hello, and she figured that was just reflex, what he did without thinking or even wanting to. He hadn't attempted to kiss her or anything. Something was off. She tried to concentrate on the chores but her imagination took over and forced her to glance at Yancy and then bite her tongue.

Terry walked into a stony silence, and Cecily ran to throw her arms around him.

"What's going on? Where's your ma and pa? I thought you'd be bringing them home."

He told what he knew and eyed Yancy when he said he hadn't made it back to the woods where Frank held them all off with a rifle.

"The Legion made it, thanks to you, and Samuel paid the price for their attendance. You didn't know anything about that?"

"No," Yancy said, feigning horror. "What do you mean he paid? What'd they do to him?"

Terry's eyes squinted as if they could determine truth by narrowing to tiny slits. He didn't believe Yancy, not the least iota, but couldn't figure why he'd lie about any of it. Something stunk, and it wasn't the manure.

"They beat him pretty bad, and Ma has a bullet wound thanks to Pa, the crazy bastard."

Cecily visualized the strong farm woman brought down by a tiny bullet, and it didn't seem possible. She was tough, the real rock of the family.

"Is she gonna be okay? Where is she?"

"Cassandra's house, and we don't know. She's running a bad fever. I came home to see about chores and to get some clean clothes. We're taking care of both of them there in her parlor."

"Both?" Yancy said, oddly disgruntled.

"Yeah, both. Strange, huh? Sam Moore and Ma lying in side by side beds." Terry gave a hawking kind of laugh at the absurdity of the situation.

"I'm not seeing the humor, Terry. Who's taking care of him?" Yancy took a seat on the milking stool and tried to ignore Terry's words. They itched at him like a raw wool shirt on bare skin.

"Shorty and Abby, mostly. Me, too, sometimes. And I gotta get back. Tell the boys . . . uh, never mind. I'll tell em when I get back. Thanks for taking care of things here. Appreciate it."

He slapped Yancy on the shoulder and left the barn, Cecily following to grill for more information.

The heifer bellowed her displeasure at the harshness of Yancy's hand as he returned to milking, and he gentled his touch.

What'd you think, fool? You didn't want him dead. Or did you? You put him right into Abby's loving hands.

After changing clothes, Terry stopped at the barn before heading back to Cassandra's, and Yancy cringed thinking he meant to clarify events that occurred with him and the Legion. To be occupied, he continued to pull at udders that had emptied of milk.

"Strange them showing up without you," Terry said.

"Well, I told you I'd get them, and I did. And I told them where to go, just in case you all would need them."

Terry nodded and chewed at his lip. Something was off kilter, but he didn't know what.

"It's getting cold. Too cold to be sleeping out here. You can use George's old room. Or Frank's."

"Thanks." Yancy spun on the stool to watch him leave and wondered why he'd said that. Why could he sleep in the house now? A trickle of fear crawled down his spine. He no longer trusted what anyone said. People lied. He lied. The whole damned world was rotten.

Sheriff Hicks was back at the hotel before Frank awoke the next morning. He slipped into the kitchen looking for a cup of coffee and smiled when Al poured one and told him to sit.

"Breakfast is ready soon."

"Everyone still abed?" he asked.

"No. Betty came down to warm Benji's bottle."

"Frank?"

Al shook her head and moved bacon around in the skillet.

"You think I could talk to Benjamin and Betty before Frank gets up?"

"Go on up. Room's at the far end left."

He grabbed his cup and left, knocked lightly on the door, and went in following Betty's command.

She grinned at him from a seat at the table where she held her son on her lap, a bottle in his chubby hands.

"He couldn't do this when I last saw him," she said.

"Drink from a bottle?" Hicks said, confused.

"Hold it by himself, silly man."

"Ah. I see."

"I missed watching him do it for the first time."

Benjamin, sitting across from his wife, looked at them like he never wanted to quit. Never wanted to let them out of his sight. Hicks didn't know how one made that kind of look or even how to describe it, but he knew Benjamin wore it on his face.

"Glad to see Benji back in your arms, Betty. You were right all along. Hope you don't hold it against me when I didn't believe you."

"Hard to do, now I got him back." She, too, wore a peaceful expression, a little like the unknowable Mona Lisa look no man could ever make on his own face. He could only paint it on a woman. "But I did before. Hold it against you. I was more than mad at you."

"I know, and I'm sorry. My defense, and I'm not sure the word is fitting, is it's one hell of a big forest to cover, and we had no way of knowing he was even in there. We tried our best."

She peered at him from eyes that said, 'I know,' and he got the point. "What are you here for, Sheriff?"

"Frank. What to do with Frank."

Benjamin got up from his chair and pointed the sheriff to it while he perched on the edge of the bed. "He kidnapped our son, Sheriff. What do you think should happen to him?"

"He believes Benji is his."

"But he isn't."

"I know it, and you know it. He doesn't."

Benjamin squeezed his forehead between fingers and thumb and closed his eyes, trying to squeeze out the sight of the old man with his son. He wanted to be kind. He wanted to care about the old man who had stolen his baby, who had put his wife through hell, who had made him crazy with grief for both of them – but he didn't know if he could.

He might still want to kill him. Even this morning with sunlight flooding the room and Benji safe in his wife's arms, he still felt like pulling the trigger, and he didn't know what would make him stop.

"What are you trying to say, Sheriff Hicks? Let's get right down to it."

Hicks stood and went to the window looking out on the lake. A few flocks of Canada geese had put off moving south and dotted the steel gray water. He wondered how it happened the lake could look inviting in warm weather and so severe and unforgiving in cold. On a winter sunless day, it looked granite hard even before it froze. He supposed that was the way of things. Nothing is all one way or the other all the time. Not even Frank. And this morning Benjamin was a winter lake.

"It's most likely going to be up to you two what happens to Frank. We could prosecute him, but a lawyer is gonna claim he's insane and a jury will likely let him go."

He glanced from Betty to Benjamin, hoping they'd consider some of what he said.

"And it's likely true," he continued. "The insanity thing. He kind of lost control of knowing who he is and what he is. You know? Been through a bit in the last few years what with Frank Jr. pretty much exiled and George dead."

The family was a mess. He rubbed his chin and looked back out the window at the geese. He was pretty sure Frank Jr. had killed old man Tatum and skedaddled. He'd needed killing, for sure, but it was either go to jail or just go, and Frank Jr. had chosen to run.

And Betty had more than a lot tangled up with the Adams men. George and the Tatums had beaten and raped her, and George was whipping her when Al shot him dead.

Why should Betty feel generous toward George's father? Why would her husband? The whole situation smelled like dead vermin rotting in the sun, and even he didn't know which way to go or what to do with Frank. It rankled, and he was kind of hoping they'd figure it out for him.

Benjamin's skin prickled and itched, and he felt the need to get on with it. "Sheriff, what do you want from us?"

Betty moved to his side. "Yes. What *do* you want?"

Hicks groaned. "I don't know. I confoundedly do not know. At first blush, it's unseemly not to put a kidnapper in jail. What he did was wrong and hurtful, but putting Frank there seems wrong, too. You get what I mean?"

He was begging for some understanding, but didn't see it reflected in Benjamin's eyes. Only Betty's.

"And if Mrs. Adams dies? What then? Still feel the same about Frank if he killed his wife?" Benjamin said.

He thought taking his son was right up there with murder. But Benji was back with them now. You don't get to come back when you're dead. And he didn't want to think the decision to prosecute or not had anything to do with color. Then again, he wasn't sure.

Hicks moved to Benjamin's side and put a hand on his shoulder.

"I kinda do, Benjamin. The man isn't right in the head. People like him are babies. They can't be expected to know right from wrong. Leastwise, that's how I see it. And I don't think his bullet was meant to kill Emily. It was to save his son."

"Well, I pray she makes it. She was doing a good thing grabbing Benji . . . trying to bring him back to us. Guess I could try to have a little charity. I'll think about it."

Betty put Benji over a shoulder and walked the room with him, patting his back and feeling like he'd never been gone, and at the same time like he'd been gone forever.

"Have you heard how they are today?"

"Samuel and Mrs. Adams? Not yet. I'm heading to Cassandra's in a few minutes, and I'll stop back and let you know how they're doing."

Benjamin called to him as he left.

"What if Frank was a colored man, Sheriff? What then?"

Cassandra met him at the door looking rested and beautiful. Hicks no longer wondered about her skills. He was certain she had powerful potions of which the rest of the world knew nothing.

"Come in, Sheriff. Coffee?"

"Please. Unlike you, I require sleep at night, and I'm suffering today." He smiled to let her know he was joking with her. Sort of.

"How are they?" Hicks asked after a sip of the strong brew.

"Still resting and recuperating. The body knows what it needs to do. But will it? That's the question."

It was a long room, and the two beds were at the farthest end, almost hidden by plants and furniture. He moved further down to peer at the still, sheet covered forms and saw Abby's head resting on the mattress next to Samuel's, her eyes closed. A light snore blew from her lips.

Shorty put a finger over his own lips telling Hicks to be quiet. He left Emily's side where he'd been bathing her face with cool water and went to the kitchen, poured two coffees and pulled out a chair. He'd been up most of the night and needed caffeine. They all had, and Abby had finally succumbed to his order to sleep but wouldn't leave Samuel to do it.

"Either of them wake up yet?" Hicks asked.

"Not Samuel. Abby's so worried she's about to shake him awake. Don't know about Emily. Her fever keeps spiking and dropping, and she babbles to Frank. Not real coherent."

Shorty tilted his head and rubbed at his neck. "Where is Frank, anyway?"

"Hotel, believe it or not. Cassandra knocked him out with something, and they put him in a room. Not up yet. I was there a few minutes ago."

"Taking him off to jail?"

"Don't know." He looked around the room like somebody was missing. "Where's Terry?"

He rapped on the door a couple of times and walked in, in the next moment.

"Where you been?" Hicks asked.

Terry glared, feeling like a criminal who needed to account for his movements.

Hicks wiped at his face. "Sorry. That didn't come out right."

Terry walked down the room to peer at his mother, put a hand on her forehead to check her fever and came back to the kitchen table. He didn't speak and waited until he was seated before responding to Hicks' question.

"Looking in on my family, Sheriff. I have a wife and two sons and a farm."

"Everyone alright?"

Terry nodded, his lips tightened into a thorny expression.

Silence fell like a dead thing, closing around them as they sipped from half-full coffee cups, and Hicks deciphered the scene through a hundred years of cumulative experience — his and others who came before him. Something was wrong. What?

"Where's Pa?"

Hicks explained.

"I think he needs to come visit her. Ma keeps talking to him. Asking for him. Maybe it'll help her."

"He shot her. Might not be a good thing to have him here at this particular point in time."

Terry stood, refilled his cup and held the pot up to offer more to the others.

"All I know is Ma keeps talking to him, calling for him. Him and a damned bird."

"Come on. A bird?"

"Yeah. 'I see the pileated,' she keeps saying, like he'd know what she means. It's his fault she's laying in there fighting for life. Damned man. He didn't deserve her. Never did!"

Coffee splashed as the cup landed too hard and sloshed its contents into the saucer. Terry cursed under his breath and looked away to see white flecks hitting the window pane. Winter's first real snow too early, and the farmer in him wondered if he had everything done.

It was up to him, now – all of it. Just him, and he didn't want to question whether or not he was ready for it. He felt like a useless boy. A stupid boy who didn't do anything right.

He'd seen his old man sitting on the ground and holding that baby, loving on it like it was his. He fought with anger and all the outlandish things he'd been feeling the whole night. Tears, for crying out loud. He couldn't get a handle on it, couldn't understand it at all. And trying to made him feel like the old man – plumb crazy.

"If you're not hauling him off to jail, I'm going to get him," Terry said, standing. He put his cup and saucer on the counter, checked once again on his mother.

Cassandra met him by the bed.

"Not yet, Mr. Adams. Give her another day to be stronger, please. At least until her fever abates."

"She might need him. She talks to him constantly." Terry didn't want to wait, but he couldn't force the issue in Cassandra's house.

"One more day." Cassandra laid a long elegant hand on his sleeve and guided him back to the table. "Have you had breakfast?"

"No. Tomorrow, then?"

"We'll see how she is. You also must see how *he* is. He may still be angry with her for taking Benji from him. That wouldn't be good for her at all."

"That's . . . Damn. The whole thing is . . ."

"I know. Sit." She gave him a cup of special tea, and he relaxed enough to look at her without resentment or preconception. He noticed her and the small things comprising her looks: the smooth, clear skin; the classical, straight nose; the composure that emphasized her elegance.

She's quite beautiful. Amazing.

Chapter Thirty-one

Frank followed her and Benji from one room to the next as she made beds, swept the floors and dusted the furniture. He grabbed the dust mop before she could and pushed it around the room with a cat taking a free ride on the mop head. Frank called him Orange Blossom and wouldn't be dissuaded when Betty told him his name was King.

"Hop on, Blossom, we're going down the hall," he said. He was all smiles and having a good time.

"Wouldn't you like to rest in your room for a while, Mr. Adams?"

"Earning my keep," he said. "You want I should carry him for a while? He gets mighty heavy. I know. We walked all over that forest together, didn't we, son."

Betty put a hand on her hip and tilted her head. "Now, you know he isn't your son, Mr. Adams. Right?"

He shuffled his feet. "It's just something men say. I know, now. I promise I do, Betty. Would you please call me Frank?"

She adjusted Benji who she carried in a pack on her back. She wasn't ready to be separated from him, not even for a moment, and she kept an alert eye on Frank as she worked. He seemed half-lucid some of the time, but she didn't trust it would stay.

Having Frank underfoot, as if nothing troublesome had occurred, gave her collywobbles, as her grandma would say. But she could deal with it. She had her baby, and Benjamin was nearby should she need him. One loud scream - or even a tiny whimper - would bring him running, she was certain.

"Maybe you should go on out to your farm, see what needs doing out there?"

"Nope. Terry can handle it. All the boys can run the farm by themselves. They don't need me."

"What boys are you talking about, Mr. Adams – I mean, Frank?"

"My sons." He grinned, his eyes sparkled, and he looked almost youthful. "The white ones."

She didn't have the heart to remind him only one of his sons still lived at the farm, and she was saved from having to explain it to him by Sheriff Hicks who poked his head into the room.

"There you are, Frank. I was looking for you."

"Why?" He stepped back and raised his hand in denial of wrong doing. "I'm working right now. Can't you come back later?"

Hicks stifled a grin and looked at Betty. "How's the babe? Glad to be home?"

"His ma is glad to have him here," she said. "Don't know if he cares one way or another. And that's the truth. Could be bothersome if I let it be." She reached around to pat the bundle asleep on her back.

"How about a cup of Al's special coffee, Frank. I'm buying."

"Well sure, Sheriff. Why didn't you say so? That alright, boss? I'll come right back after."

Betty grinned at the sheriff and shook her head maternally at Frank.

Hicks had no idea what was going on, what to do now or how to do it, but he figured the first step was to find out how much Frank knew about the last few days, how much he remembered about stealing the baby and shooting his wife. Maybe most important was what he knew, if anything at all, about the Black Legion? How'd they get out to the woods and why? At the moment, the man seemed oblivious to the past events. He lived in an imaginary world.

Al came from the kitchen with two cups of coffee and two pieces of her aromatic apple pie.

"I could put you in my pocket and take you home with me, Al. Thank you."

"Shorty might get mad."

"Damned giant."

"Shouldn't be cussing in front of ladies," Frank said, giving him a squinty glare.

"Sorry, Frank. Sorry, Al."

Hicks dug into his pie and gave up on talk until a clean plate sat in front of him. He leaned back, rubbed his belly with pleasure and picked up his cup.

"Frank."

"Sheriff."

A standoff occurred, an eye-to-eye stare down, both men determined not to look away or blink.

Hicks lost.

"Want to tell me what's going on?"

"Where? Here?"

"Sure. Start here."

"Well, I'm cleaning rooms with Betty. Nice girl. She has a baby she carries around with her all the time. It's a lot of hard work. I'd help her with the baby, too, if she wanted me to. Kind of reminds me of my boy."

Hicks rubbed his eyes and groaned.

"Do you know where your wife is, Frank? Where is Emily right now?"

Frank carefully placed his fork on the empty plate and studied it. Hicks stayed quiet and let him think. He could see him working to remember, could tell when bits and pieces of memory came to him only to be rejected.

"No. Can't say as I know. Mebbe at the farm. It's getting on toward lunchtime, so she's likely cooking lunch for the boys." He slid the fork toward the center of the plate and stared at it. Moved it again and again while he thought.

"Your wife is at Cassandra's house. She's there because she was shot and is recovering from her wounds."

Frank's chest jerked back hard enough to pull the front chair legs off the floor before they slammed back down. Hicks reached out to keep him from toppling backwards and left his hand on the arm and held it there.

"Who shot her?" He shook Hicks' arm. "Sheriff, who shot my wife? Why would anybody do that to her? She'd never hurt a fly. Can wring the neck of a Sunday dinner chicken with the best of 'em, but chicken necks are different, you know."

Hick waited long enough to consider his words and gave up trying to find a better way to say it.

"You did, Frank. She took Benji and ran away from you, and you shot her. Don't you remember doing that?"

His head dropped forward, chin to his chest. It began to swing from side to side, negating the Sheriff's words, but somewhere deep inside, the truth became his new reality. When he looked up again, liquid had formed in his red rimmed eyes, and Hicks had never in his life been more distressed by the sight of tears.

He rubbed at his chest and shoved his chair back, stood and left the table. Frank deserved privacy, if nothing else. He put his elbows on the bar and kept an eye on him from a sidelong view. A long while later, the old man joined him at the bar.

"I could use another coffee," Frank said. "With a little courage in it this time."

When he came back from the kitchen with the coffee, Hicks went behind the bar and poured a shot into Frank's cup. He slid it to him, wishing he was off duty. A bit of whiskey would go down good about now.

"Been sheriff long?" Frank asked, standing next to him and sipping from his cup of spiked coffee.

He sounded lucid, like any stranger standing at the bar with a cup of coffee, and Hicks wondered if his sense had been jarred back into place.

"Too damned long."

"Ever see anything like this before?"

Hicks looked hard at Frank and tried to gauge his rationality, his stability. He didn't need him going off the deep end. Again.

"Can't say as I have, nothing quite like it."

Frank tossed down the last of his coffee and sucked a long breath into his body, filled his chest and stood all of his six feet of length.

"Can I go see my wife?"

"Maybe tomorrow, Frank. Cassandra said not today, but Emily has been talking about you in her fevered sleep. She hasn't really woken up yet. She talks about a woodpecker, too. Remember anything about a pileated woodpecker?"

His eyes watered, and Hicks grew afraid the man would cry again. He didn't, but he nodded and whispered, "Yeah. I showed her one when we were sitting on the porch holding my . . . Benji. God, what the hell's wrong with me?"

He rubbed at his eyes and cursed himself for a fool.

Abby was forcing broth between his lips when Samuel's eyes popped open. She gasped, dumped the liquid from the spoon and tipped the cup so it sloshed into the saucer.

"Damn. I'm so sorry. I'll dry you up." She dabbed at his chin and chest to soak up the spill and then gasped again when realization came to her. "You're awake. Samuel! You're awake."

He moaned as she threw herself on him and she jerked back and apologized again. She wanted to squeeze him and not stop. But she didn't. She restrained herself, stood by his bed and stared, her eyes boring into his as if she might see his wounds healing.

"I'm so happy to see you awake."

"I do that every day." The words rasped from his throat and sounded like the squeak from a long idle, rusty hinge.

"Not really," she whispered and, having minds of their own, her lips grazed his cheek.

She felt awkward and uncomfortable, even after two days of caring for him, and wondered why. Okay, she'd said a lot of things to him while he slept, things she'd never share when he could actually hear her. Might he remember?

His eyes roamed her face and moved to the plants and flowers surrounding his bed, to the bright screen separating him from the unknown, and back to Abby.

"Cassandra's?"

"Yes. We brought you here two nights ago. You and Mrs. Adams." Abby pointed to the screen to indicate she lay on the other side of it.

"Why? What happened to her?"

Abby touched his shoulder and he winced. "Sorry. Let's not worry about her right now. Let's get you well first. Will you take some of this herbal broth? Cassandra made it for you, and I'll need to change your poultices with cooler ones, and . . ."

"Abby. Stop chattering. What happened?"

Her shoulders slumped and she deflated.

"She got shot and has a fever. Neither of you have been awake for two solid days."

"Hicks shot her?"

"No. Not him. Tell you what, Samuel. You finish this cup of tea and let me change your poultices, and I will tell you the whole story. Deal?"

He gave her the start of a lopsided grin that faded into a grimace, one side of his lips curling up and the other down, an indicator of his pain. Abby's heart clenched for him. He swallowed the tea she spooned into his mouth and slid into sleep as soon as the liquid was in his stomach. Cassandra was a firm believer in letting the body heal itself, and, according to her, it did its best work at rest. In sleep.

Abby changed the cool poultices, grew angry again over his bruises and marveled at the beautiful body they violated. She felt no shame in his nakedness. She would be the one to care for him in any condition.

She sat by his bed and watched him doze, thought about when they'd first met and he'd told her he wasn't an Uncle Tom. He'd been condescending and short with her at the time, and she with him, she admitted. In fact, she didn't like him at all, but she'd been wrong – about him and about not liking him.

She sat by his side and recounted his good deeds. He'd taken care of Al and her animals when she couldn't and never told anyone he was doing it, just surprised them all with a wagon full of chickens, the heifer and the old dog when they moved back to the farm.

"I didn't want to ruin my really good bad reputation," he said when Abby had confronted him with his acts of kindness.

And he cared for Betty when she needed help and had been kind and loving to her. Didn't ask questions, and treated her with respect. Samuel did what needed to be done like it was nothing, like anyone would do it. But he would be wrong about that.

Abby ran through the years, right up to the moment he'd turned away from her. She hadn't known why. Still didn't, but she wasn't going to let him go – unless he loved another woman. Maybe not even then. She might fight for him even if he didn't know he loved her. Because he did.

He had to.

She listened to the tick of the clock in the kitchen, to the rustle of cats weaving through the jungle of plants on the many tables, and the sedated breath coming from Samuel and Emily. If his wounds weren't so painful, she'd damn convention and climb onto the narrow bed and lie next to him.

Her lips curved in a smile at the picture she'd drawn in her mind and stayed there until the sound of quiet footsteps invaded the pleasant oblivion. Bear walked toward her with a cot under his arm.

"Gave up trying to get you to come home to get some sleep. So, climb on this." He stretched it beside Samuel's bed and pointed. When she obeyed, he covered her with a quilt. "I'll sit here and keep watch on Samuel while you catch a few."

Bear kissed her cheek and brushed the wild curls from her forehead. His half-muted gaze settled on her face, and she blinked at him and sighed and slept. She could trust Bear with anything, even Samuel.

Sometime in the night, he woke for the second time, and Bear was by his side instantly with a finger over his lips to shush him.

"Abby is finally sleeping. She needs it." He pointed to her and Samuel nodded.

"Why isn't she home in her own bed like an ordinary person?"

"Because she isn't ordinary. She's different and you damned well know it."

That was a long speech for Bear, almost a presidential address, and Samuel understood as much even in his drugged state. He blinked in response because he had no words.

"I'll need to heat Cassandra's tea."

Bear left him and met Terry at the stove already warming some for his mother.

"I'll add more to the pot," he said.

Bear hadn't known Terry well, even when he was Abby's brother-in-law. What he knew, he didn't much like, and he was astonished to see him here caring for his mother.

"Any improvement?" he asked.

His lips pinched and Adam's apple jiggled in his neck before he could put words together. "Fever broke, thank God. Didn't think it ever would."

The words caught in his throat, and Bear turned from the man to leave him privacy. He knew the Adams men wouldn't hold to tearing up. It wasn't done in their world, not so anyone knew, that is. And while Bear couldn't see the purpose in that, he'd give him what he needed. No reason not to.

"Glad to hear it," Bear told him and perused the strangely appointed room.

The rumbling purr of many cats coated the area in contentment, and Bear spent time letting his eyes roam to spot the sound makers. Two warmed the chairs at the kitchen table. One curled around a pot of basil and tarragon. Three coiled together like a pile of snakes in an orange basket on the floor. He knew there were more, but Terry handed him the warm cup and he went back to Samuel.

Setting the cup down, he took his time propping Samuel with a couple of pillows before picking it up again, all without words. He hoped Samuel would offer an explanation of what had happened to him.

Shorty told him the Black Legion had dominated the side of the woods where Samuel was beaten and were supposedly there to help a fellow Klan member – Frank. They'd proclaimed it loudly. What he didn't know was who they were specifically, how they found the place and who had sent them.

Samuel tried to hold the cup himself, but one hand was bandaged, and he couldn't manage without spilling. Bear spooned it in like Abby had.

"Not as pretty as her, I know," he said.

"For sure. Ugly as sin." Samuel didn't smile, but it was good to hear him tease.

"Not all that bad," Bear said.

"You looked in a mirror lately, my friend?"

Bear grinned and the roadmap in his beard moved as white paths in the dark forest of his whiskers altered.

"Have you?"

"That's good," Samuel said. "Got me there."

"You know who did this?"

"No idea. It's a blur."

Bear nodded. "Can't you remember anything about it? How many? What they looked like?"

"Nope. It's pretty much gone."

Bear stopped spooning. Until he could get more information, he wanted Samuel awake.

"Want to share with me the parts that aren't pretty much gone?"

"Nope."

Bear knew it was useless to push. Samuel wouldn't want others fighting his battles without him by their sides, so he spooned in the rest and let him fall back to sleep.

On the other side of the privacy screen, Terry listened to the conversation. He had some of the answers Bear was looking for, but he wasn't sharing, either. Not right now. Maybe not ever.

He needed to think.

Chapter Thirty-two

Cassandra met Frank as he stepped down from the hotel porch. He looked her over, noted the bright flowing gown and flowered turban on her head, shrugged his shoulders and let her take his arm. He'd seen her around town his entire life, and she'd become part of the natural landscape to most folks, a piece of Idlewild some respected, some didn't care to acknowledge, and others openly disparaged.

He and his buddies had snickered about her when they were young and sneaked up to her house to throw rocks that never reached. But after Cassandra started healing the sick and injured, the snickering quit and people – mostly white folks – crossed the street to walk on the other side, away from her.

Of course, they'd never admit fear. But she caused shivers to crawl down their spines when she gazed too long at them, though they wouldn't admit it – even to themselves.

Today, Frank walked by her side, and they talked about the cold weather as if it was new and interesting. She looked pretty with her smooth, mahogany skin, and it looked a lot like Benji's.

"I'm glad you're visiting your wife, Mr. Adams. She wants to see you."

"Not sure she will if what Sheriff Hicks says is true."

"And what does the sheriff say?"

Frank twisted his head to stare at her and fought the tears he couldn't seem to quit producing lately.

"Why – that I shot her. I wouldn't do that. Why would I shoot my own wife? I like her."

"We do strange things for love, Mr. Adams."

He twisted to stare at her again.

"Well, that's what I mean. I love my wife. Why would I shoot her?"

Cassandra stopped walking and turned to him, her piercing stare causing him to stumble to a halt. For a moment he felt the fear of his youth.

"What?" he asked.

"Mr. Adams, I'm not willing to play games with you. If you cause Mrs. Adams harm in any way, or if you cause a setback in her healing, you will be banned from my home. Do we understand each other?"

Frank nodded and let reality back in.

"I did it. I shot her. I just can't believe I did. I didn't mean to, but that baby was mine. She shouldn't have taken him."

"No. He wasn't yours."

A hunted look invaded his eyes saying he wanted to run from truth, but it stalked him, and he couldn't run fast enough to get away from the reality.

"You're right. I wanted him to be mine."

Cassandra threaded her arm through his once again, and they walked down the long path to her cottage. On the way, he told her all about pileated woodpeckers.

"They can lay six eggs, you know. But usually they have four. It's a lot of babies to care for."

"I'm sure it is, Mr. Adams. And you had three babies of your own to care for. That must have been a lot of work, too. A big responsibility."

"I did?" He looked muddled, but it passed quickly and he moved on to talking about Michigan whitetail deer. He patted her hand as they neared the cottage. "I know I had three sons, Cassandra. I wanted to try it again, do better this time. I get confused, but I know it, and I will be good with Emily. I promise."

"Thank you, Mr. Adams."

Emily was awake and sitting propped against several pillows talking with Terry. They avoided discussing how she'd been hurt, and she asked him to tell her about things at the farm. His brow knitted and his voice halted, but eventually he explained how Cecily and the boys were taking care of everything.

"Milking and all?" she asked.

"Yancy is helping with that," he said, wanting to skirt around any talk about him. His battle with information others wanted stilled his tongue. He didn't know what to do with his knowledge and was eager to see his father walk in.

Her eyes lit when she saw Frank, and his reddened.

"You're so pale, Emily," he said.

"Oh, I'll be up and about in no time," she said, bolstering him and taking his blame as she'd done their entire married life. "Pull up a chair." But her voice was weak, and Frank heard its quiver.

Cassandra busied herself at the stove making tea – regular tea – and put several cups on a tray along with a dozen poppyseed cookies. She knew poppyseed helped build the blood, was an antioxidant, and . . . improved cognitive function. She didn't know if it could do anything for Mr. Adams, but it wouldn't hurt.

She eavesdropped on their conversation without guilt and shook her head as Emily downplayed her wounds.

Some things never change, but just some things, thank God.

"I miss you," Frank said.

Cassandra sensed Emily's blush, and she smiled and paused before taking in the tray.

"Me, too," Emily said. "Maybe we could go home? I could recuperate there."

"No, Mrs. Adams. You're far from ready for home. Mr. Adams can visit you here." Cassandra put the tray on the small table and hustled to serve. "You're staying at the hotel to be near, correct?"

Frank nodded but looked confused. Near what?

"You're very sweet, Frank, but Terry is so busy, and he needs . . ."

Cassandra interrupted, having no part of helping send her patient back to the farm.

"Mrs. Adams, your capable son can tend to the farm for now and visit you here for brief periods. He doesn't need to be here constantly anymore. Please understand this is for your own good."

Frank took her hand in both of his. "Listen to Cassandra, Emily. She knows what she's doing. Please. I need you to get well."

Emily's eyes glowed and her skin flushed in a pretty way, not with fever this time. Her husband had just spoken highly of a colored woman. She'd not heard him do that, ever, and his words filled her with hope. And he held her hand – in front of people as if he cared about her. He said he *needed* her well, and his eyes said so, too.

Frank had scoffed at her before, objected violently to her spending time with colored friends, and he'd ridiculed her. This was a miracle, and she wanted to bathe in its beauty, bask in the joy of his change of heart.

A knock on the door drew Cassandra from them. Alma waited, a basket hanging from her arm.

"Come in. You brought goodies?"

"Soup. Same chicken soup I feed my boys when they're sick. Thought Samuel could use some. And Mrs. Adams, of course. Am I stepping on your medical toes?"

"Didn't know my phalanges and metatarsals were medicinal, young woman. You work for Abby, right?"

"Um . . . toes. I see." She gave a slanted grin to Cassandra's joke. "Patrick, actually. In the kitchen. Is Samuel ready for visitors?"

A smirk quirked the corner of Cassandra's lips when she took the basket and turned away from the woman. When she looked up, she saw Abby's piercing glare dart across the room and aim directly at Alma.

Abby leaned in to whisper to Samuel, who was awake at the moment. She stretched, rolled her head, and moved down the long room and into the kitchen.

"Think I'll take this opportune time to head to the Oakmere for some clean clothes. I'm sure I stink by now. Hello, Alma. Nice to see you. He's awake but probably not for long."

"You don't need to leave, Abby. I brought some soup and wanted to say hello."

"Of course, I don't have to, but I do need clean clothes. You can babysit for a bit."

Cassandra's grin grew and she had to pinch herself to keep from chuckling.

"Cookie? It's good for cognitive function," Cassandra said and held one out to Abby who snatched it, bit the cookie instead of her tongue, and headed to the door.

Is she accusing me of needing a brain?

"I'll be back, Cassandra. In an hour or so."

She glanced at Alma like she was giving her a time limit, and in the bed at the end of the room, Samuel's chuckle made him grab his ribs with the pain, but it felt ridiculously good.

Abby was jealous.

Sue and Sally had dressed for visiting in matching green satin dresses, and hats tilted over their eyes in a coquettish manner designed to draw male eyes. They stopped on Cassandra's porch to check their appearances and made slight adjustments to each other's hats. Sally yanked up on Sue's dress to tuck in the enormous bosom, at least for the moment. It never stayed tucked. And Sue plumped at Sally's breasts trying to coax them into some appearance of voluptuous.

Sally slapped at her cousin's hands.

"Stop pawing at me. I like the way I look just fine."

"You'd like it better with a bosom. You know, fill out that pretty dress some." Sue fluffed at Sally's dress material while staying out of range of her slaps. "But you always look nice for a thin girl, Sally. You really do."

"And you look especially nice today, Sue. Let's go in, shall we?"

"Yes, and we do look good, don't we?"

Cassandra pulled herself up to her most imperial height when the cousins entered. They would expect formal manners from her, and she certainly wouldn't disappoint them. She loved the pleasure ladies.

"Welcome to my home."

She offered them tea, which they declined; offered them tea with whiskey, and they accepted with intrepid thanks and glances at each other. They'd heard tales of Cassandra's brews.

Carrying flowered teacups on saucers, they greeted Samuel, their reason for visiting. Cassandra followed with an extra chair.

Alma was leaving, and Cassandra escorted her to the door and tamped down a trickle of annoyance, a breath at the back of her neck. It didn't warrant puzzling over at the moment, but she pushed it into the back of her mind for consideration later.

"Enjoy your visitors, Samuel," she said. "I'll be going for a walk now. Ladies, may I offer you anything else before I take my leave?"

Both shook their heads, sipped, and watched her go. Before she was out the door, Sue giggled like a schoolgirl.

"Boy, she's something, ain't she? How'd she learn to walk that way? A bit like you, Sally, only like she sorta glides instead of using her feet to get somewhere."

"Shhh. She's right out there, Sue. Hush."

Samuel chuckled and held a hand over his broken ribs.

"Now see what you've done, Sally. You made Samuel hurt himself." Sue patted his arm with concern. "Can I help you? Give you a sponge bath or a massage?"

Sally collapsed against the back of her chair and blew out a frustrated breath.

"Good Lord, save me from my cousin's ill-mannered behavior. Sue! Stop."

"You are both fine," Samuel said. "You're the best thing that's happened to me today. I mean it."

Sue puffed up and Sally relaxed.

"I knew he'd think so, Sally," Sue said.

"Of course, you did."

"He missed us."

"Of course, he did."

The day after Alma and the cousins visited, while alone, he pulled himself upright to sit on the edge of the bed. And on the following day, he moved to a chair, slowly and painfully, but he got there without falling to the floor. Moisture beaded his forehead, and his shirt grew dark with perspiration, but he needed to move in order to go home.

Lying next to Emily Adams and listening to Frank and Terry when they visited made his heart beat wildly – in anger and indecision. Bits and pieces of memory nagged at him as he struggled out of slumber each day.

They're Klan, he thought, and had access to the Black Legion. But, if the Legion had been there, who had called on them? Terry? Yancy? He didn't think Yancy alone was responsible or even had the clout, but he *had* threatened him with the Legion, and he did work for Terry Adams, a known Klan member.

He tossed the thoughts aside as the products of ridiculous, sickroom imagination, but puzzling over the events of that day kept him awake in the night. And Terry's silent movements throughout the midnight house made up pages of childish nightmares.

Samuel sprawled in the chair, his shirt unbuttoned to the waist trying to dry off after the effort of moving when Abby came through the door. While the entry was a long way from the bed end of the room, cool air blew through and he took a refreshing, but short breath.

"What on earth are you doing out of your sick bed?"

"I'm not sick. Simply in a bit of discomfort, and I want to go home. If you can't make it happen, I can."

"Quit being a baby, Samuel. Get back in bed and behave. Where's Cassandra?"

"I don't know. She doesn't report to me." Lines gathered between Samuel's eyebrows.

"She probably left her own home to get away from you and your cantankerous conduct."

Abby threw back the sheet and blanket, smoothed the under sheet, and punched the pillow to fluff it up. "Get in."

She tucked her arm under his to help and he thrust back against the chair.

"I'm not going to. I'm going to sit here, so if you want to visit, pull up another chair. And, by the way, a shot of something besides tea would be appreciated."

Abby stepped back.

"Well . . . hmmm. I see. Stubborn, aren't you?"

"You're just now figuring that one out?" Samuel shifted in his chair and stifled a groan. "Stop looking at me like I'm an insect under a microscope. Do I look like a mosquito to you?"

Abby snorted because she couldn't help the laugh bubbling inside.

"No. A giant, hairy spider, maybe. You're much too big a pain in the . . ."

"What? Neck? Me?"

"Um, I was going to say ass, or arse as Da would say."

"About that shot of something not tea?"

Abby left to find something that wasn't tea and hoped Cassandra wouldn't mind her snooping through the cupboard. Finding a little liquid that looked homemade and smelled like brandy, she poured a small glass and took it and another chair back to Samuel's space.

"What is it?" he asked as she handed it to him.

"Don't know. Try it, I guess."

One of his dark brows rose and he held the glass under his nose to sniff.

"Smells like brandy." He sniffed again. "But if Cassandra made it . . ." He tasted and moaned in delight. Sipped again and gave another sigh of pleasure. "The absolute best in the world."

He shifted so his shoulders were against the chair with his head resting on the wall, and closed his eyes, letting the breath float from his lungs. He'd never been in such total peace, so deeply serene and in harmony with the world, and he wanted to savor it.

"Don't talk," he murmured.

"Harrumph. Okay."

She waited and watched Samuel relax, muscle by muscle, and decided to try some of the drink herself. One sip was all it took before she slid down in her own chair, pressed her back against the slats and her head against the wall next to Samuel's.

They listened to gentle snores from the other side of the divider, the soft purrs from around the room, high and low and in the middle, the wind, even though none blew, the paint settling on the walls, the plant leaves growing, and believed it all not simply possible to hear, but most likely.

Abby slid sideways against him and took his arm, wrapped it around her shoulder and rested her head next to his. They remained in their tranquil state until footsteps brought them home and Cassandra spotted them entwined and the decanter on the counter.

Her smile showed a trace of concern. This would not harm anyone, but others of her flasks might.

"Did you have a nice nap?" she asked.

Abby blushed when she saw the flagon of whiskey in her hand, the incriminating evidence,

"I hope you don't mind if I helped myself. Samuel wanted something a little stronger than tea . . . and we weren't napping."

"Blame it on me," Samuel said, with nothing but good humor highlighting his words. He felt wonderful, like he had drifted with the clouds and could continue to do so until he decided to descend.

"Oh, you got something stronger than tea, alright." Cassandra's grin spread to her eyes, but she pointed a finger at them. "Don't drink or eat anything if you don't know what it is or I haven't given it to you. Not in this house."

Abby stood, sudden concern waking her fully.

"What was it? Did I poison us?"

She glanced with wide, frightened eyes, and Cassandra's chuckle was evil, if only slightly, but intentionally so.

"No toad warts or night creature innards. Not this time, but . . ." She shrugged, indicating the next container could be full of bats' eyes *and* toad warts.

"Cassandra, as much as I appreciate your hospitality, I need to go home. Any idea where my mare resides – or my auto?"

"Hotel stable," Abby said. "And I assume your automobile is at your house where you left it." She bristled, not believing he was ready to leave their care. Her care.

"Do you think Jesse could be cajoled into driving it here? I can take it home on my own. Don't think I'm quite ready for the horse."

"You're not ready to leave at all. Not yet. And the sheriff is coming tomorrow. He wants to speak with you," Abby said.

Samuel hadn't mentioned the men in the woods in an awakened state. But his murmurs while asleep led her to believe he could identify some of the Legion men who had beaten him. And the Sheriff wanted the information. He'd said he couldn't wait any longer.

Samuel stood, a slow process, but one he managed without falling or noticeably groaning, even though he turned a sickly shade of green-gray and his good hand tightened into a fist.

"He can speak to me at my house. I'd prefer it." He turned his head to stare into her eyes. "In fact, I insist."

"So, leave in the morning," Cassandra said. "You've had my special sauce and are in no condition to drive, but I'll give you a bit more if you behave and do what I say."

"I don't want to." Samuel sounded like a petulant six-year-old, and Cassandra's eyes rolled to the ceiling.

"I'll get Bunny over here."

"Damned controlling woman."

He lowered himself to the edge of the bed, bone by creaking bone, and they knew he'd given in. The threat of Bunny worked every time. She was Cassandra's sister, and Abby both loved her and was terrified of her. She thought

Cassandra might fear her, too, but wouldn't admit it, and Abby would never ask.

"You'll ask Jesse to get my vehicle?"

"I will if you stay until morning," Abby said, and part of the truth was she didn't want to give him up, send him back to his other life where she had no place and no reason to be by his side every day.

He read the truth in her eyes and let his slide closed. He didn't want her to hurt, didn't want anyone to, but especially Abby.

"Sit and have another glass of Cassandra's special tea with me before you leave?" he asked hoping to see her eyes brighten. He was rewarded with a quick tilt of her lips.

She pulled a chair close to the bed as he fell back against the pillow, and his body liquified. Maybe they were right, and he had overdone it.

Cassandra poured tiny amounts into their waiting glasses and was ready to leave them alone, but Samuel asked her to join them.

She came back with her own drink, peered behind the divider to see Emily asleep, and took the remaining chair. Samuel eyed her glass, a dark eyebrow raised.

"Won't that much of your tasty elixir impair your ability to move, Cassandra? Even breathe?"

"Course not."

"You immune?"

Her lips curled up. "It only affects as much as you choose, so be forewarned. The consequences are of your own making."

"Sometimes you're so darned . . . I don't know the word. Murky, I guess."

"Why, Samuel. You admit to not knowing a word?" Abby laughed, but she understood his frustration.

Cassandra had at times caused her to respond in the same manner. Now, included. The elegant woman masked herself in mystery and let others claw their way out of the impenetrable . . . murk.

He raised his hand as if swearing an oath. "I admit to not knowing Cassandra in the least. No one does, but I thank her for letting me stay here and recuperate. I owe you, my friend."

She shook her head. "You owe us all, Samuel."

"Us? Which us? Everybody?"

"People. Black, immigrant, Jew, Catholic. Any race, nationality and *ism* folks you can think of. You owe them."

Samuel sipped his drink and pushed his head further into the pillow. He had no inkling of the path her mind had taken, and his fled to find the tranquility her brandy had given him, the peace he found before she came home. Cassandra nudged his foot to bring him back.

"What did I do to *owe* all these people?" Samuel said, letting frustration come alive. "That's a darned lot of people."

"You were born a black man with a big brain."

When he opened his mouth to deny her words, she held out a hand to shush him. "And you let yourself be beaten by the Legion."

"What makes you say that?"

She held a finger in the air, listened and continued. "I know. I know what happens in my woods. You – of all people – should be aware of that. And you walked right to them. You should have been vigilant. You must be."

Abby's eyes followed first one and the other, unsure of what Cassandra was talking about or expected of him.

Samuel looked confused and ran a hand over his face, squeezed his temples as if his head hurt.

"So, it was the Legion?"

The words, muffled by his hand, crawled out like they'd been spoken by an old man, and Abby put a hand on his shoulder and squeezed gently.

"Do you remember? The two who threw you into the clearing wore hoods with skulls and crossbones. They shouted their affiliation like they were proud of it, threatening the rest of us scattered around the woods."

Slowly, memory returned. He saw the masks and, through their voices, recognized some of the men behind the masks. Now, he understood with glaring clarity what Cassandra meant. He owed it to people, all people, to stand against terrorists and fanatics. If not, they multiplied, grew like bacteria, and spread their disease over the country.

"They'll take Idlewild from us unless they're stopped," Cassandra said, and her black eyes bored into his, holding his gaze with her intensity.

"They as much as announced it to everyone who was in the woods that day, and they meant it. They scared me." Abby's whispered words emphasized her fear.

The door opened, and their connection broke. Samuel watched Terry wander down the room toward his mother, Frank ambling behind him, and didn't want to talk about the Legion anymore. He needed to think and to speak with the sheriff, but not here.

He was more determined than ever to go home.

Chapter Thirty-three

She met Shorty on his way down Cassandra's path, and his solid strength bolstered her and let her know the entire world hadn't changed - only pieces and parts. His serene soul was exactly what she needed. Beside him, Abby could embrace the flawless snowflakes and red-suited cardinals, the bright eyes of the does as they heard footfalls and lifted their heads from feeding to watch them pass.

Cassandra's creatures didn't flee in fear. They expected harmony in their home and would have been stunned to find it otherwise. A gray wolf crossed the path a hundred yards down from them and loped into the woods. He perched on a small knoll and watched, ready to howl an alert in order to protect the peace. He'd have been invisible in summer, covered by brush and leafed out trees, but with snow on the ground, his muted silhouette posed in majesty.

"Samuel told me about him," Abby said. "He guards the clowder. Keeps coyotes away."

Shorty's forehead wrinkled. "And how did Samuel come by this wisdom?"

"Cassandra. But he also thought she might have conjured the apparition and made up the story. He wasn't sure. He wants to go home tomorrow," she said after gazing at the wolf in silence for a time.

"The wolf wants to go home?"

She swatted his arm and then threaded hers around it to let his warmth fill her.

"And the lilt in your voice says you don't want him to leave Cassandra's."

"No. It's nice with him here, confined to a bed."

Again, Shorty's brow wrinkled and he rubbed his scalp. "Leaving that one alone."

"Brat." But she chuckled and blushed, letting her imagination run for a pleasant moment. "I promised to ask Jesse to drive his auto here in the morning."

"I'll take care of it. And I'll let Hicks know where to find him. He's been around the hotel a lot asking questions. Some good ones."

Old times scented the air and spread out around the fireplace in the Oakmere bar. Several rocking chairs flanked the hearth, close enough to warm the toes but not to burn them. The click of their in-sync movement halted long enough for a rocker to find the rhythm, and Abby's head settled against the chair back and her eyes closed.

Bear and Shorty, her da, Charles and, yes, Alma. It was *almost* like old times. She'd been staying over to help because Abby had been gone so much, and the Christmas rush was starting, even though the holiday was still a few weeks away. Abby was grateful. She tried to be.

"He good?" Bear asked.

"Didn't see him," Shorty said. Communicating like an old married couple who finished each other's sentences. "Taking his vehicle to him tomorrow."

"Guess he is then," Patrick said, "if he's driving himself home."

"One of you needs to go with him. In case," Abby said. "He may need help. He's weak, yet, and moves with great pain."

"Going home might be a good thing to do if Sheriff Hicks is coming to see him. I'd like to talk with him, too – away from the hotel."

"Want to share?" Charity asked, coming in behind the small group.

She must have walked on fairy feet because no one heard her enter, and they were startled by her voice. She pulled a chair next to Charles and ran a hand down his arm.

"Good to see you, Charles. I had to scour the town to find you."

"Did you need something?"

"Just you, sweetie. I was missing you."

"Charity, you need to go find a boy, not a grandpa. A white boy."

The runners on Abby's chair stuttered, messing with the timing. Did he mean that? She'd read his literature and hadn't gotten that message from him. She glanced sideways at Charles, and their eyes met. He lifted his shoulders in apology.

"Old and cranky."

"I plan on going by his place after rooms are done and people checked in," Abby said. "Marcus and Carl can handle things after that. I need to see Samuel is settled and has food."

"Don't trust me to see to it?" Shorty said.

"Sure, but . . ."

He stood, tugged on her braid, and ambled to the door. "See you tomorrow. Al's missing me."

Snow flew in as he went out. Winter had come while they weren't looking, full-fledged, snow laden, hard core, Michigan winter. It piled up on the window ledges and clung to the panes making folks gravitate to the fire, embrace its warmth and spiritual comfort.

Patrick sighed with regret "I'm taking my heated brick and going up to bed."

A chorus of voices agreed.

"We're closing, Charity. You need to go home," Abby said. "Actually – we're already closed. It's cold so wrap up tight." She started to walk away, but turned around. "Damn, girl. What are you doing out and about? If you take a room here instead of going home, will your mother worry?"

Abby saw the girl's eyes fill as she shook her head and regretted her quick words.

"What's wrong?"

"I wanted to talk with you," she said leaving the men at the fireside and pulling Abby with her. "That's why I came here so late. Father had friends visit and I overheard them talking."

"About?"

"The Black Legion."

Abby's skin prickled and the hair lifted on her arms.

"What does he know about the Legion?"

"Nothing!"

But Charity's single word froze in the air and caused the men to glance down the long bar room toward them.

"We need to know, Charity. Who were the friends visiting Reverend Evans?"

"Daniel Longstreet and the Rumford weasel. They closeted themselves in the library, but I overheard when I took in a tray of coffee they'd asked for. I made sure the door was open a little when I left."

Abby shivered. The Black Legion. Men who had nearly killed Samuel. She needed Bear and Charles to hear this whether Charity wanted them to or not. She grabbed her hand and pulled her back to where the men were standing and stretching, getting ready to leave or head upstairs to bed.

"One moment," Abby said. "Please wait, Da, all of you." She wrapped an arm around Charity's back for moral support and asked her to tell what she'd heard.

Charity nibbled her lip and rubbed her arms like she felt a cold draft, raised her chin and began.

"Longstreet and Rumford are Black Legion. They were talking with my father about some of the things they've done and what they planned to do in order to . . ." She hesitated and looked at Charles, apology in her eyes, and wanted more than anything not to say the words, so she didn't. She said, ". . . fix Idlewild," instead.

"I know what the Legion does, Charity. You don't have to mince words for my sake. Even people I know and like trip over words like black or negro, mulatto or African, even colored. Believe me. The words stick in the back of their throats like pus-covered tonsils."

His hands waved in exasperation as he spoke. He wasn't angry, but Charles heard her inability to say the words and knew what that awkwardness really meant – another hundred years of the same.

"It's ridiculous, Charles, but they want the negros to leave. They want this county like it was before the resort came, and they beat Samuel, would have killed him. Thought they had." Charity took a harsh breath. "I heard them bragging about it and I hate them, hate what they are!"

Gone was Charity's careless, glib tone, gone the flippant attitude, and instead the real Charity's tears fell.

Charles put an arm around her and led her back to a chair, patting her as if she was a little girl. To him, she was a naive young woman who needed her world to be simple and fun. And he was an old man who needed the same but knew the world better and had for far too many years.

"Shorty needs to hear this," Bear said, and Charles nodded.

"You didn't recognize their voices in the woods?" he asked Charles who shook his head.

"Don't know them well enough. Does Shorty?"

"We'll find out tomorrow. I'll meet him at Samuel's. We'll have a chat with the sheriff."

"My father isn't one," Charity said, sniffing back encroaching tears. "Just them."

"You did the right thing, Charity. It was hard to do, I know," Bear said.

Abby brought her a glass of sherry and went back for more when the men looked at her as if she'd beaten them with a stick. Patrick threw a couple of logs on the fire and turned to the group.

"Ye need not say the wee lass's name. Find a way to tell the tale without it." Patrick turned to Alma. "And I'm asking ye not to tell the tale at all, please, 'til it's settled. For the lass."

"I have nothing to tell, Patrick, but if you're questioning folks, you might stop at the store and see what Joe Foster has to say. Folks in the Berry patch tell me he spends time with Longstreet and Rumford. They know all about those three. Ask for Cross or Pointer over in Mecosta. They'll guide you."

"What a surprise," Bear said.

"What do you mean by that?" Alma said, tension showing in her eyes.

"Just, I'm not at all surprised about Joe. Cross or Pointer relatives of yours?" Bear added.

"Yes," Alma said, and a careful shutter closed over her eyes, barriers to any questions they might ask or want to. Her family had survived, had thrived, by living quietly. She didn't want to bring the sheriff to her relatives, but perhaps it was necessary and time. Most of all, she didn't want to invite the Legion.

Bear showed up while it was still dark, and he and Shorty ate breakfast together like they'd done for years in the kitchen of The Old Placc and before that in the Aishcum and the lumber camps.

Al piled their plates high and listened to their quiet talk – after Shorty finished his coffee, of course – letting the pleasure of memory warm her. She missed the way it had been before the Oakmere separated them all.

King and Nurse, the orange felines, clung to Shorty's wide shoulders and watched his fork move from the plate to his mouth. They'd taken a few of his bites in the past and had learned restraint so they could keep their places on his shoulders. He stood and bent to dislodge them, hugged his wife and gave her a grin.

"I'll drive Samuel's auto. We don't need to bother Jesse," Shorty said.

Bear chuckled, and Al scrunched her face as visions of him crashed in a field flashed through her mind.

"Going out," Bear said and headed to the stable.

"I'll be fine." Shorty picked her up in a hug and wandered the long kitchen and back before putting her down on the table. "Don't worry."

"I will." She yanked the ribbon from her silvery blonde hair as she did when something bothered her.

Shorty tweaked her ear and bent to kiss it.

"I mean it, Al. Don't be worrying. Gotta get the thing over to Samuel and ride back to his place with him. Wait for a chat with Hicks and then bring my gelding back here. So, don't expect me soon, and don't worry. Hear me?"

He took the worn blue ribbon from her hand, told her to gather her hair, and tied it back for her. Al tried to give him half a smile to hide the fear that lurked in her eyes.

"You'll tell me if you're doing something else?"

"Just gonna do what I said. That's all. Anything else, and I'll come tell you."

"Not looking for Legion?"

"Now, what do you know about them?"

"I heard talk."

"I'll not do anything without telling you," he repeated. "Does that work?"

Al slid from her seat on the table, wrapped her arms around the big man and squeezed, her cheek pressed against his chest, listening to the beat of his heart. She'd never known safety - until him. She wouldn't again without him, and he knew that.

"I'll be back, Al."

She patted the ribbon he'd tied, and he felt her nod against his chest.

"You even know how to start this thing?" Bear asked.

"Not an iota, but how damned hard can it be?"

They still sat in their saddles and stared at the machine. It glared back, shiny in the hazy, white winter sun.

"I know Samuel uses the crank when it hasn't been run in a while and the throttle thing on the steering column. The pedals do other things."

Bear tilted his head to look at his friend. "Other things, such as?"

"Oh, one's a hand brake, and there's a couple of gears. I'll figure it out."

They dismounted and walked around the vehicle, peered inside, moved levers and perspired in the cold air.

"Should've brought Jesse," Bear said.

"Should've bought one when I wanted to."

Shorty pushed and pulled, fiddled and swore, cranked and jumped out of harm's way, until the machine rumbled to life. He yanked open the door, squeezed into the seat, and slowly moved the accelerator lever until the vehicle sputtered forward.

Bear leaped onto his horse, which was prancing nervously to get out of range of the mad machine, and made ready to follow the smelly noisemaker. Who knew what trouble his friend might get himself into?

"You can wait here," Shorty shouted from the open door.

"Not on your life," Bear yelled. "Could really be yours," he added in a mumble.

Getting to Cassandra's house took twice as long as it should have because Shorty never moved the foot pedal out of low gear, but it didn't matter. He didn't know he should, and *he* was driving an automobile, a real auto, so the world was his, and it was good. He'd consider the bad later.

Bear followed on his mare, a grin crinkling the white lines in his beard. Life should be full of wonderous moments like these, he thought, and not what he knew the afternoon and the sheriff would bring. He pondered how to give Hicks the information on Longstreet and Rumford without bringing Charity into the conversation. It didn't seem possible, but he was going to try his best.

Samuel heard the rumble of his Model T as it chugged down the long path to Cassandra's house. He watched from the window, straining to see it creep toward him. It barely fit between the trees and brush, and he told himself not to look for scratches when it pulled up.

He gave Cassandra a one-armed hug and hobbled outside with a cane she'd made for him. Pain shredded his dignity, and it occurred to him the auto was a long way off. He didn't know if he'd make it.

"You know my appreciation," he said, his voice a worn, throaty whisper.

"And you know I'll be at your house checking on you. You should be staying put right here."

Shorty uncoiled from the driver's seat, helped Samuel in, and replanted himself in the passenger's space. Samuel nudged this, pulled that, did a couple things with his feet, sucked in a labored breath, and the vehicle turned around and took off.

Shorty's head bobbed and his eyes widened.

"Kinda fast don't you think? She has a lot of animals around."

Samuel's eyes laughed, but he slowed down.

"Didn't know it could go this fast," Shorty said, face whiter than usual. "Guess I was taking it easy on the engine, it being yours and all."

"You didn't know how to drive it, did you?"

"I do now."

They picked up Abby standing at the end of the path with a large basket on her arm and stuffed them both in the small rumble seat. Bear followed on his mare, and before they made it back to Samuel's place, the sheriff's automobile had fallen in behind.

"It's a regular parade," Shorty said.

"All we need is a balloon and a clown," Samuel said, his mustache twitching.

"You doing alright?" Shorty asked.

"Dandy." He patted his pocket and felt the flask Cassandra had given him. He wouldn't sip now, but he wouldn't hesitate as soon as he got home and was seated in his own special, horsehair-cushioned chair. He stuck a finger in the other pocket, the small one on his vest, and was comforted by the cool, smooth surface of the gold watch.

Abby invited them inside Samuel's house as if she owned it and reddened when she recognized her proprietary behavior.

"Somebody needs to do it," she whispered to Samuel when he snickered at her.

"Would you mind brewing some coffee, Abigail?" he said, "and see if there's a bottle in the cupboard, please. Shorty might need a little courage reinforcement. I gave him a pretty good ride."

"I . . . Never mind. I enjoyed the drive."

Shorty's thoughts were on his own automobile, the one he'd be buying tomorrow. Or soon.

Bear's thoughts were on Longstreet and Rumford, and the sheriff's were on wanting to finish this job and retire. He rubbed his chest, but when he thought about it, he realized it didn't hurt. It was habit, and he reminded himself he was among friends.

"It appears Emily Adams will live," he said, "so I guess we don't need to discuss that part of this whole business. It's a different situation entirely what with crazy Frank doing the shooting, and we know she's not likely to press any charges against him. And unless Benjamin and Betty press kidnapping charges against the old coot, he can do what he's doing now – playing nursemaid to the kid he stole."

Hicks lowered his head, and it swung from side to side as if it was a heavy pendulum. He ruffled his thick hair and scratched his scalp, thinking.

"So many facets to this whole thing. It's like a diamond." He looked around at the rapt faces. "Pretty fancy for an old country sheriff, huh? First, there's Frank's stronghold up in the trees. And then there's Benjamin's army, all of you who he scattered around the woods like flanking troops, and then the . . . there's the one or maybe even two sides of the diamond that bother me most."

Silence met his stare. He let his gaze follow the sound of geese and saw their broken arrow in a gray-white sky through the ceiling to floor window. His mind wandered to where Samuel could have bought a window so big. He'd like one identical to it. After he retired, he'd get one, and he'd sit and watch nothing more devious and obnoxious than blue jays.

"How'd the Legion get there?" he said, swinging his gaze back to the group. "How'd they know what was going on out in that woods and where to go? Anybody got any ideas?"

"Might want to start with Longstreet and Rumford," Samuel said.

"Why? You remember something?" Hicks asked. "You saw them?"

"Heard voices. They had hoods, so no faces."

"Voices aren't much to go on." Hicks said.

"Samuel's recollection is accurate," Bear said. "It's been confirmed."

"By who?"

"Can't say."

"That's bull. If somebody knows something, they need to talk. That's all there is to it."

Silence met Hicks' demand.

Bear didn't believe confronting Longstreet would do any good at all. He'd deny involvement, but Rumford might get rattled enough to talk. After a bit, he said so. "Head to Mecosta," he added. "See Cross and Pointer over there. They're supposed to know who's in the Legion – including Joe Foster."

"Foster?" He sounded surprised at first but then thought about it. "Of course. It makes sense, but who are Cross and Pointer? And how'd they get involved?"

"Alma is from Mecosta area. She said to check with them. That's all I know."

Hicks stared out the window again. What bothered him most wasn't so much the presence of the Legion, as horrific as that was, but how they got there. Who called on them and why?

"Tell me everything you heard, Samuel. From the beginning." The sheriff's voice was heavy with dread. He didn't want to hear about the beating or the words likely accompanying it.

"Longstreet called me a bunch of names and gave the first punches. Rumford and another held my arms. They all participated in the punching and kicking party. Guess it was required. They even dragged another man over and made him take a swing. He did, but it was a pretty pathetic blow. They laughed and called him Nancy because it was so weak, and another man made up for it on the side of my face."

"Nancy? You sure they said Nancy?" Shorty asked.

"I'm sure."

Samuel's eyes were hard, but Shorty didn't believe him, and he eyed Bear who gave a look that said he had reservations, too.

They'd pay Yancy a visit before saying anything.

Abby served coffee along with some old cookies she'd found in a cupboard for those who were hungry. Hosting in Samuel's house brought a smile to her lips and warmed her. It felt right. She stood next to him and put a hand on his shoulder after handing him his cup.

"You doing alright?"

Samuel nodded without words. He was back in the woods with the Legion thinking he'd never come out alive. Imminent death did funny things to a person's common sense. It created brighter visions, darker nightmares, longer daydreams that turned withheld desires into possibilities.

He kept himself from putting his hand over hers and holding it there. It wasn't time.

And he worried it would never be.

Chapter Thirty-four

Sheriff Hicks headed for the Adams farm. He didn't want to; the family had been through too much over the past few years - mostly brought on by themselves. Still, it didn't feel good, and he almost hoped Terry wouldn't be there.

He stopped at the barn first since the door was open, peered into the dim, straw filled room, and left for the house. Cecily opened the door and wrapped her hands around her arms for warmth. Concern clouded her eyes.

"Sheriff," she said and opened the door wider. "Is Ma Adams alright?"

Hicks stomped his snowy boots on the porch and apologized for scaring her.

"Terry around? Want to talk with him a bit."

She nodded and backed into the kitchen. Terry sat at the table, a half-eaten sandwich in front of him. Yancy sat at the other end. He nodded at Hicks and shoved his plate to the middle.

"I'll give you some privacy." Yancy rose and stepped to a bunch of work coats hanging from hooks near the door. He grabbed one and exited without putting it on.

"He going to the barn?" Hicks asked.

Terry nodded. "What can I do for you, Sheriff?"

"Couple of questions about that day in the woods."

Terry wasn't going to volunteer any information, so he waited to be asked.

"How come you found your Ma and Pa so late after everyone else had been out there for a while?" Hicks wanted to skirt around the real issues and hoped Terry might relax into the conversation.

"I was told to follow the trail. I did and ended up on the far side of the forest."

"Who told you where to go, and how'd they know?"

"Well, Yancy said where. But I followed the wrong tracks."

Terry looked amused like he'd read the funny papers, and Hicks sat back in the chair trying to figure out what was entertaining. He certainly didn't see it. Cecily offered coffee, and he took it to buy some time. He watched Terry over the rim of his cup.

"Why is that funny?" he asked Terry.

"It is and it isn't. The whole thing is as crazy as my Pa, but Ma getting shot and Moore getting beat up isn't funny."

"I'd have to agree with you there, but something apparently is."

Cecily hovered nearby, not sitting with them but not leaving the room, clutching at the edges of their conversation.

"This is the way it happened," Terry said. "Pa had been living in the woods, sneaking into the house at night and taking food and other stuff. Ma followed him one night, and Yancy followed Ma. I didn't know anything about it or I would have stopped it. Yancy was staying in the barn, so he saw her leave and followed her trail as soon as it got light."

The sheriff's eyebrow rose and he waited for the rest.

"Yancy came back here to tell me where she and Pa were, and I went to bring them home."

"How did the Legion get there? Did you call on them?"

"Nope. I didn't."

"You see them when you came through the woods behind your Pa? That was their part of the woods."

Terry shoved his uneaten lunch away and picked up his cup. Hicks knew what the man was doing, stalling, and wished he could make him talk without thinking about it first. He was stunned when Terry admitted seeing them. Came right out with it.

"Yeah. I saw them. They were almost out of sight, but I saw several mounted men heading out of the area."

"Did you see faces?"

"Nope. Didn't."

Glad Hicks had asked all the wrong questions, he pushed his chair back and put his hands on his knees. "Look, Sheriff, I went out to bring back my ma and my crazy pa. That's all. I certainly didn't want Sam Moore hurt and didn't even know he would be there. Definitely didn't want Ma to get shot. Crazy bastard."

"Take a wild guess. Who told the Legion?"

"I don't make guesses, Sheriff. That wouldn't be right, now, would it?"

Hicks finished his coffee, thanked Cecily and left, heading for the barn and Yancy. If Terry had told the truth, it made sense Yancy was the instigator in bringing the Legion into the fray, but why? What did the pipsqueak have to gain from the Legion's kind of work?

Yancy was cleaning stalls when the sheriff walked in. He blanched a sickly gray-white and kept stabbing a pitchfork into the dirty straw. Hicks made him nervous even though, in his mind, he hadn't done anything wrong. He'd convinced himself of his own innocence, so he wasn't sure why it felt so much like guilt.

"Looking for some answers, Yancy. Can you help me out?"

"Don't know, Sheriff." He dumped a fork load of straw into the wheel barrow and used the work to keep from looking Hicks in the eye. "What d'ya need?"

Hicks had been in the job long enough to recognize Yancy's pretense. It wasn't working for him.

"I'm looking for the men who beat Samuel Moore. You see who did it?"

Yancy puffed out a breath of relief. He really didn't see who hit Samuel when they were doing it. They were hooded. He couldn't tell one from the other.

Hicks put a large knobby hand on Yancy's shoulder and spun him around to look him in the eyes.

"I know you were there. You were back there with the Legion men."

"I was. I came on them but couldn't see their faces because they wore hoods. I didn't want to be there, so I left fast."

Hicks ran a hand over his face. Yancy's words rang at least somewhat true. He was a fearful kind of twerp. Hicks was sick and tired of hearing about hoods and thugs, and he was getting irate and short tempered.

"Why were you back there, Yancy?"

Something niggled at his brain and made him antsy. He didn't know what.

"I was going to help Terry, is all."

"See anyone else out there? Anyone see you?"

"Maybe the hooded men, I guess. That could be."

Sweat formed dark circles at Yancy's armpits, large wet rings of guilt hanging under his arms. Hicks took note of the stains and Yancy's nervous gnawing at a thumbnail when he stopped scooping manure and stood still. He didn't know the man well, but what he saw said culpability.

But of what? Then it hit him.

Nancy. Of course.

"You beat Samuel?" he asked, seeing Yancy's fist as some Nancy's weak hand. It fit.

"Course not. Why would I do that?"

"I don't know. Why would you? Got something against the man?"

Yancy stopped leaning on the pitchfork, took his thumbnail from his mouth, and jammed the tool into the straw again.

"You're off track, Hicks. I gotta get to work."

"Seems I heard Samuel threw you in the lake once. Why'd he do that?"

"Cuz he's an ass. I was talking with my old friend, Abby, and he comes up and . . . Never mind. Happened a long time ago."

"You hate colored folks, Yancy?"

"No! I don't hate em. But they need to know their place. That's all."

"And where is their place? Where might that be?"

"Away from white women!"

Yancy threw the pitchfork against the wall. Its prongs stuck in the weathered wood and reverberated like a church bell ringing before falling to the floor.

Hicks thought the man would have liked it to be his own chest the fork pierced, but Yancy didn't have the guts for it. He knew that. Did he have the guts to beat Samuel nearly to death with a hood over his face?

Probably not, but he'd wanted to. He knew that, too, and sorrow raised its dark head.

Hicks left Yancy to his misery.

Bear and Shorty stayed with Abby until they had Samuel settled in his bed. They didn't want to leave the bed preparations to Abby. She was their *little sister,* after all.

His bedroom had another floor-to-ceiling window which made being bedridden somewhat bearable. He could watch the deer, birds and squirrels and see anyone coming up to his house. That made him even *more* comfortable. No unknown visitors.

Abby sat by his side, watched tiny flakes fall, and sipped coffee while he ate chicken soup. Shorty and Bear shifted their feet and looked at each other, feeling like they were in the way.

"You good, Samuel? Abby?" Bear asked.

"Perfect," Abby said.

"We're heading to the Adams farm to see our old lumberjack buddy. If you need us," Shorty said, glancing back and forth, looking for a response.

Silence hung in the room and followed them to the door. They mounted and were on their way.

"What was that all about?" Shorty said.

Bear grinned. "Abby finally got what she wanted, Samuel Moore all to herself."

"Don't you be saying in bed. I'll knock you off your horse." He hauled up on the reins to slow his mount so Bear would catch up. "I can still do it, and you know it."

"Nope. Not sure about that. Married life has softened you up. Look at that big ole gut."

"My belly? You ugly old, scarred up, worthless buzzard. I oughta . . . Never mind."

They stopped at The Old Place to let Al know where they were going and headed to the farm. Small flakes meandered, but the sky said heavy snow was on the way, a lot of it. White clouds spread over a gray sky, and Bear looked up to gauge how much time until the winds picked up and the blizzard hit. It was early for a big winter storm, but it was Michigan.

Lake effect snow covered Yancy's hat and long, canvas coat well before the blizzard hit. He had gathered his few belongings, saddled his mare, and turned her west minutes after the sheriff left. He thought about finding Cecily first but decided against it. She'd cry and . . . well, hell. He didn't need a scene.

He nodded to himself and kicked his mare forward. Working as a deckhand on a Lake Michigan freighter sounded good, like it would take him far enough from Hicks, Longstreet and Rumford, and getting gone was his goal.

He feared going to jail, but thoughts of the Legion's handiwork paralyzed him. He knew Hicks would find them, and they'd find him. He wasn't waiting around for that to happen and was long gone by the time Shorty and Bear arrived at the farm, headed west toward Ludington.

Terry was in the barn and shrugged his shoulders in answer to their questions about Yancy.

"His things were gone when I came out to mend a couple of harnesses. Didn't say so long, see you later, or kiss my ass."

"Was he here when the sheriff came?"

Terry nodded. "How'd you know Hicks was here?"

"Saw him at Samuel's," Bear said.

"Told us he was coming to talk to you about the Legion," Shorty said. "Know anything about those people?"

"I'll tell you what I told to him. I saw their backs heading away from me when I was coming in from behind. That's all."

"No faces?"

"None."

"No tracks now," Bear said, peering at the heavy snowfall and the unblemished ground around the barn.

"That's for real," Shorty said.

The Old Place settled under a foot of snow. It folded over the hotel in a thick, sound-deafening blanket, white except for yellow squares scattered around the building from lamplight glowing through the window panes and painting false windows on the landscape.

Michigan winter storms enforced quiet. Solitude. Contemplation. Guests gathered in the hotel bar and spoke softly in its honor. Jackson heated toddies and cinnamon wine, captain of the room, all smiles but with a solemn air of wise introspection, too. His glance strayed to Betty who rocked in front of the warm hearth.

Al had pinned pine boughs to the stair rail and draped them over the hearth mantle, far enough from the fire to satisfy Shorty. The scene could have been in any home: mother, father, child and friends, all gathered together as early sundown forced labors to cease and folks to collect around available warmth. Rockers moved slowly, inviting soft conversation.

At the entry, Frank stamped snow from his boots, and Jackson felt cold air move through the room and slide over his shoulders. He wasn't looking forward to the trip home this night.

"How's Mrs. Adams tonight?" he asked and poured Frank a hot toddy.

"Still pretty weak. Thanks for asking and for the drink." He held the warm cup cradled in his hands, sipped and watched Benji on his mother's lap before wandering over.

"Mind if he sits with me for a bit?"

He set his drink on the floor by an empty chair, one he'd used every night since staying at the hotel, and held out his hands. Benji laughed and held his own arms out to be picked up by his favorite old man. Once there, he sat upright, pulled at the beard and chortled his glee. Frank's eyes glowed with more than the firelight reflecting in them.

Benjamin and Shorty watched and waited, never sure of Frank's stability. But since the disastrous day in the woods, he'd shown no aggression, no flights of erroneous fancy, no indication he still thought Benji belonged to him. And he was respectful toward Benji's parents.

Still, they watched.

Betty's eyes were glued to her son. She'd let people hold him – in the same room with her. Oddly enough, she trusted Frank more than others. She recognized the love in his eyes, and an essential maternal knowledge told her he'd never hurt Benji; he couldn't. Mothers know.

She smiled when Benji tugged the long, gray beard, and Frank pretended pain. The others thought he'd regained his mind, his sense, but she knew better, knew he still believed her son was his, in some strange, fantastical way. He was too clever to say it out loud, and she let him have the fantasy. And she let him be a part of her son's life.

The old man was a better father to Benji than he'd been to any of his real sons, and she knew that, too.

Betty patted Benjamin's hand. "It's okay. Our boy is in good hands. Trust me."

"I do. I should've all along. Am I forgiven?"

Betty scrunched her face at him. "Have I made you pay enough?"

"Up to you, I guess."

"Okay, last payment. Play some soft music to watch the fire by, please?"

Sweet notes floated across the room and set the mood. Conversation lagged as the music triggered personal memories.

At the Oakmere, every guest room was filled and Bear tended bar in Abby's absence. Marcus waited tables and Alma worked the kitchen and buffet with Patrick. Her son,

Carl, sat at the end of the bar waiting to take his mother home. They never let her go home alone after dark.

Patrick hobbled from the kitchen, perched at the end of the bar next to Carl and waited for Bear to see him and slide his dram of Irish whiskey down to him.

"Your ma is quite a lass," he told Carl.

"Don't think she's been a lass for a long time."

"Your family been settled in the area long?" Patrick asked, trying to make the young man feel at home. There was something prickly about him tonight.

"Why?" Carl looked sideways at Patrick as if sudden suspicion tweaked him.

"No reason, lad. Just being friendly and making a wee conversation while you wait for your ma."

Carl scratched his ear and turned away from Patrick. He didn't want to talk with the old man, not if he was going to ask questions he didn't want to answer.

"I'm from Ireland," Patrick said, a grin on his scruffy face and a twinkle in his eye. "Bet you didn't know that, did you?"

"Course I did. Everybody knows that."

"County on the sea called Donegal, beautiful Donegal. No land quite so bonnie."

"Why'd you leave if it's so great?"

"Everybody has a reason for going to or coming from a place. I wanted something better. We came to make a new life, not to run away from Ireland. Some forty years ago."

"Lots of Cross and Pointer and Berry families ran from the south to the Mecosta area." Carl stared into the glass of weak ale his mother allowed him to drink.

"Tis your family?"

"Some. Might as well be the way those people live, all knowing each other like they were brothers and sisters." Words slid off his tongue unbidden. "Settled in that area, as far over as Isabella County, and most were running from something. Like slavery. Like Jim Crow."

"Why does getting away from bad things knock you about, Carl? Seems those are respectable things to run away from."

"Can't fight if you're running." Carl wore his anger on his shirt sleeve, a young man's dissatisfaction with the life he'd been handed. "Get shot in the back that way."

"Not all lads and lasses are soldiers, young man. Some are looking for a slice of serenity, a place to lay their heads where they know they'll wake up in the morning and the sun will be shining in their eyes. They're going toward something, not running away."

"You don't know anything, mister. People need to fight some things. My grandpa is colored. My grandma is white. What the hell am I? I'm neither one!"

"I'd choose both instead of neither, son. Far as I can tell, you're a lad working on being a man. Beyond that, *what* you are is kinda up to you."

"White answer."

Carl shook his head in youthful disgust at Patrick's simplistic notion. He turned to glare at his mother as she gathered dishes from the buffet table and pushed through the kitchen doors.

"You don't understand. Nobody's calling you names, beating you up because of who you are."

"Aye. Tis true they don't beat me because I'm a leprechaun. Wouldn't have it any other way. But they did call me names and beat my kin, and Ireland has been battling for many lifetimes. I didna wish to fight."

"I do."

"Who you thinking you're gonna tangle with?" Alma came up behind, surprising both of them. "And I heard your pathetic words. Any son of mine knows who he is. You're Carl. You make *what* you are. Now get your coat. We're going home, and I'm mad at you."

Patrick smiled thinking Carl was lucky to have Alma, and Alma grumbled all the way to the door.

"Son a mine whining like a baby. I'll put you to work so hard you won't have time to worry about who you are."

"Ma, stop." He tugged her hand from his neck where she'd curled her fingers to squeeze the flesh at the nape.

"I have a good mama and a good papa," she said. "It's what they are. One is colored. One isn't, and like Mr. Riley said, you're both. You remember that."

Snow still fell, the fluffy kind, and piled up fast but made the air seem faintly warm. It stuck to eyelashes and melted on cheeks. Alma pushed her hand into the crook of her son's arm and squeezed it against her side.

"What's got you so riled up, son?"

He snorted and kicked at the snow like a little boy with a tin can.

"All this stuff going on around here, I guess. Used to be you knew what you could do and where you could go. Ain't that way anymore."

"It isn't."

"That's what I said."

"No . . . you didn't."

Carl peeked at her with a grin and took a moment for thought. "All the stuff going on around here. That old man stealing a colored baby, and now he's practically it's nanny? His white wife living at Cassandra's house. I hear she could go home now. She's well enough, but she doesn't want to. The Black Legion shit."

"Carl."

"Sorry, ma. But they scare me."

"They should. Nothing new there, Carl. They scare me, too. Stay low."

He huffed and shook his head, his fists clenched tight. "It's wrong."

"Yes, it is, but it's changing."

"Not fast enough."

"Fundamental change takes time. Has to seep into perceptions and take over. Otherwise – turbulence. Even our eyes have to change."

"Come on, Ma. Eyes?"

"Yes. How we see things. Hush now. Enjoy the snow, and don't be angry. Angry doesn't help anything at all when you don't know what to be mad at."

Chapter Thirty-five

"You need to go home, Abby. You can't stay here."

"Why can't I?"

His dark eyes snapped, and Abby grinned.

"I'm not leaving, yet. I'm going to pour us a tiny bit of Cassandra's tonic and sit in this chair by your bed to make sure you rest like a good patient."

Abby found a couple of small glasses in his kitchen and tipped the brown flask containing Cassandra's enchanted potion. It even smelled magical, like licorice and nutmeg, like the scent of fairy dust – if it existed.

"Your friends won't like you being here, Abby. You know that," he continued when she came back in the room.

She handed a glass to him and moved to the long window. Snowflakes whirled and flattened against the windowpane and piled up at the bottom ledge. She leaned against the frame, stared into the white and hoped to be stranded here, unable to leave for days, with enough snow to keep everyone else out. She'd move Samuel into the living room where the hearth would keep them warm and cozy, make soup for him and fluff his pillows. A smile lifted her lips, and a happy sigh escaped.

"Did you hear me?" he said.

"I did. They know where I am." She spun and saluted him. "Nurse Abby to the rescue. This is no different than at Cassandra's house."

"Except for Cassandra. Did you not notice no one else is here? We are alone. The two of us."

"I can count. It's just you and me. How nice is this?"

She pulled a chair up to his bed and sat, sipped her drink and refused to have the conversation. She wasn't leaving, and he couldn't make her go.

That's all there was to it.

A sip or two of the drink lifted Samuel to a cloud and his eyes went to half-mast. He drifted, the pain subsided, and he let himself watch Abby's head rest against the cushioned back of the chair, a look of serenity on her face.

When he awoke, her eyes had closed in sleep, and he could look at her without consequence. Her braid had loosened and stray locks of auburn hair framed her face. Freckles speckled her nose, and he wanted to run a finger over the creamy skin of her cheeks.

One hand lay beside him on the sheet, a capable looking hand with skin reddened from work and nails blunted and clean. Abby was no princess to be waited on. She waited on everybody else. He'd seen it and had been the recipient of it.

He wanted to pull her closer to him, show her what it meant to be loved. He knew her husband hadn't. Loving had never been his way. He clenched his teeth, and his jaws twitched in leftover anger at the stupid man. He reached for the gold watch lying on the nightstand and it clattered to the floor, waking her.

She leaped from her chair, startled and alert.

"What's wrong?"

"Nothing. Just dropped my watch. Was trying to use the bad hand."

"Don't. Cassandra said not to."

She went around his bed and saw the watch on the wooden floor, sprung open like a locket. Inside were two pictures; an older black woman and a younger white one. She picked it up and stared, fascinated.

"Who's this? I mean who are they?" she said, handing the watch to him. "I mean . . . I'm sorry. None of my business."

She fled the room, unreasonable tears in her eyes, but came to the door when he called her.

"What?"

Samuel gazed at her with hard eyes, as if glaring could pierce her mind and see the honesty in her heart. "One is my mother. The other is my sister."

"But . . . That can't be."

Abby was confused, her thoughts a jumbled mess of incoherent bits and pieces like broken china lying on the kitchen floor. Was he teasing her? Making fun of her?

"One, I understand, but. . ."

"I'm sure you mean my mother. And the other is my sister. My father was white."

"I'm amazed, Samuel. Your sister appears . . ."

"Like you." The smile he tried didn't reach his eyes. "A beautiful, ivory skinned young woman. Just like you. The difference is this. She had colored ancestry."

Had?

"I'm sorry if I sound stupid, Samuel. It's that . . . You've never talked about your family, and I know it happens – like with Charles Chesnutt. I . . . I need to shut up."

He lifted his glass, indicating he'd like a refill, and she left, poured two, and brought them back, determined to quit making a fool of herself.

Snow beat against the window pane, isolating them, making the space feel safe and private, like winter could keep misfortune from reaching in to taint them. Spring would never melt the snow and bring flowers and people and trouble.

Abby left her chair, fluffed the pillows behind Samuel, and sat next to him on the bed, leaning against his cushions. She snuggled against him – gently – and picked up the watch. She'd seen his hand caress it over and over throughout the years, and the gentle, reverent movements now made sense.

"Where are they?"

Samuel turned to see her face, his own carved from oak, his eyes from stone.

"My sister is dead. Buried beside our father."

"Oh, my God. I'm so sorry. You don't have to talk about it, Samuel. Truly."

Too late, he regretted the blunt words and put his glass on the table, picked up her hand, ran a thumb over the back and turned it over to stroke the palm.

"You work too hard, Abby." He pressed the hand to his lips and replaced it on her leg. "My father did, too. He drove himself so we could go to college, make something of ourselves. And Grace did. She made a white woman of herself, and she died for it. My father died, too."

"Oh, my God. How?"

"Trying to protect her when her fiancé found out." Heavy silence filled the room and left no space for air or breath. "Charles Chesnutt isn't the only black person who knows about passing. I didn't blame Grace. I blamed stupidity. Prejudice. Evil. I still do."

She couldn't respond for the invasion of thoughts. Samuel's inheritance, his birthright, was a legacy of mourning. Everything became clear, his words, his need to turn her from him.

She recalled the demands she'd made on him, her angry words and outlandish thoughts, and her ignorance came crashing in. Her impertinent stupidity. The same stupidity he blamed for his sister's death – she owned.

Abby couldn't stop flogging herself and didn't know if she wanted to. She had earned it, and could fill the world with what she didn't know.

"No wonder you hate me," she said, her words an agonized whisper.

Samuel's head thrust back, and he glared at her.

"What on earth makes you say I hate you?"

"Because – because I kept saying we could be together, that everything would be alright because we love each other. What a silly woman I must seem to you. No wonder you . . . But I still believe . . ." Sobs broke her words.

Samuel grabbed her neck with his good hand, and his lips on hers were hard, insistent. He pushed her against the pillows and crushed her with his body.

As suddenly as it began, it ended.

"Get out, Abby. Get out!"

She left the bedroom but not the house. Buried in his cold-pantry, she found the ingredients to make a vegetable soup and busied herself in the kitchen, blocking the words that had sent her from his bedroom and keeping them away until she could deal with them alone. She wasn't going to leave him by himself, but as soon as Cassandra came, she'd find an excuse to go.

He could be the prophet's problem.

She was much better suited to handle Samuel. Maybe she had some herbs to heal his heart and soul, or . . .

Or you should just go home and let him be. Maybe he's right and you're wrong, and he's been hurt enough. He doesn't need you adding to it.

She stoked the cook stove and the fireplace, trying to melt the ice from Samuel's words. She chopped the onions, carrots, potatoes and rutabaga found in the larder and wondered at the jars of broth she found on the shelves.

Samuel preserved food? A woman's touch? Stop it, Abby. You have a miserable, jealous heart.

She'd hung the kettle on the hanger over the hearth fire and ratcheted it up high for a long, low simmer when a firm knock startled her. Two sets of eyes peered out of woolen scarves loaded with white.

"Come in. I think," Abby said as she opened the door.

They stamped their boots, brushed shoulders and shook white stuff from their scarves before entering. She watched Cassandra and Charity emerge from the bundles of outdoor clothing.

"Found her on the way," Cassandra said. "Thought about leaving her in the snow, but changed my mind."

Cassandra's black eyes glistened with good natured humor. Part of her clowder dotted the snow-covered yard, and it crossed Abby's mind they might end as frozen effigies waiting for their mistress.

"They're fine outside, unless you think Samuel might benefit from their karma."

"Reading my mind again?" She wasn't sure if the seer was teasing or not about letting them in to visit Samuel, but she shut the door quickly just in case. He liked animals, but inviting in so many wet cats was asking for a temper tantrum, and he'd already had his quota today.

"How's the patient?" Charity asked. "I haven't visited because . . . well, I didn't want to intrude." She shuffled out of her fur lined coat and looked for a place to hang it. "It's dripping."

Abby took it from her, draped it over one of the kitchen chairs, and slid it closer to the fire to dry.

"Intrude? On whom? Want some tea?"

"We would," Cassandra said, butting in. "How is our irascible patient?"

"You said it. Irascible. And I'm glad you're here. I have to go home. Work. Da is doing it all. You know how it is."

Cassandra let Abby ramble, one brow lifted and not believing a single word of what she was hearing.

Abby busied herself, filled the teakettle and put it on the hottest part of the cook stove, set out the teapot, cups and saucers, not looking at the woman who dissected her. Cassandra smirked and pushed her into a chair, removed a packet from the pocket of her long dress and dumped it into the teapot.

"Go on in and say hello, Charity. He'll be happy to see a new face."

A breathy shriek from Samuel's bedroom startled them both, and they headed in that direction. They bumped into Charity who was backing out, one hand over her mouth and tears flowing from her eyes.

"Oh, my God. My God. Look at you. Those evil monsters."

Samuel held his good hand to his stomach as if it might stop the pain his movement caused as he laughed at Charity's response to his appearance. He knew his swollen and bruised face was shocking, but those around him had gotten used to it, and he'd forgotten how bad it looked.

"Get in here, Charity. I'm no monster."

"You're not. They are." She crept around the door again and peered at him. "Samuel, you are so hurt. Look what they did to you. I'm so sorry."

"I don't want to look, and you didn't do it, Charity. They did."

Seeing all was well and no intruders threatened mayhem, they left Samuel's room and attended to the tea.

Cassandra grabbed the kettle before it began to whistle, and Abby's gaze darted to the door, wondering how to escape Samuel's house while the seer was still in it. Abby didn't like the perceptive look in the woman's eyes, and she also didn't care for feeling like an unwanted guest, which was the sense of the moment.

The healer poured hot water from the kettle without looking at the pot it went into because her eyes were on Abby who squirmed under the scrutiny.

"I do have to work, you know," Abby said, defending herself from Cassandra's mute observation. "I'm needed."

"Of course." She put the pot on a tray along with the cups and saucers.

"I should go while you're both here."

"After your tea."

Abby fidgeted and knew she couldn't contradict Cassandra. It wasn't done. She moved toward Samuel's room, bringing another chair with her and arriving in time to hear Charity at the tail end of her story about her father's visitors, Longstreet and Rumford.

"I heard their voices, Charity. I told Hicks I did, but he said voices weren't enough."

"But I heard Longstreet admit it. All of it. I listened at the door. Wouldn't that be enough to put them in jail?"

Samuel stiffened beneath the covers.

"It might, but have you considered the impact on your father?"

Charity moved to Samuel and ran a tender hand over his bruised cheek, the salty track of her now dried tears stiffening her own, and she rubbed it away with her other hand. Resolve churned in her stomach, and for the first time since her college days, she felt worthwhile.

"I'm thinking of him, too. He needs to stop this ungodly relationship." Charity's eyes softened. "He wasn't always like this. Before he was transferred here, he cared about people. I don't know what happened. Maybe he took the transfer as punishment instead of promotion. I think Ma had something to do with that." She shifted and reached for the cup Cassandra offered.

"Think first, Charity. That's all I ask," Samuel said.

"I need to go now," she said. "I need to see Sheriff Hicks. May I use your automobile?"

Two faces swung to her, eyes wide with awe filling them.

"You know how to drive one?" Samuel asked, the first to find his tongue.

"Of course." She sparkled at him. "You wouldn't believe what I learned at college."

His good hand came up, palm out in defense.

"It's alright. You don't need to elucidate. Ignorance is sometimes a responsible state of mind."

"Would you give me a ride? I need to leave while someone is here with him," Abby said.

Without waiting for a response, Abby took the tray to the kitchen and felt Cassandra's black eyes boring into her back. She wondered briefly if she'd find actual holes there, as if the seer had thrown a spell at her, and twitched with the desire to look in a mirror.

She jerked when she turned to find Cassandra had followed her to the kitchen.

"He can't be left alone, you know. He still needs help."

"Can't you stay?"

The woman eyed her. "What happened?"

"Nothing," she lied. "I don't think he wants me here. That's all. I'll find someone else to come if you can be here for a while. Bear or Edna. Even Jesse might come for a short time."

"Fine," she said, still not believing a word she'd heard. "Send my cats in. Samuel will have to get used to them."

Charity drove expertly, as Abby figured she would, and during the ride, she came to envy the younger woman, finding she wished to be more like her – confident, smart, educated. She thought about bobbing her hair like Charity's, but nothing could make it a beautiful blonde color. She gave an unintentional sigh and Charity glanced her way.

"You okay? I admit I'm surprised you left Samuel. I couldn't be pried away from my man if he was in a sickbed."

"He's not my man. And I have things to do."

Her words held nettle stings, and Charity cowered melodramatically, almost sliding them off the road.

"Sorry," she said with a laugh. "Didn't mean to overstep. Definitely didn't mean to drive us off the road."

Abby couldn't help but laugh with her and was glad for her company.

"You didn't. But he wanted me to leave, so I'm leaving."

"Still . . . I'd stay no matter what anyone said, including him. But you're a lot nicer than I."

"Not true, Charity. You're kinder than you let on. You going to see the sheriff?"

"I am."

"See what I mean?"

Abby waved a mittened hand at the footpath and headed for the Oakmere, wondering who she could get to sit with Samuel. The answer was in the bar in the form of Jesse, Edna and Charles. She'd worry about later, later.

Charity made it to Sheriff Hicks' office without sliding into any snow laden fields and enjoyed the sheriff's surprised eyes as she parked in front. He was at the door watching snow mound and wondering if he'd make it home when she pulled up.

"You beat all, Charity. Doesn't anything frighten you?"

"Only babies, Sheriff."

"Not automobiles or blizzards?"

"No. Just babies. Got a minute?"

Hicks scratched his head, getting the sense of trouble on its way, and Charity tilted hers to look at the lush thatch of hair on his head. She'd not seen him without a hat before and wanted to run her hand through the thick waves.

"Wow. Didn't know you had all that pretty hair. You shouldn't cover it up with that big ole hat."

Hicks flushed pink and pointed to the extra chairs in front of his desk. "Have a seat. What can I do for you that was so important it made you come out in a winter storm?"

"It was fun driving through the snow."

"Samuel's auto?"

She nodded. "And he's why I'm here."

"Let me get us some coffee first. You need something warm."

When he returned and set the cups on the desk, he sat, leaned back in his worn chair and looked at her. She was an attractive young woman, and it occurred to him to wish he wasn't so old.

"So, start at the beginning, Miss Evans."

Chapter Thirty-six

"He shouldn't have withheld the evidence we were looking for, Charity. I don't know what the court will do about any charges against him, but I'll go today to ask him about the three known Legion members and make the arrests afterwards."

He handed her the fur coat and helped wrap her in it before she left the warm office.

"Give me time to see my father before coming to the house, please?"

"It'll be awhile. I need to round up my deputy and a couple more men first. Not gonna try to handle this one on my own."

She hugged him, an impulsive move that startled Hicks, but he understood. She was afraid of more than babies, and she loved her father, no matter what. The conversation she needed to have with him wouldn't be an easy one. Charity had grit, more than what met the eyes at first glance.

He and his deputy stopped at The Old Place to ask Shorty to ride along. Benjamin overheard and volunteered.

"Not sure you coming is a good thing, Benjamin," Shorty said, thinking he could become a target for the Legion.

"I disagree. I'm the perfect choice. I have good reason to be there."

They glanced at Hicks, waiting for his opinion.

"You sure about this?" Hicks asked, and gave the okay after Benjamin's nod.

He didn't have much to explain since they were aware of most details, and they left after loading the sheriff's proffered handguns and burying them in deep pockets.

At the reverend's house, Charity let them in and led the way to her father's study. Her mother was absent, but they all heard sobs coming from the upstairs, and it wasn't hard to deduce who and why.

"Can I bring tea? Coffee?" she asked.

"That might be a good thing, Charity, ease the way into conversation."

Hicks wasn't looking forward to cornering Evans, but he'd be happy to see the end of these cold-blooded, bigoted men. Their work was hateful, sadistic even, and he believed all Legion members should be in jail - or dead. Whichever. He had grown jaded over the years and didn't care which, and he'd gotten tired of thinking about them.

He removed his hat, thought of what Charity had said about his thick hair, and couldn't help the twitch of a grin when she brought in the tea tray and sat. Plainly, she intended to be part of the discussion.

Reverend Evans sat stiffly behind his desk. He didn't bother to come around it to shake hands, and that was alright with Hicks. This wasn't a social call and no amount of pretense would make it so.

"I didn't bring all these men with me just to speak with you, Reverend, but I didn't want to leave them out in the cold, either," he said, staring at the man slouched at his desk. "Thanks for seeing me. You know what I'm here for?"

Evans grunted his affirmation and Hicks took a sip of tea and went right to it since it didn't seem the man was inclined to be conversational. He didn't really blame him. It wasn't his best day.

Hicks asked all the pertinent questions, and the reverend grudgingly gave all the answers needed to put Longstreet, Rumford and Joe Foster away for a while. At the very least, it would make a dent in the local Black Legion membership.

"You don't know the names of the others who beat on Samuel?"

Evans look came close to a sneer. "Ask Longstreet."

At The Old Place, Betty and Al stood by the fire soaking in the warmth and talked about where their husbands had gone, their whispered voices holding everything from angst to hope.

"Benjamin is a soldier, Betty. He knows what he's doing." Al tried to bolster her, but she could use some encouragement herself.

"But he's a colored man, Al, and going up against the Legion is fearful. The Black Legion won't think twice before shooting a man, specially a negro. Shorty and Benjamin will, and they might think two seconds too long."

Al knew Betty spoke the truth. And while she thought Shorty capable of doing anything and everything, love made her terrified. She didn't want a world without him in it.

Betty recognized the fear in Al's eyes. It looked like her own felt.

"I need to cook," Al said.

"I know. I'll help. I'm done upstairs. Doesn't surprise me about Joe Foster, but the reverend? That's just sinful."

Frank overheard and knew right away what Betty meant. Foster was Legion. He'd been part of the force out in the woods. Frank stoked the fire and collapsed in one of the rockers. He liked it here, liked the people, the place, the conversation and Benji. He loved his son.

And he liked who he was when he was here, a nice old man without any responsibilities except loving a child. He wanted to stay and didn't care the child was different from himself. He didn't care that any of them were. He'd gotten over all that nonsense, and this was where he wanted to be.

Not the farm. Not jail.

He bundled up and went to the kitchen to tell Betty and Al he'd be gone for an hour or so. Maybe he'd stop to see Emily first, see how she was doing. She liked where she was staying, too. He smiled. It had just taken them a long time to find where they were supposed to be. Some forty-odd years.

He headed into the brisk snowstorm and caught flakes on his tongue, laughing when they stung his eyes and wondering how many years it had been since he'd even noticed snow unless it impacted the cows.

The trail to Cassandra's place stilled the whole world since overhead branches made a tunnel of the path and turned the earth to a fairyland.

Fairyland? You're going dotty, Frank. But, that's okay.

He saw Emily sorting peas at the kitchen table, one arm still in a sling tucked against her chest. He cringed as he always did when he thought about what he'd done to her. He'd undo it if he could and hoped she knew. He'd told her so, but he'd be sure to tell her again, today.

She smiled at the face in the door window and he came in, removed his boots as he'd never done before, and hung his coat. He kissed her cheek and nuzzled his cold nose against her neck until she shivered.

"What are you doing out on a day like this, Frank?"

"Came to see you. What are you doing?"

Frank cocked his head to stare at his laughing wife. She looked younger every day. He wondered if he should tell her.

"Going to make some pea soup so Cassandra doesn't have to cook when she gets home. I can do most of it pretty much one-handed."

"Can I help?"

She twisted her head to question him with her eyes before answering.

"Why, yes. You surely can."

"Name it."

Her eyes lit with fire and affection. The Frank she had prayed for was here in front of her. Where had he been for so long? For forever, actually.

"You can chop an onion because it's hard for me to do with one hand, and you can steep it in the kettle. Would that be alright?"

"You just ask, Emily. I can do it. Want some tea?"

She flushed like a girl and said, *yes*.

In half an hour, they made pea soup and drank tea. He talked about how sorry he was for hurting her, and simply talked – more than the two had in the last ten years put together.

She hurt remembering the arid desert of their lives and pushed it to the back of her mind where she would force it to stay.

"Are you going home soon?" she asked.

"No. Are you?"

She shook her head, suddenly afraid he would make her, would tell her to. She didn't want to leave. She was learning from Cassandra every day and wanted to continue. She didn't want to go back to her other sterile life.

"I want to stay," she said, willing strength into her words. "Here. Cassandra wants me to."

Frank beamed. It looked odd on such a burly man, but he looked ridiculously happy, and, because of his contentment, she was, too.

"Well, then, it all works out. I like where I am, and I'm sure Terry likes having the farm all to himself." He squinted a grin at her. "I can visit you, right?"

"I'd be mad if you didn't."

Joe Foster sneered at him when he walked into the store. Frank didn't understand why, but he didn't care, either. Joe was part of his old life, and he realized he didn't like the man and never had. His churlish behavior rubbed everyone the wrong way – and he smelled.

Frank sniffed into his glove to rid himself of the stale odor of the store and didn't waste any time saying what he came to say.

"Just needed to tell you the sheriff is coming to arrest you for the beating of Samuel Moore. You, Longstreet, and Rumford. So, you might want to get out of town. That's all. We're even now."

He turned to leave, and Joe stepped in his way.

"Hell, man. You can't walk in here and tell me to leave town. I'm not going anywhere. This is my home. I own it, and nobody can kick me out of it."

Frank slumped, disheartened. He didn't want to be here. He'd felt beholden because of the past and since Joe had been there to help him out in the woods. He wouldn't be obliged to him ever again, but this debt he had owed.

"They're coming for you, Joe. With guns. I heard em talking at the hotel, so you should probably leave out the back way."

"I'm not going nowhere," Joe snarled.

He puffed his chest, strode behind the counter and pulled out a rifle. He checked to see how many bullets it held, racked it and flicked off the safety. It was ready to fire, and Frank closed his eyes in disappointment and despair. This was not what he'd planned.

It was the woods all over again.

He knew he needed to leave and headed for the door. Outside, Sheriff Hicks and his deputy climbed out of the county auto and Benjamin and Shorty dismounted. Sorrow filled him, and the thought of Benji kept him upright when he would have crumbled.

You earned this, old man. Too little, too late.

"Get back here," Joe shouted. "You ungrateful bastard! Get back here!"

Frank kept walking toward the sheriff. Joe came to the door, rifle pointed, moving the barrel tip from one person to the next and back again.

"Put the gun down, Joe. We're gonna talk," Hicks said.

"Like hell we are." Foster pointed the rifle at Benjamin and screamed, "Colored son of a bitch! You're the problem here. Not me!"

Frank roared and flung himself in front of Benji's father before slumping to the ground. The snow bled vivid red near his chest, and the pain in his eyes was momentary, a fleeting reaction to Foster's hate before peace settled over his face and became serenity close to pleasure.

Foster racked his rifle and raised it again; Hicks fired, and Foster fell. He didn't move.

"You okay? You good, Benji?" Frank said when Benjamin knelt by his side and tried to stop the bleeding.

"I am. You saved me, Frank. I don't know what to say. Why'd you do that?"

"*You* saved *me*, Benji. Tell Emily . . . I'm sorry." Frank took a last breath.

Hicks, his gun aimed at Foster's back, turned the man over. Blood poured from a hole where his heart should have been. The sheriff didn't miss. Ever. But it didn't mean he liked it. He'd had the lives of three other men to consider, and Joe looked determined.

Hicks shot to kill, but so did Joe – first.

"I'll get Cassandra," Shorty said, watching Hicks and Frank at the same time.

"No need. For either of them is my bet." Hicks sat back on his heels and wiped a hand over his face like he could cleanse it of the last few minutes.

Benjamin closed the eyes of the man his son loved enough to pull on his beard and laugh. For that reason alone, he mourned Frank.

"Can I ask you two to take care of Frank and Joe?" Hicks said. "I've got arrests to make."

Anger boiled in his eyes, seeped from his pores, and stretched the muscles of his jaw until it seemed like his skin would split open. He'd had enough.

"Get in, Deputy."

"Wait," Shorty said. "We're going with you to pick up Longstreet and Rumford."

"Nope. Changed my mind. Not getting anyone else killed today. This is our job. Not yours."

Hick's cursed himself. He'd seen the look in Joe's eyes and, for a split-second, had thought Benjamin was a dead man and wished for his own death. He'd waited too long, and now a man was dead.

He wasn't taking that risk again.

Deputy Paterson kicked in the door of Longstreet's house with one healthy eruption of his right foot, and they both charged in, revolvers drawn and ready. The man they wanted sat at his dining room table, a newspaper spread out, his shirt unbuttoned at the collar and his sleeves rolled to the elbows. The fork continued its travel to his plate where he placed it carefully and shook his head in disgust.

"What the hell do you think you're doing, Hicks? You can't barge into private property."

Longstreet didn't have time to stand before two revolver barrels pressed against his temples.

"I just did. Get up and put your hands behind your back. Or don't. I'd prefer to shoot and rid the world of your stinking presence."

The tone of Hicks' command made Longstreet do exactly as he was told. He didn't want to die today and figured he would if he varied from the sheriff's instructions. His eyes had made that clear.

They shoved him in the back seat of the county car, hands cuffed, and buckled him to the rack made for the purpose.

"It's cold back here," Longstreet complained.

"Damned right. It's a cold day in hell," Hicks said, and chuckled at his little joke, a grim sound.

Rumford came outside right after they smashed in his front door. He knew instantly, and they had to halt his trek toward the vehicle in order to put the cuffs on.

"You'll be sorry, Hicks," Longstreet said from the back seat. "We have friends."

"I'm sure you do. You won't be having tea with them where you're going."

The deputy turned his head to stare at his boss. He'd never heard him so hard, so absolute.

Halfway back to the sheriff's office, where nothing but trees and animals lived, Hicks turned down a two-track road much like Cassandra's path, tunneled and clear of snow, and drove for what seemed miles but was likely not. It was tense in the vehicle, the air thick and pungent, and the back seat exuded the nauseating odor of guilt, fear and fury.

Hicks stopped at a place where he could maneuver the car around and swiveled in his seat. He eyed the two men in the back; one until he fidgeted and then the other.

"Cold?" he asked.

"Damned right," Longstreet said. "Told you."

"How would you feel about taking a walk in the snow buck naked? It's a long way back to town."

"You're crazy. You can't do that." Longstreet held onto his belligerence like a security blanket, but Rumford blanched whiter than his normal pasty color.

"We'd die out here," he said.

"Could happen." Hicks gave his deputy a look that said, 'don't interfere' and continued. "Human bones have been dragged up out of the woods by wild dogs before. Hell, even by domestic dogs."

He turned to the deputy with slow, deliberate ease. "Remember when Dog . . ." He looked at the back-seat men as if they were having a friendly conversation, and they needed the coming information. "That's the old hound belongs to Al Tatum. Well, he came up to the house dragging old man Tatum's leg bone." Hicks chuckled. "It happens. Strange how hungry dogs find human bones scattered here and there and gnaw on em."

"It surely is," Deputy Paterson said, drawling it out now that he understood his bosses' intentions.

"Wait," Hicks said. "He'd been already killed and buried in a really shallow grave, but same difference, I guess. Start stripping, boys."

"Our hands are cuffed, Sheriff," Rumford said, tears beginning to form in his eyes.

"Oh. Right. Well, how about you tell me the names of the other three men who were at your little party in the woods, and maybe you won't have to walk."

Rumford spilled immediately and received a kick in the leg from Longstreet. The sheriff thought they ought to patent this as a bona fide interrogation method. He didn't recognize two of the names, but he knew the third.

Yancy Black.

Chapter Thirty-seven

When Cassandra opened the door, she knew Shorty brought trouble. She could see it in his posture as he rode up to the house. He stepped just inside the door and whispered to her.

Cassandra nodded with knowledge. It was karma's way of cleaning up the world, of dispensing overdue recompence.

"I'm sorry to hear that. Justice is too late, it sometimes seems. Frank was just here helping her make soup. You should have seen her light up telling me all about it. She looked like a newlywed."

"I've told Terry. He's right behind me."

"Where is Frank?"

"With Pastor Jenkins," Shorty said.

"The colored preacher?" Cassandra's mirth couldn't be contained. "How appropriate. One more arrow from Karma's bow."

"More than you realize right now. You'll understand in moments."

Hearing voices, Emily slipped into her shoes and came out to greet Shorty with a sense of apprehension she didn't understand but felt deep in her bones.

"How about some coffee or tea, Cassandra, or a dram of brandy?" Shorty knew he could use one, and Emily would shortly.

Cassandra put the kettle on and prepared the teapot. "I think both," she said as Terry's face appeared in the window.

"Ma," he said as he opened the door, and he was by her side in three long strides.

"Nooo . . ." Emily moaned, a long drawn out word that carried too much pain, too much longing and wishing to hold onto the minutes before the words were said, before reality crushed her. Her eyes filled, and she did her best to contain the tears that clogged her throat and tangled with her breath.

She sat at the kitchen table and stared at her son, one of three she'd carried in her womb, the only son she could hold, the only one she could reach out to touch. And now she wouldn't have more.

She mused about it as if age had nothing to do with her ability to bear children. Her eyes clouded as she tried to face reality as she had her entire life. Head on.

Fertility isn't the problem, you old fool. Frank is dead. That's the problem. Your husband of forty years left you directly after you found him.

The roar of agony never came out to spray the room with the wail she heard in her head. She thought it would. Thought it must. And it didn't rupture her lungs or explode her heart.

She saw visible anguish being tossed into George's grave along with crumbles of dirt and pieces of her heart, knew she had to do it all again, and did her best to straighten her spine. Pain nestled deep inside – like a seed tucked safely in the heart of an apple.

"I'd like some whiskey," she said.

Shorty splashed a hefty amount from the bottle Cassandra gave him and put it in Emily's remarkably steady hand. He poured three others and lifted his in the air toward her.

"Here's to Frank. I liked him," Shorty said.

"I did, too. Lately," Emily said with a backward look in her eyes and a swallow. "I always loved him. He is . . . I mean, he was so handsome. So strong."

"He saved a man today. He saved Benjamin, and he meant to do it. You need to know that. And he died with your name on his lips and peace on his face."

"He would. He'd do both of those things. Thank you, Shorty, for telling me."

He refilled their cups because it seemed she wanted to talk about Frank – the good and the bad of him. She wanted them to know the one she had known for years and the new man who must have been in there all along.

They decided to bring Frank and Joe Foster to Cassandra's place for preparation. Cassandra chuckled at the idea of giving Joe a bath, saying he hadn't been clean in years, and it was high time, and she wanted to be the one to do it. She regretted her inability to hear him yelling and cursing as the soap and water connected with his skin. She'd miss the pleasure of his fury.

"You sure?" Terry asked. "We can take Pa back to the farm."

Emily shook her head. "He didn't want to be there, Terry. He liked living at the hotel and wanted to stay. In fact, he told me so just today." Her eyes misted at the memory, but she held it together.

"Then that's where he'll stay until the funeral," Shorty said.

"What will Patrick and Abby have to say about that? Might not be too good for business," Terry said.

"They'll agree with me."

And Frank went to live at The Old Place for the rest of his time on earth. In Idlewild, he became a strange kind of hero for his courageous act, to coloreds and whites alike. He had a place of honor in the bar across from the buffet, and, during the three days of his wake, Emily sat with him.

She was rarely alone. Folks joked that more people came to pay respects to Frank than would for the president. Emily didn't believe it to be true, but the number of mourners and people simply paying respect did surprise her.

Word spread fast that Frank had taken a bullet meant for Benjamin, had saved him, and folks needed to honor this valiant act whether it had to do with race or not. Whether they had liked Frank or not. Whether it changed Idlewild or not. He had saved one of theirs.

He looked good: his six-foot frame strong, his face unlined, tanned and at peace. At times, she wanted to crawl into the satin lined casket with him, curl up together and pretend they were in a bed made up with satin sheets, and they'd wake up in the morning, drink coffee, eat sausage and eggs. He would grouse about the work he had to do on the farm, and she'd be anxious for him to go do it, so she could get to hers.

Silence was her ruin, those times when she and Frank were alone in the room and stillness ran roughshod over her courage. She tried not to reminisce, tried not to see them as they were the days just before, when his heart beat strong and loving. Tears seeped when recent memories invaded, and she was grateful to seldom be alone.

"I miss him," Betty said, coming up behind her. "I think Benji does, too. He keeps looking over here like Frank should get up out of that box and come hold him and let him pull on his beard."

Betty took a chair next to Emily, Benji on her lap. She stared at the casket like words to offer his wife would leap out and come to her if she waited for them near his body. There were things she wanted to tell Emily, things Frank had said or done since they all came back from the woods, like it was a rite of passage. Things he'd told Benji or things Benji had done to him. Somehow, the old man had become important to them all – through her son – and now she missed him.

"Frank and Benji are kind of like me and lily-white Al," Betty snorted, and Emily looked sideways at her.

She ended up telling Emily all about how she and Al came to be friends years ago when Abby had asked her to be nice because Strange Al didn't have anyone at all. Betty had scoffed like that wasn't gonna happen but found herself going out to the Tatum place to help Al clean after the brothers went to jail and her father had disappeared. She grew to like Al, even love her.

"She's family to me now, and we have lots of differences but they don't matter anymore. Truth to tell, they never did. We just thought so because we didn't know better. She's a sister. Abby knew right off, but some of us have to be told. Abby always knew. Or she hoped even if it wasn't likely to happen."

Emily's eyes made her uncomfortable so she closed hers and nuzzled Benji's head.

"That's what Frank used to do. He smothered Benji's head with kisses," Betty whispered, her lips still tangled in his hair, and the floodgates of memories opened.

"I know. I saw him doing that up in the treehouse. He loved the feel of Benji's hair under his lips. Did he tell you he tried to see if the skin color would wash off? In the freezing cold creek."

Betty reared back thinking Emily meant Frank wanted him to be white.

"No. You misunderstand. He loved Benji's skin and wanted to be sure it *wouldn't* wash off. Said the baby screamed and screamed. The only time he ever howled like that, according to Frank." Emily smiled and nudged the younger woman with her elbow. "He was crazy, remember."

"Not so sure he was. But I did hear him screaming in the woods. Must a been the day they were washing in the creek, and it was good he did that. I knew my baby was still alive."

"Benji found the real Frank, the man who was inside all those years. I couldn't find him. I looked and looked. Neither could his sons." Her lips twisted as she stifled the anguish, but she turned to Betty. "Do you know, he never once changed a diaper or fed his babies until Benji? Not even once."

"I'm sorry." Betty didn't know if Emily was angry or not, but she should be. "I'm really am sorry."

Emily put an arm around Betty's back and tugged her close. "No. No sorrow. I'm glad to have known this Frank, the one who loved your son and brought us together. Sort of makes you my daughter, doesn't it, in a strange kind of way?" She squeezed her shoulders. "Have you seen the people paying respects? Frank brought the whole town out. Who would think he could do that? He was a powerful force."

"I was glad he came into our lives. I have to admit it. Wouldn't tell him so, but . . . other than Abby, he didn't care about color the truest of anyone. I mean, he saw color and it wasn't that he didn't care about it. He had a real *love* for it, for the beauty of it, for the honor of it. He did, Mrs. Adams."

Tears formed in Betty's eyes, and Benji squirmed under the unfamiliar tightening of her arm. Emily reached for him, and he went. He stood on her lap, patted her face and pulled her hair. She laughed and let him. When he settled down, Emily nuzzled the top of his head and relished the feel of soft, springy ringlets under her lips.

Abby managed to stay away from Samuel's home for an entire two days after he'd told her to get out. She battled with her resolve, fought her feelings and lost. So in the early morning, she went to check on him.

Alma heard the front door and met her in the kitchen with a finger over her lips.

"He's sleeping. He had kind of a fitful time of it."

"Did he take any of Cassandra's medicine?"

"Said he didn't want any. He wanted a clear head."

Alma chewed her lip, worrying over something she wanted to say to Abby but not wanting to overstep the boundaries of their employment relationship. She decided she'd never been very good at boundaries and jumped in.

"You saw Samuel's watch pictures, I hear."

Abby nodded and bristled knowing he'd shared that private information with Alma, but curiosity overshadowed her annoyance.

"I did."

"And?"

"And what? Lovely mother and beautiful sister. I wish I could have known his sister and hope someday to meet his mother."

Words rushed from her mouth and collided with each other in her irritation – and then she was irritated with herself.

Alma smiled. It seemed a sugarcoated smile and tweaked her further.

Was she doing this deliberately?

"Look, Alma. I'm here to care for Samuel, so if you have something to say to me, just say it." By this time, Abby's hands were on her hips, and her eyes were narrowed.

"Sorry. I've been enjoying Samuel's angst, not yours. It isn't often – in fact, never since I've known him – that someone has gotten to the man. You have. You have him in a neck hold. Good for you, girl."

Abby backed up to the table, pulled out a chair and sat. She pointed to another, and Alma took it.

"Explain, please."

"We've waited years for someone to take the wind out of his sails."

"What wind? Why?"

"Because he's so arrogant. You know it's true. Now, he doesn't know what to think, what to do. He is completely thrown. He loves you, and it tickles my funny bone."

"But . . . He . . . You . . ."

"What?"

"Never mind. He does a damned good job of pretending not to even like me. He kicked me out of his house."

"Sure, he did."

She couldn't look at Alma and stared out the window instead, intent on watching sparrows chasing a mouthy blue jay away.

"You make no more sense than he does. I thought he cared for me once."

"They had a tough time when his father and sister died. You just don't know what it's like to have your hands tied by your skin color."

"Do you?" Abby asked, her tone softening.

"Sure. All of us do. You, too. But even though I'm mixed race, I haven't come up against the harsh brutality he has, not personally. Maybe because of where I was raised. They came north after the lynching, and his mother found a place with us in Mecosta where she's accepted."

"Your father is colored?" Abby asked and wondered how she could so casually probe the woman's private life, her family.

Alma nodded. "I've never thought of my father as a black man, even though he is. I think of him as my father – a good man, a hardworking, loving man."

"Sounds like you worship your pa a little bit."

Alma stood and wrapped up in her coat and scarf. "I do. He's worthy of it. I'm heading to the hotel for work."

Abby stood and walked to the door with her. "Was there something you had to say to me?"

"I did. Just wanted to tell you he can't stop talking about you and can't stop worrying over it."

And I can't stay, and I can't stay away. Damn.

She fixed coffee, made scrambled eggs, bacon and toast, brought it all on a tray and watched him eat. When she tidied the room and opened the curtains, she felt his eyes following her and then glance away when she looked toward him. She watched him watching her from sidelong glances. They played eye tag, an adult kind of hide and seek, but neither would have admitted to the game.

"Want me to bring a bowl of warm water so you can wash your hands and face?"

"No. Thank you. I can get up to use the facility and wash up if you'd leave the room"

"You need help?"

He tilted his head and wrinkled his brow. "No. I'm capable of doing this on my own."

"Kicking me out again?"

"Just out of my bedroom, please."

From the kitchen, she listened to him move about and winced when grunts of discomfort leaked through the walls. When he finally called her name, she rushed in hoping he hadn't slumped to the floor because she didn't think she could pick him up. But he stood fully dressed, shaved, and looking fresh.

"Look at you, all grown up and dressing yourself," Abby said with a grin.

She touched a few stray whiskers on his face and clicked her tongue.

"Missed some?"

"Yes. But you look wonderful. Handsome, even. Are you going somewhere?"

"To a funeral, Miss Adams. I need to pay my respects. I hate to admit this, but I need a bit of help getting to my vehicle and to the service. Would you oblige?"

Abby kicked the leg of his bed. "Not sure I should after you mistreated me so. Get out! What kind of thing is that to say to a friend?" She grinned, teasing but wanting it out in the open, too.

"I'm sorry. Is that acceptable? Will you help me, now?"

"Maybe I should go get someone who knows how to start and drive an automobile?"

"Help me get to the damned thing and I'll tell you what to do."

"So, we're cussing, now, and today is just like any other day, huh? I go where you say, and you tell me what to do. Of course, my lord, Samuel." She mock bowed to him.

She didn't know why she needed to bait him. Perhaps she was miffed. Or maybe she was giddy with Alma's words. But most likely, she wanted him to grab her by the nape and kiss her again. No, not most likely - most positively.

"You sure you should do this?"

"Positive."

"Yeah. Me, too," she whispered and helped him with his coat.

Samuel walked into the hotel with the help of a cane and Abby's shoulder. People parted, leaving a path for him to maneuver to one of the chairs rearranged to resemble seating for a congregation.

Whispers followed them, and Samuel read unspoken apology in the eyes of white friends who gave gentle, welcoming back slaps that nearly felled him. They didn't speak of a hundred years regretted, five generations of atonement due, but the thought burned like a flame in hearts and minds. They embraced Samuel as the visible reminder of raw stupidity.

In some, remorse established itself in the shifting of shoulders, the fleeting glances and quickly lowered eyes. Embarrassment, guilt, confusion. Samuel recognized the symptoms for which knowledge and experience are the only cures.

Shorty and Bear, who had always walked the far side of the street along with him, nodded their welcomes and looked at him with affection, genuinely glad to see him healing and on his feet, no matter if they were unsteady.

Neither felt the need to display their thoughts, but Patrick looked up at him and continued the tears he'd already begun to shed for Frank. The Irish weren't afraid to show heartache or happiness.

"Ye have a rocking chair waiting for ye at the Oakmere, Samuel, right in front of the hearth fire. A seat and a glass or two of me best Irish. Ye shouldna have been treated so." He reached up to caress Samuel's still bruised face.

"I'm gonna survive, Patrick, but I thank you for the offer of a chair and a drink." He smiled at the leprechaun with fondness as natural as sunrise.

When shaking legs lowered him to his seat, he released a long-held breath, not comprehending what was going on around him. So much affection from so many people. For him. And it was real. Eyes in white faces looked straight into his. Arms went around him. Hands touched his face, and he didn't mind, didn't push them away. Of course, he didn't because they were his friends. He liked them and even loved some – if he'd admit it.

Frank's casket remained at the far end of The Old Place bar, temporarily a church, and was flanked by a dozen or so bouquets of flowers. Emily, Terry, Cecily and the boys took up the front row on one side of the aisle and Betty, Benjamin, Benji and Betty's parents the half on the other side. It looked like segregation in full bloom.

Samuel noted the colors, frowned and turned to survey the rest of the chairs behind him.

Sue and Sally flaunted integration by flanking Shorty and Al, and Edna Falmouth grabbed Al's brother, Marcus, to sit with her and Jesse. Bunny Parker refused to sit in the back row and planted herself in the front next to Emily who embraced her with pleasure. She'd come to love Jackson's beautiful, elegant mother. Bear came through the lobby door alongside big Gus, and Cassandra took Patrick's sleeve and wouldn't let go.

It seemed everyone wanted to make a liar of Samuel's interpretation of a segregated congregation.

"They're placed according to familial relationships," he said to Abby.

"Who?"

"The front rows."

"Of course. That's always the case. What were you thinking?" She looked at the front row and scowled. "Oh, Samuel."

He glanced sideways at her. She sat inches away, her arm not touching his, legs crossed and foot bobbing, a bundle of unexploded energy.

"Never mind. You wouldn't understand," he said.

"But I want to."

Confusion addled his brain, being here to give regards to a man he'd never liked, seeing folks he'd never expect to see at an Adams funeral, so many white and black people together, but all mixed up, not chunked into color squares like they should have been. Would have been a few years ago. Hell. Weeks ago.

He glanced again at the congregation, and it didn't change a thing. They were still all mixed up. His face felt hot, and he lowered his head and put his hands over his eyes.

"You alright, Samuel? You feeling sick?" Abby whispered in his ear and wrapped a hand around his back to pull him close in case he needed support. She bent toward him and peered between his fingers.

He stared at slivers of the troubled green eyes looking at him, and a smile quirked his lips.

"Are you faking illness so you can leave?"

"Would it work?" he said, a finger sliding over to see all of one green eye. "I paid my respects."

"It could work because you're not well, yet, but everyone would see you running off with me. Your bad little secret would be out."

"What secret?"

"How much you love me."

"Hmmm. And how much is that?"

She didn't get to tell him because Charity Evans breezed in on the arm of Charles Chesnutt and Pastor Jenkins bowed his head.

Emily's favorite hymn filled the room, flowing from the ends of Benjamin's fingers as if a piano wasn't needed. It was simply musical energy coming from inside of him.

When he had asked Emily for Frank's favorite hymn, she'd been forced to tell him she didn't know what it was or even if he had one.

How could you not know, Emily? What else didn't you bother to know about your husband?

When the music ended, Pastor Jenkins raised one hand to the ceiling and shouted, "Be seated!" No one ever disobeyed that tone, and every eye looked his way. Every ear listened.

"I want to talk to you today about two things: Love and bias. The Bible says this about love." He poked a thick finger at his own chest. ". . . and if I have all faith, so as to remove mountains, but have not love, I am nothing. Corinthians."

He tossed it out there like it was a little tidbit of useless knowledge he had on the tip of his tongue and they could take or leave it. But they all knew better.

The verse caused mental head scratching. It sounded like words to begin a marriage service, not a funeral.

When he continued, they understood and applauded the pastor's sermon.

"In the last little while, Frank Adams built love," he said, "and he gave love. He loved in barrels full. He loved with passion. He loved so much he stole a son so he could raise him, glory over him, look at him in wonder."

Pastor Jenkins sought Betty's eyes looking for serenity. Hoping to see compassion. He glanced at Benjamin, too, and began again.

"He brought us together with his life and with his death. Look around you and ask yourself what you see."

He paused for an unreasonable length of time, until feet shuffled in edginess, until throats cleared and neighbor rolled eyes with neighbor. Pastor Jenkins knew what he was doing, and he did it all the time. He was a director setting the stage. He was emptying the vessels sitting in front of him and standing at the back of the room so they would be prepared to fill up with his words. With his wisdom and God's love.

"Peter said, 'Truly I understand that God shows no partiality,' Acts 10, and Idlewild has none here today." Pastor Jenkins smiled and repeated from his makeshift pulpit, "Look around you."

Again, he paused until shuffles grew, and he quieted them with more words from the scriptures. Confusion reigned, but he preached on and on, quoting verse after verse and connecting love to acceptance, love to fairness, and love to Frank.

"Listen to Matthew 7:1," he said, working himself into an anger not really directed at them. He pounded his makeshift pulpit and glared. "In a paraphrase, it says how in hell can you see the speck in your neighbor's eye around the log in your own? It says you're a hypocrite . . ."

He pointed and glared until each one of them felt the probe of his pointed finger, the probability of his wrath.

". . . if you don't remove the log in your eye so you know what you're really seeing. I didn't know Frank Adams well, but I believe he picked that log out of his eye. For the first time in his life, he saw clearly. Did any of you really know him? If you like, please come forward and tell us what you know. Or sit there and talk."

Heads turned, looking for the brave soul who would speak. One moment poured into a silent minute, the only sound Benji's contented gurgle.

Betty's deep voice broke their discomfort. "He was happy just spending time with Benji. That's all I know about Frank Adams. That and he loved our son."

Jesse Falmouth stood. "He was powerful. I mean really strong. He lifted the back end of my buggy right out of a snow bank once."

"For sure," Terry said. "He carried me and my two brothers all at the same time when he wanted us out at the barn and we didn't want to go. All of us gathered in those long arms of his, and we weren't too little at the time, either. Well, we got to where he wanted us to go, that's for sure."

"He helped at my Pa's farm. He was a good farmer. Good with cows," Al said.

"He loved his wife even if he didn't know it until after he shot her." Cassandra scowled at the gasps and murmurs from the congregation. She pursed her lips and shook her finger in admonition as she looked around at them, and they blanched.

"You know it's true. Why should we lie by hiding from the truth? Afterwards, he was gentle and loving, sweet tempered. The Frank we saw recently is not the same one we saw his entire adult life. Is it Emily?"

Emily shook her head. "Not until Benji. Frank helped me make soup the other day, actually cut up the onions." Her eyes gathered a peaceful, faraway glaze before she continued. "He never wanted to seem weak. His strength . . . his authority was important. He didn't realize what power really looked like. 'Til recently."

Pastor Jenkins smiled and raised his hands like he had a revelation.

"He removed the log from his eye! Don't you see? It's plain as day, and if you can't see this, then you know what to do! Get the log out! Get the log out!"

He pounded one fist into the other over and over as he exhorted the congregation to *get the log out.* His words reverberated against the walls and rang like the clanging of a copper bell calling parishioners to lay down their sins and rejoice.

Folks tucked their hands around each other's arms and jostled one another with their shoulders. They whispered and giggled, almost quietly in deference to the fact that it really was a funeral.

Gus slipped around to where Al sat, picked her up, took her chair, and sat her on his knee like a doll. He hadn't seen her in a while and missed her.

Samuel laughed out loud, and Abby poked him, gently, with an elbow, but others were laughing, too. Tears still filled eyes, but smiles slanted their lips and lay behind the liquid floating in the eyes.

There was something perfect about this particular laying of an earthly body to rest, something rehabilitating, even revitalizing, and Samuel couldn't put a finger on it, but he felt it. It filled the room and the voices.

"What the hell is going on?" he said to Abby. "Has everyone lost their minds?"

"What do you think?" Her arm had threaded through his, and he hadn't pulled away or stared at it as if a rattle snake grew from her shoulder.

"Maybe the miracle is they found their wits. But who knows? You better get out of here while you can still go with your sanity intact." He stroked the gold watch tucked into its special pocket.

"I'm not going anywhere without you, Samuel, and not you nor anyone else, not all the Klan members, not all your relatives, not even the Black Legion can make me."

She stared him down, eyes not a foot from his. "You hear me? I got the log out."

Chapter Thirty-eight

The engine started with one crank, and Abby jumped out of its way as Samuel instructed.

"Use your left hand so it swings away from you. Hear me?"

"I heard the first time, Samuel. And I've watched you do it. I won't get hurt."

But she was nervous all the same and jumped at the sound of his voice barking at her to move. She slid into the seat with a wrinkle on her brow.

"What?" he said.

"You scared me half to death by shouting at me to jump."

"Sometimes it kicks back. It could break your arm."

"Then you'd have to wait on me." Her grin was full of mischief as she nipped at his ear.

He grimaced in discomfort and paled as he cranked the steering wheel around to head back to his house, and Abby worried he shouldn't be out of bed yet. It was too soon to know if his internal injuries were healed.

"Want me to drop you at the footbridge?"

"No. I'll walk from your place when I'm ready to go home. Bear and Marcus are covering for me."

One eyebrow rose. "I don't need a babysitter anymore, Abby. I think I can do for myself now."

"I'm coming with you, Samuel. Did you not hear me at the funeral?"

"I heard."

He pulled up in front of his house, and Abby hurried around to help him. He was tired and in pain. She could see it in his eyes, in the ashen grey of his face, in the tense set of his shoulders. He didn't even refuse when she wrapped an arm around his waist to help him into the house. He collapsed into a kitchen chair with relief.

"Hungry?" she asked.

"No. Too much food at Frank's funeral. Sit, Abby."

She heard determination in his voice and felt a prickle of fear. She'd meant what she said about not leaving him. Maybe not this night, but some night, sometime, she'd be done with leaving.

Had Alma lied to her? Had she misinterpreted?

"Want me to pour some of Cassandra's tonic first?"

He nodded. "Sure. Might be what I need."

She found the flask, poured two tiny glasses and passed him one with a trembling hand. And that nettled her.

What is it about Samuel that scares you? You've punched big men, Abby, and handled unruly lumberjacks.

She sat across from him, held her glass in two hands and tried to read his look, but Samuel was unreadable. He had practiced the absence of nonverbal cues. He was an expert, and that exasperated her, too. Her own face was a child's picture book, open and readable.

He sipped in silence, so she did, as well. He wiped the dampness from his mustache, and she patted her lips dry with a handkerchief that miraculously appeared in her hand. Had he given it to her?

When she could take it no longer, she swallowed and blurted out a jumble of words.

"Why don't you just say it? What are you thinking, Samuel?"

His lips slipped into a half grin. "I wondered how long you could sit still in the quiet."

She stiffened. "Is that what you were doing? Testing me? You're insufferable. That's exactly what you are, and I don't know why I put up with you."

"Down, girl. It isn't what I meant to do, but it did occur to me to wonder about it as I was trying to put my thoughts in order." He chuckled and twirled his glass. "You're on a short fuse. Why?"

"Because . . ." She knew he was right. But it was his fault, and she'd go to the grave proclaiming the fact.

"That's not a very informative response."

She shoved her chair back, making it scrape against the wood floor and flinching from the harsh sound. After spinning it around to face his, she plopped into it.

"You're so damned irritating, Samuel."

"Yes. I know. Going to answer my question?"

"Short fuse?"

He nodded.

"Because I bared my soul to you with a proclamation to never leave you, no matter what, ever, and you sit here staring at me, thinking and testing and . . . I don't know what all. Yes. I'm a bit tense, wondering. Waiting to hear what you think about what I said."

Samuel's long fingers wrapped around her neck and pulled her to him. His lips touched hers, and for the longest time, Abby lost the ability to think, to breathe.

Yes, a voice whispered. *Yes. This is everything.*

"You remember when we went to the theatre?" he said, his lips still touching hers.

"Yes."

"Your life will be years of that same treatment. As my wife, it will compound."

Abby pushed away from him, leaped from her chair and turned in a circle, her hands tangling in her wild hair.

"You said wife, Samuel! You said wife! Are you asking me to marry you?"

"I was thinking *you* did that, Abby."

She spun again and stopped to wrap her arms around him.

"And I'm saying, yes," he said, his mustache twitching.

She was the yin to his yang, the silly to his stuffy, the moon to his star. She'd amused him since the day he'd met her, since the day he'd told her he was no Uncle Tom, and she'd said he didn't know who the hell that man really was. She tested him, pushed him, and he needed her and wanted her. The hell with consequences and other people.

"We'll make it work," she said. "If crazy Frank Adams can change people's hearts, we can, too."

He leaned back to pull the watch from his vest, caressed the shiny top and opened it from the back side where the pictures lay. He began talking about his life before Michigan, about the sacrifices his sharecropper father and mother had made, about learning to walk on the other side of the street and cross when necessary for safety.

Samuel's eyes grew hard in the telling of parts of his life, and they grew soft in the sharing of others. His dark skin left no doubt who he was, and he'd been carefully taught by his mother how to survive in Jim Crow south.

His eyes glistened when he explained about losing his sister and father, but briefly, and when she prodded for more, he shook his head.

"Another time."

"Anytime, Samuel. I'll be here."

"I know. You said that."

"You've given me everything I could ever want. Thank you."

"You've got to be careful when you ask for the moon, Abby, if you don't know what it's made of."

He wrapped both her hands in his and held them tightly, held her eyes, too, so she couldn't look away. He needed her to hear his words. He smiled, but Abby wasn't sure what it meant.

"It isn't green cheese. It's disparagement so constant and complete you question the value of an entire race of people, even question your own worth, your own value. Think about that," he said, and when she attempted to disregard his words with ones of love, he stopped her.

"Don't, Abby. You must listen to me because I know, and you don't. It is the truth; I went to that place, and it was the worst day of my life. I'll never do it again. I became arrogant instead. Still want the moon?"

Crocus blossoms in Nirvana had been out for a week or so, their riotous color competing with Canada geese honking for attention. Abby stepped out the back door, and the lemony sweet scent of Michigan's early flower hit her hard; she filled her lungs with its memory. In her rubber galoshes, she walked the Aishcum Hotel grounds and stalked the daffodils, snowdrops, and hyacinths she knew would be there – if they hadn't been buried in weeds.

She followed the path both she and her mother walked when they wanted solitude, the one that meandered through the copse in back of the stable and still showed signs of use. Where the canopy of branches filtered sunlight, clumps of snow claimed winter had yet to give up, and the ground remained frozen. In the soggy pathway, though, her boots squished as muck sucked at each step.

She felt like a child again and happy to have come alone. She'd needed to touch her old home again, to breathe in the dusty, vacant scent of the hotel, revel in the musty stable, its dirt floor littered with old straw, and remember Marie, the mare old age had claimed a while back.

She left muddy boots at the door and climbed the stairs, holding on to the bannister she used to slide down. It was cool under her hand and glossy smooth from years of guests' hands polishing it as they went up and down the stairs. Looking over the railing into the lobby, she saw Shorty, Bear and Yancy stomping their dirty lumberjack boots outside the door and hollering her name. She gasped, and they disappeared.

But they hadn't. Bear was at the Oakmere, and Shorty was with Al at The Old Place. Only Yancy had disappeared, and she paused to wonder where he went. Gone like her ex-husband, Frank.

She bypassed all the doors except the one on the end, hers since she'd grown old enough to have her own. The room was unchanged since the day she and her da left it and moved to Idlewild.

Instinctively, she looked at the window seat for the afghan her mother had crocheted before she'd been born. It always rested on the pillow-lined bench, folded and waiting to comfort her, but it had gone to Idlewild to their new hotel – now The Old Place – and then on to the Oakmere.

If her dream materialized, it would come back here to wait in a place of honor on the window seat once again.

They would knock out a wall or two and make a real home with a bedroom, living room, and washroom all their own. They could live like the rest of the world and still run a hotel, a small one. A great number of guest rooms weren't needed for what she had in mind.

She pulled the dust cover and sheets from her bed and opened the window to let fresh air cleanse the room. She washed the sheets and hung them in the sunshine behind the house, thankful the clothesline was still there and hadn't rotted away. She stepped back from the flapping linens and called herself a fool for the wide grin. Had she actually been gone for years? It didn't seem so. Part of her had always been here in the soil and soul of Nirvana.

Upstairs again, she whisked the cobwebs away and washed the walls, windows and floor, polished the furniture, and stood back to appreciate the room, her room, one she would gladly share with Samuel so it could be theirs. It tasted like home, like pancakes and sausage, like colcannon and friends.

She stood in front of the sparkling window, reached around her back, and tilted sideways to stretch muscles unused to the labor. Nirvana spread out in front of her, a tiny village limping along like an old woman with creaking bones, but content and wise, not fractious and mean spirited.

Across the way, she saw a few folks on Main Street and wondered where they headed?

A shabby general store still operated, one selling boots, shovels, canning jars and a few groceries. Abby remembered the candy counter from her youth and herself standing in front of it for a long while making penny candy decisions. She saw a light in the barber shop, but the pole outside was grayed and peeling instead of the bright red and white it had been.

A livery and blacksmith shop at the end of the street posted a sign on a window thick with dust and grime telling customers to knock at the door of the house next door if they wanted anything. He should sell gasoline, Abby thought, not horse shoes.

Nirvana rested. Perhaps it slept. But it wasn't dead.

A motor car rumbled up the road and sputtered to a stop in front of the hotel. Abby glanced out the window to see Samuel unfolding from the front seat. The top was down, in honor of the warm day, and he lounged against the auto and let his gaze roam the small village of Nirvana.

She admired his elegance before shouting his name.

"Up here. Come on up and tell me how wonderful I am."

"I can't tell you from here?"

"No."

He wrapped his arms around her as soon as he entered the room, and his lips found hers.

"See?" she said when she could speak. "You needed to be up here to do that."

"I see your point. You've been working."

"Do I smell?"

Samuel grinned. "Yes. You smell like Abby, and you have smudges on your face."

"Well, yours is beautiful. I can't believe all the cuts and bruises have fully disappeared."

"Would you still want me if they hadn't?" He pulled her closer to nuzzle her neck.

She leaned away and raised her eyebrows. "You know the answer to that question."

"I do. I just don't know why. Now, what did you want to show me?"

Abby clapped her hands together like an excited little girl and grabbed one of his to drag him out the door and into the next room.

"These walls come down so we have a big space that takes up three rooms, and we'll have a living area, washroom, and bedroom. Down at the other end of the hall, we do the same so Da and Bear have an apartment to share, but with two small bedrooms. All the other rooms stay the same for paying guests."

She hauled him downstairs to show him where his office would be in a soon-to-be walled off corner of the bar.

"We don't need a bar this big because most of the folks staying here will be overflow from Idlewild. So many people are vacationing there, The Oakmere and The Old Place are always full, so we'll take the extras, give them breakfast in the morning and drinks at night – I think. Although, Nirvana residents might enjoy a dinner here, but nothing fancy. Between Bear and me, we can do it all without having to hire anyone."

"You don't think Patrick might have something to say about all this?"

She glanced at the bar and ran a hand over the fine gleaming oak. She saw her father as a young man wiping down the bar and doing it all: the cooking, bartending, changing out the rooms and taking care of a little girl. He did it with a healthy dose of Irish blarney and without complaint.

"He's been at this a long time, Samuel. He'd never be the one to bring it up, but I can see he's tired. If he wants to cook a few dinners, he can. Here he won't have to unless he chooses. That's the beauty of it."

Samuel smoothed his mustache and looked around at the beautiful wood floor and bar, the big windows, and the tiny town a short distance away. It was quiet. He could hear birds chirping and squirrels scolding. He could work here. He could live here.

"We'll take a small cut from The Old Place and the Oakmere. We'll live just fine."

Her words were tiny with hopefulness.

Abby bounced from foot to foot and wrung her hands waiting for a word from him. She'd been so certain it would be the right move. Her da couldn't run the Oakmere without her, and she no longer wanted to. Shorty and Al could. She wanted a smaller place, a quieter place, a real home, and Samuel. A life with Samuel. She wanted Nirvana for them.

"I like it," he said.

Chapter Thirty-nine

She flung open the bedroom door and Al and Betty rushed in. Al pushed a small bouquet at her, several Dragon's Mouth orchids tied with a faded pink ribbon, and Abby grabbed her in a hug.

"The flowers are beautiful, Al, and is this what I think it is?" She fingered the worn ribbon and peered at her friend.

Al nodded.

"My God. I gave this ribbon to you years ago. I can't believe you still have it."

"I use it."

Abby stepped back in time, and sweet remembrance painted her face with something not happy and not sad. Her expression said she struggled with wanting to be in that earlier day forever and wanting to move forward to her new life with Samuel. A battle waged within, and she wondered if all brides fought this same war. She shrugged the skirmish away and sniffed the fragrant wild orchids.

"I thought you were going to quit working for me because I made you tie back your hair. How many times did you pull the ribbon from your ponytail so you could run off to the pantry and hide from talking people?"

"Plenty. I still do."

"I think you liked your hair down so you could hide your face behind it."

"Still do that, too." Al grinned, her head nodding, her white hair moving like a lazy ocean.

Betty stepped forward with a blue velvet neck ribbon she'd worn when she married Benjamin.

"Something blue," Betty said. "And you borrowed Al's old ribbon. Now you need something new."

Shorty slipped in the doorway beside Bear who held a wrapped package close to his chest.

"This is new," Bear said and held it out to her.

A gold watch pin gleamed in her hand when she unwrapped the box.

"You pin it on your dress," Shorty added. "And it opens just like Samuel's, so think about whose picture you want in there."

"What do you know about Samuel's?"

"He had a talk with us. Wanted your brothers to know everything." A sparkle lit Bear's eyes.

"We *are* family, Abigail," Shorty said.

"It's beautiful, Shorty, Bear. Thank you. Thank all of you. You're going to make me cry."

"Have you seen all the folks at the pavilion?" Shorty asked. "We ran out of chairs, and people are spilling out onto the lawn and sitting on blankets."

Abby went to look out the window and Bear followed and stared at her. She looked beautiful with her long, auburn hair flowing down her back, her green eyes sparkling with unshed tears.

A grin showed lopsided on his face, and she didn't know if he was aware of the two-sided nature of his smile. Was he not happy for her?

He saw the liquid and teased to dry her eyes. "You want to count?"

"How many people are out there?"

He shook his head. "How many fingers and toes do you have? Enough?"

Her hand went to her mouth, and she gave up trying to suck back her tears.

"Oh, my God, Bear. I don't have enough fingers and toes. I'll have to use yours, too, and Al's and Shorty's and Betty's."

"Remember when you couldn't fill one hand?"

"I do."

"You made it happen. You're something else, Abigail. Samuel better know that."

"But I didn't do it. Idlewild did. You and Shorty did. And Cassandra and Jesse. And Frank."

"That's true. They're ready, Abby. I'll walk you to the pavilion."

Shorty took her other arm and they walked into the sunshine, Al and Betty following. They handed her over to Patrick, and he led her to Samuel who waited in front of Pastor Jenkins.

"I'll not be giving the lass to you, like they always say," Patrick told him and placed Abby's hand in Samuel's. "I'll just be sharing."

Reverend Jenkins wore a grin stretching for miles across his cheeks. He'd been waiting years for this day, knew it was coming long before either of them did, was fairly certain the first time she came to one of the church services – at Bunny Parker's house, he recalled.

She'd been the only white face there and was scared to death of us, he pondered in amused reverie, and came out of his trance when feet shuffled and throats cleared with intent. He lifted his shoulders and cleared his own.

"You ready for this, Samuel?"

He could only nod because speaking had become impossible.

"You ready, Abigail?"

"I am."

"You sure?"

Abby glared, and he began.

She slipped into a long white nightgown the cousins had given her. It was diaphanous in the glow of several lit candles that painted the walls with moving shadows, and she felt like she might as well have not put on anything at all. She'd have to remember to tell the ladies. Sue would giggle, and Sally would nod with knowledge.

She folded back the quilt and fussed with the pillows, moved the candles further from the bed, and checked her hair once again in the mirror. It looked as it had five minutes prior, hanging down her back in an insurrection of curls. Samuel liked her hair down.

When he still hadn't come to her, she sat in the window seat and stared out at Nirvana. Only a couple of lights shined from the village, but stars decorated the night as if celebrating their wedding with bright, twinkling baubles. A last-quarter half-moon hung in the sky, so she knew it neared midnight, and she wondered where he was and checked her new watch. Should she call downstairs to him? Get into bed? She nibbled at a cuticle, stopped and rubbed her neck.

An odd thump at the door startled her, nearly tumbling her from the window seat.

"Who is it?" she barked as if she had no idea they were the only people in the hotel.

"It's me, silly. I have no hands so I had to kick at the door."

She opened it to see Samuel in a satin jacket holding a tray with two tall crystal glasses, a plate of fruit and cheese, and a rose. A bucket swung from his other hand, and it carried a bottle moist with condensation.

"Oh, Samuel. How thoughtful. And beautiful."

"It seemed the thing to do."

She cleared a place for the bounty on the dresser, and he poured clear bubbly liquid into the glasses. He handed one to her and stared into her eyes, taking in the green of them surrounded by pale ivory skin, the deep auburn tresses hanging over her shoulder, and the would-be puritan gown.

"You look stunning, Abigail." He clinked his glass against hers and sipped.

"You do, too, Samuel. I didn't know men could wear such beautiful fabric, but it suits you." She swallowed.

His mustache twitched. "You won't make me wipe the bottom of my glass on the sleeve of it?"

She chuckled. "Not tonight. Not if you behave."

They sipped again, and Samuel was glad to feel the beginning inner glow of the champagne.

He was afraid. Of her. Of how she looked. Of them. He knew her strength but didn't know if he could match it. And he was terrified.

He sipped again, and so did she.

She moved to the window seat with the plate of berries and cheese and placed it in the center with room for both of them on either side. Samuel took her cue and sat.

He put a strawberry in her mouth, and she giggled and gave him one. Back and forth they went until Samuel relaxed and crossed his legs in the elegant way Abby loved.

"This was a great idea, Samuel. I love it."

"Thank you. Would you like a refill?"

She held out her glass and he got up to fill them both.

"Bear told me he might kill me today," he said and handed her the champagne.

"Why might he do that?"

"If I disappointed you in any way."

Abby leaned back against the wall making up part of the cove in which they sat.

"He would, too. And he could. Bear is strong. He fought a bear and won, you know. Did I ever tell you about tending to his wounds for days and days?"

He shook his head, and she gave him the story, her voice a soft breeze, serene and unhurried.

"By the way," she said when the tale was finished, "Cassandra made it clear I am to understand how special you are. I believed her when she talked about a potion which would take me out of this world if I failed you in any way."

Samuel chuckled, a soft, amused sound that covered her skin with little shivers.

"She loves me like an attentive aunt. Bunny, too. I'm surprised the cousins didn't talk to you."

"They did, but they're torn because they love me, as well."

"I heard. You definitely know how to get to people, Abby."

The sun peeked at the horizon, and they saw it from the window seat. A second bottle of champagne had helped loosen their tongues and their reserves, and conversation gave strength to their understanding of who they were at the moment, who they had been in the past, and who they wanted to be.

A half-moon hung in the early morning sky and both of them reached for it.

The Real Idlewild

Idlewild lies on the southern edge of Michigan's Lake County which was originally called Aishcum after a Pottawatomi Indian Chief. The county was organized by a group of Civil War veterans who settled near Baldwin and Luther. A variety of tales surround the growth of Idlewild, but few disagree it originated under the guidance and ownership of four couples with a single dream – a peaceful resort for African American families.

The 2700-acre plot of land was purchased in 1912 and homesteaded for three years. Immediately after, lots began selling for $1 down and $1 a month to black men in the largest cities of America. WWI interfered as men went to war, Spanish Influenza decimated cities, and Jim Crow tried to subjugate black Americans. Because of the nation's unrest, they needed a place where they could play together, and they found it in Idlewild.

In its heyday, between twenty-five and thirty thousand people vacationed in Idlewild and its surrounding small towns. Over three hundred businesses were black owned, and hundreds of cottages had been built. They held philosophical discussions and musical events at several Chautauqua during the summers, and welcomed famous entertainers and political and literary greats such as W.E.B Dubois, Charles Chestnut, and Madam C.J. Walker. It quickly became the biggest resort in the nation – black or white.

During the 20's, our nation suffered unequaled hatred at the hands of the Ku Klux Klan. Riots, marches, cross burnings and lynching proliferated. The Black Legion was born, a group of men more violent than even the KKK, and added to the nation's pain. Jim Crow fought reconstruction and hollow emancipation laws and made it impossible for black men, women and children to live free as Lincoln intended.

Yet Idlewild persevered in its serenity and its determination to remain an oasis in the middle of chaos. The small town of Idlewild was a living, breathing egalitarian dream.

In the 30's, The Negro Motorist Green Book was written providing a guide to African Americans who traveled the roads of America. Victor Hugo Green, the author, helped travelers by letting them know where they could safely go, stay and eat during the Jim Crow era of horrific discrimination. Idlewild was listed in the Green Book and provided a haven and paradise long before and after the book's creation.

Black and white people shared the resort. I know because my mother went there, and she is white. She loved dancing at the clubs and has fond memories of time spent there with her three sisters. Everyone I interviewed for the Idlewild Series had positive commentaries about the peaceful relationship between the races. The small Michigan town was an oasis and was integrated before the word became an uncomfortable dictate by law.

Early in its development, Idlewild became a mecca of understanding, love and tolerance. Its bright moon rose for several decades and set with the civil rights act of 1964. The battle for equal rights, for compassion, knowledge and understanding continues across the nation. My sorrow is that Idlewild, as the living example to us all, died.

TO MY READERS

I hope you enjoyed reading *Ask for the Moon.* I loved writing the Idlewild series, meeting new friends through research, and gaining perspectives because of all three.

Through reading novels, I gain an understanding of worlds I never knew, and through writing, I can live in those worlds. I can taste unfamiliar food, hear language I never understood, smell and touch foreign objects. Through the agony and wonder of writing, I can become the stranger, even if for only a moment before she slips back into her own skin and out of my grasp. But I keep her essence as part of my knowledge, and I am grateful to her for that opportunity.

Thank you for spending time with me.

Go to www.julisisung.com for news. If you leave your email, I will let you know when the next book is available.